THE CHILDREN OF MENLO PARK

THE CHILDREN OF MENLO PARK

THE THRILLING SUPERNATURAL ADVENTURES OF KATE WARNE, LADY PINKERTON VOLUME ONE

JESSICA NETTLES

Charlotte, NC

FALSTAFF
BOOKS
WWW.FALSTAFFBOOKS.COM

For Maeve and Stuart, my own magical children.

Kate Warne, Senior Female Detective for the Pinkerton National Detective Agency, glanced up from her work as Shadow, her partner and liaison between the Pinkertons and the mysterious group known simply as The Brotherhood, stepped out of a dark corner of their shared office on Washington Street. He became more solid as he moved closer and into the warm gaslight that glowed around her desk. His appearances from the darkness had become less disturbing during the years she'd worked with him, and she'd learned to be prepared for almost anything when he'd return in this manner. She pulled a small brush from a lower drawer in her desk and handed it to him.

As he brushed away alley dust from his dark suit pants, she continued clicking along on the Hammond #2 typewriter she used for all of their reports.

"Did you see the girl?"

He hung his coat and hat and picked up a stack of letters out of the slot in the pigeon-hole cabinet by the office door. "There was a fire. She came to town with the Halvard boy."

"How many dead?"

He took out a slim letter opener and began slicing open one of the envelopes. "Only the parents. She saved the boy and the horses and drove them into town despite her hands being burned. She either can't feel the pain or was focused on getting to safety. The boy was crying, but she was as calm as you or me."

"Mr. Edison said she might be that way." She tucked her report into the vacuum chute to Allan's office and was thankful for the conveyance. Dealing with the man himself was not something she was keen on at the moment. Things had been awkward since her funeral. She hadn't reckoned on how disturbed and confused her former companion would be when she arrived at the office a few days after she was buried. Her body may be done, but her spirit was not. She'd made the decision to continue in the Inside, the world of the living, within days of her arrival to the Outside, the world of the spirit. Now, she was sure she'd miscalculated a few things in her haste to continue doing what she loved best.

Her partner continued to sort through the mail. "We need to extract the girl before she lights up an entire town."

Kate sipped from a porcelain teacup ringed in pink roses. It had always been her favorite pattern. "You make this sound like she is on the attack."

Her partner tossed empty envelopes into the trash bin the nearby trash bin and stacked the letters on his desk. "She's already killed two people. Three if you count O'Neill."

Setting the cup on her desk, Kate pulled a cover over her typewriter. "Did it look like she set the house on fire on purpose?"

Her partner shrugged. "There's no way to be sure at this point. Or maybe ever."

"Sounds a bit like O'Neill's death. No way to know, which is why I find your connecting the girl to his demise disturbing at best."

Shadow arched his eyebrow and smoothed his mustache in that way he did before a rousing discussion. This is one of the things that she appreciated about having him as a partner. He was always up to counter her claims. Three hundred years of experience with people and argument made his viewpoint more challenging to come up against than most men, even Allan. Noticing that her cup was empty, she called up a matching pot. She thought better with a cup of tea. One of the perks of being a ghost is that she could use some of her energy to conjure things she loved most from her former Inside life. While she could manipulate items in the Inside world, she still used the typewriter on her desk, being able to have tea at her desk was a bit of a luxury. The aroma of bergamot wrapped around her like a comforting blanket, and she smiled. *This should be fun.*

Her partner sat down at his own desk. "We both know O'Neill didn't just plunge into the river on his own."

She poured steaming liquid into her cup. "He suffered from melancholy, did he not?"

"Not when he was on a case." The gangly detective pulled a bottle of Four Roses whiskey, his favorite, from a small glass-doored cabinet behind him.

"He was a bit of a bulldog like President Grant. I will give him that much."

Her partner continued. "O'Neill visits the farm. Twenty-four hours later he is floating in a creek only a mile from the Halvard property. There were no gunshot wounds, no knife wounds, and the lady at the hotel in town said he never came back after leaving to go to the farm. If that girl felt the least bit threatened who's to say she didn't follow him long enough to find time to shove him into the river?"

She laughed at this bit of conjecture. "You cannot be serious. O'Neill was almost as tall as Pinkerton. She's not a big girl, is she?"

Her partner shook his head. "Just a slip of a thing, but with a bit of stealth and good timing..." He made a hand motion indicating going off a cliff.

"Even with my level of skill and ingenuity, I'm pretty sure I couldn't shove Pinkerton off into a river, even if I wanted to."

Shadow chuckled as well. "Maybe after he'd had a few drinks? Wait. What was it the notes said about not looking her in the eyes?"

She picked up a file from her desk and rifled through it until she found what she was looking for. "'Agents should not make eye contact with subject.' Something about bad luck following. If he looked the girl in the eyes..."

"Seems a bit far-fetched. O'Neill was new to our unit, right?"

"We deal in far-fetched, remember? And yes, this was his first solo case with us."

"Perhaps he saw this like you do. Far-fetched. There aren't many agents on staff who deal with the sorts of cases we deal with. Allan swore O'Neill would be a good fit. If O'Neill's death is connected to the visit, then it could have been caused by lack of understanding of the situation on both O'Neill's and the girl's part. I doubt she intended for him to die."

"Even if his death is accidental, I have a suspicion that this fire is less of an accident."

"Maybe you can ask her when we bring her in." Kate turned the last page back. "This is odd."

Shadow came around to look over her shoulder. "What are you looking at?"

"It's what I'm not looking at. It's what's missing from this file." The lady detective flipped through several typed and handwritten pages.

"There's Edison's letter." He pulled it out from the file.

"And what's left of O'Neill's notes about how he found the girl." She laid a small notebook emblazoned with a single eye.

Her partner took the empty folder from her. "But no interview notes."

"So, O'Neill never visited Menlo Park at all?" This was not protocol. Kate checked her desk to be sure the interview notes hadn't slipped out. "There are no notes from Pinkerton saying not to visit the client, so why didn't O'Neill do the interview?"

"I'm not sure, but perhaps we should do it for him now." Shadow joined in her search and even checked under the typewriter. "Should we ask the man upstairs?" He pointed and scowled in a way that made her laugh in spite of herself.

"No. I have no desire to rile an already unhappy bear." She studied the notes in the file again. "Go ahead and check things out. You can get there faster than I can. See what the inventor says. While you're gone, I'll go through the file once more to see if I missed anything."

Shadow put on his black overcoat and bowler hat and turned down the gas sconce so that one corner darkened. He parted the darkness and stepped into the Paths to make his way to Raritan, New Jersey the small town near Edison's Menlo Park.

Blue-gray light fluttered, and the corner began to close. The glow brightened to the point that Kate had to cover her eyes with her arm. After a moment, the sconce popped hard and a heavy thump followed. She made her way, half-blind, to her partner's part of the office and his body crumpled at her feet. The darkness was heavier in the corner since the gaslight was out. She knelt beside him and leaned close to his face. Still breathing. His body faded in and out as though he were moving through the Inside and Outside at the same time.

From her previous experience, she knew that touching Shadow wasn't the best idea, so she used a pencil to tug his watch from his vest pocket. Clicking the pupil of the Pinkerton's Eye opened his watch. Twelve o'clock sharp, just like when she'd checked it all those years before on the train in Baltimore with Mr. Lincoln. When her partner came to, he was convinced that Mr. Lincoln was dead at the Ford Theater in Washington, D. C. The future president had to bring him a drink and sit with him to convince him that he was Inside and well.

The worst part was that she couldn't follow him. A good partner should be able to follow if there is trouble. In a usual stepping out, all Kate would have to do is check his notes, which he often left for her, and go to the physical locale where he was headed. That was easy. Time travel was not. Since her demise, Kate could travel up and down her own timeline because it was hers and it was complete. But she could not just show up on other timelines where she'd not been when she was Inside. After Baltimore, Shadow told her that the members of the Brotherhood were unable to travel in time, and he wasn't sure why he could.

At this point, the best she could do was pour him a drink and hope that he would return soon. Kate glided back to her desk and continued to peruse the case file. If anyone had entered the office at that moment, they would have thought a window was open and a breeze was fluttering the papers on her desk. Most people on the Inside couldn't see her unless she decided to present in a corporeal form. It took a lot of energy to do this, but the longer she worked on the Inside, the stronger she became. Kate laid several photos, including one of a dark, handsome man posing with something that crackled with electricity. The name on the back was 'Nikola Tesla.' She had no idea why he was included in the file.

A groan rose from behind her partner's desk. If Kate had been one who was easily startled, she might have screamed. Instead, she brought him the shot glass as he sat up and scratched his head. The scent of bourbon burned her nose and made her eyes water.

She was far from being a Prohibitionist, but since her move to the Outside, certain scents were stronger. Bourbon was a spirit that, like her, crossed between Inside and Outside easily. "How was your trip?"

"Not what I planned," He took the glass, and knocked the contents back in one gulp. She took his arm when he struggled to his feet.

"I saw the girl, the one they call Thirteen. She was at a train station with a group of other children, but she looked younger."

"I wondered if you'd gone to the past again." She steadied him and he grabbed the back of his chair, which rolled forward, causing them to stumble forward together. "Tell me more once you sit down."

The watch dropped straight down on its chain and dangled around his mid-thigh as he held onto his desk. Kate pulled the chair back and he sat down and fiddled with the distinctive timepiece.

"You checked the watch?"

"It's not often you leave your body behind when you step out. I suspected you might have gone to the Ford Theater again."

"Smart lady."

She sat back on the side of his desk. "I have my moments, m'dear."

"I didn't end up in Washington though." He checked the watch, which was now showing the correct hour, clicked it shut, and placed it back in his pocket.

"Where then?"

"A train station at Raritan Township."

"So, you ended up where you intended to go."

"In a way. A man with a group of children waited there in the dark. He wore a suit and looked as though he was prepared for a trip. The children were in sleeping gowns and long johns but not much else. A train marked "Orphan" came up, and they all boarded but the gentleman."

"Late pickup." Kate sipped a cup of tea.

"The odder part came after the children rode away." Her partner poured a second shot of Four Roses. She crinkled her nose at him.

"Do tell." "A black train pulled into the station, and he got on board."

Kate set her empty teacup on the edge of her desk, and it faded away. "The Brotherhood is involved?"

He took a drink and slammed the glass down harder than she expected. "No one will answer when I ask if we are."

This was surprising. The Brotherhood shared everything as a collective. She didn't understand how this worked, but what one knew, all should know. Then again, her partner had kept secrets, so how was this different?

"Who was the man?"

"Not sure. When he spoke with the children, I thought I heard an accent. Maybe Southeastern European."

Kate picked up a photo from her desk and held it up. "His name is Tesla. He works with electricity. No shock there."

A wry smile crossed her partner's lips, and she handed the image to him.

"What does Tesla have to do with children and orphan trains?"

"And why were you pulled to this girl's past?"

"Perhaps we need to focus on Tesla instead of Edison?"

Kate took the photo from him and replaced it in the file. "Or maybe we needed to see a bigger picture. Mr. Edison asked us to find this one girl. Why? What about the other children who got on that train? Why not hire us to find them all? And why would this man," she tapped the folder, "be taking this girl and these other children to an orphan train?"

7

"He's moonlighting? I don't know. It doesn't make much sense to me, but then neither did the Baltimore Incident 'til years later."

She made her way to her desk and put the folder in the leather briefcase Allan-Mr. Pinkerton-had given her when she became the senior lady detective at the firm. "I'm thinking we don't want to wait years to find out."

"At least we know where the girl is for the moment. I doubt she will be going anywhere soon with those burns. Maybe if we can talk to her, she can tell us about her family."

"Family?"

Her partner took his bowler off the floor and brushed it off. "That's what she called the other children. Her family."

"They're all related?"

"I don't think so. Not in the truest sense. They were a rather diverse group from what I could see."

Kate straightened her desk as was her custom before a trip. "What if bad things happen while she's with that doctor? We need to extract her soon. I'd hate to have more fires or folks floating down creeks." she said, shifting focus back to the girl.

"No one else will be floating down any creeks, Mrs. Warne." The person she least wanted to see leaned into the office. Allan Pinkerton's broad form filled the space of the doorway. "The girl caused a fire?"

Shadow offered the oversized chair that was meant for their supervisor. Pinkerton settled into it, stretching his long legs across the floor.

"*Mrs. Warne.* My, we are formal today, *Mr. Pinkerton.*"

"Serious times call for serious addresses." The playful burr of his voice never failed to weaken her knees a bit in spite of her effort to stay focused and professional. He was relaxing and teasing her like he used to, which was a step up from the mixture of confusion and grief she got from him over the last month or so. Perhaps he was settling into their new arrangement. Or he'd read Shadow's report and was engaged in the case, which was much better than engagement with her.

Their eyes locked and the mischief that twinkled behind his faded into the sadness she'd become accustomed to since her return. She turned away. The room became less solid and less real, and she was back in her bed. There was a doctor, who shook his head and retreated from the room. Allan sat next to her, his warm massive hand cradled her tiny hand. *Why is he here and not with his family?* In one corner, Shadow stood, not saying a word. She wanted to adjust his tie. Her chest ached and rattled with each breath. She couldn't sit up because she had no energy. She closed her eyes. The pain lifted and her strength and energy returned. She awoke and sat up, her hand still in her paramour's. His eyes were wide at first, and she thought she'd surprised him with her abrupt turn for the better. Instead, he was sobbing. He laid down her hand and leaned into her lap. She tried to cradle him, but her arms went through him. *I'm...dead.*

Kate looked at her partner and returned to the present. He cleared his throat as he studied the pages on his desk, and the lady detective wasn't sure if he was coughing past the liquor or was as uncomfortable as she and their lead. "There are more children involved."

His words pulled Pinkerton's attention away from Kate. "How is it that you two know about the other children?"

"Was that in the report you are holding on to, *Mr. Pinkerton?*" She sipped her tea as the world around her solidified and her heart quieted once again.

"O'Neill mentioned other children, but Edison was more concerned about this girl. I have no idea why. But maybe you can make the connection since my news is already old."

Shadow updated their supervisor on what he'd seen at Raritan Station. The large man stopped him when he mentioned the black train. "Why didn't you tell us your people were connected to the case? You're our bloody liaison for Heaven's sake."

"I didn't know."

Kate braced because she knew what was coming.

Allan shook the report at the liaison. "What do you mean you didn't know? You're talkin' mince, for Christ's sake! All of you are connected."

Shadow's expression never changed. "The war changed many

things, even the Brotherhood. You saw how scattered we were at Appomattox Courthouse when the treaties were signed."

The Scotsman's face flushed. "We were all scattered that day. That doesn't explain the lack of communication now."

Kate's partner ignored the man's bluster. "In a general sense, you are right. We share all things. In a more specific sense, there are those who are motivated and make decisions apart from the rest of us." He stood up and leaned into his supervisor's face. "So, no. I have no idea what one of our trains was doing in Raritan picking up this man or if my brothers know anything about these children."

The burly man muttered something under his breath that Kate could only guess was the sort of foul language that he knew shouldn't be spoken in front of a lady, even if that lady was fond of wearing pants and camped with Union soldiers. She focused on her partner. "Why would a faction of the Brotherhood be interested in these children or Mr. Tesla?"

"I will have to ask, but an answer isn't likely if the faction isn't talking."

"The war's ended. Factions seem to defeat the purpose of your organization."

A wry grin crossed the Brother's face. "Tell that to your congressman, *Mrs. Warne.*"

She arched her eyebrow. "Will it make a difference, *Mr. Jones?* Kate turned to her superior, who was still grumbling. She stomped her foot to get his attention. "Do you have O'Neill's report? It's missing from our file. We need to make up for lost time."

Pinkerton cleared his throat and he flushed anew. "It disappeared after O'Neill died. I can't find it."

Kate hated being stonewalled. "Do not play games with me, Allan. If this is about…"

The man balled his fists. She'd pushed him too far. "You think I'd cripple this case over that?"

"You have been rather distressed as of late."

"And you believe that my distress would cause me to play games and keep information from you?" He marched toward the door. "I have a business to run. I don't have time to ruin a case because I'm upset over my best agent coming back to work *after she's died*. That's not fair, and you know that, Katie."

The lady detective cringed. She hated that name and hated herself for provoking him. Words failed her, and the silence hung over them like a brewing thundercloud on a summer day.

Shadow said, "Since there is no report, we should visit Mr. Edison."

His suggestion hung between them until she reached for her briefcase and began to fasten the straps and click the locks on the front. "I can take an airship this afternoon and meet you there. Is there anything else, sir?"

Allan Pinkerton left the office without a response. She looked up and caught a glimpse of his bearded face, which was wet with tears.

Her partner shuffled papers on his desk. "That went well."

"He is possibly the most frustrating man I have ever dealt with." She shouldered her bag and approached the lanky detective. He looked like he wanted to say more. Before he could, she asked, "Are you better?"

"I believe I can travel down the Paths safely now."

She straightened his tie and patted it. "No more random time travel. I won't be around to pour you a shot this time."

"I'll meet you at the station on time, at the *correct* time. I promise. Stay out of trouble."

She laughed in spite of her mood. "As if."

2

Kate walked to the Home Insurance Building on LaSalle, which was the home to Chicago's first airship port downtown. While many people believed that the dead can travel anywhere they want instantaneously, Kate had not found that to be universally so. Travel in the Outside was only a little more flexible than the Inside. In the Outside, she could move instantaneously inside the Pinkerton headquarters and also to her small apartment if she wanted to go there. Places that were part of her heart drew her as though she were wired to them. To go anywhere else, she had to travel like those bound to the Inside. She preferred traveling on the small commuter airships that ported from the top of the skyscraper because they were faster and more comfortable.

By entering from the Outside and not manifesting during the trip, however, she didn't have to pay fares as those Inside did. As much as Allan was a law-abider, he was also enough of a skinflint to accept this bit of financial advantage.

Once she floated past the conductor and found her seat, she pondered the case so far. What sort of girl is this Thirteen anyway? The notes were vague at best, and that missing interview...O'Neill knew better than to not include it in the file. She hated having to go backwards in order to move forward.

The steward pushed a cart of teacups down the aisle. He paused by her, and Kate reached for a cup, but stopped short. A floating teacup would also do nothing but disturb the entire car. No need for that. Instead, she called forth her own familiar pink and white cup and a matching teapot. She sipped and watched a red-headed young man wearing a crisp blue uniform following the steward. He took the tickets passengers pressed into his gloved hand. As he paused at Kate's seat, he shivered and turned pale, making the sprinkle of freckles on his nose stand out. She remembered him from the last trip she took for another case in New York. He tapped the steward's shoulder. "There's that cold spot again, Lenny. I swear I feel it every time I fly this route."

"You need more sleep, Will."

Kate touched the young man's hand, as he walked away. He paused, looked back at her, shook his head, and moved on. Messing with the boy was unkind, but it was fun just the same.

The ship lifted from its moorings as the engines fired on either side of the craft. Several passengers gripped the arms of their seat or their travel partners. She continued to sip her tea while watching the city spread below her as the ship rose. Seeing Chicago from the air reminded her of the first time she saw the Inside and Outside at the same time. Both worlds resided side by side most of the time. Insiders couldn't see this because for most there was a veil that blocked the view of the Outside. She'd not known this 'til she died, and her veil was lifted and she learned that both worlds interconnected in ways she'd not expected. People and creatures of every era, known and not so known, were visible and living side-by-side as if nothing were unusual. Once she decided to live in both worlds, she'd had to learn to focus on the present moment or be pulled into the cacophony of history that played out before her.

She closed her eyes after the ship passed over the city and rose to cloud level. These trips were notoriously boring, which was advantageous in most cases, including this one. She went over the case in her head. The missing interview nagged at her. She had no reason to believe that it was taken out on purpose, but at the same time, O'Neill was not known to be sloppy.

A scream pierced through her reverie, and she stood at full-ready, derringer drawn. The passenger compartment was filled with dead passengers.

"Porter?" She made her way toward the front of the cab. The ship tipped forward and she slid through Will the porter, whose eyes were no longer troubled, but blank and staring into the distance.

She used a seat to steady herself as she stood up. *If everyone is dead, why can't I see them here in the Outside?*

She peered out one of the passenger windows and saw a blood-spattered full moon hanging against a black curtain sky. The red stains flooded the silvery orb and flowed down it like waterfalls. A bell tolled thirteen times, shaking the ship mid-air, and shattering the window in front of her. A dank odor rose around her.

In her experience with the supernatural, she'd learned that various creatures smell specific ways. Nosferatu, or vampires, tended to smell like gardenias or citrus and pine (the ones in the South could also carry a magnolia scent). Skinwalkers tended to smell like the animal they became. This was neither Nosferatu nor skinwalker, nor anything she recognized. As the odor passed over her, a panic began at her core. Whatever this thing was, it was hungry for her and for anything around it.

Thousands of eyes glowed from behind the waterfall of blood, all of them fixed on her. She tried to turn away and saw a square of stars cut through the black curtain sky. She reached for the comfort of the familiar twinkles, hoping that they would lead her from this place. Her hopes were dashed as tentacles tore through the opening, blocking off her view. They stretched and wrapped around the airship, and it shook mid-air. Rope, wood, and sheeting from the exterior hull rained past her window. People screamed around her as the passenger deck floor crumpled under their feet. The ship was pulled toward the opening.

All of the sadness she felt about dying and Allan and his response to her return washed over her. It deepened her terror and she found herself on the floor curled up sobbing. A rich mocking chortle echoed over the scene, and she felt the ship being towed through the darkness.

The laughter stopped her sobbing cold. A fire rose inside her. Whoever was laughing was directing their contempt at her and her decision to come back from the Outside. It had taken everything she had to face Allan once she'd returned. She'd worked hard to make it clear that this was a work choice, not a choice about their love. The sadness faded to frustration over his inability to let their previous situation go. *He is so damned stubborn.* That was followed by massive self-doubt and the words "selfish" and "cruel" whispered around her and turned back into giggles. The fire in her soul rose up once more and she got to her knees. "I don't know who or what you are, but this ain't your funeral. It ain't your business. Leave me alone!" She cringed at slipping into Confederate speak, but all of this stripped her past polite words.

A sharp whistle cut through the air and a man in a crisp blue suit walked through her. "Next stop, Raritan, New Jersey. Return flight to Chicago will be tomorrow morning. Please purchase tickets as you leave the station." She crawled back to an empty seat as her fellow passengers began to disembark as if nothing had happened. The sun sparkled through clean, unbroken windows, and the porter made his way through the gondola assisting passengers as he should. As the ship docked, she spotted Shadow at the edge of the landing pad. Unlike most men she knew, he did not carry a briefcase. Instead, he wore his bag on his shoulder. He swore it was more comfortable and could hold more things. She stayed in her seat until the ship was empty. Even if the ship was in one piece, she was not and needed a moment to gather herself.

Shadow saw Kate from his position on the landing pad. He waved, but she didn't see him. As usual, she waited until all of the others had exited. She told him she didn't care for the jostling that went on at disembark. He was sure that she also didn't want to cause a panic if someone saw a ghost. The conductor stood outside the exit, blew a whistle. The lady pilot came down the stairs as she pulled her goggles off and tucked them in her side pouch. She strode past Shadow, and he tipped his hat.

Kate tapped him on the shoulder. "What do you know, Joe?"

He cleared his throat and turned. "Not as much as you, I suspect."

She slipped her arm through his. There was no reason for doing this since no one could see her unless she willed it, but it was an old habit and a pleasant one at that. His partner's grip was tense, and she gazed at the sky as if she expected something to swoop down on them.

He patted her hand. "Are you okay? You look like you barely escaped with your life. Surely the pilot wasn't that bad."

"It wasn't the pilot." She pulled him away from the crowd to the far corner of the station. "You probably shouldn't talk to yourself that way in public."

"I doubt they even noticed me, dear Kate. Now tell me what's going on." She shivered a bit, which surprised her partner. There were not many things that disturbed Kate Warne either before or after she'd had the veil lifted.

"I had a vision of rather Biblical proportions." She explained what had happened as they walked to the local hotel.

"I don't recall tentacled creatures coming through the sky in the Bible."

"True enough. Now that I'm not afraid of my impending forever death, I'm drawn toward the tolls of the bell," said Kate.

They made their way down the street. A little girl waved at them. "Thirteen...is there a connection, you think?"

No one else seemed to notice his partner. "I didn't see any children, but that number keeps coming up in the investigation. The Universe repeats things for a reason in my experience."

Shadow checked in and explained that his wife had missed her airship but should be along the next day. The man at the desk didn't ask questions but gave him two keys for two rooms anyway.

Moments later, there was a tap at the door that joined the two rooms. Before he could answer, Kate floated in looking much more settled than at the station. She'd changed into a blue suit dress and hat.

"You didn't have to knock."

"Now how nice would it have been if I'd seen you in your skivvies, Mr. Jones?" She sat down in the one ornate chair in the room.

He sat on the windowsill. "Wouldn't have been the first time."

She arched her eyebrow and her pale green eyes sparkled as her now familiar teacup appeared in her hand. "I'm not that sort of woman, sir!"

His partner was attractive in a practical sort of way. Her hair was eternally chestnut and tucked in a soft bun under a modest blue hat that sported fashionable ostrich feather.

"But you are the sort who wears pants and lives in tents with men."

"That was for a good cause." She sipped her tea to hide her smile. This made him smile.

"And this frock?"

"You should recognize it. It's the one you and Allan picked out for my funeral."

"Why wear it now? Seems rather a morose choice."

"I like the outfit, though not as well as my pants, and it's not every day one gets to visit Menlo Park."

She conjured up a second cup, and he accepted it. "Do we have a plan if we learn nothing from this visit?'

"We continue to track the girl until we can get her to talk with us. I find it worrisome that O'Neill made such a basic mistake."

"Was he hiding something?"

Kate shook her head. "No. I don't think he would do that. Allan is Edison's friend though."

Shadow put down his cup and it faded away. "Pinkerton wouldn't hide things for his friend. You know that better than anyone, Kate."

"All avenues must be pursued, but you're right. He wouldn't do that, no matter who it was." Her own cup faded as well.

"Then we have to conclude that the interview either wasn't done, or it was stolen."

"Perhaps our interview will shed some light on all of this. I believe we should make our way to Menlo Park, good sir." His partner rose and picked up her briefcase.

Shadow checked his watch and offered his arm "Shall we?"

3

Minutes later, the detectives stood in front of a two-story farm style house on Christie Street. Train rails curved in parallel to Lincoln Highway, moving away from Menlo Park and town. Shadow opened the gate and stepped aside for his partner to enter.

"There's no need for this. You're the only one who can see me."

"Old habits die hard. It seems a waste that you've dressed to the nines and are invisible."

She took his arm when he offered it once more. "Old habits die hard."

The farmhouse was the only building on the property that felt homey, with its broad front porch that contained three rocking chairs and large windows with red shutters. Small clapboard factory-style buildings filled out the property. Cold, electric light filtered from the sparse structures through the few windows that dotted their exterior. Kate closed her parasol as Shadow knocked at the screen door. A young boy with his right arm in a sling came from the darkened interior of the house. "Are you Mr. Jones?" His eyes were dark and sad.

"Why, yes. I have an appointment with Mr. Edison."

The boy glanced back into the hall. "He's expecting you." Shadow paused to hold the door, but Kate shook her head. Without a word, he stepped in front of her. The boy reached to catch the door before it hit her and held it. *He can see me.* She put her finger to her lips and shook her head. He glanced around again as if he was afraid of being caught. He reminded her of some of the animals she'd seen at Lincoln Park Zoo. The same savageness mixed with fear. The boy ran down the hall. "I'll get Mr. Edison. You stay there."

Her partner took her arm for a moment. "Will he say anything?"

"I'm pretty sure he won't say a word. Wonder what happened to his arm?"

"Maybe he fell from a tree or a horse."

"He doesn't strike me as a boy who climbs or rides. There's something wild about him. Someone much larger could have broken it?"

"We shouldn't assume such things without evidence."

"Could he have been one of those children at the station?"

"He favors one of the boys I saw. I didn't get a clear view. If he is one of them, how did he end up back here?"

Before she could venture a guess, the boy returned and led them to a formal sitting room. He looked at Kate as though he wanted to ask a question but couldn't find the words. The wood floor from the hall echoed with footsteps, and his eyes got wide. He gulped and ran out of the parlor.

A low-grade hum caused the hairs on the back of her neck to tickle. It spread through her body like needles pricking her from head to toe. The sensation settled for a moment before clustering at the center of her chest.

"Do you feel that?"

Shadow looked up from his notebook. "No, but you look flushed."

She put her hand over the heavy lump under her ribcage. "I feel a sort of sharp tingle right here." The pricking spiked and the needles exploded down her arms. Her hands faded to the Inside.

"Perhaps you should sit down?" Her partner was being kind but not so helpful. The pain flooded down her legs. She couldn't stop herself from fluttering between Inside and Outside for a few moments. The needling hurt no matter where she was.

Before the conversation could continue, a man with tousled hair and a stern look entered the room followed by another man who wore glasses and had a sharp, well-groomed goatee. Kate stayed Outside even though the chance that the men could see her while she was Inside was slim. She saw the man with the goatee arch his eyebrow as he locked eyes with her for a moment. For a moment, his sharp features blurred, revealing gray skin and a gold reptilian eye that contrasted with his more human brown one.

"Mr. Edison." Her partner shook unkempt older man's hand while the bespectacled, smaller man scanned the room as if he were expecting something or someone else.

"I explained everything to Mr. O'Neill when he visited two months ago. There should be a transcript of that interview in your files, Mr. Jones." Edison spoke in a voice that was sharp and loud, as though he were lecturing instead of having a private conversation.

"The transcript is missing, sir. Possibly some inefficiency on the part of our agency."

The inventor's second gestured for everyone to be seated, but he continued to stand. "Where is Mr. O'Neill, Mr. Jones? Wasn't he the lead on this case?"

The inventor pointed to the dapper man, who seemed a bit distracted. "I'd like you to meet Mr. Harry, my assistant." He tapped the bespectacled man who smiled on cue in a way that was congenial but closed.

"Secretary, sir. I wouldn't presume to be your assist---"

"He is my assistant." Mr. Edison gestured for the detective to sit, but Shadow ignored him as he reached out to inventor's second to shake his hand.

Mr. Harry ignored the gesture, his eyes locked on Kate. "I'm also missing O'Neill's lovely partner...what was her name again?"

Edison looked puzzled. "He didn't have a partner on this case."

"Of course. I'd forgotten that. Said something about his partner being dead, I believe."

Kate sat down in the rocking chair, and the prickling settled in her chest once more. Mr. Harry moved behind the chair and pushed it as if he was bored.

Her partner kept a placid demeanor and didn't give any sense that she was there. "She died of tuberculosis."

"How tragic. Losing a partner must be difficult. I am so sorry for the loss."

Shadow returned his focus to Mr. Edison. "Mr. Edison, how exactly did the girl go missing?"

"Just like I told Mr. O'Neill, we woke up one morning and she'd gone. No letter, no goodbye. Just gone."

"That makes no sense." Kate muttered.

The next push was more forceful, and she almost fell out of it. Her head began to ache and for a moment, she saw the square nose and dead eyes of an alligator in her mind.

The assistant growled. "You're different. Who are you?"

A solid wall of pain squeezed around her chest like a corset that was pulled too tight. She must have gasped because Shadow turned, but she shook her head.

"How quaint. Trying to protect your Mr. Jones, I see. That is what partners do for one another, correct?"

Mr. Harry placed his hand over her wrist, pinning her arm. His hand was colder than any dead body she'd touched when she was Inside. He leaned in so close she could feel his breath move her hair around her face. "I am the future, the past, the gate," he whispered. "We shall return, and the world will be different and magnificent. You pitiful creatures will be a part of this."

The room around her fell away and she was right back in the vision from the airship. She floated past the opening as the same tentacles wrapped around her and her rocking chair prison and pulled her toward a pinprick of light that seemed miles away even though she could feel its heat. The blood-soaked moon loomed behind the door in front of her as the tolling bell began its ascent to thirteen tolls. Around the tentacles, there were thousands of eyes and sharp, gnashing teeth snapped under them. The prickling exploded inside her and she felt as though she were being devoured from the inside out. She opened her mouth to scream but nothing came out. Rage rose over her fear, and she began to struggle. If she ended up being eaten by whatever that thing was, she'd never forgive herself. As well-armed as she was, there was no way for her get to her weapons because she was so tangled in the writhing, heavy arms of the door creature.

Everything around her dimmed and turned gray. She could hear Shadow speaking in the distance. Her scream caught in the back of her throat and turned to a squeak. A sound, like the closing of a door, clicked in her head, and the moon and tentacles disappeared, leaving her back in the rocking chair in Edison's parlor.

Shadow saw Edison's second put his hand on the arm of the chair where Kate had been only moments before, shaking her head despite her pain. The dapper man gave him a condescending look. Shadow ignored the man's demeanor. Perhaps Kate had left to look around on her own. One of the excellent things about Kate being his partner was that she could go places without restriction since she could enter from the Outside. Whatever was causing her pain was in this room, she'd avoided it, and he was relieved. He turned his mind back to the client.

"Was the girl friends with any children in Raritan?" He thought about Tesla and the children on the platform and remembered that the girl named Thirteen called them "family."

"Mr. Jones, she was an asylum child."

"I'm not sure I follow, sir."

The older man leaned in close to the detective. "Her mother was an inmate at an asylum with no chance of release. I found the child when she was six or seven while touring a facility that was converting to electricity. Children like Thirteen don't make friends easily, so no. She had no little friends in Raritan and didn't go to school in town. She was tutored here at Menlo Park."

Shadow slid away from the man. "And her name? Most children aren't known as numbers."

It was clear that Edison was growing tired of the questions but wanted to try to be polite. "That was what she was called at the asylum. She wouldn't answer to anything else, so we continued to call her by the number."

"She had no other family?"

A look of pity crossed the inventor's face. "Asylum children never have family. Most aren't even acknowledged as people. We offered her a much better life."

"If you offered a better life, why would she leave at all?"

"The girl is troubled, Mr. Jones."

The Pinkerton wanted to ask about the other children who Thirteen called family at the station that night, but he had no idea how he'd explain seeing them or Tesla.

"That seems like a given. What sort of troubled?"

Edison clinched his fist and sighed. "As I told O'Neill, that has no real bearing on my finding her."

Mr. Harry spoke over his employer. "She caused conflict here at Menlo Park."

The inventor scowled at the man. "Conflict is the wrong word. Things happened. Several things. On the surface, they were unconnected. Our cat died suddenly. The chickens wouldn't lay eggs, mirrors shattered for no explainable reasons after she left the room. Some of the people here at Menlo found themselves with broken legs or equipment after interactions with her. There were never any clear explanations. Her presence seemed to cause bad luck."

Like O'Neill's death.

The detective closed his notebook. "You're a man of science and you can't come up with a better term than 'bad luck?'"

Edison's impatience was becoming more evident with each question. His assistant was no better.

"There is no scientific explanation for people like Thirteen."

"People? There are others?" This could be the opening Shadow was searching for.

The great inventor got up and began to pace as though he was giving a speech. "You've met people who are different, I'm sure, Mr. Jones. Some are better at certain things than the rest of us. Others seem to have bad things happen around them all the time. They are all around us and look no different than any of the rest of us. There is a potential in these people that is fascinating."

"So, you were studying her potential? For what reason? How is being studied going to give her a better life?"

Edison paused and put his hands together. "Getting rid of whatever it is that causes bad things to happen around this child means that she can have a better life. In order to help her, we had to apply science, which means study. Surely you can understand, sir."

"Applying science to debunk superstition and the things we don't understand. Seems reasonable."

It was time to be direct. "Were there other children you were helping to have a better life, sir?" Edison's lecture face dropped. "What about that boy who greeted me at the door earlier?"

The assistant took Shadow's arm. The man was stronger than he looked. "He answers the door and reminds Mr. Edison to eat, which is a step up from living in the woods, I'm sure."

There was a knock, and the boy entered the room as if on cue. "Mr. Edison, you have a meeting in town in ten minutes."

The Great Inventor cleared his throat. "As you can see, he does his job quite well." The assistant rose from the couch and pushed the rocking chair from its arm one more time. Shadow stood and shook the older man's hand once more.

Edison made his way to the exit. "I do hope you find the girl soon. We want the best for her, you know."

The detective adjusted his coat. Kate had been gone a while now. "Could I take a look around the facility? I'd like to talk to the people she interacted with."

"Many of those people are no longer with us," said Edison's assistant.

"Give him the tour and answer any questions. He may be able to learn a few things that will lead us to the girl."

The odd little man nodded. "Mr. Jones, follow me." Shadow glanced back at the chair, and for an instance thought he saw Kate. She faded in long enough for him to see a look of terror on her face.

"Are you looking for something, Mr. Jones?" The assistant guided him to the door.

"No. Just admiring that rocking chair. I think it moved."

"How odd." They exited, and he shut the door behind them. Shadow fought the urge to take one last glance. As the two men made their way to the front of the house, The boy scurried back down the hall away as if he wanted to get as far from them as possible. Once they were outside, the bespectacled man began what sounded like a rote spiel. "Menlo Park holds many wonders of the modern age. Mr. Edison takes pride in the fact that this is a hub of research, invention, and progress, which draws intellectuals from all over the globe."

"Does that include a man named Tesla?"

The assistant paused as if he wasn't used to being interrupted. "Mr. Tesla is one of those people who are no longer with us."

"Bad interaction with Thirteen?"

His companion's demeanor dropped from professional boredom to downright icy. "He was asked to leave."

"Why?" Shadow pushed.

Mr. Harry turned on his heel to face the detective. The man's pupils were horizontal slits surrounded by brown-gold irises. Impatient hunger danced behind them. "Because he asked too many questions." He blinked, and his pupils were once again round and dilated, but a dissatisfied glint remained. "But then, questions are your job, aren't they?" He turned and walked as if nothing had transpired.

The man's shift was alarming, but Shadow didn't want to give this...whatever he was...the pleasure of his discomfort. Instead, he pressed forward. "Do you have a forwarding address for Mr. Tesla? I'd like to ask him some questions."

A low-level growl emanated from his guide, and he clenched his fist. "I'm afraid he didn't leave one. Now, if you're done with that line of thought, let's proceed." With that, the two of them entered a building marked with a number three. Nothing of what the strange fellow droned on about during this tour answered any more questions about the girl or her bad luck.

The sharp prickling in Kate's chest disappeared, leaving a hum in its place. That secretary was close by, but she suspected he'd turned his focus to her partner. *Maybe he thought I would be taken care of,* she thought. She pushed her hand through from Outside to Inside. For the first time she could feel the veil that parted the side-by-side worlds.

A small voice rose behind her. "Who are you, ma'am?"

She turned to find the boy with the broken arm. His face was gaunt and there were dark circles under his eyes. The fact that he could see her even when she was Outside didn't surprise her. Children tended to see past the veil. Some even had playmates on the Outside till they grew older and started believing that these friends were imaginary.

The lady detective knelt in front of him. She wanted to whisk him back to the hotel and take care of him but wasn't sure if he or she would be safe. "I'm Mr. Jones's friend. Can you tell me where he went?"

"He's with Mr. Harry." He clenched his fist and trembled when he spoke the name.

"Did he do this?" She touched his arm and braced for the answer.

He pushed her hand away, eyes wide. He glanced all around her as if he expected someone to jump out and attack them both. Then he backed toward the door, his eyes settling on her. He stopped at the door, used his good hand to turn the knob, and paused.

He nodded, and then bolted into the dark interior of the house.

She could have given chase but didn't want to scare him even more.

"Poor, kid."

Perhaps the reason for Thirteen leaving was becoming clearer.

Who is this man? Was he some sort of construct built in the lab or a supernatural creature of some sort? She was not eager to get close enough to find out at the moment. A construct couldn't send her to a different realm with the touch of a hand. The boy was also a mystery. He was as much animal as person. She wondered what transpired between him and the assistant that would have ended in a broken arm.

Staying Outside, she left the house and choked back her outrage as she wondered if Edison knew how Mr. Harry treated the children. There were three large structures that filled the back of the property. Kate could hear buzzes and crackles as well as other work sounds like hammering and sawing even though she was Outside. Acrid smells of fire and chemicals rose around her as she made her way around buildings, hoping that Edison's mysterious assistant didn't sense her skulking about. The curious thing about the Outside was that, for the most part, it was the same as the Inside. Same sounds, same textures, and same view, so Kate saw everything that anyone else would see as they walked through the property. The main difference was that, usually, she also saw her fellow dearly departed, as she'd heard folks on the Inside call them. These were people and creatures that had come to the Outside like she had. Most of them knew they had passed and chose to stay in the Outside to make a new life for themselves. She'd seen everything from schoolmarms to giant elephants with enough fur to make the richest women gasp.

Menlo Park was empty of such things. She was alone in the Outside for the moment. *Perhaps it's all the electrical experimentation going on.* As she continued through the property, the oddity nagged at her but there was no clear answer.

She walked alongside a building labeled with a large, painted 2 and spotted Shadow and Mr. Harry turn the corner opposite her. She pulled back, not wanting to be spotted. Once they were out of sight, she took stock of the area. *Where would the children Shadow saw have lived?* The numbered buildings seemed to be laboratories based on the sounds and activities coming from the Inside. *That boy would know,* she thought, but knew he'd never tell her. The main house was large, but not large enough for thirteen children.

Just past Building Three, she tripped over a dirt-stained metal plate and fell. As she picked herself up, she saw that the plate had a lock on it. She knelt down in the dirt and examined it, shifting from her afternoon dress to Levi's and a blue work shirt. *Well, damn.* Having a random door in the ground was odd. Having a lock on it was odder. *All the ingredients necessary to make a curious person, like myself, want to know what's under there.*

She could pick the lock, but that might take a while, which didn't matter unless Mr. Harry came back this direction. There was also a chance the lock had been built on site, which meant that her tools might not be up to the task. The faster, easier method would be to simply use some energy and pass through the door. Of course, if the secretary was close, he might sense the fluctuation of energy between Inside and Outside. Both were risky options, but she had not become the senior female detective at Pinkerton's by choosing safety. She glanced around and the grounds were empty except for a few scientists crossing from one building to another and phased down through the door. She glided down onto a set of dusty stairs into a dark hallway. The darkness pushed against her, challenging her presence. She continued to move forward, ignoring the silent threat. She was dead, so there was no need to be afraid. She thought of the tentacles again. *Except for that. Universe-ending monsters are frightening even if I have crossed the mortal coil.*

What she thought might be a cellar turned into more of an underground barracks. There was an open area and then a corridor that led farther down into the ground. She followed it even though the lighting was dim at best. Without hesitation, she entered a few of the locked rooms, finding in each a small cot and a washstand. *Did the scientists sleep down here?* As she made her way down the passage, she saw an open door. A sort of musty scent wafted from it.

The room contained a table with a cabinet behind it. On the table was a book. A series of metal latches held it closed. At the center of the cover was the face of an angry gargoyle with snakes surrounding its head. *Medusa?* Kate backed against the wall as a familiar prickling in her chest rose again. *Had Mr. Harry come looking for her?*

The prickling danced down her arms and legs, and the room crackled with the same energy she'd felt in her vision. The pain she previously experienced rose through her once again, and the book shot a bolt as black and shiny as obsidian at her. She threw herself to the floor and it exploded against the door with a resounding boom. If the residual energy hadn't pierced through her and cleared her thoughts, she would have been worried about the attack being heard. She was glad it'd not struck her dead on. Even while she was dying, she'd not felt such a sharp, deep agony. A low-grade prickle rose inside her again, as if the book were revving for a second attack, so she dove under the thick oaken table. The book shook and the metal latches tinkled and rattled. The door was only a few feet away, but she wasn't sure if she could crawl through it before whatever was guarding the book took another shot at her. She'd fought a lot of odd folks in her day, but she'd never fought a locked book before.

As Kate crouched under the table, Shadow's voice echoed into the room as if he was close. She almost called out but was interrupted by Mr. Harry's voice. This gave her pause. Her partner bedeviled the man with questions. It was one of his best tactics. Ask questions until the subject breaks. He must think something was enough off about the secretary to justify this. Of course, none of it mattered as long as she was trapped by the gargoyle on the book.

The men's voices faded, and she was left with her opponent. No chance for help now. The pain subsided and the shaking on the table ceased. *Maybe that thing believes I am gone.* She shifted her weight and bumped the table. The book came back to life. The table shook harder than before, and Kate rolled into a fetal position and fluttered Inside and Outside as pain threatened to tear her apart. *What happened to no more pain, no more tears?*

As she attempted to gain control of herself, she got angry. Every time she fluttered, she could see herself lying under the table, holding her knees like a five-year-old. Anger gave way to fury. Who the hell was she anyway?! The rattling stopped again, and the pain and fear subsided. Now was her chance. She got on her hands and knees and skittered out from the protection of the table. She might not survive what came next, but it was better than doing nothing. She spotted a small rock in one corner of the room. She crawled across the room, grabbed it, and threw it at the book. The rock bounced off it and hit the floor. Nothing else happened. She unpinned her brown feathered hat and threw it. Before it could reach the table, a black bolt reached out from the center of the book and the hat fizzled and faded away. A wave of agony made her wish she'd stayed under the table.

"Don't like Spectrals, huh?"

Once the book calmed once again, she checked out the room. The exit was close, and she might be able to leave without the book. Given that the book attacked her and that she was certain it had information about what was going on with the children here at Menlo Park, she couldn't convince herself that leaving it behind was in any way good. Anything that made her feel the way that thing did deserved to be defeated. It might also reveal how and why the so-called Great Inventor had thrown in with the likes of that creature posing as his assistant.

One edge of the book was hanging off the table, opening a possible option she'd not considered.

As long as it doesn't see me...

A single, satisfying thump sounded after she tilted the table causing the book to fall off onto the dirt floor. *It's always the stupid simple stuff that works best.* The needling pain subsided and more of her strength returned. *Now that I've got it, how do I get it out of here without it destroying me.* She couldn't just conjure up a bag. The gargoyle would just try to destroy the bag the way it had done her hat.

Surely there is something I can use from the Inside to wrap the beast. She materialized and after a quick search discovered a thin blanket on a cot in one of the cells. Once she returned, she slid it under the book, taking care to not put her hands under it for the gargoyle to see. A single sharp pain cut through her as she secured the blanket and slung it over her shoulder. Victory was hers. She couldn't help but hum a little tune she'd learned in the Confederate camps as she headed down the corridor and back to the surface. Just before she opened the cellar door, she heard the secretary's voice once again and the book shuddered and struggled. She pushed the makeshift bag against the wall with her hip so that if the gargoyle started screaming no one above would hear. The two men above her had a conversation that took an eternity.

The lady Pinkerton waited an extra few minutes after that was done to be sure that Mr. Harry was gone. If her partner was smart, and he was for the most part, he'd head on back to the hotel and wait for her. She attempted to phase through the door, but the book shuddered, and the door solidified. Kate pulled hard and the door thinned out. Before she could stop herself, she lost her balance and fell backward. The wrapped book smacked her on the chest and fell to the ground. Once she caught her breath, she looked around, grabbed the bag, and scrambled for Christie Street. There was no way to know if anyone could see the bag fluttering between the Inside and Outside, but she couldn't leave it behind.

Shadow walked along the tree line and she caught up, book in tow. "Mr. Jones."

Without a pause, he walked into the tree line, and she followed. He gestured to the make-shift bag. "What's that you have there?"

She dropped it at his feet. "A rather deadly trinket I found while you were hobnobbing with that thing upstairs."

"Upstairs? Wait. You found that cellar door, didn't you?"

Kate tapped her nose.

"There's a maze of rooms that I didn't get to see much of while I was down there, except the room where this book was out on a table. You'd think they'd keep something that dangerous locked up. Damned thing tried to kill me for good down there," said Kate. "Being almost destroyed twice in one day isn't my idea of a fun time."

"Twice?" The long-legged detective knelt to get a closer look at the blanket covered book. He started to unwrap it.

"I wouldn't do that here." Kate picked up the package and swung it over her shoulder again. "Mr. Harry trapped me somewhere that wasn't Inside or Outside. The place had the same bleeding moon and bell tolls. The major difference was that the tentacles tried to pull me to wherever they came from."

Shadow brushed off his pants and offered to take it from her. "Could he have caused that vision in the airship?"

She passed it to him, and they made their way back to the main thoroughfare. "Doubtful. He looked surprised when he spotted me in that chair."

"But then why did you feel that prickling in your chest before he arrived?"

A few wagons passed them, and several people crossed back and forth as they spoke. All she could see were Insiders. "Maybe it's some sort of warning system to alert him and disable Spectrals that crossed onto the property. He was surprised when he saw me and made damned sure to let me know that I was not welcome."

"Which means he knows you're a Spectral and have powers that allow you access to most everything if you want."

She nodded. "He sent me to something with lots of tentacles. I thought it may just devour me straightaway, but then everything turned gray, like clouds, and I was back in the chair."

"Is that how you managed to escape and find your little treasure there? Or did I manage to distract him?"

"You and your barrage of questions. I heard some of that. Impressive work, detective." The world around her went fuzzy around the edges and needles danced up her back.

Shadow didn't notice. "It seemed to deeply annoy him, but it didn't make him reveal anything of use, I'm afraid."

The scene faded out once more and more prickling and pain moved through her as she found herself alone Outside. The streets were empty. She looked up into some of the windows of the houses and buildings around her and saw a couple of fearful faces peering back at her. Other buildings were boarded up and abandoned. A hard tug brought her back to the active, noon-time street they'd been traversing. Her partner was holding her hand.

"What the hell just happened? I thought you were going to faint for a moment."

"Something's wrong in this town. On the Outside." She told him what she'd seen.

"This place should be teeming with Spectrals."

"Yes. But something is messing with them."

"Maybe this book?"

She looked blanket wrapped artifact without touching it. "It's possible. It certainly wanted to destroy me."

"Well, we can't take it back now." Her partner opened his bag and stuffed the still-wrapped book into it. Muffled screams rose from the book as he latched the bag shut.

"I'm not sure that thing likes you any more than it likes me."

"It doesn't have to like me." He took her arm and shouldered the muttering package. "It just has to leave you alone. How do you feel?"

"Better.

He squeezed her hand. "Good. I need my partner to be around so this case can be solved."

The screaming subsided as they approached the hotel. Her partner opened the door for her. "It's calmed down. Wonder what it's up to and why it hasn't attacked you?"

"Maybe it hates Spectrals and nothing else, or it doesn't know what I am."

They lowered their voices as they crossed the lobby and made their way up the stairs to their rooms. "Well, since it doesn't have anything against members of the Brotherhood, perhaps you could manage to get it open. In all fairness, this is Brotherhood-level nonsense, don't you agree?"

He scratched his chin the way Allan did when he was puzzling through a line of thought and then switched to a familiar Scottish burr. "I was afraid you'd say that, Mrs. Warne."

She punched his arm as they entered the hotel.

4

Once they got to the room, Shadow pulled the book out of his messenger bag and dropped it on the bed. The book grunted and a mixture of leather, mildew, and some unknown spice wafted up and inundated the area. Kate felt like she'd just walked through a rosebush and had run into every single thorn it had.

"It senses me." She backed into a corner to avoid more pain and then faded Outside. The silence unnerved her as much as the pain.

Her partner opened the adjoining door to her room. "Go in there and wait."

She was able to come back Inside once he shut the door. "I don't want to just cower while you have all the fun."

He crossed his arms and stood in front of the exit. "Tell me about what you saw before it attacked you."

"The lock looks like a gargoyle. No, more like Medusa...it has snakes around its head. The eyes are jeweled, I think. It shot black energy bolts at me and anything I called up from the Outside. Those bolts disperse and destroy things from the Outside."

"And you want to go back in there to have all the fun?"

"I should have a chance to get it back for trying to murder me."

Kate tried to push past her partner, but he didn't budge, which didn't surprise her, but did irritate her. He stood like one of those wooden statues in front of some general stores. She threw up her hands and sat down in a chair that matched the one in the adjoining room.

"I don't want it to get a second chance. Look, I've already lost you once to something I couldn't fight. This time, we have the upper hand, but you have to step aside. You already tricked it and learned some of its weaknesses." Shadow leaned against the door. "You can't always be the hero, dear Kate. I'm your partner. Remember, this is *our* battle now. Not just yours."

Had any other man said this to her, she'd probably have conked him. Shadow was different. He never patronized her. They'd worked as equals since the first day he arrived at the Pinkerton office to help her investigate secessionist activities in Baltimore, Maryland. While she attended social events as a flirtatious Southern belle and rooted out information about a plot against Lincoln, her partner managed to discover and dispatch an organization of insurgent werewolves who planned to attack West Point.

"I don't want to be the hero. I just want to kick the hell out of whatever that thing is." She fiddled with her skirts and hated how much she sounded like a whiny child.

"That's no way to treat a book, you know." Humor danced in his dark-brown eyes. A familiar scream rose from the other room. Her partner opened the door and the familiar tingle of pain returned for Kate. "Maybe it will like me better. I am quite charming at times. Stay in here and let's see how it fancies me." She closed the door enough to buffer some of her pain but peered through the crack. If it got the best of him, she needed to be ready.

He reentered his room and removed the blanket from the book. The eyes of the lock glowed green, but nothing shot at him. Shadow stumbled back and then shook his head.

"Damned thing tried to knock me out." He rolled up his sleeves and leaned over the book.

"Be careful. It's a wily thing." Kate warned from the other room.

"It reminds me of some of the books Old Franklin had in his library in Philly."

"Are you saying Mr. Franklin was a magician of some sort?"

"Ben dabbled in many things, so it wouldn't shock me in the least." He examined the lock. "The lock was machined, so not as old as the book. Someone has kept it clean too. Recent signs of bluing. This should make it easier to find a master for it." He pulled out a ring of keys from his jacket. When he leaned in and touched the lock, Kate noticed that the color of the eyes changed from emerald-green to ruby red.

"Be careful, it doesn't like what you're doing."

Her partner's hand shook hard, and he dropped the keys to the floor. He knelt to pick them up and doubled over for a moment. Kate clutched the doorknob as a wave of pricking pain washed over her as well.

Once it'd passed, Shadow got to his knees and took a deep breath. I'm not a Spectral if that's what you're trying to decide." He grabbed the keys and returned to the book.

The first key snapped before he could even try to turn the lock. Shattered pieces of the key spat out, bouncing off his nose. The book laughed and spoke a garble of unintelligible words. The tone made the hair on Kate's neck stand. What she saw next made her want to run.

A creature rose behind her partner. It's backward bending legs that reminded her of crickets. When it spotted her, it's face split in half with a grin of sharp teeth. A chittering growl rose from its blue-green chest. She held on to the door and unholstered the derringer from her boot.

"Shadow. You may want to stop."

Her partner didn't hear her and pulled out another master key to stuff in the mouth of the Medusa. "Look, you chalker, I know you can't hurt me."

"You're talking to the wrong thing. There's something behind you." She flung the door wide but before she could fire, the creature disappeared.

She checked behind her in her room but saw nothing. *Where had it gone?* Shadow, who was completely focused on his task, muttered and cursed behind her.

"Damned thing is eating my keys like candy."

Before she could reply, a grin appeared to float over her bed. Familiar blue-green scales flooded underneath the curve of pointed teeth. The face and bulbous eyes etched in the face, and all was rooted with the cricket-legs with hooves. The lady detective leveled the derringer at the thing.

"You know that creature that was behind you, Shadow?"

"Any idea where it could have gone?" He shook his diminishing key ring.

The creature jumped down from the mattress and leaned close enough for its breath to blow through her hair. She willed herself Outside to no avail. With that avenue spent, she slid toward the wash table at the other end of the room as it slashed at her. It followed, turning its back to the door to her partner's room. Saliva dripped from the corner of the thing's mouth as if it was hungry.

Shadow entered the room, pistol ready, and it turned to meet him. Instead of attacking it grew toward the ceiling and backed into a corner as it assessed both detectives.

Her partner didn't take his eyes from the oversized demon-looking thing. "Ever seen anything like this before?"

"I was hoping you had." Her hands shook as she kept her inadequate weapon trained on the beast.

"Well, I have. In the other room. Just now."

The creature roared, making the furniture shake around them. It launched a long, out-sized arm toward Kate. Shadow stepped in front of her, and its hand stopped within inches of his chest. Kate saw the fingers turn red, like they were being burned. The mottled skin on the creature's arm began to turn red and sizzle. The creature yanked back from her partner and Shadow stepped forward, aiming his pistol at it.

A light shone from behind demon-like thing where the wall of the room should be, and Kate could feel a pull coming from the other side. The wallpaper smoked, spreading an acrid smell into the area. Her attacker folded at the middle of its back and bared its teeth before being yanked through. Kate held onto the iron fore board of the bed and grabbed at Shadow's hand but missed it. He didn't seem to feel the pull of the light and fired at their adversary. The sound of the weapon was muffled, and laughter poured into the room once more before the light extinguished leaving them alone.

She collapsed against the rose-lined wall. "You made quite the impression on that thing."

He sat down on the bed. "Was it something I said?"

She moved to the wall where the light had poured through moments before. It left no evidence of it ever being there. "You have no idea why it reacted that way, do you?"

"No more than I understand why the things connected with that lock and book want to destroy Spectrals." Her partner searched the bed for anything it may have left.

"Don't put another of your keys in that thing. No telling what will come after us next time."

"I'm thinking we're done with keys. Time to bring out the big guns." He exited, pistol still in hand and approached the book.

The lady detective scurried after him. "Please tell me you aren't going to shoot it."

"Give me credit, Mrs. Warne." With that, he holstered his pistol and began rummaging through his bag. Kate felt the pain surging as she crossed the threshold and backed away to the relative safety of her own room. This time, she didn't close the door.

Her partner pulled out a sturdy pair of wire cutters. The cutters shone like new, and the blades looked as though they'd just been sharpened. The blades sank into the clasp like it was butter. Kate's vision fluttered and, for a moment, she thought she was going blind. The pain was so strong that it knocked her down.

She struggled to her feet in time to see an arc of black energy throw Shadow across to the other corner of the room. A corona of dim gray burst around her partner as he banged against the wall. Through the haze, she could see him struggling to not embrace the darkness that wrapped around him.

Before she moved, a door appeared in front of her, and the creature from moments before reappeared, reaching for her with burnt claws. Tentacles tried to wrap around her as she skittered back. The language she'd heard in her vision flowed from the door in a rhythmic chat joined with the scream of the lock and burned into her being. She swallowed her terror as she was torn between both worlds at the same time. One wet, brown tentacle wrapped around her waist, and pulled her toward the creature that had now opened its mouth revealing row after row of spiny teeth.

"Shadow!" The chanting paused and the tentacle around her waist loosened just enough for her to pull free and run toward her partner. Just before she could reach him, a large hand grabbed her bustle and pulled her back toward the growing creature in the other room. *Damned fashion.* She willed the skirt to fade, leaving her in her pantaloons, and had to step forward to keep from falling on her face.

Kate scrambled between the book and the gray dome. The book's energy burned around her, but she held her ground and reached for Shadow.

"Take my hand." She pushed her hand through the cloudy dome. The darkness burned up her arm, but she ignored the pain and found Shadow's hand. She pulled hard enough that he stumbled and fell against her and into her arms. He grabbed onto her.

A tentacle wrapped around her corseted waist and yanked her out of Shadow's embrace back toward the creature's slathering maw of needle-teeth. The bizarre words that flowed around her got louder and made it stronger. The tentacle tightened and shook her like a rag doll. It pulled her closer to its maw and for a moment, her head spun. When her vision cleared again, she saw the chatelaine purse she'd worn with her outfit lying on the bed. Its brown leather and beads were as solid as if it should have been from the Inside. By all rights, it should have disappeared when she lost her skirts. Then she remembered what it held. She kicked the creature in the chest and the tentacle loosened enough for her to lunge for the bed. She scrambled for the bag on the mattress. The long arm of whatever this thing was wrapped around her waist and yanked her back in as it roared with frustration. Her arms were free, so she snapped open the bag and pulled out a rustic, deer antler knife with an edge that shined like a star that had been a gift from her dear friend in Savannah, Don the Knife. When he'd given it to her, he called it God-Killer, but wouldn't tell her why. She slid the knife between her waist and the pulsing arm around it.

"Damn you, beast. You will let me go this instant!"

She turned the thin, bright edge of her weapon toward the tentacle. The blade sang as it sliced through her captor's arm as though it was the most tender of steaks. The creature howled with anger and pain. Its former tentacle flopped onto the wooden floor with a nasty *splat* as blood and green gore covered what was left of Kate's clothing. Kate never let go God-Killer as she fell away from the now raging beast. She sat up in time to see a second tentacle reach across the bed and wrap around the book.

"Oh hell, no."

With her last bit of energy, she lunged at the tentacle with her still-shining weapon and stabbed the creature once more. It dropped the book and howled as more green mess coated the walls. She crawled across the floor and pushed the tome behind her against the wall in spite of the pain it caused. Her angry, wounded opponent pushed the bed to one side as if to give itself more room for the final kill.

Kate's hands shook as she pointed the knife at the thing.

Calm down, I'll help.

She wasn't sure where the voice came from, but her hand stopped shaking.

The tentacle-beast stopped cold when it saw her blade pointed in its direction.

"Why isn't it attacking me?" She wasn't sure if speaking out loud was the right thing to do.

It knows what I am and where I come from.

The blade pulled her toward the creature. She moved faster than she'd ever moved before and landed two slices into the monster chest. Her opponent looked as shocked as she felt.

It put its hands on the wounds and greenish blood flowed between its fingers. The chanted language stopped and was replaced by a howling wind. A silver-blue door opened over the bed and the wind sucked the angry, injured creature backward into it. Once it was past the threshold, the light and the wind snapped off.

The lady Pinkerton slumped against the wall, and her weapon slid into her lap. The blade was warm, but sparkled, unblemished by the green blood of the creature.

"What the hell are you?" She rolled the knife in her hand.

The maker warned you that I was special.

"He never said you were alive."

For him, that's a given.

"There's no metal I know of on Earth that can talk and attack at its own will."

Who says I was made of material from this world, child?

Kate shoved the knife into its sheath, not knowing what to make of the answer or the fact that she'd just had a conversation with a weapon. This was something to talk to Don the Knife about when next they met.

She faded to the Outside and was relieved to find no evidence of the thing lurking there.

Kate scrambled to her partner, who sat against the corner where he'd been trapped moments before, his face paler than usual. As she joined him, he laughed and turned his head away from her. She looked down at her lacy bloomers dotted with tiny roses and covered with monster guts.

"Mrs. Warne, your fashion sense is impeccable but inappropriate, don't you think?"

"I may have lost my skirts, but I won the battle." She transitioned to a simple pair of dungarees and a work shirt with boots. "Let's take a look at what I managed to cut off…"

The tentacles that she'd sheared off moments before were gone as was all the gore that had covered the area.

"Housekeeping will be pleased."

The book, however, was still against the wall, the Medusa facing toward her. The lock lay next to it on the floor, the clasp sheared into two pieces. Its eyes were no longer green or red, but clear stones filled with silver needles. Tendrils of smoke wafted from its mouth. The room was quiet. The prickling and pain that the book should have caused her was gone. She reached for the tome, but Shadow, who'd gotten up and joined her, took her arm.

"That thing just tried to kill both of us."

"I think you released whatever was trying to kill us when you cut the lock. The eyes look different."

The lanky detective stepped in front of her and tapped the book with his toe. His protectiveness aggravated her but also made her appreciate him even more. The book didn't respond or hum or act in any way that a book shouldn't.

"How do you feel?" He looked back at her.

"Being near it doesn't hurt anymore."

He knelt down to inspect the face on the cover. "The eyes are different now too. They look like quartz crystal."

Kate moved closer, but her partner put out his hand. She pushed it aside. "I think we got rid of the part of it that was bent on killing me."

Shadow nodded and picked up the book, placing it on the bed. "And angered someone who wants and needs the book as well. Two different attacks. The book and whoever sent that tentacled nightmare."

"If it's Mr. Harry, why would he need this book?" Kate picked up her bag from the bed and her sheathed knife away.

"And why would he involve Mr. Edison, who is a mere human?" Shadow followed her.

"The larger question is does this connect with the missing girl and the children you saw when you went to the station? If it does, we need to figure out how. For all we know that thing is hunting them down."

"But why would it hunt these children?"

She called up a cup of tea and took a sip. "If that girl brings bad luck like Edison claims, then maybe the other children do similar things. What if that cryptozoological nightmare of a secretary is working to create an apocalypse of sorts?"

"But why go to all the trouble to work with Mr. Edison. Doesn't he want to make the world a better place?"

"Edison is experimenting with electricity. Is it possible that there are energies even more powerful that have yet to be discovered? Maybe the book will offer a clue." She led her partner back to his room and picked up the book. Whatever energy caused this to happen and whatever fueled that door that opened over the bed is much more powerful, don't you think?"

Her partner took the book from her and turned it over to examine it. "It could be that the electricity that Edison works with catalyzes whatever Mr. Harry is using."

"I doubt this energy needs a catalyst."

He laid the book back on the bed, "Perhaps the thing with the children has nothing to do with the offer to tap other energies. Do you think the old man knows what his assistant is?"

"You saw what he looks like under that sharp-dressed-man guise, huh?"

Shadow nodded. "I don't understand how an alligator man taps this sort of energy though."

"He said that he was the gate when he caught me back at Menlo Park. My presence infuriated him, so he tried to scare me. He could be some sort of cultist who has it out for Spectrals." She took her turn at the window not wanting to admit that the secretary had scared her.

"Those of you on the Outside tend to see more than those Inside, so you could be a threat. You can move between planes in ways that not even the Brotherhood can move. As far as a cult, I've never encountered a cult amongst the alligator people that taps this sort of thing. This is different."

Kate nodded. The alligator people of the Golden Isles at the coast of Georgia had many powers, but none of them involved destroying the planet. They were brutal but kept to themselves for the most part. They also wouldn't survive this far north. "Mr. Harry is probably not one of them. He is something else. It could be he's manifesting as something we can understand. At any rate, we have his book, and I imagine that he knows and is properly peeved now that we've driven off his minions. We need to make a quick retreat."

"If he can call minions like he just did, then retreat may not matter."

She pointed at the book in her partner's hands. "True, but since the lock is burned out, traveling may make it harder for him to follow."

The lady detective was about to close the curtain again when she saw the sharp-dressed Mr. Harry enter into view. He glided around a group of ladies without a tip of the hat as if he were focused on his prey. She gestured toward the window and her partner joined her. He said, "Check out time."

"Too bad. You didn't even have time for supper." She closed the blinds, and he grabbed the book.

"Perhaps I should carry this." He slid it into his bag. Kate extinguished the gaslight by the door, allowing her fellow detective to melt into the darkness and away.

A deep-throated growl came from the other side of the door. Not wanting another fight, Kate phased through the floor. She found herself at the back of a large kitchen. Even though she was Outside, there should have been the usual bustle of people and food expected for a saloon. Instead, the kitchen was empty except for a heavy-built woman covered in flour who was kneading dough on a wooden table. When she laid eyes on Kate, she froze.

"No!" The woman backed away from her and picked up a wooden spoon.

The detective raised her hands. "I won't hurt you."

An angry roar echoed from upstairs. Kate felt prickling at the edge of her mind again. *But we got rid of that...*

The baker crouched and looked up at the ceiling as what sounded like furniture was being thrown around. "Oh gods, he's here."

"Who?"

The woman backed up against a cupboard. "The Devourer. Don't you hear him?"

The door slammed hard and then along with the prickling, Tinny, off-tempo notes accompanied the heavy steps coming down a set of stairs to the back of the kitchen.

"He's not after you. I took something from him. Something very valuable and now he's angry." The lady Pinkerton stepped in front of the woman.

"It don't matter. We're Outsiders. He'd be after you no matter."

"What do you mean?"

The tinkling music got closer, and a foot appeared on the stair just below the floor. She grabbed the baker's hand. "Let's go." They exited into the tight alleyway behind the hotel. Kate scrambled and dove into what turned out to be the town stable. A couple of horses whickered but none panicked. The scent of horse dung was a comfort despite the ticking pain that danced, once again, up her arms and legs. Not far away, a door slammed open, and the weird tune flowed out.

Her companion trembled and moaned. "We going to die for sure."

If they died for sure, that would be it. No Outside or Inside for them.

She grabbed the woman by the face and looked in her eyes. "What you said back there. What does he have against Spectrals?"

The baker pulled away from her and spat. "Nothing. He doesn't hate us. He eats us! Have you seen anyone on the Outside in this place?"

Kate sat back. Menlo Park was empty and so were the streets on their way to the hotel. This woman was the first she'd seen the entire visit. "No one except you."

"I know you're around here close. Make it easy on yourselves, ladies."

Her companion pushed her out of the stable on the opposite street from where he was coming. "I don't know who you are, but you seem nice. Get on out of here. I'll manage." Their scuffle caused the horses to skitter around in their stalls. One muscular chestnut whinnied.

The detective grabbed her hand. "Come with me! I'm going to Chicago."

"He's already taken my family. There ain't nothing left for me." The woman pushed her out onto the street. An angry roar tore through the alleyway and she said, "Go now!"

Kate ran faster than she knew she could. A shrill scream rose from behind her, and the Outside shuddered as if it was going to tear apart.

The need to get away overcame her desire to turn back. She didn't stop except to throw up at the edge of town. The woman was gone-gone, and it was her fault. When she found an empty seat aboard the airship, she closed her eyes, trying to unhear and unfeel everything that had led to that final moment in the stable. An innocent bystander had died because she'd provoked Mr. Harry. She summoned a cup of tea, but her hand shook hard enough to make even that one respite impossible. She'd seen men die in battle during the war, but none of that prepared her this sort of final death. She wept as the airship made its way to Chicago, Allan, Shadow, and safety.

5

Shadow stepped into their office, took the book from his bag, and placed it on his desk. He'd studied many supernatural texts in the almost three hundred years since he and the Brotherhood had been called to service, and he was familiar with many of the languages used to invoke and provoke all manners of spirit and power. This book was written in none of those languages. The letters were hand-scripted, and some pages were illuminated with bright colors and large, complex symbols. Other pages had drawings of creatures that reminded him of the way ancient Egyptians told stories. One drawing showed a circle of people looking up at a door in the sky. The next showed them kneeling before two alligator-faced creatures wearing crowns. One was smaller, and Shadow assumed it was female, but since both were wearing gold robes, it was hard to tell. The word 'Yog-Sothoth' was written in red over the door. He flipped through it again, stopping at a page with circles and numbers. Then he moved back to the page mentioning 'Yog-Sothoth.' America was home to many creatures and spiritual oddities, especially since the war, when both sides dabbled in things that were in no one's best interests.

Before he could continue, there was a tap at his door. His superior leaned in. "No Kate?

"She's on the airship. I will meet her at the station in a bit." The Brother examined the tome, continuing to flip pages back and forth in search of more connections.

Pinkerton joined him and scratched his beard. "It would seem you have found a piece of trouble. Was that at Menlo Park?"

"Kate found it by accident after provoking Mr. Edison's assistant, who is, shall we say, unusual."

The senior detective winced. "She's rather good at that, isn't she?"

Shadow didn't reply but turned back to the book.

Pinkerton tapped his fingers on the table, and said, "There is no use in burying yourself in that book after a sideways comment like that."

The Brother didn't look up but continued taking notes as he turned the page. "She wants to continue working. It's what she loves."

"Well, I can't manage it. I see her, and all I know is that I want her again."

The ageless liaison put down his pen, but still refused to look at his employer. "You should take this up with her."

An uncomfortable silence settled between the two of them. Even after a few centuries, the liaison was unsure how to respond to lovers' quarrels. This quarrel was even more complicated by Kate being Spectral, and his partner. He'd worked hard to not become involved in what she and Mr. Pinkerton had before she passed away. The one time it had come up in conversation, he told her to trust her instincts. After that, he just made sure to stay clear of the entire situation. It made him uncomfortable, just like this moment.

The next page in the book revealed a drawing of a circle. Around the circle were Roman numerals in parentheses and the corresponding words for the numerals in Latin.

Pinkerton cleared his throat, leaned closer to the book and traced the circle with his finger. "Pre-church Latin?"

"Yes, but it's a bastardized form. Can you read any of it?"

Allan shook his head. "The language I learned in school is nowhere close to that." He moved his finger back to the circle. "The only things on this page that make sense to me are these numbers. Language may change, but numbers don't." He began to read like a schoolboy would. "Unus, Duo, and Tres. . ." he read until he got to "Tredecim."

"Thirteen." The men glanced at each other.

"The girl?"

"So, it does come back to her." Shadow moved to the cabinet and pulled out two glasses and his whiskey. After pouring for both of them, he continued to examine the page headed by a writhing bundle of snakes coming out of a dark circle. There were more words he could not read around the sketch. Below it was a door emanating a bright light, indicated with lines around it. The huge bundle of snakes was at the center. Figures of people, lots of people were rising toward it and into the light. In the margin was scribbled "Power=light. Death=light."

"Death? But what death?"

Movement at the top of the page grabbed his attention. The snakes were reaching out at him, and cerulean light poured out from the doors where the lines had been moments before that was so bright he covered his eyes. His throat tightened and he couldn't speak. As the light changed from a cerulean to a pale eggshell blue, he grew weak and had to hold on to the edge of the table to stand. The snakes wrapped around his chest, some squeezing while others slithered down his legs. Pinkerton leaned over the page, not seeing a thing that was happening next to him. A massive cobra was the last snake to lift from the page. It opened its mouth, fangs dripping with milky death, and sunk them into his shoulder. At first, he wasn't sure if the scream was his or something else, but it echoed around and inside what was left of his being. Then the giant cobra ripped away from him and the snakes released him, convulsing like they'd been shocked.

"You cannot be here. You are empty," said a voice through the echoes. Shadow stepped back and felt the wooden floor beneath him again. He was himself. Pinkerton glanced up at him, pointing at the margin notes. "So, what do you think this means?"

Shadow slammed the book shut. "You didn't see all that, did you?"

"I don't know what you mean."

He passed his superior a shot of whiskey and knocked back his own before pouring himself a bit more. "There were snakes and light right here. I very nearly got eaten just now."

The larger man stared at him and scratched his beard. He reopened the book to the page they'd been examining. "The only place there are snakes are on this—well I'll be damned."

The snakes were no longer at the top of the page. Instead, the word, EMPTY, was scratched in red where the snakes had been. Before Pinkerton could say more, Shadow tore the page out of the book, and shredded it into bits that rained into the trashcan by his desk. Then he closed the cover and sat down.

"What did it mean by EMPTY?" Pinkerton poured himself another shot and sat in the oversized chair meant for him.

"I have no idea, but it made the snakes back off like I was spoiled meat, so I have that going for me." He had no desire to explain to Pinkerton why this declaration was upsetting to him. His soul or lack thereof was a personal affair.

Both men drank in silence until his superior cleared his throat. "Tell me about your trip to Menlo Park."

Shadow checked his watch and reached for his hat. "It will be a much better story if Kate tells her portion of our adventure. Her ship should be docking shortly."

The large, bearded man plunked his shot glass on the desk next to the book and exited, looking frustrated. Shadow put on his hat and coat and stepped out to the airship station.

Shadow lied about the time of the airship's arrival, but he didn't want to talk about Menlo Park without Kate being in the room. She was the one who'd found the book and faced Mr. Harry, the lock, and whatever that was that came from that door in the hotel. He'd just been along for the ride. He also needed a chance to tell Kate what had happened back at the office. He had no idea how he'd become empty again, but he'd learned that gaining half a soul was not the burden he'd been led to believe it would be. In fact, it'd given him a better understanding and connection to the people he was created to protect. He was sure it made a difference in his role as Special Liaison to Pinkerton's Supernatural Unit and his partnership with Kate Warne.

The rise in supernatural activity and encounters after the war had caused Pinkerton to see how having a few investigators available to handle such cases would be beneficial, especially since some of those activities were less than benign. In all fairness, the New World had always had supernatural creatures and activities, even before the coming of the Europeans. The Brotherhood had managed to hold back and even create treaties with certain creatures long before there was a Pinkerton's or even a United States. This became more difficult as more people settled and moved into places that were once protected. The real shift happened during the war. The Brotherhood discovered certain generals on both sides making pacts with powers and entities that promised to tilt battle in their side's favor. Between pacts being broken, forgotten, or fulfilled in unexpected ways, many things as supernatural as the Brotherhood but not nearly as benign had risen and become part of the American fabric.

Shadow had seen revivalists preach God's judgement on the American people for the deeds of the generals from their stumps on hot, humid evenings. People needed a simple explanation for the supernatural shifts and the malignant creatures that changed the fabric of the country. The wrath of God seemed to comfort those who were willing to believe that the country needed to be punished for the sins of the enemy's generals. Many people living in the United States had no idea that most of the creatures they saw had always been around them. The only difference was that the creatures that had lurked at the edge of awareness no longer had to lurk.

A couple of centuries ago, Shadow saw the pamphlets created about the New World by those interested in creating an adventure for would-be settlers There were prints of wood carvings showing men tied onto spittles over a huge fire while groups of women and children waited with knives and spoons. Explorers told stories of strange glades of magical waters and people who hunted only at night. What neither explained were the actual supernatural creatures that lived in the lands they gave and sold to those from the Old World. The problems worsened when Old Worlders arrived on the shores of the New World, often with Old World creatures in tow.

The War Between the States was not the war that mattered in all of this. The war that mattered ended almost three hundred years before with the carving of a simple word on a tree. Unfortunately, the Europeans could not heed a simple warning, and the first wave of arrivals began shortly afterward. Some would say that this shouldn't have happened, but Shadow was not in that company. Without this catalyzing moment and the ones that followed, neither he nor his brothers would be here in the present. This would most certainly be detrimental to the current situation, no doubt.

Whatever was happening had no connection with anything he'd encountered in all of his three hundred years. He'd never heard of this Yog-Sothoth before in all his travels. He had heard of men who lived in the swamps of Alabama and Georgia who swam and hunted like the alligators that populated those areas, but none that had ever taken on the visage of a human. They stayed close together away from most humans unless provoked.

He stepped out onto the platform from the darkest corner atop the new ten-story Home Insurance Building on LaSalle and Adams, away from the gathering crowd. The chatter of people, excited to see their loved ones, flowed over him. He couldn't help but smile. As he joined them, he wondered to himself, *How does this make me so happy when I'm supposed to be empty?* A whir of engines drew his attention and he watched as the airship docked. He would take the longer walk back to Washington Street and catch Kate up on what had happened. Maybe she would have some insight.

6

The droning sound of the engines was little comfort to Kate. *There was no need for him to kill that woman over me.* She considered what the woman had told her. *What sort of creature eats Spectrals?* Perhaps her partner would know. He was more learned in such matters.

She smiled at the thought of Shadow. She had no doubt he would be waiting at the station when she arrived. He always met her like the consummate gentleman he was. She enjoyed his old-school manners even though she was rough and tumble and not what most would define as a lady.

She wondered if Allan would join him, but the answer was obvious. For such a brilliant man, he was being more than a little thick about their relationship since her return. There was no way they could continue as they had been before she got sick. Even if she'd survived by some sort of merciful miracle, she wasn't sure that the relationship would have continued. There was talk around the office, but she didn't care about that. People could chatter all the livelong day about her. Being scandalous was nothing new for Kate Warne. She could have blamed Allan, but he never once put her on the back burner for cases or treated her small force of women like they were anything but top-notch investigators. She had loved him, but as much as she hated to admit it, she loved her job more than she loved America's First Detective. She hadn't understood that till she went to the Outside.

She spotted her partner in his dark suit and bowler hat as the airship docked at the top of the Home Insurance. Some would disdain his predictable actions, but she understood there was more to him than the patterns he kept. Most of their clients and some of their coworkers never saw the reality that lay beneath that veneer. *They have no idea.*

He tipped his hat and reached for her bag, but it dissipated. "I forget you can do that."

"Part of the privilege of living Outside. Just glad I'm safe and sound. Others aren't so lucky, I'm afraid."

He offered his arm. Predictable, indeed. "What happened?"

"There was a woman in the kitchen downstairs."

"You went through the kitchen?"

"I had no choice. He was in the hall outside the room."

"The woman was from the Outside. She was terrified, but she helped me."

"And?"

"He ate that woman."

Her partner opened the gate for the elevator leading down to the street ten stories below. The lady detective hustled into the compartment, and he closed the gate before anyone else could enter. A few people scowled at him as he tipped his hat, and the elevator made its way down. He turned on her.

"He did what?!"

"She lost her entire family to him. On the Outside! I wondered why there were no Spectrals in Raritan."

"I've never heard of a creature that eats Spectrals."

"He didn't just eat her. He tore her from reality." She sobbed, unable to hold back anymore. "She shoved me into the street and instead of helping her, I ran away. My God, I ran away, Shadow." She collapsed on his chest.

He pushed the up button and several people groaned as the elevator began to ascend once more. "Sorry, forgot my bag."

He tried to put an arm around her, but his partner backed away and turned toward the wall. "I hate crying in front of you."

Shadow pulled out his handkerchief and passed it over her shoulder. "If you hadn't run away, he'd have eaten you too."

"Pinkertons don't run away." She took the white linen and dabbed her eyes.

"You saw how well that served O'Neill. Now let's get back to the office. Allan wants a full report. Then I want to show you what I found in the book. Maybe it will give us a clue about why Mr. Harry eats Spectrals." He pushed the button, and once again, the elevator headed for the ground floor. Kate straightened her shoulders and handed him the now-damp handkerchief.

Once they were on LaSalle, her partner continued. "Speaking of the book, I may have torn out and destroyed a page."

"Why would you have done that?"

He relayed what had happened while he and Allan were perusing the pages.

"Allan didn't see a thing? Lughead!"

"All he saw was the word EMPTY on the page."

They turned onto Washington Street, which was busy at this time of day. "But that's true, isn't it? You told me once that the Brothers don't have souls. That means you're empty."

"Since the war, it's a bit more complicated than that," he said.

They entered their office and settled around the book. "Explain what you mean by 'complicated.'" Kate could tell he didn't want to pursue this line of thought even though he was the one who brought it up. Despite his discomfort, she wanted to understand.

He cleared the whiskey and shot glasses that were left from earlier. "Please keep this to yourself, but I have half a soul, or rather *had* half a soul. My brothers do not know."

This wasn't like hiding a train or a partnership from the whole. "How could they not know? I would think they'd feel a soul in their midst."

"Part of the magic, I guess. The warlock told me that they wouldn't know."

She conjured a teacup and took a sip to hide her irritation. "So, now there's magic involved too. What did you do to get a soul? Because if I recall, we were partners, and I don't remember you consorting with warlocks or witches."

"I helped a group of warlocks to end the war and repair some of the lingering damage. It happened while you were working down south. There was no other way."

"Why didn't you tell me?" She sat down on the chair meant for Pinkerton.

"It didn't change our relationship nor keep me from being a good partner, and it did good for everyone, which is part of my oath to the Brotherhood."

Kate leaned toward the lanky detective. "A group of warlocks gave you half a soul as payment to help them end the war, and now you've gone and lost it."

"That does seem to be the case."

"Souls don't just come and go."

"I know. The entire thing upset me so badly that I destroyed the page. It seemed rigged to attack and eat a soul now that I think on it." He stared hard at Kate. "Sounds familiar."

Kate sat her cup on the desk. "Wait. You said Allan was there with you. Why did it come after you instead of him? He has a soul, I assume."

"Maybe I touched it first and triggered it."

The dark-suited detective flipped the pages past the one he'd destroyed. His partner stood next to him and checked his notes.

"Shadows die, don't they?"

"No. They just fade away."

It was a joke among his brothers. Kate didn't laugh.

After a sharp knock, Allan Pinkerton entered with several pieces of paper and an envelope in his oversized hands. When Kate met his gaze, he dropped the envelope. Kate reached down and picked up the yellow package and sighed as she placed it on Shadow's desk. Shadow gave her a look that said patience. Allan stood by the desk where the book lay open.

"While you two were in New York, these things were delivered. You may find them curious."

Shadow perused the telegrams while Kate conjured up more tea and tried to pull herself together. She'd had more than enough drama in the last twenty-four hours.

Her partner passed her the telegram. "The girl wasn't taken in by the boy's family. Looks like she's on the move."

"Shadow tells me that you had much to share about the trip to Raritan, Kate."

Time to act professional. "Strange goings on, sir." She reported all that had happened.

Their superior sat down and stretched his legs. "Your partner destroyed part of that book you found."

"I know." Kate flipped through the book until she found the drawing of the alligator-man. "This looks like some of the drawings of the gods from Egypt."

Her partner tapped the creature on the page. "He looks like someone we've met."

The lady detective traced the shape of the creature with her finger. "Are you saying he's a god?"

"I think he's an avatar, a representative here on earth, which is why he can change how he looks. He reminds me of Sobek, an ancient Egyptian god."

"Sobek is a river god and has no current followers that we're aware of. He also has no minions like that thing we fought in the hotel room." Kate paced and tapped her foot. None of this line of thought made sense.

"Maybe he's standing in for a different god. One we aren't familiar with. One that feeds on the souls of others."

"Why would a god eat Spectrals?" Kate stopped at the book once more.

"Maybe his god is dying or needs energy to resurrect. That's what sacrifices were meant for in ancient times, no matter what the texts may say." Shadow leaned against the table.

"A dying god with tentacles? I don't recall reading any stories…"

"Maybe this is a story that hasn't been told yet. Our mythologies tell stories about gods that have interacted with us, people, over our histories. One thing to keep in mind is that most stories of dying gods end in the god being resurrected. If we follow that line of thought, then who does this avatar want to resurrect?"

Kate discovered the page with the Roman numerals and started counting. "Thirteen."

Her partner showed her his notes. "Pinkerton and I were discussing this before you returned. There could be a connection. Thirteen could be important to his god, or it could be random."

"Nothing about this feels random anymore."

Allan joined them and put his shot glass on the page. "You're saying that Edison is harboring and aiding this avatar that's going to resurrect a god? Thomas wouldn't even believe in such a thing."

Kate removed the glass and put it on her partner's desk. "Harboring, yes. Aiding? I'm not so sure. Your friend may be the Great Inventor, but I'm not sure he has any idea about his assistant."

"I will say he was in an awful hurry to finish the interview though. He wasn't keen on my questions about other children," said Shadow.

"That boy was scared." The lady detective sat on the edge of the desk.

Her partner sat next to her for a moment. "You think he knows Thirteen?"

She nodded. "Without a doubt, but I'm not sure going back there to question him is such a good idea now."

Allan scratched at his beard. "Now that you've managed to steal a book from and provoke this alligator-avatar-man so well, what's your next step?"

Kate tapped the XIII on the page. "Find the girl and the rest of the children. Perhaps one or all of them know what's going on with Mr. Harry."

Her partner closed the book. "If she does, will she talk?"

"We won't know until we find her. If they know what Mr. Harry is up to, then she may resist any attempt to bring her back to Menlo Park."

Allan made his way to the exit. "You know, all of this could be nonsense. Thomas could genuinely be helping these children."

Shadow followed his superior to the door. "I think it's more than coincidence that I saw thirteen children boarding an airship, that the girl's name is Thirteen, and that there are thirteen people in a circle on this page all facing what is probably a form of our Mr. Harry. If we find the girl, even if she knows nothing, we will have completed the primary mission and can focus on the supernatural portion of the case."

Pinkerton pointed at the envelope that lay unopened. "Until that time, perhaps you should open the envelope I brought in earlier, Mrs. Warne."

Kate reached over and opened it. After a quick scan, she read aloud:

Dear Mr. Pinkerton:

My associate and I have information about a group of children that are in great peril and need to be found. It is at great risk we are contacting you.

Because you are known as a man of honorable reputation, we would like to warn you of a certain Mr. H and inform you about his true connection with these children and with other less than honorable activities. These activities are not just a threat to the children, but to the entire United States.

An airship will arrive at midnight on May 1 at the LaSalle Street Station. No tickets are needed. Your associates should be at the station before it arrives. You will be flown to my current location, and we will discuss what I know.

NT

"NT." She pulled the case file from her briefcase and found the photograph. "Nikola Tesla?"

Allan took the letter from her hand and perused it. "Thomas swears he's a crackpot. Said he's gone mad."

Shadow moved behind his partner. "Mr. Harry told me Tesla asked too many questions."

Kate took the letter from her lead and folded it. "I wonder what Tesla has to say about him."

Pinkerton said, "The airship is a Brotherhood *modus operandi*. Is there something you're not sharing, Mr. Jones?"

The lady detective put away the photo and the letter. "All of this does seem a bit orchestrated."

Shadow closed his eyes for a moment, as if in deep thought. Kate had seen him do this before to connect to his brothers and ask questions. They shared memories and ideas, which is why her partner's ability to keep parts of his life from them was unusual. She waited for the answer they sought, and when he spoke, his voice echoed and sounded like many voices. In moments like this, he wasn't just a Brother, he was the Brotherhood. "An airship is on its way to take you to Colorado. We took an interest in Tesla a while back because of his radical ideas about electricity. He's no threat but considered useful."

His voice returned to normal. "I didn't say anything about Tesla before because our interest in him was low-level at best. This new interest is not explained. Someone is keeping it from the rest of us."

Kate moved close to her partner. "More secrets in a place where there are none. Why?"

His eyes darkened and he clenched his fist. "If I knew why, then I'd have been in on this secret before now!" Kate was shocked by the sharpness in his voice. He stalked away from her to gaze out on the street below. His face was flushed.

She followed him and touched his shoulder. "Maybe they didn't tell you because Edison is our client."

"The Brotherhood is cracking and splitting. We're supposed to share everything."

"Like the way you've shared that time travel thing you do?"

He straightened his shoulders. "That's a personal matter."

Arguing the point wouldn't help or move the investigation forward, so she changed focus. "We're going to meet that airship and fly to Colorado to meet NT and his associate. It won't take long to figure out if he's mad or someone worth talking to. Then we'll ride the airship back and continue our investigation. During that time, no doubt, you will be updated on his value to the Brotherhood. In the meantime, before the airship arrives, let's look at the book some more and prepare questions for Tesla."

Kate moved back to the book, but her partner stayed at the window for a while. Allan had left at some point during their discussion without saying goodbye, which was fine by her. The lady Pinkerton didn't understand everything about her partner or his Brotherhood, but she did understand when he needed space. She flipped through the book taking her own notes and left him to brew for a while. They could regroup on the airship.

7

Dear Samuel:

I write with great concern and hope that you, my friend, can help me in this time of need. I have made some decisions which put me in grave peril, the likes of which I cannot explain in this time or place. An airship will arrive in Hartford on the 8th. You must be ready to come aboard when it docks. Once you arrive, I will explain everything.

Nikola

Samuel Clemens had many friends, but none of them had managed to cure his digestive problems until he met Nikola Tesla at the local gentleman's club in New York. Sam mentioned his ongoing intestinal distress, and the Serbian said that he had just the thing to cure it in his lab around the corner. "A bit of vibration and you will feel better."

He followed the young man to his lab where Nikola asked Sam to stand on a metal plate. The author was fascinated with inventions and scientific advancements, and he was delighted to be a part of this experience. If it also alleviated his uncomfortable situation, all the better.

The young scientist flipped a switch from across the room. Sam relaxed for the first time in maybe a year as the plate began to hum and tickled through his boots and resonated through his entire body. Muscles he never knew he had turned to butter and grew warm. He closed his eyes and enjoyed what felt like the best massage he'd ever had.

"When I tell you, step off the plate, Samuel," The Serbian's voice spiked just above the ongoing vibration. The scruffy adventurer sunk into peaceful, comfortable thoughts that blanketed his mind. Time didn't matter anymore, only comfort. As he sank deeper into his reverie, he heard, "Now. Get off now so nothing terrible happens."

Nothing terrible could happen. This is---

Before Sam could finish his languid thought, he felt something warm run down his pants. The younger man pointed to the back of the lab and the exit to the latrine in the alley. He returned from the place of comfort in his mind and ran for the door in search of the first outhouse, not caring that his white suit was ruined.

Nikola cured Sam's terrible constipation, and after that, Sam supported his friend even in his maddest moments. The author became privy to many of the inventions his friend worked on in his lab. Some seemed for the greater good while others were toys. Or that's how Sam took them. He was sure that Edison and Westinghouse would be outstripped by his friend if they kept bickering long enough. Time would tell.

The tone of the letter surprised him. He wondered what sort of peril Tesla was in and if it had anything to do with his work at Menlo Park.

He made his way through the foyer. "Livy, I'm going to go see Nikola."

She scurried down the broad stairs leading to the upper floor. Her countenance was less than encouraging. "More drinking and playing with dangerous toys?"

He handed her the telegram. "No. He's in trouble this time, Liv."

His wife scanned it and rolled her eyes. "Probably from drinking."

"Yes, probably from drinking." Sam took the paper from her and tucked it in his jacket. "Nevertheless, he is my friend and has asked me for help. I am obligated to---"

"Bring him more of that Four Roses? Get into trouble with him? You can't keep doing this, Sam." He started upstairs and she followed. Her stomps made her feelings more than clear, but he couldn't help but be tickled by them. She loved Nik as much as he did, and her protest was out of concern for them both. He began to pack. Every shirt and pair of pants he added to his bag, she pulled out and folded in that neat way he could never manage.

While she reorganized his clothes, he lit a cigar and took a puff. "If I led a sedate life, you'd love me a whole lot less."

"You may charm audiences all over the world, but it won't work on me. A sedate life means you'll live longer." She snatched the smoldering stub from his fingers. "Then again, you may not if you keep smoking in the house!"

"I can't charm you because you were charmed years ago, my love." He leaned over, kissed her cheek. She turned away with a girlish giggle he'd found so delightful ever since they first met. He placed his shaving kit and an extra box of cigars in the bag and then grabbed her around the waist. She leaned into his embrace and adjusted his tie.

"If you insist on visiting your little friend, please promise that there will be no trouble. I worry."

"No troubles. I promise." He pulled her close with one arm and kissed her again.

She pulled his free arm around to find his fingers crossed. "Irascible."

"That does seem to be the final definition of who I am, my sweet."

"Go on, you fuzzy old beast."

He leaned down and kissed her once more on her forehead. They made their way downstairs. As he reached the gate outside, he turned, and she waved. "Telegraph when you arrive."

"I'll try."

She put her hands on her hips and laughed. Both knew he was lying.

The ticket officer stared at Sam through the glass. "Mr. Clemens. I have no idea what you mean. There is no airship on the schedule just for you." The man flipped through some papers on a clipboard. "Is this one of your pranks?"

Sam pulled out the telegram and showed it to the fellow. "It ain't no prank. My friend sent me a telegram that I am to board an airship from this station today!"

"Maybe the prank is on you this time, sir. Would you like a ticket to New York City?" He got out his stamp and a wide ticket for his well-known client.

"No thank you, sir." The author tucked the telegram back in his pocket and walked away.

The fellow behind the glass had a point. Perhaps this was one of his friend's attempts at humor. If it was, he'd failed. He glanced behind one of the large doors at the depot, expecting to find the strange little inventor crouched and snickering about the little scene with the ticket officer. No Nik. Sam sat down near one of the large windows that gave visitors a view of the comings and goings of the airships that frequented the station. He dozed in the warmth of the sun and the drone of incoming ships.

"Mr. Clemens! Mr. Clemens!" Someone spoke too loud and shook him by the shoulder.

He opened his eyes and found the ticket clerk in front of him, looking anxious. "Pilot just came in looking for you. He's waiting at the gate now, sir."

Sam picked up his bag and shook the man's hand. "Told you it wasn't no prank, son." He reached into his coat, pulled out a 10-cent piece. "For your troubles."

He left the uniformed man and headed for the gate. It was at the far corner of the terminal. A man wearing a brown coverall and goggles that were cocked up over his hat waited. Sam towered over him.

"You're takin' me to see Nik, huh?"

"Only if you're Mr. Sam Clemens, sir." Stroking a gray mustache that hung past his jawline, his slanted eyes revealed that he wasn't convinced of that assessment.

Sam pulled the telegram from his pocket and handed it to the man. He studied it for a moment and handed it back to him. He picked up Clemens's bag and led the way to a black airship tucked away at the back of the air station.

"And you are?"

"Sho, your pilot." The author noticed that the man's left leg hitched for a moment, and it looked as though the small man would lose his balance. He heard a whirr and slight hiss as his companion adjusted the weight of the bag.

The author reached to take the bag from him, but the pilot shook his head. "Compensation for an old war injury. I got this, thank you."

"Where are we headed, Sho-my-pilot?"

"I can't tell you that. I got my orders."

"Nik's orders?"

The pilot didn't answer, but instead fumbled with some keys. When he found the one he wanted, he continued up the stairs that led to the ship. Sam followed and noticed that they were far away from the other ships.

"So, whoever you work for is secretive. I'm sure my friend appreciates that."

"Wouldn't want folks to get riled up seein' a black airship. Might think we're pirates or something." The Japanese man unlocked the door and held it as the author entered.

"Wouldn't shock me if you were."

The pilot followed. "You wouldn't be the first to say that. I'll show you to your quarters. You're welcome to join me on the bridge for takeoff. I'm afraid you'll have no company besides mine for the trip."

The offer pleased the scruffy man. He'd not had the chance to see the bridge of an airship before and wondered if it would be any different than the steamboats he'd steered in his youth. Perhaps this fellow wasn't so bad, even if he turned out to be a pirate. "That won't be a problem seeing as you probably have stories to tell. I brought some bourbon along. Pretty sure Nik won't mind if his gift is open as long as it ain't emptied by the time we arrive."

After settling into his quarters, which were larger and more ornate than he expected, the men made their way up a ladder. Sho spun a wheel on the ceiling and pushed open a round door. Sunlight flooded down on them as they made the final climb. As Sam entered, he saw a dark wooden wheel taller than the pilot set into the pale wooden floor. Just as he expected, there was a compass the size of a man's head mounted next to the wheel. What he didn't expect were the metal cabinets covered in gauges, dials, switches, and levers under the massive windows that circled the bridge. He could hear a steam-powered engine from somewhere below and assumed that it contributed to the warmth of the room.

He lit a cigar. "You some kinda inventor or something, Mr. Sho?"

His new friend took a clipboard from the wall and began pushing buttons, pulling levers, and taking notes. "You could say that. Today, though, I'm just a pilot." He gestured to the wheel. "Hey, could you man the helm momentarily?"

The lanky author stepped up to the wheel. It'd been a while since he'd stood behind one, he'd never handled one this magnificent. Sho moved around him and flicked some switches. The floor shook as the engine roared to life and pulled out from the dock. The way it floated felt similar to the way some of Sam's ships felt as they launched.

"What now?" The author felt silly having to ask, but he wasn't clear on the rules of the air.

"Grab that handle to the right and pull back but not too fast or too..."

Sam pulled it back and the ship rocked. In an attempt to stabilize, he pushed the lever forward, but slower than before. The nose began to tip and threw his new friend to the floor. "Sorry. Got excited." Now that he understood what the lever controlled, he pulled it back, keeping the movement slow and steady until the nose was level again. He was afraid to let go of it for now. "This ain't much different than a steamboat."

The small man got to his feet and his leg whirred and growled a bit. He joined his pilot-in-training. "Keep it steady. You know, maybe I should hire you as a co-pilot."

Sam stepped aside and his companion took the wheel. "Let's see what Nikola needs first. You have any idea what's going on with my friend?"

The pilot turned the wheel to the left, adjusting course. "All I know is that I'm supposed to take you out to Colorado to meet Mr. Tesla. The Brotherhood didn't say more than that."

"Who the hell is The Brotherhood?"

"That's a long story." He pulled up on the lever and they began to ascend.

"We have a long trip. Humor me." Sam sat down in an oak chair with curved arms carved like dragons next to the metal cabinets. It was upholstered in reds and golds and ended up being quite comfortable.

"They are the good guys, I assure you. They are interested in most folks who can help this nation. Your friend is one of those folks, Mr. Clemens."

"Call me Sam." He reached into his pocket offered the man a cigar.

The Japanese pilot took the stogie from him. After the author lit it, he inhaled and blew out a smoke ring that was bigger than their heads.

"As I was explaining, The Brotherhood watched your friend while he was still in Serbia. Once he decided to come to the United States, they watched him even closer."

"You still haven't explained who they are exactly." The scruffy haired man took another drag from his stogie.

"Why, they are the guardians of your country."

"I thought that was the job of our military."

"The Brotherhood handles more delicate matters and assists the military at times. Not many civilians know about them."

"But you do."

The small man blew out another huge ring. "If one is employed by such an organization, it would play out that one would, no? I build and fly their airships. I deliver precious cargo—"

"Like me?"

"Your friend requested that we retrieve you. It was a reasonable request, so yes, you are now precious cargo."

"What sort of mess has he gotten into this time?" Sam stretched out his legs but tried not to be in his pilot's way.

"We're not yet sure if he's gotten into a mess yet." The small man adjusted the wheel and lever. "We first contacted him when he arrived in America. We needed someone with his skills to monitor some possible rising assets."

"But he told me Edison searched him out."

"In a way, he did. He was given information about the Serbian and his research. This piqued the inventor's interest. If he hadn't acted on the information, we would have found a different way to place your friend at Menlo Park."

"So, Edison was in on your plan for Nik?"

"No. We routed the information in a way that covered The Brotherhood. We wanted to monitor how he was developing his plan for the practical use of electricity. This plan allowed Mr. Tesla access to tools and a lab and allowed us to watch from a distance."

"I would assume that you all saw that Edison is doing well. He's wired up New York City quite efficiently, I'd say."

"He is also careless. Many areas in the city have caught fire because of his generators. We knew that Tesla had ideas that could make Edison's work safer for public use, and we'd hoped that the older man would listen and make proper changes to protect people."

The scruffy author took another puff as he took in this information his friend hadn't shared. "You keep saying we. Are you a Brother?"

The pilot shook his head. "Not exactly. I was recruited by them during the War Between the States and became an operative. If you join Tesla, you'll be an operative as well."

The ship bumped and shook for a moment. Sho gestured for his companion to take the wheel and then went to the panel behind him.

"Your friend learned that his employer at Menlo Park was less than thrilled with listening and wasn't interested in stabilizing his electrical system in New York City. It became clear that Edison was more of an idea thief than a fellow inventor."

The author held the wheel steady as the clouds rolled past the windows. "Nik wrote me about the thievery. He said that was why he was leaving."

"His departure was caused by several factors. The thievery was only a fraction of what escalated his departure." Sho continued checking dials and gauges before reappearing at the wheel.

"Was it his drinking? Livvy always said that would be the end of him." Sam stepped aside.

Sho took his place. "You know he doesn't drink when he works."

The author settled in the carved seat once again. "Edison was hard on him. He might have started." He took a draw from his stogie. "So what happened?"

The Japanese pilot turned to him. "He did something that, at first glance, is very good. He rescued some children."

"What about at second glance?" said Sam.

Turning back to the wheel, the small man blew another smoke ring. "Edison is concerned enough about one of them that he's hired Allan Pinkerton to find her. If the other children are like her, we could have real trouble brewing."

Sam leaned back against the side of the control panel. "Damn, Nik. When you do things, you go all the way, son."

"If he'd told us what he was up to before he put them on that train..." The pilot adjusted their course.

"Asking for help is not a strong point for Nik. The fact that he sent me a letter is shocking."

"The Brotherhood encouraged him to contact you."

"By encouraged you mean made him, which sounds ominous."

Sho moved to a panel of dials on the wall. "No one forced him to do anything. I'm not sure that's something anyone could do to Mr. Tesla. We expressed our concerns about him working alone and asked that he choose a partner he could count on. He chose you on his own. I'm here to make sure that you arrive in one piece and in a timely manner."

Sam took the wheel once more. This was something he could get used to. Livvy, however, might have other ideas. Sam clapped his new buddy's shoulder. "You are fine company, good sir, and so is your lady."

The nimble pilot checked the large compass ensconced in walnut next to the wheel. "We should be landing in the next hour."

Scratching his graying hair, the famed writer moved to a window. "The prairie is fading, and the mountains are rising. Don't crash into the sides there. I don't want Nik to have to explain to Livvy why I died a fiery death out here."

"I've been flying longer than you can imagine, my friend. We'll land safely. I promise."

8

The air was chilly but not unpleasant as the author and the pilot exited the ship onto the platform atop what Sho had called The Antlers. A huge snow-capped mountain towered over them like a grey blue wall. The two men crossed the platform to the other side where the city spread out like a patchwork quilt. There was a street that stretched from the front of the building where they'd landed to well past a hill that rose above a square brick building at least half a mile away. On that hill was a tower that made the slope seem higher. A sphere sat atop it. Sam had seen this design before. "Nik's laboratory is over there, isn't it?" He pointed toward the unusual structure. "I thought you said he was hiding."

"People around here don't ask many questions," said Sho. "They got their own troubles and the rumor that Mr. Tesla is mad keeps most from investigating."

The author scratched his head. "Folks may get interested if they find out I'm here."

The Asian pilot handed him his bag. "Then don't let them know you're around. Stay close to him. Maybe he'll tell you more than he tells us. We need to know what he's going to do next." He pulled out a stogie and lit it.

Sam shook his head and frowned. "Oh, hell no. I won't spy for you and yours. You can just tell your Brotherhood to go stuff that idea where the sun don't shine."

The smaller man puffed a smoke ring that floated out and over the city. It hung over the sphere at the tower. "We're not going to force you to do anything like that." Then he opened a pocket on his leather vest and pulled out a black card with gilded lettering. "If you do end up feeling like you need help or are concerned about your friend's choices, here's how to contact me. You may need an ace in your pocket."

The author tucked the card in next to his stash of cigars. In the distance, a small figure walked up the road toward the hotel. It looked like his friend. Sam shook the pilot's hand and rode the elevator down to the massive lobby of The Antlers. The place lived up to its name, as the walls were covered with the antlers of many native and non-native animals. Were he giving one of his famous talks, no doubt he would have lodged at this fine establishment. He made his way to the carved cherrywood bar to wait for his friend.

He pushed a glass into Nikola's hand when the younger man arrived. "What have you gotten into this time, Nik?" The scientist was tall and dark and, in contrast to Sam, his hair and mustache were combed and trimmed with precision. Nervous energy danced beneath the man's brown-black eyes as he shook hands and accepted the libations offered by his dear friend.

"Nothing that you cannot help me with, my friend. I am glad Mr. Sho flies quickly. We have much to do, but we cannot talk here." He finished the drink and the lanky author picked up his bag. They made their way to the laboratory. The view along the way stretched for miles, and they passed a few houses and buildings, including the brick building the older man had seen from the platform. Children were playing outside, so he assumed it was a school of some sort.

As the scientist unlocked the door of a tiny house under the massive metal tower moments later, Sam stopped him. "What in the blazes have you gotten mixed up with, Nik?"

Nikola led him inside and shut the door. "Edison stole from me, so I stole something from him."

"Come on. That ain't your style."

"The children were in danger. I saved them. I stole no other property from that man. There were strange things going on at Menlo Park, my friend." He showed the older man a cot and Sam set his bag next to it.

"It's a lab full of scientists and inventors. Of course, there were strange doin's." The author pulled out the half-full bottle of whiskey from the bag.

Nikola gathered a couple of glasses and placed them on the table. "That is not what I mean. Those children...he had them in cells beneath the ground."

"How the hell did you find them then?"

Disdain spread across Nikola's face. "I followed a man called Mr. Harry. He is Edison's assistant. He was odd. Many of us didn't care for him, but Edison revered him even though he didn't do more than take notes and remind him to eat."

The author laughed and knocked back a shot, "The lot of you are odd."

"He is reptilian. His eyes were like lizard eyes. He watched all of us with those eyes. He would be around when Edison wasn't."

"Could be one of them frog men from California."

"No. He is not a frog man. Those are just a lie you made up."

"That was no lie! I saw 'em myself." Sam raised his hand to the sky for effect. Nikola didn't laugh and looked pale and more nervous than at the hotel. This was no joke.

"He would look at us like we were nothing more than prey."

"He's arrogant, so is Edison."

The scientist poured more liquor and passed another glass to Sam. His hand shook. "This is not arrogance. Papa would have called him a demon."

"That's pretty superstitious talk from a man of science, Nik."

Nikola ignored the jab and continued. "I followed him down into a cellar. There was door on the ground, but I didn't think much of it until he opened it one evening when I was watching him. The door was unlocked so I climbed in after him. I don't know why he didn't notice me."

"I've never known you to be so nosy."

"It was more scientific curiosity, my friend. If he had new technology, I wanted to see it. Instead of science, I found the children. There were thirteen of them. One of the older ones, a boy, called to me. He begged me to help them and told me bad things were coming if they stayed there. Before he could explain more, I heard Mr. Harry coming down the corridor behind us. I promised to help and managed to escape before I was caught."

Sam pulled out a small notebook and a pencil. This was a better story than he'd written in a long time. Nikola continued. "I began to work on this problem when I was not working on electricity projects. I stole some keys from Edison's desk, hoping one of them would fit the lock on the cellar door and on the cells.

"Didn't he notice?"

"He did, but no one thought to search me. I found this odd but didn't question my luck. I did not go that night. I waited a week and contacted my friends in the Brotherhood. By this point, my disagreement with Edison grew. He lied to me, and I quit. I had to help the children then or there was no coming back at all."

"So, you rescued thirteen children and then left. That's all?"

"Yes. I put them on an orphan train and then the Brotherhood took me away. I do not know why he hasn't come after me."

"Your telegram said you were in grave danger."

"The Brotherhood wanted to make sure you'd join me. They want someone to keep an eye on me because they know that I'm interested in discovering more about the 'bad thing' the boy spoke of. They also want to distract me." He clinked the shot glass with his finger. "If you are here, then I am drinking and not focused. Except they are wrong."

Sam poured another shot and lifted his glass, "Here's to underestimation!"

His friend's eyes narrowed. "Now, you are a writer and I am an inventor. While we are both clever, we still need help. We need detectives. When I visited Chicago once, I met Allan Pinkerton. I wrote him a letter."

Sam lit a cigar and offered his friend one, but Nikola declined and made Sam put his away. The older man forgot that his friend didn't allow smoking in the lab. "Allan Pinkerton is coming to help us?"

The inventor shook his head. "He is too busy, but he is familiar with The Brotherhood and has a liaison who works in his office. I received a telegram from Pinkerton, and he is sending this person to us. An airship should arrive from Chicago soon and then we can learn what our next steps should be."

9

Shadow checked his watch as they entered the Home Insurance Building. Even though it was a quarter till midnight, and no airships were scheduled after dark, the door to the elevator was unlocked as though they were expected. They stepped onto the platform ten stories up, and a soft whirr indicated that a ship approached for docking. "Punctual as always." He clicked his timepiece shut and tucked it away in his jacket.

Kate held onto his arm and patted his hand. "Mr. Jones, you seem in much better spirits."

"I came to the conclusion that change is inevitable, even for the Brotherhood and for me."

"Secrets are expected then?"

He shuffled his feet. "I'm not sure."

Once the airship docked and the stairs came down, Shadow allowed his partner to enter first. The man who greeted her could have been her partner's twin. He shook her hand and led her inside.

"You must be Mrs. Warne."

"And you must be one of Mr. Jones's Brothers." Her partner joined them in the foyer.

The man who resembled Shadow looked uncomfortable. He

78

should know her as well as her partner, but he didn't act that way. "I see we're using our street names tonight."

"Seems the most appropriate approach, Mr…"

"Mr. West."

Shadow cleared his throat, and Mr. West stepped away from Kate and toward his brother.

West began. "Without light."

"There is no darkness." Her partner responded.

"Without darkness."

"We have no purpose."

"My Brother, Shadow." The detective's twin grabbed his hand and clapped him on the shoulder.

"My Brother, Shadow." Kate's partner shook his brother's hand vigorously.

"Because one of you is not enough."

"Are you escorting us to Mr. Tesla?" asked the lady Pinkerton.

Both brothers laughed.

Mr. West led them deeper into the gondola. "I see why you like working with this lovely lady. She cuts to the chase."

"Her direct nature makes many conversations much easier."

Their companion opened a heavy-looking arched door. "The direct answer, Mrs. Warne, is that I am escorting you to see our Mr. Tesla. He is to be joined by a companion who is sympathetic to his cause." They followed him to a wide, curved window set with several comfortable chairs. Once they were seated, the man pulled a chain. In the distance, a bell chimed. Not long afterward, the ship lifted away from the Home Insurance building into the sparkling night sky over Chicago.

Her partner's face flushed. "A companion? Why wasn't I informed? This information directly impacts…"

"I'm sure you were, brother. Perhaps you are slipping and being distracted from your work." West nodded toward Kate. "It has happened to a brother before."

"This is not like that Betsy Ross business."

Kate cleared her throat. His brother should know the nature of their relationship. "My partner has been left in the cold without important information more than once. Shadow had to ask about Tesla yesterday when we received his letter. He was not informed. Why is the Brotherhood so interested in Tesla right now? My partner tells me that you all have been watching him for some time."

"We've been watching Edison for a while, and Mr. Tesla has been part of that. He is inventing items and dabbling in sources of power faster and more successfully than any other New World —I mean United States —inventor to date."

"Edison is creating things to make the world better for everyone. Without him, New York City would just be another city of gas and fire. Why would he or any inventor need to be watched by you?"

The Brother put his feet up on an empty seat. "Without him, many of the fires that are ravaging parts of New York City wouldn't be happening. What concerns us more is his dabbling."

Kate leaned forward, pushing her point. "Dabbling is a part of invention. You don't think Edison was dabbling with evil magic books like this to help the girl?"

Mr. West dropped one foot to the floor. "Magic books? It would seem you've kept something from us as well, my brother."

Shadow looked down at his feet. "There's nothing to report as of yet. It could have nothing to do with what Tesla found. Since you mentioned this, explain, please, Mrs. Warne."

The irritation was palpable in her partner's tone, and she wished she hadn't mentioned it. Instead of addressing this, she explained the book to Mr. West, but did not mention the missing page or the message her partner had gotten from the creatures inside.

"The girl could be crucial to whatever event this book addresses, but I'm still not sure how Edison would play into anything mystical. It seems rather odd for a scientist of his ilk to partner with something that is clearly supernatural."

"Edison wants things that are bigger and brighter, but there's an undercurrent to his work. We've seen lots of turnover at Menlo Park. Scientists come and go."

She stood up to gaze out over the starlit landscape below. "How is that connected to what we've seen? He invites them to use his facilities. They do their work and then go home. Isn't that how it's supposed to work?"

"Not if Edison releases new inventions claiming they are his not long after the inventor or scientist leaves. This doesn't happen every time, but it does happen consistently enough for the Brotherhood to take note."

"They could have arrangements."

Shadow interjected. "Most of them don't, Kate, and because Edison submits the paperwork for patents, he can claim ownership and there's nothing anyone can say or do."

"Edison is a thief and a liar. I can buy that, but that doesn't mean he'd become friends with some sort of cosmic monster that has nothing to do with science."

"And yet his assistant, the man he works closest with is just that, isn't he? We were watching the inventor to make sure that his work, stolen or otherwise, didn't lead him somewhere destructive. Tesla's discovery of the children shows us that Edison has made steps that increase the level of danger he represents. We can't prosecute him for the thievery because that's out of our jurisdiction. Now that he's crossed supernatural lines, we are concerned."

"And you used Tesla to get close to him?"

Her partner said, "It was easy to encourage Edison to hire Tesla. He needed someone to improve the direct current generator plants used to light New York City. Tesla wanted space to work on his own projects. We made this happen."

"During this time, he saw things?"

"Yes, including these children who were locked up like slaves. He had no idea how or why they were there but insisted that Edison's assistant was in charge of them and that he had to save them."

"Did he confront his employer?" Kate conjured up a cup of tea. "Would you all care for some tea?" Neither man was interested, but she continued to sip.

"By this point, Tesla had seen what Edison was doing with the patents. They also had their first argument about direct current. Why would you go to someone who you didn't trust?"

"Does he believe that Edison knows, then?"

"He isn't sure what was going on with the children but is convinced that Edison is up to something bad. He said he would explain when you arrive."

"Where would someone get a group of children so easily?" Kate asked. "Are their parents dropping them off with the Great Inventor with the hopes that their illnesses are cured by electricity?"

West joined her at the window. "None of them have families that we can locate."

"Are they ill?"

Her partner took her other side. "Define ill. Remember that Thirteen causes bad luck. In some quarters, that is an illness of sorts."

"Best we can figure is that the children are from asylums and prisons. There are no records of them, and if they came from those places, there wouldn't be," said West. "Most families don't take in asylum-born children."

Kate paced back and forth. "He told you that he's trying to help Thirteen with her bad luck. There are twelve other children locked away in a cellar that he failed to mention."

"That word assumes he knew they were there."

"Remember that boy with the broken arm, Shadow? What if he was one of the thirteen who got on that train?"

"It's unlikely, but then this case seems to thrive on the unlikely. How would he have gotten back?"

"This goes back around to why Edison wants Thirteen back but didn't mention the others" The lady detective turned back to a previous topic." Do you think the children told Mr. Tesla anything?"

"I doubt there was time."

"Tesla may not have told us everything. He's a private fellow and gets touchy when we push him too much."

"He will have to answer questions if he wants to save these children and himself."

The lady Pinkerton sat back in the leather seat nearest the

window. The trip had better be worth all this. There was a girl out there who was in trouble and needed to be found before more people were hurt or killed by her wake of bad luck.

The airship docked near a small town surrounded by prairie grass. Kate stepped out to stretch her legs. In the distance, a train whistle pierced the serenity of the early afternoon. Her partner joined her as he adjusted his hat.

"I thought I'd head to the sheriff's office if they have one. Check to see if there's been more unusual activity before we launch again. Care to join?"

She took his arm. "It's good to know that the Brotherhood doesn't know everything."

"I suppose." He got a far-off look. She was unsure if he was worried or just not amused.

"Did I say the wrong thing?"

The gangly detective picked up his pace. "No. This isn't about your joke. One of my Brothers shared some information about a brutal attack close by."

"Is this relevant to our case?"

"Possibly. A woman was torn apart by someone or something."

Kate scurried to keep up with her partner. "Could be a werebeast of some sort. Sounds like the right *modus operandi.*"

"There's also a young boy missing."

"The boy could have been taken by a pack and things got out of hand?"

They stopped outside a rough looking shanty with a star on the door. "Perhaps."

"Or maybe our girl has caused some mayhem in search of her siblings.?"

"This doesn't seem accidental." He opened the door and she entered first. The interior was simple, but neat. There was a heavy table with a cane-bottom chair behind it. Further back she could see one area with rustic bars and a heavy door with a lock. The whole place smelled of strong coffee and cigarettes. A tall, blond man sauntered up front. His demeanor was serious but warm. Shadow showed the man his card and inquired about the attack.

The sheriff stared at the card a minute and then flipped it onto his desk. "Someone invited a Pinkerton to the party. Must be more than a wild animal attack. Coffee?"

Shadow accepted and continued as the man poured from a metal pot that sat on a small iron stove in the corner. "We aren't sure yet and thought we'd see you before we head up to the site."

The sheriff offered a ladderback and the Pinkerton sat down. "You need a guide to get you up there. The woman who died, Annie Dougal, was a piece of work. She and that fella, Brody, caused lots of troubles wherever they went. I figure that one of 'em provoked a werebeast. Of course, most folks don't want to believe those sorts of things are out here, so if I said that out loud to most folks, I'd get laughed right out of town."

The dark-suited detective sipped from his tin cup. "Then why tell me?"

"Mr. Jones, I figured that you may be more open since you brought that lady there with you. When do you plan to introduce her?"

Kate offered her hand, and he took it in a much more gentle way than she expected. "Kate Warne, Pinkerton's Agency."

"Donnie McClain, ma'am. My family, we got the Sight. Don't talk about it much because folks out here don't cotton to such things. I've seen haints, but never talked to one." He went into the empty cell and got a third chair so that she could sit. "Hope this is comfortable enough for you."

She accepted the seat. "Now, what about this werebeast...have you seen it?"

"No, but I dealt with a pack of 'em back east before the war. Most don't want nothin' to do with folks and try to stay away. Once you provoke one though..." He shook his head. "Smart ones move after somethin' like this. At least that's what happened to the ones back east."

Shadow sipped coffee. "There was a boy living with Dougal and Brody."

"An orphan train stopped about a year or so ago, and Brody took that kid. I think he and Annie needed someone to work their farm, but I gotta tell you, that boy was scrawny, so I doubt he was much help. I ain't seen Brody in about six or seven months. Last I heard before this was that Annie and the boy was still in the house, but when we got there after the attack, we couldn't find the boy, and Annie..." The man turned a pale shade of green. "You sure you want to go out there? I mean, I can take you, but I ain't sure a lady should be there, you know?"

Kate tried to refocus him. She did want to go out there. "What about jurisdiction?"

McClain cleared his throat. He finished his cup of coffee in a gulp. "The Brody place is out in the middle of nowhere. The U.S. Marshal won't be here for another two days, so me and the fella in Wellston are lookin' into the situation. Wellston ain't gonna buy the werebeast idea. He's a little too Baptist, if you know what I mean."

A few minutes later they were following the long-legged man into the woods at the edge of town. Just before they left the road, the lady detective caught a glimpse of a girl in a blue dress and bonnet walking ahead with a determined stride. She nudged Shadow.

Examining the ground, her partner pointed at some older foot-prints that could have been from a dog or maybe a wolf. "What sort of werebeast do you think it might be, Sheriff?"

The blond man examined the prints as well. "We got wolves nearby, so maybe there is a pack of weres that roam the area too."

Shadow brushed the dirt from his knees. "These are from one dog or wolf or something. Wolves, even werewolves, hunt in packs. I don't see any other prints but these."

The lawman nodded. "The prints here seem small. I think the boy had a dog, but I ain't sure."

"Could have been passing through or an associate of Brody who wanted revenge." The Brother paused as something or someone scuf-fled under some brush close by.

Kate drew her pistol, and McClain reached for the rifle on his back. Shadow faded out into a darker area under some trees.

McClain gazed into the brush and trees. "It ain't no were this time. It smells too clean."

Kate gave him a sideways glance.

"You ain't never been near one have you, ma'am? Well, they stink different than any other creature. I can't explain it. All I know is that there ain't no were stink."

Shadow returned from the cover of the brush and canopy of the trees. "It was a couple of boys. They looked spooked."

"Did you?" Kate crossed her arms.

"I didn't have to. They were scrambling away like they'd seen you."

Their blond companion lowered his weapon. "Folks are talkin' about this in town. No doubt they came for a look." He glanced back toward town. "Poor, stupid kids."

"There were just boys?"

"Yes. You don't think she's here?"

The lady detective put away her weapon and started moving toward their destination. "Maybe?"

Her partner pushed past their guide. "We should hurry."

McClain scratched his head. She moved back and took his arm. "I suggest we follow." They scurried to catch up to Shadow.

"Couldn't you just pop over there, ma'am?"

"Spectrals don't just pop into places like people on the Inside believe. We have to run, just like you."

"Good to know."

Her partner stopped at the edge of a clearing, and they joined him.

"God have mercy." The scene before them had little mercy to spare.

10

A white clapboard house was marred with a large brownish red stain that covered the side door and flowed down the three steps beneath. It wasn't shiny, so it'd been there a bit. Small handprints left in the same brownish red spotted along the wall. Something light and sort of stringy hung from the top corner of the doorframe. A spring breeze lifted the long stringy stuff lightly in the breeze. Kate made her way into the scene and began to take notes. McClain got in front of her.

"Ma'am, I don't think you should—"

Kate stepped around him. Her partner pulled the man aside. "Let Mrs. Warne alone. She's studying."

"Mr. McClain, I know you say you think this was the act of a were-wolf, but it seems a bit more..."

"Brutal?" His face was pale, but he joined her in the middle of the horror. She tucked the notebook in her belt and made her way up the steps. Then she touched one of the child-sized handprints.

The lanky lawman knelt down to see what she was doing as her partner joined him. "She ain't exactly delicate, is she?"

"It's not a word I'd use for her."

She glanced back toward them. "You may want to be careful. There are teeth out there."

McClain grew as pale as Shadow and picked up a rather large tooth.

"Yeah. This ain't like any were attack I ever seen. You're right, ma'am."

"Looks like whoever did this was dragging something along here. The hands are small."

"Our girl?" asked Shadow.

Kate fiddled with the strand of hair stuck to the top of the door. "Doesn't seem her *modus operandi*, does it? Plus, these are too small to be a young lady's."

The sheriff approached the steps but didn't join her on the stoop. "A child did this?"

"These could be the boy's, but I can't say if he did all of this." She went down the steps and leaned to get a look under the house. "Wonder if he's still here somewhere."

She made her way to the back of small house, and her two companions followed her. They found a fresh shallow grave under a tree behind it. McClain knelt and dug it out easily with his hands. It was the body of a skinny black and white dog. There was a bullet hole in its head.

"I think this was the boy's dog. I remember seeing it once or twice when they was in town."

A crash came from inside the rickety gray barn toward the back of the property. Shadow drew his pistol. Kate gestured for him to put it away and pointed at the handprints. If the boy was in the barn, the last thing he needed was for more adults to put a gun in his face. She pulled the sheriff close. "What's the boy's name?"

"I dunno. Brody and his woman didn't come to town lest they were causing trouble. The boy wasn't with them much when they did."

Kate moved to the entrance of the barn. "We don't want to hurt you, son."

No response.

She scanned the dim interior of the structure, looking for any hint of the boy or anything else that might be lurking.

"Kate!"

The two men rushed around the corner of the barn toward the tree line. When she caught up, her partner pointed. "I'm pretty sure our girl headed out there."

"Any sign of the boy?"

McClain shook his head. "What was that girl doing in the barn?"

"Looking for the boy."

"No doubt she's wanting to find the others. Maybe to protect them from Mr. Harry and whatever he's got planned."

"Should we give chase?" asked the sheriff. The lady detective didn't answer, but instead led them around to the back of the barn. The door hung on one hinge and swung in the breeze. There was a sharp scent in the air as though it had rained even though the sun was shining. They'd lost both children.

She said, "Mr. McClain, whatever did this is gone now. I don't think you'll have more troubles of this sort."

"This goes beyond troubles, ma'am. What'll I tell the marshal?"

"Clean this up and tell him it was wolves. Let's check the barn one last time." She entered the barn. Drops of bloody mud speckled the straw strewn on the floor. Shadow picked up a shovel with small brownish handprints on the handle. "Looks like he buried his dog with this."

Kate approached a mound of hay that was scattered and smeared with mud and blood and bits of gore she had no desire to touch. "What kind of child is able to bury his dead pet after witnessing something this horrific?"

Shadow didn't answer until he moved farther in. "There are footprints back here."

As she headed toward her partner, she saw the sheriff enter the barn. "Sheriff, I wouldn't if I was you."

There were three distinct sets of footprints. One set looked as though the owner's feet were bare. Traces of blood, mud, and unidentifiable gunk surrounded them. Another set was deeper. These were shoe prints rather than footprints and they were adult sized. Neither led outside the barn. The third set, however, did. These shoeprints were small, almost dainty, and close together. Kate followed them out of the barn and to the edge of the trees, just as she suspected they would. The girl. She returned to her partner who was examining the other two prints.

"So, the boy and the owner of these prints didn't leave."

"Not the same way the girl did."

"Perhaps a portal like the one we saw at the hotel." The rangy detective brushed off his pants as he stood up.

"It would seem that way. I don't understand why Mr. Harry didn't take both children when he had the chance."

"She got away and the boy didn't?"

A retching sound came from the front of the barn. Kate rolled her eyes. "Mr. McClain, are you feeling well?"

After a couple of more coughs, the man answered. "Better now, ma'am. If I may say so, you are made of steel."

"Should we track the girl?"

"My bet is that she's headin' back for the next train out of town. One of us should be aboard to keep an eye on her."

"What about Tesla?"

"Mr. West and I can handle that. Take a ride back east, Mr. Jones. Message me when you find out more about our Thirteen."

McClain was waiting for them near the edge of the woods. He wiped his face with a red handkerchief and sipped something out of a canteen. "I ain't never seen the likes."

"Nor have we, Mr. McClain, but your community is safe now. I can guarantee that whoever or whatever did this is gone."

"You don't know what did this either?"

"I'm afraid I have a notion, but you won't like it." The man offered her the canteen, but she pushed it back. "It was the boy."

"A scrawny half-fed boy like him?"

"Someone shot his dog, and then it was buried. I don't think that the person who shot the dog buried it. I think the boy did."

"But that don't mean the boy...he ain't a werepup, that much I can tell you. Good God, woman, if he did all this, he's tougher than any creature I've ever seen."

"That would seem so."

"But there ain't nothin' left of Annie Dougal, and she wasn't a small woman." The blond lawman scratched under his hat.

Shadow leaned against a tree. "Maybe this boy is something different, and more of a killing machine than your werebeast.".

"He couldn't have gotten far. We gotta find him." Readjusting his hat, McClain moved toward the woods. Kate stopped him.

"I don't think he's here anymore. We're not sure where he's gone, but we know he won't come back here. There's no use in giving chase."

"What can I do?"

She led them back to the path to the main road. "Get a posse and clean up this mess before more folks come looking."

Her partner was quiet for a moment then announced. "My Brother is ready to launch at your arrival."

"Keep me posted." She adjusted the liaison's tie and patted it. "I'll see you soon." He entered the darkness of the forest and faded from view. Once he was gone, she took the sheriff's arm and started walking back to the road.

"Where'd your partner go, ma'am?"

"He's following our lead to the train."

"And he left you behind?" Judgement crossed the man's face. "Mighty ungentlemanly."

"He knows I can handle myself, Sheriff."

McClain glanced back at the bloodied house. "Yes, ma'am. I believe he's right."

Once they arrived in town, Kate hurried to the airship and Mr. West. Moments later, she and the mysterious Brother were on their way to Colorado.

11

Duo came back to the world the way he always came back to the world: naked and cold.

A familiar voice cut through the haze. "Welcome home, Two."

"I didn't mean to go white, sir." He shivered even as his shoulder burned like fire. His fists felt crusty as he rubbed them against his face. When his vision cleared, he saw streaks of brown and clots of something he knew wasn't dirt. The last thing he remembered was Mikey dancing around the yard. *She didn't have to kill him. He never did nothin' to nobody.*

"You murdered that woman outright. Be glad that you are here, because otherwise you'd be dangling from a tree." That wasn't Mr. Edison. Duo backed to the far corner of his cot and clutched the blue blanket that covered him.

Mr. Harry leaned close. His eyes were golden and cold as ice.

"Leave me alone."

Mr. Harry gave a low bellow. Duo responded with a roar, but that didn't stop his assailant. The man's face lengthened into a flat, blunted nose and his hand became clawed and rocky. A wide gray-brown tail pushed from underneath his coat. The boy clawed at the wall behind him in an attempt to get purchase and climb away from the reptile-man.

A scaly hand grasped his thin ankle and started to twist his leg. "I could end this misery for you right now."

"Is this the cure you told me about?"

The assistant hissed and pulled the boy hard enough that he was sure something must have broke. "There is no cure."

The door to the small cell opened. "You can't eat this one, Harry. Not yet." It was Mr. Edison.

The assistant turned faster than Duo knew a man could. "We need his energy."

"For later. He'll join his sister and a few others when it's time.".

"Feeding on Spectrals isn't enough. I can't open the gate."

"We won't discuss this in front of the boy." Edison stepped around the half-man/half-lizard and reached for the small figure on the cot. Duo swung at him with his small fists, but the older man jumped back before he could make contact. The assistant bellowed one last time before exiting. The inventor pushed a button on the wall, and a young woman dressed in all black entered and wrapped Duo in a towel. As she led him to the baths, the scent of sweat hung over them. He couldn't help but shiver.

1 2

I have several things you ought to see, Mrs. Warne." Mr. West placed a folder on the desk where Kate worked on her report for Allan, who would want all the bloody details. Kate wasn't sure how to explain a woman being torn limb from limb by a small boy. She opened the folder and flipped through several of the articles. "These all involve children."

"Oddities, no?"

"Much like what we just left."

Mr. West poured some coffee from an urn. "My kind have seen many horrors in all the years we've served this country, but we all agree that few if any natural creatures we've encountered can do the sort of damage that was done there. Mr. McClain was convinced it was a werecreature, was he not?"

"Until he got a closer look at the scene. Interesting fellow, that sheriff."

"We will be calling on Mr. McClain very soon. He could be of service to the Brotherhood."

She studied the articles, and one titled "Boy Merged with Tree" grabbed her attention. A young teacher couldn't find the boy after recess. One of the children, unnamed, led her behind the building where the lost boy was discovered his arms reaching out and his face frozen in a wide-eyed scream. According to the teacher, when she tried to pull him out of where she thought he was stuck, she saw that green-grey bark grew from where his pants should have been up past his heart. New formed branches grew out of his arms and shoulders. Tiny green leaves sprouted from the branches and the tips of his fingers. Chartreuse lines crossed and jagged under the skin of his face like a miniature root system. A sign hung around his neck with the word "monster" scrawled in childish writing. The story did not mention the victim's name, nor did it reference the child who led the teacher, a Miss Rogers, to the tree.

"The girl, Thirteen, causes bad luck. It would seem she isn't the only one of the group with powers. Those powers could be something that Mr. Harry back at Menlo Park is interested in. I thought that perhaps he was eating the children, but that doesn't make a lot of sense. Instead, he could be eating their powers."

"To what end?"

Kate dropped the article back in the folder. "He told me he was the Gate when he held me hostage back at Menlo Park. Gates are portals that one can travel through. It's possible that he needs the energy to become large enough for someone or something to travel through. He eats Spectrals because he doesn't have access to anything more powerful yet."

"If that were the case, and I think you do make a strong one, then why didn't he just trap them like he trapped you?"

"The living are different. You have two parts—flesh and spirit. Once the flesh dies, then what's left?"

"The Brotherhood is extraordinary, ma'am. We aren't of two parts."

"So, how do you cross over to the Outside?"

"We don't. We are of the darkness, charged with the duties to watch over the people who live in this land. We have to blend in. Flesh, blood, heartbeat - why are you surprised? Your own partner is one of us. By now, you know he is not human."

"He has said that you just..."

"We fade away into our collective."

The idea of fading into a collective was hard to connect with, and she wanted to ask more questions. Instead, she turned her focus back to Mr. Harry and the previous discussion. "He has to use a tool to trap and take Spectrals. I saw him with a box back in Raritan. Perhaps it's harder when you have to kill the flesh and then catch the spirit?"

"Do you think Edison built that box for him?" The Brother sipped his coffee and sat across the table from her.

"I can't be sure. Without Tesla's information there are holes in the story that make it weaker than I like." Kate conjured up her usual tea and a plate of shortbread. She offered it to the man who resembled her partner in so many ways and continued to read through the article in the folder. She must learn if this was connected to Menlo Park.

Shadow stepped out onto the platform before the train stopped and blended into the small group of people who were waiting either to see a loved one or to get on the next train. Thirteen exited and glanced around as if getting her bearings. The sign on the depot said "Brainerd." She strode toward the general store. He followed her and crouched under a window at the side of the shop.

The girl approached the counter, and a man wearing tiny round spectacles and an apron greeted her. She took off her bonnet. "An orphan train stopped here a year or so back. Do you remember the children who were taken from the platform?"

The man tapped a rough pencil against his clipboard. "Well, there was a young fella, 'bout your age, but he don't live here. He went off with that Dr. Lazarus and his wife. They're peddlers. Guess they needed a strong set of arms."

Thirteen opened a small pouch from her skirts and asked for a bag of rock candy. Her attendant scooped out the sparkling sugar treats. He handed her the bag. "There was another one. She was younger. Sweet lil' kid but had some hard times."

"Where does she live?"

"Right now, she's livin' with Miz Price just outside of town." He pointed toward the right of the front door.

She thanked him and headed out. Instead of going in the direction the man had pointed, she made her way up a hill at the edge of town. A white sign bore the words "Food and Rest" and an arrow pointed at a two-story house. The warm fragrance of cornbread hung in the air. Good cornbread was hard to resist, but the detective didn't want to startle the girl and have her bolt like she had before. Instead, he faded back into the shade of a couple of buildings near the foot of the hill. A broad-shouldered man with a red-brown beard and wearing a tin star on his chest led a small blonde girl dressed in a calico frock past the sign toward the house. A mark on her neck peeked over the collar of her dress.

A black number 10.

Shadow followed them to the back of the house. The lawman knocked on the back door and a young woman with brown hair and a gentle smile answered. She looked tired and was covered in flour. The young man took off his hat.

"Miz Price is gone, just like the rest."

"That doesn't make sense, Horace. Folks don't walk away like that. Widow Price would've never…"

"I found Lil' Deci sitting on the front porch swing, kicking her legs saying that they all go away. Not sure what she meant by that. I am sure she needs to eat and I could use a bite myself."

"Why don't y'all come on in. I'll make you a plate."

The little girl took the woman's hand as they entered the house. "I love you, Miz Moira."

A blue aura rose around the girl when she said those words, but it faded as she and that Horace fellow went inside. Shadow embraced the darkness behind the house, and he faded into the kitchen where they'd gone. As he materialized, he saw the blue aura once more.

"Come on, Deci. Let's go out front and eat with everyone else. This is better than sheriff food by a long shot."

The girl made eye contact with the Pinkerton, who had faded back into one corner. Her eyes shifted to a more reptilian gray. He was sure she growled at him as she exited the room.

"NO!" A voice cried from the dining room. Miz Moira dropped a plate and raced out to see what had happened. Shadow faded from the kitchen to the adjoining room to check out the commotion.

Thirteen bolted out of the house with Deci in tow. "I'm so sorry!"

The young sheriff gave chase and Shadow followed, out of sight. Once the girls were out on the street, Deci pulled away from Thirteen. Instead of running, she turned on the older girl and said, "I love yo—"

The older girl slapped her, and she fell backwards into the dirt. She held the girl marked 10 down and reared back to continue the assault when Horace grabbed her hand and pulled her off.

"Stop." The tall girl in the flowered skirts didn't fight him but turned in his grip to face him.

"How many folks in your town are missing, sir?"

Deci wailed as she darted to the porch where Miz Moira stood and wrapped her arms around the woman's legs.

The sheriff didn't let her go. "That little girl ain't got nothin' to do with that.".

"She's my sister. I know what she does. How many of those folks did she live with?"

Shadow noticed that for all her crying, Deci's face was dry. She stomped her foot. "That ain't my sister, Mr. Horace. She's crazy. I met her back on the orphan train."

The young lawman released Thirteen's arm. "Well, now this is one fine mess we got here. Maybe both of you need to come to my office so we can work this—-"

Moira scooped up the small girl in her arms. "This poor little girl has been through enough for now. She just lost her folks and now this girl tries to take her away."

"Miz Moira, I'm awful hungry. I ain't eaten all day." Deci curled up in her protector's arms. Her would-be sister rolled her eyes. The flour-covered lady carried her inside.

"You come right back in here and eat you some biscuits and gravy."

"I love you, Miz Moira"

"Oh honey, the whole town loves you." Before they got inside, the girl's face stretched to a scaled snout, and she growled. Thirteen clenched her fists but the lawman took her by the shoulder and guided her further into town.

"Well, ma'am. Looks like it's you and me for now. What's your name?"

"Treze...Halford. And those folks of hers aren't lost." She glanced back at the house like she might bolt again, but her shoulders dropped as the sheriff led her away.

The dark-suited detective took the opportunity to get a closer look at Deci. He knocked on the front door. A moment later, Ms. Moira appeared.

"Ma'am, do you have a room to spare?"

Moira allowed him in. "Dinner has just begun. Please sit down and after you eat, we can get you registered, Mr..."

"Jones. Andrew Jones."

Deci clung to her skirts as she showed him to a communal table that was not yet full. The lady poured him fresh coffee. She shuttled back into the kitchen with the tiny blonde girl in tow.

"You here about those missing folks?" A rough looking fellow slid onto the bench next to him.

"I just got here from back east." Shadow sipped from his cup.

"Whole families, widows—all gone with no leavings to track."

"Where do you think they could've gone?"

"No one knows. We thought maybe the first few folks had just packed and gone west. Then Jack Verner came to town last summer sayin' his goats had gone missing. Said everything was fine 'til they took in that girl what just went with Miz Moira. No one thought much of it because Jack was a drunk. Next thing we know Jack and Lacy was gone and Arlene McTavish done took the girl to her house. Bet you socks she and Hollis are gone now too."

"But she's just a little girl."

A scream came from the kitchen. Thirteen, or rather Treze Halford, burst into the dining room with the sheriff in tow. He had his pistol drawn. "Where the hell are you off to?"

99

Shadow faded and entered the kitchen. His head rang and he heard the voices of his brothers call out. He embraced the darkness to ease the way his mind felt. He wondered if he was at a ley line crossing.

"I love you, Miz Moira." Deci stood on the top of a small table surrounded by chopped ingredients. The detective's head echoed when she spoke those words A blue light shone from the girl's chest. Tendrils of blue wrapped around the young hostess. The skin on her hands were blistered and smoking as she clung to the pipe behind the huge iron stove.

Shadow understood why Treze hit the so-called sister. The elder girl grabbed a wooden hammer from the table and threw it past Deci.

"STOP IT NOW, TEN!"

As Deci dodged the weapon, she stomped her foot. "But I love her and want her in me."

Treze charged her sister, but Horace reached to stop her. Instead, he stumbled and fell on top of the girl. They both struggled to get up.

The light from Deci's chest reached the corner, cutting into the darkness where Shadow hid. This was no normal light. It didn't just enter the shadow, it sucked the darkness away, and the detective was torn from his hiding place and ended up on the floor at the child's feet. She was more blue light than physical at this point, but his impact knocked her off the table. When she hit the floor, the light shut off. The detective scrambled to her body.

Horace leaned over him. "What the hell is she?"

Treze crawled over to Moira, who was screaming and crying next to the hot stove. "She is my sister. Now does this town have a doctor?"

Horace went to the door to the dining room. "Hey, doc, you here?"

An older man dressed in black entered. "Miz Moira? Oh my! Let's get you on over to my place so we can get those hands bandaged." He half-led, half-carried her out while she still wept and screamed.

Deci began to stir and put her hand to her head. "What happened?"

Shadow sat back away from her. "You fell off the table."

Treze looked down at him but didn't meet his eyes. Surprise

flushed over her face. This man - he's been following me. I keep seeing him places."

"Who are you anyway and how'd you get in here?"

The detective handed Horace a card. "Andrew Jones, Pinkerton National Detective Agency. I came through the door. Just like you."

The young man examined the card. "THE Pinkerton's? I heard there was some other folks using that name and causing troubles."

Deci sat up and looked around. "Where's Miz Moira, sister?"

The older girl's shoulders tensed. "Oh, so now I'm your kin? Can I have a biscuit?" The child stood up and reached for a biscuit as if the answer to the first question didn't matter.

Horace took her hand and pulled her to face him. "You almost killed Miz Moira, Deci."

"But how could I have done such a thing? I was in here getting some dinner and then I woke up on the floor.". The girl's face was crossed with confusion.

Treze moved to her other side and took her face in her hand. "Don't act like you don't know exactly what happened."

The confusion melted and was replaced by innocent sweetness that didn't reach her blue eyes. "You know you're my favorite sister."

"What about that light that came out of you?" asked Shadow.

Treze grabbed Deci's hand and ran for the back door.

The detective and sheriff followed the girls into an alley between the saloon and the adjoining stables. The young lawman stopped him before they went farther. The girls rounded the back corner.

"What've you got to do with those girls anyway, Pinkerton?"

"Long story. Keep up."

A light exploded ahead of them, and the air tickled with the same energy Shadow felt in the hotel room back in Raritan. When they rounded the corner, Treze was on the ground weeping and her sister was gone.

The girl scrambled to her feet and ran, but Shadow called out, "I don't intend to hurt you, miss."

She stopped but didn't face him. The bearded lawman approached her. "Where's your sister?"

She looked down at her feet. "This ain't your concern."

"I just saw the craziest shit I've ever seen, and that kid you call sister nearly killed my friend Moira." The young, bearded man towered over her, but she kept her eyes down and didn't budge. "Ain't you even going to look at me, Miss Treze?"

"You wouldn't want that, I assure you.".

Shadow put his hand on the man's shoulder. "Listen to her, Sheriff."

"This ain't your concern any more than the sheriff's here. None of this is. Why do you keep following me?"

"Mr. Edison hired us to find you."

"If he was so keen on finding me, why didn't Mr. Harry take me just now?"

Shadow had no answer. The girl stomped away.

Horace cleared his throat and headed toward the street. "Well, you didn't kill Deci and now that she's gone, there ain't much more I can do here.".

The detective glanced at the girl, but then followed the broad-shouldered sheriff. "Can I ask you a few questions about the situation?"

The young man nodded but kept walking. Shadow glanced back but Treze was gone. Two children from his vision had disappeared since he'd found Thirteen again. There were few coincidences in his experience.

"I'll catch up with you. That girl. We need her after all." The Pinkerton faded into the dimness of the alleyway.

Horace headed toward the saloon. "I think I need a drink."

13

S orry, sir. There's no train going east till Thursday. You want a ticket?" The man behind the counter searched through the schedules. Shadow didn't have time for this.

"I'm not interested in a cabin, but I am looking for someone who might be. Young girl with brown hair, about this high." He held his hand just below his shoulder. "She probably didn't look you in the eye."

"It's been quiet since this morning. I heard there was a fuss over at Moira's. She okay?"

"Kitchen fire, I think. Miz Moira burned her hands." Shadow tipped his hat. "Much obliged for the information."

He headed back to the boarding house and tried to figure out how he'd explain to Kate that he'd lost the girl and another child along the way. His partner would be understanding, but it would complicate an already complicated matter. Once he arrived, he saw the girl, Treze, perched on the porch swing.

"Decided not to walk?"

She kicked her legs and moved the swing but didn't answer.

The detective sat down on the painted steps near her. "Mr. Edison says you're dangerous."

The girl stopped mid-swing. "He's right. All of us are, except maybe for Three."

"Was Mr. Edison helping all of you?"

She fiddled with her blue skirt and stared at her hands.

"Why did you come back here? You could've gotten on a wagon if you didn't have any more money, I'm sure."

"Someone has to take responsibility for what happened in that kitchen this morning. I'll work off the debt owed to Miz Moira and then start searching again. One or two of us can't stop him."

"Mr. Harry?"

She nodded.

"Why didn't he take you just now?"

"I don't know."

"Does Mr. Edison know?"

Treze headed for the screen door and paused. "Apparently not or he wouldn't have hired you, right? Look, I'm staying here to help out Miz Moira because my sister is a monster. Unless you have real questions, go away and tell Mr. Edison that I won't be returning for his help." The screen slammed hard, and he heard her latch it.

He stood outside but didn't attempt to follow her. "Mr. Harry will be there every time you find one of your siblings. He's tracking you somehow."

"You're mad. This whole thing, my whole life…mad."

"Like your bad luck or Deci being part lizard and eating people or whatever that was back at that farm? Mr. Harry wants your siblings for a reason."

The girl backed away. "I need to cook. Please just go back to Mr. Edison and relay my message. Good day."

The Pinkerton sat on the swing as the morning air warmed and reached out to the Brotherhood.

Mr. West's voice was close enough that it felt like he was on the porch. "Do you intend on sending her message back to Edison?"

"Not yet. I'm more concerned that she's going to go off and find more of her siblings. She said something about one or two of them not being able to stop Mr. Harry."

"Kate is sure that Edison knows."

"I am still not convinced. Thirteen isn't exactly a font of information on that front. Find any more interesting news stories?"

"No, but we have landed for refueling. Kate is going into town."

Shadow saw the sheriff strolling up toward the porch. "Once I'm sure the girl is staying here, I'll catch up with you all. Tell Kate to be safe." He could almost hear his partner's laugh as he severed the connection.

"No train?" The lawman leaned against the post at the steps.

Shadow shook his head. "How is Moira?"

"Resting. I stopped by Doc's. He said he'd send her home in a spell. She's not happy about missing the lunch crowd."

"I don't think she needs worry. Treze is back in the kitchen. Says she owes that much to Moira."

"What the hell happened back there, Pinkerton?" The boyish sheriff scratched his beard.

"I believe that the girl is leading a creature to her lost siblings. She doesn't believe this, but this is the second time I've seen that blue door since I've been following her."

"Is all of her family as scary as Deci?"

"We haven't encountered all of the girl's family, so we aren't sure. We won't be until we have more information."

Horace sat down on the steps. "I guess you'll be staying for a while?"

"Perhaps not. Can I count on you to keep an eye on her for a spell?"

The lawman laughed. "You want me to keep an eye on her? She may kill me."

"Doubtful. I think she likes you. I need to catch up with my partner before she gets to Colorado Springs. Once we get back, we'll know more about the girl and her siblings, I suspect. Maybe we'll have a clue about why they are so important to Mr. Edison."

Shadow tipped his hat and walked between two buildings into the shade created by the two roofs meeting. He parted the darkness and found himself falling into space rather than walking the paths. When he opened his eyes next, he was gazing up into a starlit sky.

14

ealings, fortunes, and miracles! Come see them all this
afternoon right on the square! Let Dr. Lazarus show you
the way to true life and true living! Show starts at 2
o'clock. Not tomorrow, my children, but TODAY!" called the young
man wearing red and gold robes and a matching turban.

Kate stepped out of his path, but not before he shoved a flyer into
her hand. He'd seen her, which was amazing enough, and the page
tingled just for a moment. At the other end of town was a vardo, a
wagon painted in reds, blues, and yellows. The flyer in her hand read:
"Come See DR. LAZARUS at HIS MYSTICAL MEDICINE SHOW!
The wonders of the Orient and beyond await!" In the center of the
page was a man with a curled mustache and blue turban, arms raised
and a huge grin on his face. When she glanced up, she saw the man
himself come out of the painted vardo wearing a blue and gold robe.
He whistled and a moment later the boy in the turban raced past her.

"I wouldn't have thought you would be interested in medicine
shows, Mrs. Warne," said a voice from behind her.

"Mr. West, I thought you were staying behind."

"Sho assures me that he won't leave without us. My brother is with
the girl Thirteen." Mr. West tipped his hat as a group of young ladies

walked past them. "She is less than forthcoming concerning her situation with Edison. In the meantime, another of her siblings was taken through the blue doorway."

"How is he following the girl?"

"Edison?"

"No. Mr. Harry. Keep up, good sir."

"Shadow says he doesn't think Edison knows what his assistant is doing."

"We could be facing a situation of the right hand not knowing what the left hand is up to. I find that difficult to believe considering the control Edison seems to exert over Menlo Park."

Kate glanced at the ornate wagon. The older man was moving crates and tables with the help of the younger man. The flyer in her hand fluttered and faded from Inside to Outside and back. Most objects could move between the realms but were grounded Inside. A woman stepped out, wearing a red scarf over her head and a sari of jade green silk. She brought the boy tea in a fine china cup and fussed over him for a second. Worry held in her dark eyes even as she laughed and kissed Dr. Lazarus on the cheek. Then she made her way to what the detective thought was a table by the stage. At first, it looked as though the woman was going to take tickets, but instead, she picked up two wire sticks. Flowing, metallic tones rose as the woman struck wires stretched across the top of the table. Kate felt drawn in and wanted to get as close as she could to the stage and to the enchanting music. A muted glow rose around the woman as she continued the tune.

"Mr. West, would you accompany me to this show?"

He didn't answer. Kate turned to look at the gathering crowd around her, but he was nowhere to be found. Her relationship with Shadow had taught her that sudden disappearance was not uncommon for those in the Brotherhood. Assured that Sho would not leave her behind, she joined the crowd gathering around the small stage at one end of the street. She pushed her way to the front of the crowd to get a clear view of the stage, which was now empty except for boxes of so-called elixir and a table swathed in a rich, blue velvet piece of cloth. Very few shows Kate had seen had such finery. The wagon was spotless and well-maintained. Nothing dirty around here except the audience who'd gathered here after dinner instead of returning to work. Dr. Lazarus must be finding great success.

The young man who'd been passing flyers earlier bounded to the front of the stage. "Good day to each of you! Today, you will see miracles! Illnesses will fade. Youthfulness will return. The future will be made clear! And now, I give to you our very own master of miracles, the one and only Dr. Lazarus!"

Dr. Lazarus burst onto the stage resplendent in his blue and gold robes, balancing a turban on his bald head that was twice as large as his assistant's. Kate saw sweat dripping down the man's face even though he was dressed cooler than most of the audience. Both men bowed and waved until the clapping stopped. The turbaned showman pulled out a white scarf, wrapped it around his left hand and tapped it three times. When he lifted the scarf, a small white canary took flight and swooped around the heads of the people in the audience. They clapped. His son stepped back and opened a small cage where the bird lighted inside and stayed for the rest of the show. Kate could see where Lazarus hid the bird in his robes, but the man had such a pleasant energy that the small fraud didn't worry her.

Lazarus walked the edge of the stage, never taking his eyes off the audience and said, "Welcome one and all to my show. We've traveled from afar to be with you today! My wife, son, and I have spent time with swamis in India, visited the ancient tombs of Egypt, and spoken with the wisest men in China learning the medicines and curatives guaranteed to--"

"He's a liar!" A deep voice echoed from the back of the crowd. Kate tried to locate where it came from.

"--make you feel like you're—" Dr. Lazarus continued over the voice.

The crowd parted and a small but sturdy-looking man in a fur coat and hat strode toward him. His dark beard and angry eyes made him look like a small bear. Kate put her hand on the pistol she had hidden beneath her coat.

"This man killed my horse!" He threw a bottle at the stage, barely missing the good doctor. The bottle shattered as it hit the back of the ornate wagon.

"Sir, I don't know who you are, but my curatives are not meant for —"Dr. Lazarus, backed up as the man stepped onto the stage.

The boy stepped between them. "Sir, I'm sure we can help your horse. Where is it?"

Kate noted a grin that passed between Dr. Lazarus and the boy as the rough, fur-clad man led him to the horse, which was lying on the ground behind the crowd.

"You can't help him 'cause he's dead." The scruffy man crossed his arms.

"Perhaps he's just asleep." Kate rolled her eyes. Boy was stealing lines from Jesus himself. The old snake oil peddler walked past her, keeping up with the scene. Kate had seen enough of these shows. Plants like this were common, but effective. If the crowd sees a miracle, belief in the product and show is assured.

The boy knelt by the horse on the ground. For a second, he fluttered between the Inside and Outside, something Kate had not expected. No one else seemed to notice this. A look of panic washed over his face until his eyes landed on Kate.

The showman interrupted her observation. "Do not fear! In the Near East, my young son, Seth, learned the mysteries of many worlds including the next world. In Ceylon, he learned the ritual of resurrection from ancient Buddhist monks. They called him Dali Hoko, the greatest healer of his generation."

The boy broke Kate's gaze and pulled a small glass sphere from the sleeve of his robe. He began chanting over the horse. As he leaned over the unmoving animal, his collar slipped and revealed the number three tattooed in black on his neck. She stepped back. The boy was one of the missing children!

He snapped his fingers in front of the horse's face, and murmured, "Come on, sweetie. Come on back," but it didn't respond. Murmuring rose from behind her, and he looked back at her, sweat rolling down his cheek, hand shaking.

The snake-oil man continued. "We must have complete silence. The ritual is not complete without your silence and cooperation." If he knew that the horse was dead, he didn't let on.

The burly customer pulled a pistol and cocked it. He pointed it at the boy. "Raise my damned horse, you charlatan."

"The boy can't focus if he has a gun in his face."

"Maybe I should point it at you then. The horse don't matter anyhow. I'm here for the boy."

The boy? Before Kate could pull her own pistol, the ruffian fired on the good doctor. The crowd screamed and the boy leapt up and threw himself in front of the older man. He flickered between the Inside and Outside before he dropped at his father's feet.

The showman looked down at his boy. "Well, shit."

Even with the rising confusion, Kate was able to level a shot at the retreating assailant. The bullet hit his arm, causing him to drop his own weapon. He looked around but didn't seem to see her at all. Grabbing at his bleeding wound, the man pushed through the crowd, which rushed toward Kate and the fallen boy, slowing her ability to pursue the man. She went to the Outside, but a group of people surrounded her there as well. By the time she pushed past them, the man in the rancid furs was gone.

The voice of a woman cut through the chatter and screams of the crowd. It echoed even in the Outside. Kate turned as the crowd parted to reveal the woman with the green sari and red scarf pushing her way to the fallen boy, weeping and chanting in what sounded like a Central European dialect, but she wasn't sure. The boy flickered between the worlds once more and then the flickering stopped. His face was gray in the wash of colors around him.

Why did the ruffian want the boy?

Kate stayed in the Outside but followed the weeping woman. Insiders could be seen from the Outside, but the colors they wore were dimmer. Usually. The woman Kate assumed was the boy's mother shone as bright as the rest of the Outsiders. The boy stayed gray before blinking out of sight. The crowd gasped and Kate reentered the Inside. His body lay unmoving on the ground, but the woman had stopped weeping. Instead, she was chanting under her breath while the crowd pushed to get a better view of the spectacle and the victim.

Kate flashed her badge at Doctor Lazarus. "Who was that man?"

"I don't know." He glanced around at the crowd. "We didn't exactly have time for warm introductions."

Of all the ways I've come here, this has to be the worst.

Seth opened his eyes to the familiar white space of what he called the Terminus. It wasn't quite Inside, but it wasn't Outside either. Thirteen doors were around him. He found the door marked with a 3 that matched the one on the back of his neck. He stood up and brushed off his robes. The bullet in his chest fell out and away, melting into the floor. No one at Menlo had ever tried shooting him. Now that he'd experienced it, he wondered why, especially since so much shooting went on in the world.

The room felt fuller than it should for a moment. Someone was watching him.

Hello?

No one answered, but he was convinced he was being watched as he took out a ring of keys, which he could only access in the Terminus. He glanced around at the other doors for reassurance more than anything else. None of the other children were here. Relief followed by discomfort washed over him. If none of them were in the Terminus, then who was watching? No one else could come to this place as far as he knew. His door dinged, reminding him that he need not linger.

He found his key out of the thirteen on the ring and as it clicked in the lock, he could hear Preacher Butler, one of Dr. Lazarus's friends, singing, "When I hear that trumpet sound/gonna rise right out of the ground." He wondered how anyone would know about that who hadn't been to the Terminus. Maybe that guy John who wrote the Revelations had a terminus. A horn blew from somewhere and everywhere, Inside and Outside, and Seth walked through the door.

People surrounded him, but his eyes fell on one face-his adopted mother's. She bent over him, hands over her face, wailing. The heat from the sun beat down on Seth's chest and he knew that someone, probably his father, had torn his shirt off trying to get to the wound. Seth sat up, took a deep breath. He put his hand on the cold body of the poor beast beside him.

"Damn, Pop. That man killed his own horse."

The crowd gasped, the weeping, chanting woman screamed, and Dr. Lazarus sat down hard on the ground, eyes wide with surprise. This may have been the first time he'd seen his pop speechless. A young brown-haired woman stood between his family and the crowd. She was transparent but solid. "Who are you?"

Without missing a beat, the boy got up. "I'm the Dali Hoko, don't you know?" He moved back toward the poor horse. No animal should have to deal with a shitty owner who kills it. He knelt by the horse. The crowd was silent. His father came up behind him, but Seth put out his hand to keep the old man back. It wasn't that he had a thing to hide, but that he needed to focus. Seth had no idea where horses went when they died. Was there a terminus for animals? He hoped so.

He touched the chestnut horse. Warmth flowed through him and words that he didn't understand flowed out of his mouth. This was new. There was no room or keys, only a bright light that enveloped him and the fallen beast. The warmth spread into the chest of the horse, and its body shuddered. The Dali Hoko fell back at the old showman's feet as the horse got up and ran in the opposite direction.

One lady started clapping and jumping up and down. The rest of the townsfolks followed suit. There were only two who did not clap. The mysterious woman he could see through and his mother who was wiping her eyes.

Seth grabbed his father by the hand and bowed. "Miracles can be yours, too, if you listen to the wise and learned Dr. Lazarus!"

The snake oil salesman bowed once more to hide the confusion, pride, and concern that welled up inside him. There was no way explain what had happened. It's not everyday someone dies, comes back, and raises a horse from the dead as well.

———————

Kate noticed that the boy's mother picked up two small items from the ground after the boy performed his miracle. What the boy had done with that horse wasn't one of the usual tricks she'd seen in these sorts of shows. Something had gone wrong with the original bit, that was certain. He'd died. She'd seen him in the Outside for a brief moment. Then he'd gone, but not back Inside. His concern for the horse when he'd come back to life was also real. None of this made much sense to her until he turned, and she saw a number tattooed on his neck.

The boy's mother grabbed Kate's arm. "You can't take my boy. Go tell your master that we had deal."

"I don't have a master."

Kate winced as the woman's grip tightened around her bicep. "As my beloved would say, 'Like hell.' You are from Outside. Do not tell me you have no master." She released Kate and moved toward a tent with townsfolks lined up at the front of it. "You tell him," she said as she slipped between the silken fabric panels of the back of the tent.

Kate blended into the crowd as the show continued. The boy went through the paces as if nothing had occurred, but she caught looks of concern cross Dr. Lazarus's face more than once during the show. People bought trinkets, bottles of tonic, and fortunes for the rest of the afternoon. She needed to check on the airship and Mr. West, but that could wait. Kate made her way to the tent bearing the sign "Mystic Mona Sees All." Perhaps she could find a way to make Mystic Mona see good sense and talk to her. She passed the line and stepped into the tent.

The inside was dim and filled with sandalwood smoke. A small metal lamp flickered, casting dancing shadows every time Mona moved. She leaned over four Tarot cards the customer had drawn. A smaller version of the wired table sat next to her. She hit a tone and then began.

"The first is Inverted Fool. This card tell about you." Her accent thickened as she settled into her role of fortune teller. If the detective hadn't just argued with the woman, she'd have thought she'd just arrived in the United States.

The young woman looked down and shifted in her chair. "I'm not a fool.".

"We human. Are all fools at time, especially the young, eh? I have been fool myself. There is no shame. Only lesson, no?"

The would-be sybil hit some lower notes on her instrument and then gestured with one stick to a second card that showed a cloaked figure with his head down. Two cups were standing, but three were spilled on the ground at his feet. A Roman 5 floated above him. She said, "The next is the Upright Five of Cups. What have you lost?"

The woman pulled out an embroidered handkerchief from her skirts. "Henry…he left me to work at the railroad…I lost our baby last winter…he never came back after the baby died. How did you know?"

Mona took the young woman's hand. "I know nothing, little one. You pull these cards. You know story. Spirit knows story. I just help. For your loss, I am sorry." The next note she played was brighter and louder. "Next is Upright Nine of Wands. Your mind. The loss hasn't weakened it."

"My ma says that too."

"Your mother, she is wise. Finally," Mona played the previous series of notes, a measure that was haunting and uplifting at the same time. A sense of hope washed over Kate and the darkness on the customer's face lifted a bit. The older woman pointed to the final card, "Spirit speaks."

The pale young woman glanced around as though she expected to see the spirit. Mona tapped the table with her stick, pulling her client's attention to the card once more.

"Is it going to tell me the future?"

"No. Spirit knows no future. You make future. This is Inverted Eight of Swords."

Kate saw a blindfolded and bound woman surrounded by eight swords.

"It's upside down. That must be bad."

"No. No. Spirit sends special message. You brand new. Start new life. Accept new life. Live well."

"I'm scared, Mystic Mona. I have nothing."

"You have your mama, no? She will help. No more fool for you, eh?" She led the woman to the front of the tent. Before exiting, the woman hugged the fortune teller. "Thank you."

Mona said something in Prussian and smiled. When the woman exited, she latched the tent opening and turned to face Kate.

"You will not take my son!"

Wind rose around Kate and lifted her off the ground.

"If you'd let me explain—"

"There is no explaining. We had deal." The woman lifted her arms and pushing into the air. The lady detective was pinned to the ceiling. She tried to phase through the force holding her to no avail.

"You are the second person in a week who has managed to trap me, Mona, and I find that most annoying. For the last time, I am not going to take your son. I'm here investigating for the Pinkertons. We're looking for a girl who has a mark on her neck much like your sons. I stumbled on you all by accident."

"But you are from Outside—"

"There is no ruler of Outside who I've met."

The wind stopped, but Kate hung at the top of the tent. "More lies."

"No. I promise. I just want to help the girl. And now your son."

Kate was thrown to the ground but not hard. "Not you. Another lie told by the boy's father," said Mona.

"Dr. Lazarus?"

"Another. It is a long story for another time." Mona helped Kate get off the ground. "So, you look for a girl like my boy. There is no other like him. But now I must work. Come back after the show."

Kate thanked her and hurried back to the airship. A few more hours was all she needed and then they could be on their way to Colorado Springs once more.

15

K ate returned to the ship and found Sho climbing along the hull of the ship.

"What ho, Captain?"

He stopped, waved, and scuttled down to meet her. He bounced a little hard when he dropped to the ground, and she thought she heard some gears grind a bit. He muttered to himself, "Need adjust that soon. Don't feel right." He tipped his hat. "I need a few more minutes and we'll be ready, ma'am."

"No worries. I've latched on to a lead and need a few more hours, if you're amenable. Have you seen Mr. West?"

"I thought he went into town with you.".

"He was with me, but only for a few moments. Then he disappeared. I thought he may have come back here."

"Haven't seen him. You know how it goes with the Brothers."

"They come and go at will. Perhaps he noticed something that would help us with the case."

"Like your lead?"

"Yes. If you see him, tell him I've found a boy that I think is one of the Menlo children. I'm going back to town for more answers." Kate turned back toward town but stopped. "Did you see a man holding his arm run past the ship about an hour ago?"

"I don't recall seeing anyone like that, but then I was inside doing minor maintenance, so I may have missed that spectacle."

"Too bad. I wanted to get another shot at him."

Sho raised his eyebrow.

"Long story. I'll fill you and Mr. West in when I get back."

The crowd had thinned by the time she arrived at the vardo. Seth passed out bottles of tonic while his father took the townspeople's money. The line to Mystic Mona's tent had only one person left, so Kate stepped past the men to see her. A shadow passed over them and when she looked up, she saw a large figure in flight, too high for her to make out any details. Could have been a condor.

Dr. Lazarus called the wagon as the last of the crowd moved on. "Hey, Mona isn't doin' anymore readings today. We'll be back in town in a month."

She turned to him and smiled. "She asked me to come back after the show."

He put down a bottle and scratched under his turban before removing it. "You're that Pinkerton lady. What do you want?"

"I had some questions about what happened this afternoon."

"There was nothing fake going on if that's what you're worried about. My son is 100% the real thing, ain't you?" He nudged the boy at his side. The boy pretended not to see her.

"Your wife is scared of something. I'm here to help her."

The snake-oil saleman's face got hard and his eyes turned almost black. A man in overalls pushed some money into his hand. He pushed aside his anger and gave a wide smile as he gave his customer two bottles of his elixir. The lady detective took this as a chance to head on to the tent. She made it about ten steps before the fortune teller's husband shouted, "Stop right there, missy. My wife fears very few things. We'll go to the tent together. Now."

He stepped off the platform and took Kate by the arm. He wasn't rough at all, but he stomped and rushed her to the tent. The joviality he'd shared with his audience was not evident in this moment.

He shoved her into the tent. "Deborah! This woman says she is here to help you." The table and chair were folded and lying on the ground and there was a red and gold case on top of the folded table. Since his wife was no longer there, he pushed the lady Pinkerton out the back and led her into the wagon that was parked behind it. Deborah stood over a boiling pot of water whispering in her own tongue. The water hissed and dark blue steam streamed into the air.

"He saw the boy, Thomas." Her eyes were red from crying, and she passed the man a triangular amulet with a white stone shaped like an eye. Kate was sure that was one of the things she saw the woman pick up off the ground earlier. "He is blind for now, but he'll try again, I have no doubt."

Thomas threw the eye on the floor and crushed it under his book. "Now he'll be blind longer." He put his arms around his wife and forgot Kate for a moment.

She sat down and cleared her throat. "Who are you talking about?"

The miraculous young man bounded in. "I was about to ask that."

"Seth…" Mona scurried to the boy and held him close.

"I felt someone watching me after I died. Wasn't that you?"

The woman sniffled and led him to an empty chair at the small table. Determination, anger, and sadness shone in the fortune teller's eyes.

Kate made her way to the door. "Perhaps this isn't a good time."

"No. This is the perfect time." The fortune teller gestured for her to sit down despite her husband's protest. "Especially since you may be able to help."

The older woman took her son's hand and squeezed it while Dr. Lazarus brought a pot of tea along with some cups and joined the group. He was not pleased but accepted his wife's request. She poured a cup and passed it to him. When she offered a sugar cube, he held up his hand. "No, sugar."

"Ah yes, you are sweet enough." The two of them held hands. Her fear and his anger lifted as they gazed at each other for a moment.

"This is no time for your charms, woman. Don't we have some cookies or something for the young lady?"

Kate accepted the warm cup when her host offered. "There's no need to put yourselves out. What happened out there?"

The showman reached for a tin of cookies from a shelf behind him. "You saw the show same as the rest. That man shot Seth, then the boy got up, and healed a dead horse. Show goes on. End of tale." He took a few bits of shortbread from the tin.

"The boy died, Dr. Lazarus. I saw him come to the Outside and then disappear."

"You don't know that..."

"Ma'am, my name is Seth, and you're right. I died right there in front of everyone."

The fortune teller took a few cookies and passed them around the table. "She is from the Outside too, Thomas."

He poked their visitor's shoulder. "She's solid. How?"

"I am here because I want you to see me. Your belief that I am here helps me solidify."

The boy finished his cup of tea and poured a second for himself, waving off his mother. "That guy who shot at Pop said he wanted me. Is Mr. Edison sending folks to hunt me and my brothers and sisters now?"

"If he is, we haven't been told. Based on what we've discovered so far, he doesn't need to send mountain men to hunt you all."

"Edison? You mean Thomas A. Edison, inventor extraordinaire?" Thomas punched Seth's arm. "You never told me you knew him!"

The boy rubbed his arm. "He's my past. You say to focus on the future, remember?"

"But..."

"This Edison man has nothing to do with what happened today." The older woman took the cookie tin from her husband, who picked out three more cookies. He tried to pull it back, but she slapped his hand and put the can away.

"Then why did that man out there shoot at Pop?" Their son leaned toward his mother.

"The amulet belongs to someone I left behind when you were born. I find...found it next to you when you died today." His mother touched his face and the worry from earlier returned to hers. "It allows the one who owns it to see whatever he is looking for. It means he's seen the boy."

"I picked that man myself from the bar this morning for the show." The boy looked ashamed. "We mean no harm when we do that."

His pop grunted. "No need to explain our methods to the young lady."

"He took my money and then came to the show."

"You paid him to kill the horse?"

Seth's eyes widened. "No, ma'am! I didn't know he was going to kill that poor animal. If I had, I wouldn't have chosen him. We don't need but one crazy in the show." He patted his father's hand.

"That crazy puts food on this table and gives you a place to sleep. Keep that in mind."

"As long as I lift and move boxes after the show."

"Truth."

"So, who owns the amulet, ma'am?" Kate sipped her tea.

The fortune teller covered her face and wept. Her husband put his arm around her. "You don't have to tell if you don't want."

She brushed his arm away and straightened her back. "The boy's father."

Confusion crossed Seth's face. "Wait. I didn't know you 'til you picked me off that train platform a couple of years ago. How do you know?"

The showman crossed his arms and said, "Mystic Mona knows all." Then he winked.

The woman punched her partner. "This is no time for laughing. Seth, you are a special boy. I knew this the first moment I held you after you were born. Then they take you away. I watch for you everywhere me and the old man travel. Then, when I find...found you standing in front of all those farmers I said to myself, 'Deborah, your miracle has come.'"

Her husband, with a roguish grin, took her hand in his. "I thought I was your miracle."

She punched the showman again, and he mock-winced.

The boy got on his knees next to her as she grasped his hands. "So, you really are my mother? But who took me away all those years?"

The older woman kissed his hands. "When I came to America, I was lost. I barely spoke English and my powers were not yet in full bloom. I met someone who said he could help me control my powers more."

"Couldn't you see your future?"

"Just because you can see doesn't mean that you believe, my dear one. Choices change the drift of the future, so there are many possible outcomes. At that time, I just saw the happy possibilities. I had support and a teacher. For a woman with no means, this was important. I loved him."

Kate knew this story well. She'd encountered many women in the course of her career and life who had been cornered by the lack of education, money, and friends or family. Her own story could have turned ugly had Allan Pinkerton been less willing to take a chance the day she marched into his office.

Deborah continued, "I thought he loved me, but he asked me to do things that were wrong. We hurt people." She began to cry, and Thomas took her hand. Leaning on his shoulder she said, "And when I wanted to leave, he forced me to stay. Not long after, I found that I was pregnant. He put me in an asylum to protect me."

Thomas tapped the table. "That was where I first found her."

"You were in an asylum, Pop?"

"I was in jail. The asylum was on the same island on the Hudson. Most people never escape that hell hole. But most people aren't me and your mother. You were born there." A mixture of pride and sadness crossed his face.

"Why didn't you take me with you?"

"They took you away from me. Said I was dangerous. Then your father came looking for you."

The snake-oil salesman's eyes darkened, and he trembled as if trying to hold himself together. "I almost killed him right there, but my beloved made me promise not to, and made him vow to not look for you. Guess I get to take my gun and go hunting now."

The fortune teller let go of her son's hand and pulled at her spouse. "No, Papa!"

"None of that 'no, papa' nonsense. He broke the promise."

The lady detective plunked her cup on the table to get their attention. "Why does he need the boy?"

The old showman pointed at his son. "You saw what he can do in the show. Who wouldn't want that kind of power in his back pocket?"

Seth stood up. "I can leave. It would be safer, wouldn't it? I need to go find my sister anyway. Been dreaming about her lately."

"And what if that scruffy fella shows up again? Or your birth father comes after you? You have no idea what you're up against. No. I won't let you go. Sit down."

The detective attempted to redirect the conversation once more. "Seth, where did you get that number on your neck?"

He reached up and scratched it. "I don't remember much, but I think it happened when I came to Menlo Park. I was maybe four. We all had one."

Her partner would say that the universe often conspires to pull pieces of the puzzle together. Even though she didn't believe this herself, in this case it would seem that had indeed happened.

"What do you know about the girl, Thirteen?"

His father took her cup off the table. "Does this have anything to do with what happened today?"

"It may."

The young man sat once again. "She is my sister. At least, that's how we saw ourselves. All of us. She's looking for us, isn't she?" His parents were surprised, and so was the lady Pinkerton. "I've been dreaming about her. She's in trouble."

"Seems trouble follows in her wake."

"She doesn't mean any of it. She can't—"

Kate took his hand. "I know. We also think that someone at Menlo is using her to track the rest of you. So far two other children with your markings have been taken after she found them."

"Where is my sister now?"

"She's about four days ride back east from here. In a little town called Brainerd."

The boy stood up. "I have to go to her."

"I already spoke my mind on the matter." The snake-oil salesman gave him a stormy look, but beneath the sternness was a wave of worry.

The boy headed for the door. "I need some air."

16

Seth sat down on the steps of the wagon and put his head in his hands. *Thirteen, where are you?* His mind wandered and he saw flashes of a woman with bandages on her hands, the scent of biscuits, and the bearded man he'd seen in his dreams. Fear and sadness washed over him, but there was something else he'd never sensed in his sister. He reached out to her and for a moment, he heard a song they used to sing when they were trying to be happy. The song faded, and he saw a creature with a boxy nose and rough gray skin wearing a calico dress and matching bonnet smiling at him. Her voice was sweet and musical. "I miss you, Three. You need to come home."

He was drawn to her, not out of concern, but by the glowing door that had opened in her chest. He grabbed the step. "Stop it."

Anger flashed in her amber, reptilian eyes. In a moment, she stood close enough to him that he could smell rotting flesh mixed with the sharp scent one smells after rain. Her face split into a grin of pointed teeth as she touched her snout to his nose. "Make me, brother. Oh. You can't stop me like you want, can you? What was it you used to say? Family don't hurt each other. I'm family, ain't that right?"

"Why do I need to come home?"

"Isn't me missing you enough?"

"I'm not going back with you or anyone else he sends. Tell the old man that he can save the world without us."

She simpered and reached for him. "But I love you." The pull got stronger and his grip on the step loosened. The blue light surrounded him with a warmth and comfort he'd always wanted. As he reached toward it, he heard a shuffle behind him followed by the scent of sandalwood and spice. His head cleared and he found himself on the stairs again, holding on for dear life as his mother sat next to him. She passed him a cup of coffee.

"What is wrong?"

He put one arm around her and hugged her hard, then took a sip of the coffee. "This is strong enough to slap the long-johns off Paul Bunyan." It was one of Thomas's jokes. He waited for the payoff.

"I would pay to see that, my love." She leaned into his embrace. "But you do not answer my question."

He looked down into the cup. "I don't know why Pop is being so hard about this. Thirteen is my family as much as you are."

"You love her, no?" She pointed into the wagon. "That old man in there loves you too. He is afraid."

Her son pulled away. "Pop isn't afraid of anything."

"He is loud. He makes jokes. All to hide."

"But he fought in the war. He told me about him and Sarge."

"And you think he wasn't scared?"

Seth hung his head. "Do you ever have dreams that tell you things you don't know?"

"You speak of prophecy?"

"If you mean old-time religion prophecy like your friend, Preacher Butler, talks about, no," he said. "I mean do they tell you about people or places, things that you need to know to help people? Do you see people you don't want to see?"

Deborah was silent, then she put her hand on his. "Dreams are powerful. Sometimes they lie, and sometimes they tell truths. Most are about you. What are you dreaming about?"

He told her about the visions he'd just had. "Thirteen is safe. I can see her, but I can't get her attention. The same is not so for my sister,

Ten. She's watching Thirteen. If the lady detective in there is right, then Thirteen is finding and losing us. I don't understand why Ten is calling me."

The fortune teller didn't answer right away. "All of you are connected, no?"

"I can feel most of my brothers and sisters."

"And you said you reach out?"

"I do that best with Thirteen. I haven't reached out to the others in a long time, and until now, none have reached out to me."

"You want to help this, girl, Thirteen, no?"

"If I can just get to her."

Deborah leaned over and kissed his temple. "You are a good boy. I will go in and talk to the old man. He will listen to me. In a little while, you will come in and tell him about what you have seen. He is an old fraud, but he understands much about the true oddities of this world. He will help you. Now go do your chores, my son, before I feed you to crows."

His mother left him on the steps, and he was comforted that she understood, at least a little. In spite of being afraid to get too close to them, Seth loved her and the stubborn old man he'd left grumbling in the caravan. He also loved the life she'd pulled him into and didn't want to leave them. But after seeing Ten, he didn't have much choice but to do so. Deborah and Thomas, with their laughter, stories, and even their stubbornness, had made him a better person. Maybe that was what love was.

Whistling, he went to care for the horses as the sunset began paint the sky in rose gold tones. Maybe his mother could talk some sense into the old man.

Thomas slammed his fist on the table. "Absolutely not!"

Kate was more shocked by the old woman's suggestion than by the showman's response. Deborah let her husband rage as she prepared supper. As he stalked past her, she put another cup of coffee in his hand. "You are being foolish, my love. It will ease the boy's mind."

"No. I will not hypnotize my own son." This time he slammed the cup down. Coffee splashed on the newspaper lying on the small table.

"Look what you've done, old man." His wife turned, picked up the paper, wiped the table, and refilled his cup in one fluid motion.

"No sugar." He sipped the refreshed cup.

"Aren't you sweet enough?" She checked the small stove and stirred some beans.

"Where's my supper?"

"Soon, my love. The boy told me his sister needs him."

"We need the boy too. I may be as handsome as the first day you met me, but I'm not as young and need help with moving things. Then there's the show. Can't do the show without the Dali Hoko."

Kate interjected. "As I said, my partner is with the girl now."

"See, her partner is with the girl. No need for Seth to go racing to her side."

Deborah set out wooden bowls around the table and cleared the paper off. "We could hire a hand while he's—"

"Hire a hand?! And pay him with what? Pancakes?" said Thomas.

"If the boy went, he wouldn't be gone forever."

The showman took his wife by the hands. Sadness and fear washed over his face "Remember that man from this afternoon? What if there are other men looking for Seth? He's safer with us."

"None of them can kill me if that's what you're worried about, Pop." The boy stood in the door, his hands dirty.

"You been listening?"

Seth looked at his feet. "Maybe."

Thomas clapped the boy's shoulder. "A fellow after my own heart," He pulled him to his seat at the table. "You. Sit."

Seth did as he was told. "I know you're worried about me."

"Damned right."

His wife tutted at his language as she continued at the stove. "Now, Thomas…"

"I just want him to know I'm serious."

The detective leaned close to the boy. "Why do you want to go to Thirteen?"

"If what you say is true, then The Calling is coming soon. She'll need me. I've dreamed about her and some of the others."

"So, you want to go save this girl?" His father scrabbled around in a box.

"There is no saving Thirteen. I want to go help her before she causes anyone else bad luck."

The older man went through the pockets of the caftan he wore on stage. "If I helped every woman I dreamed about—"

Deborah snapped a drying rag at him. "If you helped every woman you dreamed about, I'd be a widow with a wagon and two horses."

"True."

"What do you mean the time is coming soon?" By this point, Kate had her notebook out.

"I'm not sure. It's something we were told over and over again by Mr. Edison and Mr. Harry. We learned about the things that we did or happened around us and that's what they would say."

His mother served the bean soup. "All the more reason to hypnotize him, Thomas."

"All right. I'll do this only once, but only because I want to see how this plays out." His father pulled out a Chinese coin on a chain that he used in the show earlier. He muttered, "Woman never fails to get me into crazy messes."

The fortune teller sat down next to her son. "I heard that, old man."

Kate knew from other shows she'd seen that a good hypnotist could cause people to act like chickens or sing songs. She hoped Thomas would be able to do more than that.

He stood in front of Seth, swinging the amulet back and forth. Symbols were stamped around the outer perimeter of the metal circle. As it moved back and forth, the detective was sure the symbols sparkled in copper. A ripple from the Outside tickled down her arms from the direction of the stove. She saw a tiny smile on Deborah's face.

"Watch the amulet, boy. Just relax. Focus on the amulet and my voice and stop trying to figure out how this works." The salesman turned to Kate. "And that goes for you too, missy. Don't think I don't know you're studying me."

The boy's breathing slowed, and his eyes shut. Thomas snapped his fingers.

"Open your eyes. You are back at Menlo Park."

"My family."

"Tell us about this Calling you've been told about."

Seth's body slumped, and his breath was shallow. His spirit exited his body, and he sat next to the detective. "I'm not supposed to tell. He said he'd kill us all and start fresh."

Thomas didn't seem to hear him.

"Edison?" Kate asked.

"Mr. Harry."

"What's going on here?" His father poked his body, and then listened for a breath.

Kate turned to the showman and smiled. "Seth relaxed more than you expected and has exited his body."

Deborah gasped and cradled the boy's body close to her.

Thomas dropped the amulet on the table. "I knew this was a bad idea."

"He's not dead. He's afraid." Kate took the hand of spirit Seth and looked him in the eyes. "You are scaring your parents. Mr. Harry isn't going to kill anyone if I have anything to say about it. He already tried to kill me twice and failed." The spirit-boy let go of her hand. Surprise crossed his face and he fluttered again. "Now get back in your body and talk to them." She nodded at Thomas who pulled his wife away from the boy's body.

Seth's eyes popped open, and he responded to Thomas's original question in a flat tone. "It is a time when all men will have light and power. The world will be bright as a morning star. In one moment, all will see and never fear the night again."

Deborah raced back to his side and slapped at his face. "He's still hypnotized, Thomas."

The showman picked up the amulet and stared at it for a moment.

While all this was going on, Kate cut in with her own question. "How will this happen?"

The boy sat up as if he were in a classroom and reciting important information. "The power that brings eternal day must be balanced and held. You must use your powers and be strong. You and Thirteen are the balance."

Thomas snapped his fingers and the boy's eyes opened. He turned to Kate. "You are more miraculous than me!"

The detective laughed.

His father snapped again. "You said something about a power that will bring eternal day. Any idea what he meant by this, son?"

"I remember those words, but not what the power would be. There's a lot that I've forgotten since we left. The pieces I do remember are odd at best."

"Did you ever see a special book at Menlo Park, Seth?"

"Mr. Harry had one book that he wouldn't let us look at. He kept it in a room that he locked. He told us it was going to help us call the power to us when the time came. He treated it the way some folks treat the Bible. Like it was holy or something."

The old showman put away the amulet. "That's crazy."

"You watched your son come back from the dead, but you say this is crazy? Can you stop this, Seth?"

"I don't know. If I can be with Thirteen, we may be able to help stop whatever will happen. I will leave in the morning."

His father sat down to eat. "You aren't leaving without us."

"This isn't your fight, Pop."

The man pointed his spoon at the fortune teller. "The moment that woman over there brought you into this vardo, it became my fight. We head to Brainerd tomorrow."

Kate stood up and shook their hands. "I will let my partner know to expect you. In the meantime, I must get back to the ship. I have an appointment in Colorado."

1 7

Long after Deborah and Thomas had turned in for the night,
Seth sat on the steps of the wagon gazing at the blue-purple
sky of three am. He couldn't sleep knowing that he'd finally
get to see Thirteen after all this time. He also worried about his
brothers and sisters who he couldn't find. Some were as unstable as
Ten while others were just beginning to learn of their gifts.

A slurred, stilted voice broke his reverie. "I'm here for you, boy."

"Who's there?"

Out of the darkness stepped the scruffy mountain man from the
show. He stunk of something earthy and rotten. The butt of a rifle
peeked over his shoulder. In a stiff sort of motion, he reached for the
young man.

"Wrong caravan, sir." He stepped out of the large man's reach and
into the wagon, shutting the door before the man could move up the
steps. He leaned against it to keep the man from getting in. "Pop."

The older man's snore hitched. "I know I said we'd go to Brainerd,
but I need another hour of beauty—"

A shotgun cocked outside, and the showman sat straight up on the
edge of the bed.

"You got to the count of ten before I fill your wagon with lead.

Can't all of you come back to life." The words slurred at the end. Seth had experience with drunks, but this was a different sort of slur and mush. Thomas put his finger to his lips, and then winked. If he'd had a white beard, he'd have looked like Santa in his red long johns. *Pop must have one hell of a plan.* Thomas nudged Deborah, but she slapped at his hand. "Don't break my concentration, you idiot." She started singing in Romani. The snake-oil man pushed his son aside and opened the door just a hair. He projected in his Dr. Lazarus voice. "Before you start counting, good sir, could you give me time to put on some pants?"

"One...two.."

"I think that's your answer, Pop."

The older man closed the door. "You have to applaud his spirit."

"He's gonna kill us in—"

"Six...seven...eight..."

His father put on his pants. "I'm surprised he can count that high."

Deborah song got louder as their visitor continued to count.

"Pop, what's the plan?"

Thomas slid on a shirt and buttoned it.

"Nine..."

A red glow exploded through the windows. Seth scurried to one and a curtain of red light rose from the ground. The man screamed. That was followed by a heavy thump.

"Holy shit, Pop!"

The light from the curtain revealed the mountain man lying on the ground in two halves, shotgun unfired by his side. Thomas led Seth out of the wagon to get a closer look.

The boy knelt as close to the body as the curtain would allow. "This was the plan?"

"That man won't shoot my boy again." Deborah stumbled down the steps and fell to the ground. The curtain fizzled out. She was pale and breathing hard like she'd run a long way. Seth scrambled to her side. "You made the curtain?"

She waved toward the boy and her arm flopped in his lap.

He cradled her. "And it did this to you?" His pop took her hand and brushed the hair from her sweaty face.

His mother leaned into her son's chest. "I would do it again if it saved you."

"How did you do that, Ma?"

Thomas put his hand on the boy's shoulder. "Do you think you're the only one who does special things in this world, boy? She's been doing this stuff longer than you've been alive."

"But I thought she just saw the future."

"How long do you think a witch would last in proper society? There are parts of this country where they'd put a noose on her faster than you could say your name. Soothsaying is amusing. Witchery, not so much."

She pointed at her husband. "So, I take up with the old man over there, and we put on a show. People like shows. Now stop with all this chatter. There is more to do," She stood and would have fallen to her knees if Seth hadn't been there to catch her.

"Sit back down. Pop and I got this. Right?"

The older man glanced at the sky and around the wagon. "We need to get moving now before the sun rises. I'll hitch the horses. You go move the body off the road. Don't forget to get his shotgun. We will need an extra weapon, I suspect."

After carrying Deborah back inside, Seth went to what was left of the mountain man. The stench was overwhelming, even after he covered his nose, and he threw up.

"Pop, get over here quick." He wiped his mouth with his sleeve.

As he got close, Thomas covered his own nose.

"Good God. You'd think he'd been dead a while. Wait, where's all the blood?"

"Ma's magic wouldn't take it away, would it?"

"I don't think so." Thomas picked up the shotgun.

Seth covered his nose with one arm and reached down to touch the man's hand. It was colder than any dead person's hand he'd ever touched, which was amazing since that was the most stinging and bitter cold of all. He pushed past the bitter frost of death and found himself in a white room with no doors. What was left of the mountain man's soul hung upside down. Worms with human faces crawled in and out of the spirit-carcass. He turned and closed his eyes, repulsed and angry that he could do nothing to help the man.

"You came to visit me. How decent of you. I see your ma is sticking to her deal." The boy knew who it was before he opened his eyes.

"Your deal with my ma doesn't matter. It's my choice now."

A black-clawed hand grasped him by the chin and forced him to look up. Blood trickled down one side of Seth's neck as a claw dug into his face. Seth thought his neck would break before he could look into his father's face. When he did, golden eyes glowered down on him, set into a chiseled face with edges sharp as stone. Leathery wings spread from his shoulders. Whispers swirled around Seth's head in voices he recognized and then didn't. Glowing eyes of all sizes glared at him as he rose higher and higher off the ground.

"Using stubbornness to mask your fear. You're so much like your mother it's delicious." Visions of Deborah being hurt and maimed flashed through her son's head. He struggled to free himself from this thing that was his father by concentrating on a door—his door. His father faded away to be replaced by a large white door. It opened before he could touch it and revealed the familiar room with thirteen exits. He stepped forward, but stumbled and fell through the floor, down, down. He bounced on the floor face down. When he got up on his knees, he was face-to-face with the rotted mountain man, who still hung from the ceiling like a slaughtered animal. He tried to stand but was yanked up from behind and something held him by his collar. "You need not try to escape. I can reveal who you really are, what you really are, my son."

The boy pulled hard and reached for his door, but his feet wouldn't move. He looked down and saw a mass of giant, black-glazed centipedes flow through the white walls. They surrounded his feet and held him in place. Their metal legs clattered against the surfaces they crossed, and their front claws curved into sharp wires. As they climbed his pants, sharp spines tore through the dungaree fabric into his legs. He cried and whimpered as pain rose through his lower body

A pungent scent wafted around him as several of the centipedes crawled over his chest and around his neck. Frustration and anger flooded past the pain, and then, for some reason, he couldn't help but quip, "So, I'm really the king of centipedes?"

The boy's lack of paralyzing fear didn't seem to please his captor. "You will be dead unless you call them down. What a waste that would be."

Instead of saying a word, the young man dropped to the floor and laid back into the writhing mass of centipedes. The poison entered his system as they attacked him using the needle-like claws at the sides of their heads. Some began to burrow into his legs and chew into his flesh. His heart began to race, and his blood turned to fire inside him. The keys for the Terminus formed in his pocket in slow motion, and he leaned into the pain that could be a bridge back to his door.

A clawed hand yanked him from the floor and shook him like he was a rag doll. The boy convulsed, half aware of what was happening. His hand fell from his pocket, still holding the key that would allow him to live. He was lifted to face his captor, who took his lifeline from him. "You won't be needing this now."

Seth choked on a scream.

His father twirled the keys and dropped him to the floor like trash. "Since you have your mother's inability to follow instructions, I will make this simple for you."

The creature spread his wings. Hundreds of eyes, of every shape size, and color blinked and examined his son up and down with contempt. The room, the centipedes, and the monster who was his sire faded. Instead, figures rose before him. Thomas and Deborah.

"Once you understand who you are, you won't be needing these two anymore." The figures melted into pools of flesh at his feet. He found himself outside the wagon with this winged creature. The camp was surrounded by a red dome, and Seth realized that this was what his mother's red curtain looked like from outside the wagon. He and his so-called father had traveled back in time somehow. The mountain man's body was on the ground next to his shot gun. The dome dropped and he watched as Thomas exited the wagon followed by a more corporeal form of himself. He wanted to warn them but the poison coursing through his body stilled his tongue and made it hard for him to move. Instead, he was silent as his mother stumbled out of the wagon and passed out. Every nerve in Seth's body screamed and burned. Once again, he leaned into the pain, reaching for death, calling for Terminus.

Seth turned to the tableau of Thomas, Deborah, and his corporeal body kneeling around the dead mountain man. He raised his flaming hand as the pain escalated once again. There was only one release. A single note sang over the roaring agony inside his mind. He turned away, marching toward the center of town.

The fire in his veins ignited on his skin and burned till it shone like his father's. Before he could stop himself, he pointed at the wagon, and it exploded. Some of the pain subsided. He turned to his captor and pointed his finger, pushing his pain toward the creature, but there was no explosion or flame. Instead, pain ripped through him as though the destruction he wished on the thing who was his father was redirected.

The creature pushed down his arm. "You will hurt as long as you fight this. Embrace the destruction and live."

Seth wept and groaned until a scream echoed around him and he wasn't sure it wasn't his.

"Burn it all down!"

Pain subsided as each building flamed up and exploded in front of him. He roared with delight until a tinkling tune rose above the destruction fueled him. Through the fog in his mind, he reached for the notes of a half-familiar song and clung to them. The father-creature twirled the keys as they made their way to the center of town, unhearing and unaware.

With the music came a cool, flower-scented breeze that pulled Seth from the searing pain welling inside him once more. Steam blinded him as tears rolled down his face, mixing with the screaming heat that he now emitted. Another wave of anger flushed through him, and the pain of the fire behind it was more intense than the pain of the centipede poison. The music and sweet fragrance were replaced with a scream and the acrid odor of brimstone as fire climbed through his chest and into his throat.

Lava flowed from his mouth, igniting everything around him except his father, who rose from the ground, fueling the flames of the burning town with each flap of his eye-dotted wings. The demonic figure clapped and howled as though he were at a show.

"Tap into the rage, boy. Death is yours!"

Seth, who was now cognizant enough to see what he'd done, turned and spat lava at his father. The airborne creature held up a hand, and the molten rock stopped mid-air. It rained back on the boy and engulfed him. Flame, pain, and rage melted his body away. He was hell and everything should die. He roared and pounded the earth around him. Fire emanated in all directions, consuming everything.

Something floated atop all of the din around and inside him. It was *her* voice, so sweet and soft. He reached for it, craving relief.

Ma?!

The familiar sound of her cimbalom rang out around him, and she sang a song he knew deep in his soul. He saw a tiny baby with light hair, and he lay at the feet of a beautiful woman wearing scarves. He rocked back and forth with the music because he was the wee child. Her words circled around him:

"Haida Liulu
Dormi in pace
Măuca țe ț-a face
Așernutu' pe păântu'
Sădormi ferit die vântu'"

He sang with her, his tears flowing into the lava, cooling it into a magma crust on his body. Her voice soothed the rage and fear that fed the fire. The magma began to drop from his body, which was no longer wounded. All the flames were extinguished as he watched his mother walk toward him down the middle of town. Golden light surrounded her, and her eyes shone with the same light. The music followed her even though he didn't see her mouth move.

"Stop that noise! He's mine, woman!" His father swooped down in front of Seth. He created a barrier between mother and son with the wings of a thousand eyes.

Her hair flowed and the red, gold, and blue scarves she always wore whipped in the winds that rose around them. She looked like a goddess. "You know, I spend a lot of years trying to find my boy. Then I find him after I quit looking. It is the way, no?"

"You said he was mine. You promised. We made a deal." The creature grew to monolithic size, but the woman never flinched.

"I was young and thought I had no choice. I know better now." The witch leaned down to look past the massive wall of wings. "Hello, Seth, my son." She flicked her hand and the creature stumbled back. She ignored his scream of frustration as she offered her other hand to the boy she loved most. He took it and the last of the pain ended. The embroidery on her dress and kerchief sparkled and the bright golden light flowed up his arm. His heart slowed and his mind cleared.

"He is grown now. Deal is off."

The creature shrunk in Deborah's light. Its skin dulled and the eyes spread along his appendage rolled and turned red. He charged her, but she pointed at his chest. "I will blind them all, *diavol*."

The sky above them flashed. The *diavol* lifted off the ground before he disappeared in the cobalt sky. "This is not over, *draga mea*."

Deborah and Seth floated over the wagon. The boy spotted the halves of the mountain man on the ground beneath them.

"How can you love me after this, ma?"

She squeezed his hand harder than he thought possible. "How can I not?"

"But I'm this thing, this horrible thing."

"Do you believe this?"

The boy pulled from her and turned away. He fell on his knees. "You saw what I did to that town. To the wagon. If you'd not come, I'd have killed you and Pop."

Light moved from her and wrapped around his shoulders like one of her hand crocheted shawls. Memories flooded his mind. Dancing with Deborah after a show. Helping Thomas move boxes and telling jokes. The once dead horse from earlier. Behind all of those memories rose the gleaming black creature vomiting fire and brimstone over everything.

Deborah's song rose and shattered his vision, bringing him back to the bubble. "Both sides are you, my little one. Only you know which one you will be forever. Time is short. We must return or the old man will wonder where we are."

The golden light rose bright around them and then he was, once again, kneeling next to the stinking corpse on the ground. Deborah pulled out a bag and began chanting and sprinkling a circle of herbs around the body, causing the stench to subside. Thomas hugged Seth hard when he stood up.

"You okay, boy?" The showman put his hands around his son's face and looked into his eyes.

"Yes, sir."

The older man released him. "Is your father gone?"

The boy glanced around. "For now." He looked at his feet. "I'm sorry...I burned the caravan, sir."

The showman leaned close. "You did what?"

"I became this demon and set it on fire. Then I burned the town. Oh no. Those people...and he has my keys now." The boy started to sob.

His pop turned him toward the wagon.

"I don't know what you are on about, but the wagon is right where we left it when Ol' Stink Face over there dropped by earlier."

Words failed the boy. The rolling home was in order down to the curtains inside. He looked back toward town and every building was where it should have been.

Deborah pushed a cup into his hand. Rose and mint warmed the air around him.

"We need to move this carcass and leave before the sun gets high. I'm not keen to answer questions about dead mountain men."

His pop's eyes sparkled as the two of them dragged the body as far from town and away from the road as they could. Thomas could find humor in the darkest places, which is one reason Seth loved the man so. It took them several trips to get the dead man out of the road since bits and pieces of the corpse kept falling off. The stars were fading as dawn approached, making the sky more azure and gold.

"Hurry up, boy. Folks are gonna be comin' to market soon. We need to be long gone."

The young man looked up at the sky. "What if he sends someone else?"

The show man clapped him on his shoulder. "We have our secret weapon."

"He'll be expecting her to fight next time."

Deborah stopped them at the door. "No one who touched that body is coming in this house till he's clean of that stink!"

Thomas rolled his eyes.

"I saw that." His wife smacked his bald head.

I t was well after midnight when Kate heard the thump outside her cabin on the airship. The sound was out of sync with what she'd grown accustomed to hearing during a flight. *Maybe that fellow who killed his horse stowed away.* She grabbed her derringer from the fold-out table by the tiny fold-out bed and made her way to the door. With her back against the wall, she cracked open the door and saw a body prone on the floor.

"Shadow!" She put the gun down and went to her unconscious partner. His pocket watch had slipped out of his vest pocket onto the floor, so she knelt and picked it up. Instead of the hands pointing to twelve, like it had when he'd had one of these spells before, it was now at one. He was time traveling again. She tucked the watch back into the pocket of his vest. She was certain he wouldn't want his brother to find him in this condition, but she wasn't so sure she could move him. When she touched him, her hands didn't pass through him like they had in past episodes. Grabbing under his arms, she pulled him out of the hall.

"You'd think he'd be lighter since he's not all here." Kate muttered as she pulled him onto her bed and went to the ornate miniature liquor cabinet tucked into one corner of her cabin. His shot would be ready when he returned at the very least.

The crickets chirped in the dimming light of dusk. Shadow breathed in air that was thick and scented with pine and sea salt. He opened his eyes and found himself in a glade thick with loblolly pines. Stars streaked across the dark blue sky and two bright silver comet-like lights whooshed past him around the edge of the trees with an echoing rhythm. Their power was palpable even though there was no heat emanating from them. Despite the dim of the evening, he couldn't part it to find the paths again. He stood up and a little girl in a white ruffled dress approached him. She had black hair, pulled back with a large red bow. Her eyes were blue and her face radiant.

"You came!" The child threw herself around his waist.

"Uh, yes. Here I am." It wasn't often that anyone hugged him, and this girl was strong. "How did I end up here?"

She giggled in the infectious way some girls do. "I called you and now you'll be safe."

Shadow knelt down and took the girl's hand. "You called me? Who are you?"

She pointed up. "The sky is falling. We're all being called together, and I like you and want you to be safe." She danced around him until her skirts billowed out. "I'm Oona. That's what my aunties call me. It's German, just like them. I'm not German though."

As she turned, he could see the number 1 on her neck.

"What's that on your neck, Oona?"

She plopped on the ground and covered the number with her hand.

"Couldn't protect myself then. They gave me the number."

"Mr. Edison?"

She nodded.

"Mr. Harry?"

She started screaming and rocking.

A new girl rose from behind Oona. She was a photographic negative of Oona with white hair and skin dark as the deepening night sky above them. Her eyes of sky blue shone in bright contrast.

"Look what you've done." She embraced Oona, who continued to rock back and forth.

The detective sat down on the ground. "I don't understand."

"You grownups never do!"

The pale girl wiped Oona's eyes and pulled her close. "I protect others."

"And I protect her."

The dark girl poked her paler self. "I told you not to bring him here."

"I'm sorry my question scared you. I was trying to help."

The first Oona took his hand. "May the circle be unbroken."

"How do you know about me?" The Pinkerton let her play with his fingers because he wasn't sure what to do.

The dark girl started brushing her other's hair. "We know lots of things."

Her lighter self kicked her feet. "The door will open. The monster will come. People will die."

"But what about the others?"

"The others?"

"Your brothers and sisters? My friends? Everyone?"

"They can't find us here. We will live," they said in tandem.

Dark Oona put the brush away in her skirts. "We can't protect everyone. Not powerful enough."

The roar of water intensified as if the ocean had moved closer. It was constant until an explosion shook hard enough to knock Shadow to his knees. Screams cut through the night air and the ground shook hard with explosion after explosion. He got up and ran for the edge of the glade, protected by the two gleaming comets.

"You can't keep me here. I must help them! My partner—"

Light Oona glanced behind her as if the scene were right there. "None of that is happening now."

"But the explosions! The screams."

"All things happen at all times."

The girls must have created a bubble to float on the edge of time, thus all things were happening. As long as they stayed here, time could happen without touching them. As much as he needed them, he understood why Dark Oona wanted to cocoon her other self this way. He was sure that her/their help would be vital to stop Mr. Harry and whatever was coming. If he could figure out how to take her/them back with him or how to convince her/them to take him back, he might be able to convince Thirteen he was on her side.

The Pinkerton got to his feet and brushed off his pants. "We can help each other, girls. Come back with me. I can take you to Thirteen."

"We've seen her already." The girl in white joined him. Her dark sister followed.

"Troubles follow her as always."

"If you join her and I can find your brothers and sisters, we can stop whatever it is that's happening out there." He pointed past the trees.

The girls spoke in tandem. "You don't know that."

She were right. He had no idea if she could stop whatever was coming. He thought of his friends during the Revolution, well before Kate and Pinkerton. He'd had a similar discussion with Ben and Thomas one night over ciders. The Brotherhood stood behind the Yanks with odds as bad as here. Except there was no unknown monster involved.

"I was made to protect all people in this land. That includes you and your brothers and sisters. If I hide here with you, I can't do that. You don't have to go, but you do have to send me back. If you do come with me, however, I will promise to protect you. Whatever that is needs to be stopped. Someone with your powers could help us. It's your choice, though." He attempted to open the darkness to the paths, but to no avail.

The second Oona took her sister's hands. "He's telling us truths, sister. We need to go back and help."

Light Oona got paler. "I can't. I'm scared."

Her dark sister slapped the girl. "Yes, we can. You heard Shadow. He's protecting us!"

The girl in white wiped her tears with her sleeve and then took her dark self's hand. She opened the circle and took Shadow's hands. "May the circle be unbroken." Nothing happened.

Light Oona stomped her foot. "You have to say it too."

"May the circle be unbroken."

Her dark other yanked his arm. "No, you dummy. You have to say it with us. And say it like you mean it."

"Not like a grown up." The dark girl snickered.

They said the words together, and the two shimmering comets orbited closer and closer until they were brushing the sleeve of Shadow's jacket. A third comet joined them, a jet of black smearing between the silver twins.

The Oonas said in tandem, "Take us down the paths."

Shadow wasn't sure this would work, but he reached out to the dark comet and opened it to reveal the paths he was so familiar with. "Don't let go."

The three of them stepped out and fell and fell and fell.

19

K ate considered calling Mr. West in but was sure that her partner wouldn't want that. She had no idea how she'd explain what Shadow had done or was doing anyway since she wasn't sure herself. Instead, she pulled up an upholstered chair and waited for him to return.

What if he doesn't return? She pushed the thought away. "You'd better come back. I don't want to have to tell your brother."

As if in response, two bright orbs appeared above him and began to circle the perimeter of the room. A black orb appeared and followed the silver orbs that had tails like comets. Two young girls appeared on either side of Shadow. One had hair the color of corn silk put up in neat curls and white bows, which matched her white dress and boots. The other wore the same outfit but all in black. Her curls were blue as the midnight sky. She looked down at her partner.

In unison, she asked, "Why is Shadow lying on the ground?"

"Who are you?"

The girl with sable hair ignored her question. "We pulled him out of his time, silly. Give him a second."

Her fair double looked the lady detective in the eye. "We are Oona."

"Both of you?"

"Of course!" They both giggled.

Shadow groaned and his partner scrambled to help him as he tried to get up.

"Where's Oona?"

"The girls are here. She said they pulled you out of time. I'm not sure I know what that means, but that doesn't matter. What matters is you're here."

Her partner got to his feet and brushed off his pants. She called me to their hiding place. Where was it again?"

The light girl hugged him. "My safe place away from the monsters. We wanted Shadow to be safe too."

"How did you know about my partner?"

"From my dreams. I know about everyone who will participate in The Calling." The dark girl spoke with her other.

"Are there monsters in The Calling?"

She both nodded.

"What's being called exactly?"

Dark Oona looked at her sister. "We promised not to tell."

"Well, it's too late now, isn't it?" The lighter girl curtsied to Kate. "You're prettier in person, ma'am."

"You dreamed of me?"

"And we know you're a Spectral."

"What about The Calling, Oona?"

"I wanted to save you all, but she," Dark Oona pointed to her photo positive, "wanted to save Shadow most because she likes him best."

Kate brought the Four Roses from the table and handed him a shot glass. At this moment, she wasn't sure that she didn't need one as well.

Her partner knocked back the whiskey. "You told me that you weren't strong enough to save us all."

"I may have lied. Sorry?" Light Oona took the shot glass from him.

The lady detective pulled the girl's dark other to one side. "Please explain The Time."

The girl glanced at her other. "You shouldn't have lied to him."

"Stop!" Her voice echoed and both girls jumped. "Tell me what I want to know right now."

Her partner set the whiskey bottle on the table. He looked like he'd just watched her sprout horns. "I would do as she says."

Dark Oona sat down and kicked her feet. "A door will open and what is supposed to be good will destroy people and things."

"Who's opening the door?"

Light Oona grabbed the lady detective's arm. "We aren't supposed to tell anyone. It's a surprise."

Kate pulled out the book from Menlo Park and opened to the page with thirteen people. "Does it look like this?"

The pale girl gasped and backed as far away from the book as she could get in the small cabin. "It's what we saw, Oona, in our dreams."

The dark girl took in the page. She counted each figure and then put her finger on the central figure above them all. "Yes. This is The Calling. All of us gathered to open the door."

Shadow stood behind her. "Is that Mr. Harry?" He braced for the lighter girl to scream. Instead, her other nodded. "You know it's him."

"What is he doing?"

"He's being the gate, of course." Dark Oona traced around the edge of the page.

"For what?"

"There are no words except power, death, and madness." The light girl took her sister's hand and pulled it away.

The long-legged detective sat down near the girls. He made them look tinier than they were. "Why does he need you and your brothers and sisters?"

The darker girl pushed her other away. "His time among people has weakened him. He led Edison to each of us with the intent of using our energy to strengthen himself."

Kate poured a shot for herself. "I thought he ate Spectrals for energy."

"It's true, but there aren't enough around him to give him the energy he needs for The Time to begin."

"So, he's going to eat you all then?"

149

"We help him. He gathers us around him and…"

"Except now he can't since you all were spread out and lost." Kate closed the book.

The girls nodded. Dark Oona said, "He won't be as strong without all of us. That's why I pulled out of time and hid. I protect us from being used."

Light Oona shook and covered her face. "I dreamed that lots of people were going to die because of what he opens the gate to. I tried to find all of the others, but some are gone."

"I'm not strong enough to pull who's left out of time," said Dark Oona.

Her other kicked her. "Tell the truth. Some of them you don't want to find."

"Ten would eat us. She almost did before we left home." Her sister/self skipped away.

"She isn't our sister."

Kate's partner knelt in front of both of them. "How did you pull me out?"

Light Oona took his hand again. "I saw you in my dreams. You're in almost all of them as of late. I like how you shine." She pointed at Kate. "I saw you, too, but you're a Spectral, so time is different for you."

Her dark other took his other hand. "I wanted to save you because I knew you could help us if we had to stop hiding."

"I begged her to bring you to us," said the lighter girl. Both giggled.

Shadow squeezed their hands. "He's using Thirteen."

"We know," the girls spoke together.

"She is our caretaker and is connected to all of us," said Dark Oona.

"We don't know how that works exactly," said her lighter self.

"Doesn't she bring you bad luck?" asked Kate.

Both girls shook their heads. "Not to us. She loves us. She's never caused us any trouble."

A knock broke the conversation.

"Kate, are you awake?" It was Mr. West.

Shadow put his finger to his lips and shook his head. His eyes danced with a panic Kate had never seen him display before. Had he done something wrong in bringing Oona?

She signaled to her partner that she'd handle things and moved closer to the door. "I'm here. Shadow came in a few moments ago." Shadow threw up his hands, and she shrugged. What else could she do? There was no hiding the girls now. "We're discussing the girl in Brainerd."

From behind the door, Shadow's brother answered, "I shared the information with you already, brother, but I wanted to speak with Kate as well. I felt a shift in the paths earlier. You were gone and then back and there were others on the paths with you."

Kate let the dark-suited man in. The Oonas, who had decided to sit on the bunk, waved at him and giggled.

"He looks like Shadow," whispered Light Oona.

Her dark other nudged her. "They're brothers, silly."

Mr. West crossed into the room and studied the children. "The paths are open to wanderers now, I see."

"We aren't wanderers. Shadow brought us here," Dark Oona stepped in front of her other. "We want to see our sister, Thirteen."

"The paths are only for the Brotherhood. All others die."

"Do we look like Spectrals, sir?" asked the dark girl with white hair.

"Sister be polite," said Light Oona. She pushed past her other to face the man. "Your brother was protecting us. He did what he should have done."

Shadow spoke up. "She joined her powers with mine and we ended up here."

His brother circled the girls. "You keep saying she when there are two."

"We are Oona."

Kate took West's arm and led him to one of the red upholstered chairs near the window. Her partner joined them.

"What you have done—"

Kate called up a teacup and pressed it into his hand. "Is the best he could. These girls, Oona, could answer some of our questions."

"Take us to Thirteen," said Light Oona.

The lady detective passed both girls a cup and motioned for her/them to join the adults. "I'm not sure this is a good idea. We think she draws Mr. Harry when she finds you all."

"Shadow promised he would protect us. Are you saying that your partner lies?" The dark child sipped from her cup while her sister gazed into her own cup.

Mr. West slammed his fist on the table. "None of this matters at the moment. My brother broke a law and took a chance with your lives." He stood up and paced as if that would strengthen his point.

"This child called for my help. Is that not what we were made for?" Shadow got up and stopped his Brother mid-step. They stood toe-to-toe. "We have an obligation, and that's more important. I'm pretty sure this is one more secret we can keep, right?"

Mr. West didn't answer. The air in the room became chilly, as he made his way to the door. "Once this gets out, I'm not sure what will happen. Secrets don't keep well." He exited.

"What do we do now?" Kate put her hand on her partner's.

"We do what we promised and take her/them to her sister."

"You made that promise. What if Mr. Harry comes like he has for the others?"

"I'll do my best to stop him. You heard Oona. He's weak."

"What if she are just guessing? She is a child."

Dark Oona kicked Shadow. "*She's* right here, sir."

Her pale other stood in front of the lady detective and crossed her arms. "I can decide where I want to go and how safe I am. As long as I have her, I'm safe. Take me to my sister."

The lanky detective set the dark girl on his knee. "If you're worried about him eating me, remember that the book called me empty not so long ago. Maybe that emptiness will save me again?"

His partner spoke over the lighter girl's head. "Don't make me have to train another partner in the middle of a case or join me here in the Outside. You promise."

"Brothers don't die." He put the girl down and got to his feet. "Come on, girls. Time to go."

The lady Pinkerton straightened his tie and handed him his hat. "Meet us in Colorado Springs when you can."

"I'll watch over him, Kate." Dark Oona embraced her before taking his hand.

Light Oona grabbed her other's arm. "I thought you only watched after me."

Shadow took both girls' hands and they made a circle. "We'll watch over each other. Are you ready?"

"You have to say it right this time." The pale girl gave him a stern look.

The three were orbited by two silver orbs and a black orb. Her partner's voice rose above their whoosh. "I'll see you soon."

"May the circle be unbroken." In a flash, Kate's compartment was empty once more.

2 0

Two silver orbs and one black orb whooshed past the stoop of the boarding house as Treze stepped out with a bucket on her arm. The hair on her arms stood up and the number on her neck itched. She dropped the bucket. As it clattered down the steps she ran back into the house and shut the door.

Little One. At any other time, she would have chased the twin orbs, calling out to her younger sister, but she wasn't about to allow Mr. Harry to take another of her siblings back to Menlo Park. Her mind wandered to Two and she held back tears.

The itching subsided a bit. She peered out the kitchen window, but no longer saw the orbs. That meant they were coming. She had to be gone by then. Grabbing her bonnet, she made her way back outside, clinging to the shadows. Giggles tickled the edge of her mind. She scurried down the hill toward the tracks at the back of town and saw Mr. Jones with her sister. *How did he find her/them?* Leaning against the side of the red depot wall, she watched as she headed for the front steps of the boarding house.

"I thought you were staying for a spell?" She couldn't help but relax a bit at the sound of the sheriff's voice. He leaned against the depot wall next to her and she looked up into his bearded face.

"Something has come up. I can't stay."

"Are they your sisters?" Horace nodded toward the small group heading up the hill.

She nodded. "I can't let her see me."

"Bad luck again, huh?"

"The worst of all. Mr. Harry will come back. It'll be my fault."

The sheriff crossed his arms. "So, you believe Mr. Jones?"

"I don't know. I just don't want to take the chance."

"Where are you going to go?"

Treze stared at the ground. "If I lead him to all my family, then I will be the cause of the worst thing of all."

"Their deaths?"

"No. Everyone's."

"You can't protect everyone, Thirteen." The girl and the sheriff both turned to find a pale girl in curls and a white dress standing on the street.

The older girl pushed past her friend. "Why did that man bring you here? Run as fast as you can. Mr. Harry will get you." She pulled the bearded lawman forward. "Tell her, Horace!" She glanced behind her, expecting blue light to start flooding the shaded alley.

Dark Oona stepped from behind her light self. "We're not afraid, sister." The light girl trembled but nodded in agreement.

Horace backed away from the girls. Treze pointed at him. "He's not family and even he knows to be scared. What's wrong with you?"

The dark-suited Pinkerton joined the group and took the girls hands. "We can face him together."

Their older sister reached up and scratched the number on her neck.

"YOU? Take them away now before he can find them! I thought you wanted to help."

"We can face him." The Oonas reached for her, but she backed into the alley. The sheriff caught her shoulders.

Shadow said, "Two was gone before you found him. Ten went because she wanted to go. I could have been wrong. Maybe you don't guide him to your siblings. Maybe it was coincidence."

"I don't believe in coincidence, Mr. Jones. Bad luck winds blow around me at all times." She shrugged off Horace and pushed past them toward the train station.

The lawman called after her. "There's no train passing through for another two days."

The girl gripped her blue skirts, and the number on her neck went from black to red and back again. She turned on her heel and ran up the hill to the boarding house. At the gate she turned back to the group. "Then I guess I'm going to go fix dinner for folks. You may as well follow. If he shows up, at least you'll have a full belly to face him with."

―――――――

As they followed, Shadow could hear the words "stupid' and "get killed" and "all my fault" wafting back from the girl. Dark Oona took the sheriff's hand and skipped as she headed for the gate.

"Is she always this confusing?"

The Oona(s) giggled in tandem. "Of course. She's Thirteen."

Dark Oona kicked a rock. "She don't need to worry. He ain't coming for us. If he was going to come for us, that one," she pointed at her pale self, "would be screaming by now." She tugged at her companion's much larger hand. "I'm glad my sister made a friend."

"I wouldn't say we were friends. I just want to make sure that she's safe. It's my job. Why do you call her Thirteen?"

"That's her name." The dark girl paused and then continued, "I bet she doesn't call herself that now. I mean, I don't call myself One now that I'm in the world."

Shadow opened the gate for the pale girl, who turned around to join the conversation. "Our name means one. The aunties told us so."

The sheriff took the gate from the Pinkerton and held it for his dark companion. "Her name is Treze. I don't know what it means."

"I like it!" Both girls jumped.

As they made their way to the house, the detective followed behind the children. "Do you have a plan, Oona?"

She skipped up the stairs of the boarding house and sat down on the swing. "Wait for dinner. Our sister makes fine biscuits."

Her/their companion crossed his arms. "Stop playing."

Dark Oona kicked her legs to move the swing. "We aren't, Shadow. We found our sister. Now we have to wait."

"For what?"

"For whom." Light Oona corrected. "Our brother is coming soon." She leapt from the swing and spun around. "And someone sparkly is with him. I love her already."

The two of them began whispering together in a language that Shadow didn't recognize. The dark one hopped down from the swing, and she hopscotched to the kitchen door. The detective opened the screen for her/them, and he gestured for Horace to follow.

Dark Oona held up her hand. "You stay there."

"I thought we were waiting."

"You are waiting. We are going to talk to our sister."

"Alone," said Light Oona.

They skipped and giggled as she went to the kitchen. The detective closed the screen.

The lawman leaned on the porch rail. "Not often a grown man gets pushed back by a child."

Shadow peered after the girls. "I'm not so sure she is a child, Mr. Stewart." Then he stepped inside the dining room, which was not well lit at this time of day.

His companion followed him. "What are you up to, Pinkerton?"

He ignored the sheriff and faded from the room to the corner of the kitchen. Light Oona glanced his direction but did nothing to indicate she knew he was there.

Treze stirred at an iron pot and took a large knife to the table at the center of the room. "Why are you with that man?"

"I called him to the circle. He can help us!"

The older girl sliced pieces of pie and placed them on tin plates for her sister(s). The detective could smell warm apple and cinnamon. "You could call all of us to the circle if you wanted."

Dark Oona dug into the treat as if she'd not eaten in days. "We can't find all of us, sister."

"Some of us are dead." Her other fiddled with her piece.

Treze slammed the knife into the table. "You take that back. That's a lie."

Light Oona nibbled on the pie at the end of her fork. Her sister's violence didn't faze her. "Listen to your heart for one second."

"I can't find them because they are too far away. We scattered when we left the train. That's all!" Treze plopped into an empty chair and put her head in her hands.

"How many did Mr. Harry find and eat?"

The lighter sister dropped her fork and started to wail.

Dark Oona comforted her other while Treze wept.

The pale girl took a deep breath and took her older sister's hand. "I saw Shadow when we were hiding in the circle. His light is brighter than all of our lights, even Three. I think he can help us."

She pulled away from Light Oona and scowled. "He's works for Mr. Edison, you ninny. Do you want to go back to Menlo Park?"

The darker girl slapped her hand against the table hard enough to shake the plates. "Would I have let her call Shadow if I thought he'd hurt her? There is no betrayal in Shadow's heart."

Before Treze could retort, the girls eyes began to glow. Dark Oona grabbed her other's hand and reached toward her older sister. "Take it now! Hurry. Two needs us."

The girl pushed back from the table. "I'll make things bad, like always."

Shadow struggled to get to the three of them, but the darkness held him in place.

Dark Oona's eyes stopped glowing and turned as black as her hair and dress. She stomped her foot and stretched out her hand once more. "Things are already bad. Take. My. Hand."

Treze joined the half-circle. Silver orbs swooped around the room in a wide orbit. Dark Oona's eye color changed from black to the brightest of blues while her other's eyes turned golden white, like her hair. Treze screamed. "Go back. He's going to kill us all!"

Something slammed against a hard surface and a massive animal howled from inside the circle of silver and children.

The girls whispered in the mysterious language they spoke. The dark one intoned, "We cannot leave him lest he die by his hand."

Shadow squirmed against the wall, pinned like an insect in a collection. "Let me help you."

None of them answered.

Treze began to hum a tune Shadow had never heard. The Oona(s) sang in her/their personal language. The harmony was sweet and precise, like she'd practiced it many times before. At first, their voices were soft and subtle. He felt his shoulders drop and tensions he didn't realize he carried melted away. With each successive verse, their voices grew louder but kept a gentle tone.

A naked boy, who couldn't have been more than ten or eleven years old, flickered in the center of the circle. There were scars covering his pale skin, and new scratches and bloody lines crossed his back. He growled and grunted like a wild animal, and when he turned toward Shadow, his eyes were white embedded in puffy, blue-black sockets. Dried blood caked under his nose.

The silver orbs grew smaller and began to circle him. He clawed and grabbed at them as they swirled around his body. The swelling in his face receded and white eyes shifted to brown. As the girls continued to sing, his breathing slowed as well.

He crawled to the pale girl and pulled at her skirts. "One?"

She broke the circle and reached for his hand "I'm here! Take my hand."

"ONE? Where are you?" The broken child skittered around the edge of the circle as if he'd lost her. The sisters had stopped their song.

Treze stomped her foot. "Keep singing!"

The older girl and Dark Oona began again. The palest of them called out to the howling boy on the floor, who flickered in and out as if he were between Inside and Outside. "Two. Follow the stars."

"STOP PLAYING TRICKS ON ME!" The boy's eyes went white. He grabbed the cot in the room and threw it against what Shadow assumed was a door. Treze stepped between the silver orbs and slapped the boy as he turned, teeth bared and shoulders hunched.

The boy's eyes changed back to brown again. He grabbed his sister around the waist and sobbed into her flour-covered skirt. "Thirteen." She patted his back and returned to the circle with him in tow. Just as the girls broke the circle to check on her/their sibling, the door burst open, and Horace sprang in. The boy pulled away, hunched and growling like an animal. Treze stepped between them

"Not a good time to come in, Mr. Stewart."

The lawman backed away. "Is that another family member?"

Treze nodded and hummed the tune again. Shadow fell out of the corner and stumbled into the sheriff. The boy ran back to his sister and hid behind her. Horace took off his long coat and passed it to the girl.

"Boy is cold and naked."

She grabbed the coat and wrapped the boy, who kept his sister between himself and the men. A whimper rose from under the massive coat. She stroked the boy's dark hair. After a few moments, he peeked out from around Treze. The swelling around his eyes receded and some of the fresher injuries on his shoulders began to heal before Shadow's eyes. *Is the boy a werecreature?*

He pounded his sister with his small fists. "Why did you come? Mr. Harry could have killed you!"

She grabbed his wrist and he struggled for a second. "Hush, boy. Rest and don't worry about me. He won't eat me, not yet."

"I'm sorry," He hugged her again.

Dark Oona joined the two of them and rubbed his back. "Nothing to be sorry for. You're with us now."

The boy cried, "I killed that woman on that farm. I killed her with my bare hands."

Treze took his face in her hands. "You didn't mean it. Simple as that."

"Yes. I did. She killed my dog right in front of me. Then I killed her. So, it ain't simple as that, sister."

The lawman and detective glanced at each other. The boy had

admitted to a murder. Shadow wondered if this qualified as justifiable.

Treze took the boy by the hand and led him to the back porch, gesturing to the girls to pick up a wash barrel near the door. "We can talk more about this after a bath. I'm sure that Mr. Stewart and Mr. Jones will keep this to themselves."

"I'm a monster," said her brother.

"Aren't we all?" She picked up a bucket and glared at the two men in the kitchen.

21

M r. West, did you see this article?" Kate examined the Nebraska newspaper she'd picked up earlier.

He glanced up from writing in a small notebook. "No." Since the episode with Shadow, he'd answered most of her questions in single-syllable words. He also paced the sleeping cabin corridors at night, which would have been disturbing had she slept.

"'Boy Found in Tree,'" read the lady Pinkerton despite her companion's lack of engagement. "At first glance, the whole thing sounds silly. Lots of boys climb trees after all, so my first instinct is to think that he crawled into a hollow and got stuck, but that's not what the story says."

He didn't respond. She continued.

"The paper says that when they found him, he wasn't stuck in a hollow, but grafted into the tree and that they had to cut the human parts from the trunk of the tree. Of course, he was dead."

He didn't answer but turned back to his notebook and started writing again. She put the paper down, moved to sit across from Mr. West, and grabbed the notebook from his hand. "You will stop this nonsense right now."

"My brother has put me in the precarious position of hiding something from the Brotherhood, and you support this. In order for me to keep this secret, I have to work with you. This does not mean that I have to converse with you in a social situation nor be more than civil while traveling with you." He reached out his hand. "My notebook, please."

She handed it back to him. "This article involves work, so stop being a pig-head and listen. We have to make another stop before Colorado Springs."

"This is all very curious, but I'm not sure this is any more than a ridiculous story to scare people."

"He's either one of the children we're searching for, or he pushed one of the children into using their power. Since you weren't talking to me, I already directed Sho to take us there."

Mr. West laid down his pen. "It would seem that I'm not in charge of this ship anymore."

"Thank goodness it's not far off our course to Colorado Springs. I'm glad you understand." Kate folded the paper and left it on the table.

A bell chimed, and she adjusted her hat. "I believe we're landing right now."

The town didn't have a newspaper, but it did have a telegraph station in the train depot. Kate stepped up to the ticket window and focused so she would be noticed.

"Where to, ma'am?"

"I see you have a telegraph there."

"Yep. I'm the best operator in these parts. You want to send a message?" He reached for some paper.

The lady detective put the newspaper down on the counter and pointed at the article. "You write this?"

The man leaned over and pulled out some wire-rimmed glasses. "Sure did."

"Tell me more."

"You a reporter or something? Everything I know is right there."

She flipped out her Pinkerton's badge. "I was sent to find out more about this situation by a client since it is so unusual."

He crossed his arms. "I didn't make it up if that's what you are implying, Miss Pinkerton."

"I don't doubt the veracity of your tale. I need to know who found the boy. Who witnessed the event?"

The man glanced out the window and pulled down the blind, gesturing for her to come around the corner. She followed but not before unholstering her pistol. No telling what this rascal might be up to. A door opened at the end of the hall. "Get in here!"

He put up his hands when he saw the derringer. She signaled for him to lower them by lowering the weapon. "A precaution, sir."

He offered her a chair and then sat at a green desk. "The boy was found behind the schoolhouse by young Miss Rogers, the school-marm. Classes were canceled the entire week."

"Does she know how he ended up in the tree?"

"She and the sheriff both have been all clammed up about it. Boy was Arnold Melton. Folks are nice enough, but their boy hadn't been right for as long as I can remember."

"I don't understand."

"He was a bully. My kids wouldn't walk to school alone because of him. He was pure mean. Lots of folks feel like he provoked some spirit or weird creature and that was it."

She took out her notebook. "You got spirits and creatures around here, sir?"

"Ain't never seen any in these parts, but since the war..." He glanced around as if he expected someone to appear.

Kate had heard this over and over again. The world had gotten stranger since the war, but at the same time, more folks had moved farther into the west where there were things and people easterners had never encountered before. Sometimes it was hard for the average settler to distinguish between things they'd never experienced and the kind of weird this man was talking about. In this case, however, the man could be more on target in his assessment than he understood.

"Do you think Miss Rogers would speak to me?"

"She's been quiet about all of this. I learned about most of it from my girls. They were scared but happy that Arnold got his, so to speak. If you visit her, she'll be polite, but I don't know what she'll say. You could try visiting his folks."

"No use in upsetting them." Kate tucked away her notes and shook his hand. "I'll go see the schoolmarm and maybe the sheriff."

"I hope you find what you're looking for young lady." He took out a card. "Here's my card," The card dropped to his desk. His office was empty.

The detective made her way to the schoolhouse via the Outside. Talking to the schoolmarm or the sheriff would be useful but going to the victim himself might be even more useful. If he would talk to her.

The one-room schoolhouse stood on top of a hill at the other end of town from the depot. Train tracks made a lazy curve just before the building. Not far from the schoolhouse sat a small blue house with a dainty porch. Behind both buildings was a small stand of trees. One was cut at odd angles. Chips and chunks lay on the ground around what was left.

"Arnold Melton?"

There was a chance that the boy had left the area, but since the boy had only died a few weeks ago under traumatic circumstances, she had a hunch that he stuck around.

"They send you to tell me to move on? 'Cause I ain't gonna move one inch till I get that little bitch back in full," a voice came from behind the tree.

He must have already upset the Outsider community. Fast work for a new spirit.

"No one sent me. I've come to ask about the circumstances of your death, Arnold."

A boy, no more than about fifteen, appeared in front of her, too close for comfort. His hair was parted in the center and dark under a coat of some sort of pomade. He had an inkling of facial hair fuzzing under his nose. Although he was dressed in his Sunday best, the glint in his eyes said church was not for him. "Who's asking?"

Kate stepped back to assess the boy. He was lanky and had a swagger to him that reminded her of Billy the Kid. Billy had been better looking though.

She showed him her badge. He put his hands on his hips and laughed. "Well, damn. They got folks on the Outside too."

She ignored his amusement. "Tell me what happened."

"Girl lured me out here during lunch. Said there was something I should see."

"Who?"

He looked at the tree and paled but regained his swagger and looked her in the eyes. "Quinn LaMoux. She'd been teasing me for months like all the other girls in class. She was the only one I'd not caught, you know."

"Caught?"

"It's all a game, ma'am. They make a fella crazy and then run away 'til I catch 'em. I figured she wanted me to, you know, do what everyone knew I did with girls. When we got back here, I told her what to do. She started crying. She said she wanted me to see the monster. After that, the world got weird."

Kate fought to keep her hand from her pistol. She doubted anyone from the community would come to see what had happened.

"How did it get weird?" Her hands shook and rage flushed through her.

"She hit me in the head with a stick so hard I lost some teeth. No girl ever hit me like that. It ain't part of the game. I lunged at her to try and take the stick, but my pants fell down. She kept hitting my head 'til all I saw was stars. Next thing I know, I'm against the tree. I thought she'd tied me, but I couldn't move, and my pants were gone. I couldn't breathe and things got dark. When I woke up, I saw my arms crusted with bark and my head was clotted with some sort of golden tree stuff. I was naked! She'd hung her writing board around my neck, and it read "monster" in big letters. I want you to know my pa did not understand and had the menfolk cut away pieces of me, so my ma didn't have to see me. That girl murdered me, ma'am. Plain and simple." He faded away and Kate pulled her pistol. Something blew on the back of her neck and grabbed her shoulders. "Of course, then I learned there were nice people here I could play games with." She turned but not before he put his hands around her throat. "Like you, Miss Nosy."

The detective released all her rage in one fluid motion and kicked him hard, which, despite his deceased status, caused enough pain that he howled and released her. Before he could gather himself, she pushed him down to the ground and put the heel of her boot on his throat, grinding it on his Adam's apple. His swagger was replaced with terror as she leveled her pistol at his head.

"Let me explain something. You turn up anywhere near me or any other of the ladies of the Outside, I will know, and I will come for you. You don't want to know what comes for folks like you who end up leaving the Outside over your style of games." She had no idea if she could remove someone from the Outside, but she wasn't about to let him know this.

"You can't kill me. I'm already—" He coughed and struggled, but she pushed harder, making him gag.

She cocked the pistol. "Wanna find out, son?"

If he'd been less frightened and more experienced with how the Outside worked, he would have known to dissipate. "You have one hour to leave. If you're smart, you'll find a way to make a new life that doesn't include hurting people." She doubted he would succeed, but she continued. "In no way will you attempt to contact Quinn LaMoux. I am lead detective for the Outside. If there is a next time, I will show no mercy." She raised her boot, pleased that her heel left a mark in plain view, and kept her pistol trained on him as he scrambled to his feet. For half a second, she saw a scared little boy with big green eyes, but she didn't flinch. In her experience, reality blurred around people like Arnold, sometimes shaped by the person's own warped view of their lives.

He scuttled away from her. "You're nuts, woman. Pointing a gun at a kid."

"Once I knew someone who called himself a kid, but he was like you. He stopped being a kid long before he looked grown." She fired a shot at his feet. "Now git." He yelped and ran as fast as his long legs could take him.

"Mighty impressive, ma'am." Kate turned, pistol at ready. A tall, gray-bearded man leaned on a cane and tipped his hat. "Didn't think we'd be shuck of him."

"He's young and easily frightened." She holstered the weapon.

"You hope for better from kin-folks. I wish I understood why he was like that."

"If he's yours, I'm sorry you had to see all that."

"He hurt a lot of folks. I hoped that passing would have cleared out some of that ugliness. It does sometimes, you know." The man leaned forward on his cane. "Is it true you can watch him anywhere?"

The lady detective felt bad for that lie now. "I don't know."

The man clapped her on the shoulder and laughed. "You were convincing, that's all that matters. He will run for a while yet. I'll send out some trackers I know and have them make him nervous for a spell."

She shook his hand. "Thank you. Now I have a girl to see to."

He tipped his hat again and walked into the fog that had begun to form on the edges of the trees. She stepped back to the Inside to find Miss Quinn LaMoux.

22

Quinn sat back against the wall and stared at the heavy door of her cell at Menlo Park. She'd come full circle. *If everyone was nice,* she thought, *no one would get hurt.* Arnold Melton came to mind. All she wanted to do was make him stop. She lost control when he wasn't nice. Thirteen would have said she'd done the right thing, but she needed to learn to control herself and be less intense. If she had, a boy wouldn't have become one with a tree behind the schoolhouse and she wouldn't be in this cell right now. Mr. Harry showed up at the foot of her bed that night after everyone else was in bed. She expected him to just eat her then and there, but instead he grabbed her by the throat in his clawed hand and pulled her through to the cell where she gasped for air long after he'd gone.

Steps echoed down the corridor, and Quinn glanced out of the small window at the top of her cell. There was a purple flower just outside it, and beyond that was blue sky. She'd already been given breakfast, so it must be midday.

Keys rattled and she turned over on her bunk groaning. It was the oldest trick in the book

"What's wrong, girl?" It was the nurse.

Quinn groaned. "My stomach's been hurting since after breakfast, ma'am," she said, rocking back and forth for full effect. She could feel her neck tickling in anticipation.

The woman scurried to her side. Just before she reached it, Quinn rolled over. "Stop."

Her would-be helper stopped mid-step. The girl crawled off the cot, rebraided her ebony hair, and brushed her skirts. She took the key ring from the woman's belt.

The dark-haired girl patted the woman's head. "It's nothing against you, ma'am. You're nice. I just want to leave. That's all. I have things to do, just like you." She slipped out and locked the door behind her.

She'd learned many things while living with the LaMouxs. Mother LaMoux was determined that Quinn be a lady in spite of living in Nowhere Special as New York, Nebraska. As such, she learned to walk without making a sound, so as to not disturb Papa when he worked. Mother made her practice daily, and now, perhaps, this would pay off in ways the good lady would never expect.

The corridor was lined with gas lamps that flickered and made dancing shadows along the walls. She wasn't sure how long the nurse in the cell would be bound by her word. Her power had never been consistent, and often depended on the force behind it. On a good day, she'd have hours. On an off day, it could be moments. She thought about Arnold. That was an extraordinary day.

She passed a large steel door with no handle. Random voices and sounds came from the other side, so she straightened her back and made her steps soft enough that she was sure Mother LaMoux would have clapped and smiled. Once she made it past that obstacle, she sped her steps, turned a corner, and began feeling along the wall of an unlit corridor until she felt a grate. Three told her about it once when he managed to escape and explore one evening. She smiled at the thought of her older brother.

Quinn had no idea what was behind the grate or where it led, so her plan could be stupid. In fact, it probably was, but she was willing to take the chance. It opened without a sound, and she crawled in, catching the grate with her feet so it wouldn't clang.

The vent was smaller than she expected, and the walls began closing in on her. If Mr. Harry found her, that would be the end of everything. There was no escape. She almost turned back, but then heard Three telling her to breathe in his calm voice. She took a breath. Then another. She began to crawl forward.

Time and location lost meaning for her before long. She tried to think of what she'd do when she found a way outside. She imagined the trees and the flowers and the warm sun. At one point she thought she heard the rhythm of running feet above or below her somewhere. Maybe that nurse had been released. She kept crawling, following the tunnel as it turned and snaked through the walls. The tunnel was flat for a long time and then it started to incline. She crawled up. At the top she was able to stand. She looked up and saw an arch of light. Her eyes adjusted, and she noticed metal rung lined up the wall toward it. *Maybe this is outside of Menlo Park.* She began to climb the cold metal rungs that were just in reach for someone her size.

She ascended on the bars toward the light until she reached the top. A ring hung from the hatch that blocked her escape. Quinn wrapped one arm around the top rung and grabbed the ring. She struggled to turn it, but it refused to budge. She looked back down into the darkness and got dizzy. Her foot slipped and had she not had a firm grip on the rung, that would have been then end. She swung her foot back on the rung and steadied herself. When she looked up again, the ring was turning on its own. Not wanting to find out who was on the other side, she lowered herself down the way she'd come, hoping the darkness would hide her. When her feet touched the ground, a metal creak echoed down from the hatch and light spilled around her, blinding her for a moment.

Footsteps echoed in the confined chamber. She backed against the wall, and her hand found a doorknob. She turned it and fell backward as the door opened into a new room. Around her, four metal towers rose toward the high ceiling. She scrambled to the door and slammed it shut but couldn't find a way to lock it. She turned and discovered a man-sized cage at the center of the room. There was no time to process what any of this could have been. She ran and hid behind one of the towers. It wasn't the best choice, but there was nothing else she could do.

After a few minutes, she heard the door open. A familiar voice said, "Hiding in this room wouldn't be a safe choice, my dear."

All the tension melted from her shoulders as she recognized the voice. She ran to the old man. "Mr. Edison. It's you!"

He hugged her. "Of course, child. Who else would it be? I don't understand why you would want to leave at such a critical point in our plan."

She pulled away. *What was he talking about?*

A second voice came from outside the still open door.

"It wasn't very nice of you to stop Mr. Edison back there, Five. He wanted to help you since you were lost."

Quinn looked from Edison, her trusted friend to Mr. Harry, who closed the door and locked it.

"I thought you were here to help me."

The Great Inventor didn't respond. Instead, he pulled her toward the cage, which Mr. Harry was opening.

She yanked from Edison's grip and said, "Stop." The inventor froze mid-step and even the particles of dust around the room froze. She made a run for the door beyond the towers, but before she reached it, she heard an angry bellow and a hand yanked her and spun her around. This just proved how tired she was. If she hadn't used all of her energy to climb that ladder, she may have been able to stop the loathsome assistant. He slung her into the cage and waited for Edison to be released. It took a full five minutes.

Once the inventor was able to move again, Mr. Harry said, "I think she's gotten stronger, sir."

The scientist moved to one wall and began flipping switches. "That bodes well for what we will face during The Time, does it not?"

The towers popped and crackled around Quinn, who sat up, putting her arms around her knees. If only she'd not fought when Mr. Harry turned up at the LaMouxs's house. If only she'd been able to convince them to leave after what happened with Arnold. Even though it was a stupid, useless gesture, she stood up, shook the cage door, and screamed.

The inventor tapped her fingers with his pencil. "Step back from the door. Time to test your strength."

She resisted the urge to snatch the pencil and throw it at him. "I'm tired, sir."

"And whose fault is that?" Mr. Harry kicked at her through the bars. His employer pulled him back and gave him a clipboard.

"Stay in the center of the cage and don't touch the bars. We need you at the Calling." The older man turned some dials and unlocked the door that would have been her escape route.

"You know how strong I am." The hair on her arms stood on end.

The assistant scribbled some notes and followed the elderly gentleman. "Do you think she can hold back the electricity?" She couldn't hear the reply as the door slammed shut.

The room glowed purple, and the towers began to crackle and pop. Her hair stood on end, surrounding her head like a crown. Edison's secretary was right. This was her fault. If Arnold had left her alone, she could have continued to pretend her powers weren't real and that all of the things that happened at Menlo Park was a nightmare, but nothing real. The LaMouxs would be alive, and she'd have been able to continue a normal life.

Energy lit up the bars of her prison. The intense heat made her skin redden. She stamped out sparks that lit on the edge of her skirts. While she kept herself away from the current the best she could, she saw a girl appear near one of the whining towers.

"Little girl, get out of here!"

The girl turned and Quinn saw that this wasn't any girl. It was One. The last time she'd seen her sister, she'd been a head shorter. A branch of green lightning launched from the tower closest to the pale child in curls.

"Run, One! Oh God, Stop. Stop." She focused on the arm of energy, unsure if she was fast enough to make it do her will.

All of the sound cut off around her and the bolt heading toward the young girl bounced against an unseen wall. It spread out in the room like summer sheet lightning. One ran through the energy wall and headed for the cage. Before Quinn could stop her, the girl gripped the bar of the cage and the electricity lit her up. She dissipated like steam.

Quinn sobbed and screamed. One more death she caused. She grabbed the gate. Nothing mattered now. The current danced along her arms. Her hair broke free of her braids and stood like porcupine quills on her head. Her frock rose along with her hate for her captors. Quinn struggled to release her grip, but the current held her in place. She leaned into what she thought might be death. Despite the current's hold, she wasn't on fire, and she felt no pain. Only sadness and exhaustion.

"Well done, Five. Well done." Mr. Edison clapped as he approached the cage.

His assistant scribbled on a clipboard. "I was wrong. With a little more control, she'll be the perfect tool for holding him in place."

Tool?! The notion that she was just a tool infuriated her. Her shoulders began to shake, and tears burned down her face just like when she'd taken down that sniveling excuse for a human, Arnold Melton. Her outrage refilled her empty stores of energy as she remembered how he laughed at her, thinking he had gotten the best of her, just like these men who should be her guardians.

The metal clip ripped off the board and smacked the glasses off Mr. Harry's face. He tried to grab it, but sparks burned his hand and he jumped back. He glared at her with reptilian eyes. The box of switches on the wall behind Mr. Edison began to sizzle and shake as hard as Quinn. The old man reached to pull a large lever on one side, but his assistant dove, taking them both to the floor as the smaller switches shot like bullets over them. They ricocheted off the cage and failed to reach the girl.

She screamed, "Monsters. All of you are monsters!" Every gauge on the box and in the room cracked and shards of glass rained on the men as they covered themselves with their jackets. Blood ran down in then rivulets down their exposed hands.

The towers whined at a high pitch and the electricity around her body popped hard enough to shake the cage. She rose off the floor, supported by the same field that killed her sister moments before. She ripped her hands off the bars, pulling parts of them with her.

She threw the white-hot metal pieces at the men. They bounced off the wall of switches and dials. "Leave now."

Green sparks sprayed from the towers and cascaded to the floor.

The inventor ran for the exit. "She's killing herself. No one else will be able to hold him when he comes. We need her power. Stop her!"

The room shook as she burned through the top of her prison. Her hair was a halo of gold, green, and purple and her dress crackled in blue.

Mr. Harry shifted to his reptilian form, but his feet melted to the floor. He freed them but slogged to the door as if he was caught in quicksand. The door closed behind him just as the towers shivered and exploded in front of the angelic figure of their captive. Her body dropped to the floor, and a second explosion shook the doors and knocked the men down.

———

Fresh air tickled Quinn's nose when she awoke. It smelled like a huge storm had passed over while she was asleep. She remembered the towers exploding around her in a bright flash of white-purple. She merged with the power that had once been terrifying and it erased all of her anger, fear, and pain. The scene ripped open, revealing darkness and millions of stars. The girl flew through them. She wasn't sure if this was death or if she was somewhere else, but she didn't care. Something called to her, and she followed until the stars and the planets fell from her sight and she tumbled down, down. She landed behind a lady who studied an oversized book.

23

Kate knocked on the door of the schoolhouse and it swung open.

"Hello?"

Some papers rustled at the front of the room and a small, blond girl stood up behind a massive oak desk. She couldn't have been much older than Arnold Melton. "Can I help you?"

"You must be Miss Rogers. I came to enquire about—"

"About Arnold Melton no doubt. Simon should have never sent that story to the newspapers." The young teacher crossed her arms and frowned.

"I'm not a reporter." She handed a card to the young lady. "I'm a Pinkerton, and I'm working on a case that may what happened with Arnold Melton."

"How did you know it was her?" The teacher studied the calling card.

"It doesn't matter. Do his parents know?"

The girl didn't answer right away. Instead, she laid the card on her desk and shuffled papers. "Mr. Coleman—the sheriff—-and I decided it was best to keep silent about what we saw that day. The boy's father saw the boy's remains in that tree, but I have no idea if he understood why he was...well..." She blushed and dabbed her face with an embroidered handkerchief.

"Naked?"

The young teacher nodded.

"Where is the girl now?"

"She hasn't come back to class since that afternoon. I tried to call on her family several times, but they never answer. They even stopped coming to church."

The lady Pinkerton stood up and shook the teacher's tiny hand. "Perhaps I can call on them before I leave town. Can you direct me?"

Ms. Rogers wrote directions on a piece of paper from her desk.

"Doesn't the sheriff think it odd that the LaMouxs aren't taking callers?"

The teacher walked her to the back of the schoolhouse. "He thinks they probably left town, but I'm not so sure. Every time I've gone calling, the place feels odd. I can't explain it. Maybe you'll feel it too."

"It was good of you to take time to speak with me, ma'am."

"I hope you find what you're looking for." She shook the lady detective's hand.

"So do I."

The robin-egg blue house trimmed in delicate white gingerbread at the apex of its roof and along the gutter line of the porch stood out among the simpler cottages that dotted the street. A once well-cultivated garden of coneflowers spread a patchwork quilt of color in front of the house. Kate saw weeds rising between the blossoms. In a few more weeks, the plot would be overtaken.

When she stepped onto the porch, she could feel remnants of joy and contentment clinging to the structure. A fiddle played and two female voices, one high and one with a richness that came with age sang along. The tap of dancing rose under her feet and the detective couldn't help but hum along to the catchy tune.

She knocked on the door, and it swung open. The music cut off as an undercurrent of emptiness and terror wafted over her. The sharp contrast made her step back, and she thought about the bloodbath she and Shadow found when they tracked Thirteen to that farmhouse.

The dissonance between the house and the porch was jarring. Ignoring her best judgement, she stepped over the threshold and into a dark hall leading to the back of the house. To the left was a parlor decorated with two upholstered wing chairs and a child-sized rocker. The drapes matched the blue flowers on the wallpaper. Dust had begun to layer on every surface in the room. A small wedding portrait of a blonde woman wearing a summer frock and hat and a dark-eyed man with wire-rimmed glasses standing behind her sat on one table. A fiddle sat in its case on the mantle of the fireplace, waiting to be lifted once again. The warmth that should have permeated the space was missing as though it had been removed by force.

"Hello?" Kate entered the Outside.

Her voice echoed, but no one answered. Terror washed over her again, but despite the urge to run, she stepped into it, letting it move through and past her as she entered the parlor, which smelled of salt-water and chum. Kate shivered, terror welling from inside her this time. Mr. Harry.

She stopped looking for the girl. She was gone.

"Mr. LaMoux? Mrs. LaMoux? My name is Kate Warne. I'm here to help."

The wall next to the staircase going to the second floor was decorated in embroidered samplers, including one that bore Quinn's name. It lacked the grace of its companions but used similar colors and motifs.

Nothing was out of place in the bedrooms. No sign of struggle or anything that would indicate that this family had faced anything out of the ordinary. Kate came back downstairs. The kitchen and rooms to the back of the house were as still and empty as the upstairs. When she came back to the parlor, fear welled up around her again. Whatever had happened was concentrated in this part of the house.

If they were dead, there was a chance they stayed around like

Arnold had. It was easier to transition when you were close to what you were familiar with. "Mr. LaMoux? Mrs. LaMoux?"

The emptiness of the room when she crossed through magnified and overwhelmed the lady detective. The raw chum smell intensified, and she gagged. Someone or several someones had been torn from this space. She went back to the Inside and her nausea subsided. She didn't remember this stench back at the hotel, but then she'd not stayed long enough to smell anything.

The front door clicked as she exited the house. She'd lost another child and more people had died because of that alligator-faced monster. There was no use in speaking to the sheriff. Let the community think the LaMouxs had moved on to avoid conflict.

Sho was packing some tools in a bag when she reached the ship. The look on her face must have been enough, because he scrambled to pack the last remaining things. He let her board first.

"Are you okay, ma'am?"

"We need to get to Colorado Springs before more people die."

"That doesn't answer..."

"I'm not okay, Sho. In fact, I'm perfectly terrible. Can we go now?"

She left him standing in the corridor and headed for her cabin. The magnificent sunset that painted across the sharp-edged Rockies was lost on her. After a good cry, she opened the book from Menlo Park and searched for anything that might reveal Mr. Harry's weaknesses.

The hair on the back of Kate's neck stood up. She closed the book in case she'd managed to trigger something the way Shadow had when he'd looked at it.

"Help me." The air smelled the way it should after a storm. The detective turned. An angelic figure reached for her. Lighting crackled around them when she touched its fingers, and she wasn't sure if she was Inside or Out for a moment. She closed her eyes and when she re-opened them, the angel resembled the girl she'd seen on one of the cabinet cards back at the LaMoux's house. Perhaps the girl was dead and not sure how to traverse the Outside yet.

Kate got the girl's attention and said, "I need for you to focus on me."

Her vision settled for a moment and the child's features became more distinct. She'd been crying. While the detective held Inside, her visitor fluttered around her edges.

"Can you tell me where you are?"

The girl's voice fluttered. "Mr. Edison put me in a cage."

Edison.

"Are you there now?"

"I don't think so. I see you and there are stars around me." She solidified for a moment and then fluttered and glowed once more.

"I'm going to try and pull you to me. Don't let go."

She pulled hard enough that her new friend fell through her and on top of the book. Her angelic features faded and revealed a child in a torn frock. She was shoeless. Her ebony hair was free and hung to the center of her back.

Her new companion crawled off the table and shook her skirts. "Am I dead?"

"No. Not at all. We're Inside."

"Wait. I went through you. You're a ghost! Oh no! Did I kill you? I didn't mean to."

Kate sat in the red upholstered chair near the window. "You had nothing to do with my physical demise, Miss LaMoux."

"How do you know my name?"

The detective showed her the newspaper article. "Your Miss Rogers was worried about you."

"I can't let anyone hurt me again, ma'am. That's why I ran away." She covered her face and began to flutter from Inside to Outside once more.

Kate pulled her hands down and leaned close. "I'm not sure how you managed to reach out and find me, but now that you're here, you're safe." Quinn solidified and sat in the chair close to the book. Shadow would tell his partner not to make promises she couldn't keep, but until she understood what this girl could do, having her upset was not a good idea. Instead of worrying what her partner would say, she called up a pot of tea and two of her favorite rose-covered cups. The girl's hands shook as she accepted the beverage, but she relaxed after the first sip. One more bit of strangeness to explain to Mr. West.

24

Shadow left the boarding house and found his way to the local saloon to sort out what he'd witnessed. It wasn't the supernatural element of the events that bothered him. Three centuries had taught him that the New World was filled with all manner of unusual creatures and activities. The War Between the States had done nothing but exacerbate the weird nature of the country. It wasn't even the violence he'd seen in the last few days. What troubled him was that all of this was being enacted by children.

"A mule skinner please. More whiskey than blackberry." Shadow handed the bartender four bits.

The sheriff sat down next to him. "What the hell just happened back there?"

The saloon keeper plunked a beer in front of Horace without saying a word. A moment later, he brought the detective a copper cup.

"Oona can call people from other places. She called me to help out."

"Our little town ain't used to the level of oddity these children have delivered." The young lawman took a draw from his mug. "How am I going to protect folks if every time I turn around, I have another child who murders folks visiting up at Moira's?"

Shadow downed the mule skinner and ordered a second. "At the moment, we need to trust the girls. It seems they know how to manage their own."

The sheriff slammed his mug on the counter. "And what if that boy back there wakes up in the middle of the night and goes on a rampage?"

"How well do you shoot, Mr. Stewart?"

The bearded man's hand trembled as he lifted the mug to finish off his drink. "I couldn't shoot a kid, Pinkerton."

There were many young men who had become the law in towns across the territories who were like Horace. No doubt the man had been chosen as sheriff because he was young and strong. Not every town had the luck of hiring a man of experience like Tombstone had.

The Pinkerton patted him on the shoulder. "I don't think that boy back there is going to go on a rampage of any sort. He was scared. You saw how he looked. Someone hurt him."

"Mr. Edison?" The saloon keeper plunked another mug in front of the sheriff.

"I won't know until I speak with young Two."

"Are there more?"

Shadow nodded and finished off his drink. "Edison gathered them, then someone released them thinking it was the right thing to do." He wondered if Mr. Tesla understood the ramifications of what he'd done that night two years before.

"Was it?"

"That remains to be seen, Horace. Right now, we need to protect the ones who have gathered and figure out what happens next. We can talk to the children in the morning after breakfast. Perhaps their combined stories can give us a sense of what they mean by The Time."

Shadow stood up and put on his hat.

"Where're you heading, Pinkerton?" The bearded man rose as well.

"I need to talk to my partner."

"Can I join you?"

"I appreciate your offer, but right now, those ladies up at the boarding house need you more. I'll be back before breakfast."

Horace's shoulders slumped a bit, but once they were outside, he made his way toward the boarding house. The Pinkerton headed for the shaded alleyway.

He stepped out into Kate's cabin. She took notes next to the open book. He couldn't help but flinch at the sight of the thing and fought the urge to slam it closed. A young girl was sleeping on his partner's bunk like she'd always been there.

"Came back to go another round with your brother?" Since his partner returned to work, he couldn't sneak in on her at all.

Shadow sat near the window behind her. "No time. Looks like we've both been busy."

She kept writing. "Young Quinn came to me, a bit by accident, you could say." She turned around in her chair. "You said 'we.' What's happened, Shadow?"

"The girls found their brother."

"Oh good, Three and his family made it to town. They traveled fast."

"Three?"

"Their brother. He lives with a family who own a medicine show. I met them…you didn't read the report, did you?"

"I've not had much time since you left. They call this one Two. He confessed to tearing that woman apart. If I hadn't seen him raging, I'd have scoffed at the notion. He can't be more than nine or ten, and he's scrawny."

She patted his hand. "Let me tell you about Five." She shared the girl's story.

After she'd finished, he leaned back and put his feet up on the ottoman. "So at least three of these children are capable of extreme violence."

"Quinn swears she just wanted to scare the boy."

"Two said something similar. Called himself a monster. I can't say his assessment is incorrect. He rages like an animal, but I still have a hard time believing he caused that much destruction."

"Keep in mind that the wolverine is small but can tear apart a bison for supper."

"The wolverine is built to kill."

Kate touched the pot left on the table from earlier and steam rose from its nose. She poured tea into her cup and conjured up a second for her partner, who accepted. "Who's to say this boy isn't? We don't know much about these children at all. The best I could get from Three's mother is that some men in an asylum took him from her after he was born."

"There is a market for asylum babies. Women there have them, and the facility administrators find ways to rid themselves of these children." Her partner took a sip.

"Are there records?"

"What they do is only marginally legal at best. The families are too poor or too scared that the child will be like the mother."

"Did Edison buy these children?"

"That's a good question, but without records or anyone talking about these things, it isn't a leap I'd want to make. Should I take her back with me? I'm sure Oona will be thrilled to see her/their sister."

"I want to talk with her some more. Get to know her. She may be able to fill in some more of the gaps. Three, the boy I was telling you about, said something about what they call The Calling, which is what they are all supposed to be working toward." She caught him up despite having sent this in the report.

Shadow took the book from the table. He flipped to the page with the numbers and the creatures at the top of the page. A small hand pointed at a page.

"Oh, that's what's going to happen when we gather together for The Calling." The dark-haired girl pointed at the figure marked with a V above it. "That's me."

"Do you know what Edison has planned?"

"He says there's a new form of power. I guess he thinks it's better than electricity. Mr. Harry is supposed to help by opening a gate."

"What comes through this gate?"

The girl pointed at the winged squid with glowing eyes at the top of the page. "I think he calls it the Old One."

Shadow knelt next to her. "Any idea what this is?"

Kate traced her finger along the margin of the page and said, "I've heard terms like this, usually ascribed to gods, but I've never seen a god that looks like this."

"It's like that tentacled creature that attacked us in Raritan."

The child recited, "The Old One isn't here yet. He's coming soon."

Shadow studied the page again. To one side of the creature Quinn called The Old One was a blue rectangle and an alligator-man with tentacles running the length of its body.

Kate pointed at one side. "Look, it's missing a tentacle."

Her partner paused and arched his eyebrow. He pushed past the observation and asked, "Why use Edison?"

Kate tapped her head. "He has one of the greatest minds in the world. He also seems to have found a way to find and gather people who do have supernatural leanings." She poured Quinn a cup and conjured up a plate of sandwiches.

"It just seems odd, doesn't it? Edison meets this Mr. Harry and learns he has powers like a god. Why not just harness that power if the old man is wanting to experiment with something more powerful than electricity?"

"Because Mr. Harry offered him someone who has more power."

Shadow stepped back from the book. "None of the children we've encountered would be able to contain something like that. How is someone who causes bad luck or goes into a monstrous killing rage going to help when this Old One arrives? It makes no sense."

"There were more of us, sir. Some of us never made it out of Raritan."

Kate checked her notebook and found a page. "All of the cells I saw were empty. I didn't see any children when I found the book."

"They're all dead and eaten, ma'am. When the weaker ones failed, he, Mr. Harry, got to eat them. He said they made him stronger." The girl nibbled her sandwich. "Mr. Edison wanted to stop once he saw there were only thirteen left, but then there was this book. Mr. Harry insisted that thirteen of us were all that were necessary."

"Are you saying he's a cannibal?"

Her partner took a sandwich. "It's not cannibalism if the meal isn't your own species. But if he was eating the weak ones, there is no guarantee that he'd end up with the right children for the job. What if some of you weren't useful?"

"It's not as random as you think, sir."

Kate changed the direction they were going. "What is your job? I know you can tear holes in space and time."

Shadow paused mid-bite. "What?"

"I bind people and things." The girl finished her sandwich.

"Is that what happened to Arnold?"

Quinn poured herself more tea. "I didn't plan for that to happen. I just wanted to freeze him against the tree long enough to hang a sign around his neck and reveal him for the monster he was. When that man put us on the train, I decided then that I wasn't going to stand for anyone hurting anyone else ever again."

"What do we do now?" He slurped from his cup.

There was no reason to keep the girl on the airship and run the risk of having another disagreement with Mr. West. There was something that stuck in her craw about his last interaction with her partner and his subsequent response to their continuing investigation.

She answered. "Does your brother know you're here?"

"I didn't see any reason to share this visit. I was just checking in with you."

"Let's keep it this way." She handed him his hat, which lay on the table.

He took it from her and gave her a questioning look. There was no time for details. "Miss LaMoux, how would you like to see your brothers and sisters?"

The girl's demeanor brightened at the suggestion. "I'd like that a lot. We're safer when we're together."

"Mr. Jones will escort you, but do as he says and don't go tearing any more holes in the universe, okay?"

The girl laughed as the Brother offered her his arm.

"This is going to cause more trouble for you, isn't it?" Kate brushed off her partner's shoulder.

"Probably. I'll just blame you. You've corrupted me, Kate Warne."

"What are they going to do to me? I'm already dead." She turned down the lamps in the room, and he and his companion faded into the darkness. Once they were gone, she gazed out the window, wondering what surprises Mr. Tesla would offer.

2 5

Shadow stepped out into the alley by the train station and led his charge past the saloon and the general store. When they reached the hill going up to the boarding house, Quinn made him stop at the gate.

"What's wrong?" Nothing seemed out of place. The stars spread across the open sky. The moon was full enough to bathe the scene in shades of silver and gray. The town was quiet except for the chirp of crickets in the grass. All the lamps in the boarding house were dark.

"I haven't seen any of them in two years, and except for what happened with Arnold, my life has been excellent. Now all that has been ripped away, and I have no choice but to return to a life that wasn't so excellent."

She was right. Of all her brothers and sisters, she'd won first prize in the fair of life. They both sat against the gate.

"You've come all this way to see them and be with them."

"It's true, but I also miss Mother and Father. They gave me the best life, Mr. Jones." She leaned on his chest, and he offered a handkerchief.

He let her weep. He wasn't sure what he could say or do except be with the girl. His partner was much better at this. Once the girl had settled and wiped her eyes, he got up and offered his hand. "As I see it, you have two clear options. You can go see your brothers and sisters and help them, or you can ask me to take you back to Kate. I can't just let you wander off into the prairie on your own."

She took his hand and giggled. "I wouldn't wander off into the prairie. That'd be silly." She sniffled one last time. "Miss Kate doesn't need me slowing her down more than I have. The Calling is almost here. My family needs me."

"Oona—One will be delighted, I'm sure." Her guardian opened the gate and she entered first.

"She is delighted by most things she loves, sir."

"Then at least you know where you stand with her."

"My mother would find her scandalous at first, but in time she would love her...both of her." She started to cry some more.

One thing Shadow never had been able to get the hang of was comforting people. He and his brothers were created to protect, but not so much to offer comfort. After living for so long among them, Shadow understood that offering solace was part of the human experience. In spite of all this, he had no words to offer her. Instead, he put his hand on her shoulder and she wrapped her arms around his waist and sobbed into his vest for a while. He watched the stars until she was done.

Thomas checked the wagon one more time, and his wife followed behind. She kissed him, and he climbed onto the front and picked up the reins. "The boy needs to be with the rest of his family, and I intend to get him there even if takes all night."

Seth hugged Deborah and climbed up next to Thomas. "I'll sit with Pop, so he doesn't fall asleep." The boy set the gun that once belonged to the undead mountain man across his legs. They'd been traveling all day and even though his mother thought they should take their time, the old showman insisted that they continue.

"I ain't going to fall asleep. You act like I'm an old man or something."

His son nudged him. "If the boot fits."

"I can use it to kick you back to your ma, mister."

The sky was cobalt blue when they arrived in Brainerd, which was smaller than most of the towns where did their show. There was a strip of wooden buildings down the main thoroughfare and one brick building with arched windows and a sign labeling the town. At the top of a hill, the boy saw the house from his dreams.

"That's where my sisters are."

The old showman stopped near the center of town and climbed down from his perch. "Don't look like anyone is awake yet. We'll head up after the sun rises. For now, go get some rest."

"I can't sleep. Too excited." The boy stayed put.

His pop rubbed his eyes and patted the horses before heading toward the back. "Suit yourself. I'll see you in a few hours."

Seth watched the house for movement. He sensed more of his siblings, and they all felt stronger. Maybe that Miss Warne was right. Thirteen was a sort of draw for the children. Maybe Mr. Harry was biding his time, which could end up being a big mistake. The boy leaned back, comforted by the stars above and the warmth of his brothers and sisters.

Quinn cried herself out before they got to the porch, and because Shadow didn't want to disturb the sleeping occupants of the house, he settled on the swing. She curled up next to him and fell asleep. A few hours closer to sunrise, the thump of horse hooves and the creak of wagon wheels broke his reverie. Even in the early blue-gray of morning, the colors of the wagon were bright. The driver climbed down from the seat and headed toward the back. His partner stayed. Shadow noted the rifle on the young man's lap. He didn't sense trouble from the new arrivals, so he relaxed. He heard a door clatter at the back of the house, but by this point the sun was close to rising, and he was sure it was Treze, gathering eggs and preparing for breakfast. He set the swing moving with his foot and waited for Horace to arrive. Shadow liked the young lawman. Lesser men would have run away after what had transpired in his town over the last few weeks. This could be due to courage or plain inexperience, but nonetheless, he found it admirable.

He thought about what Kate had told him. If what she said was true, this could be something that not even the Brotherhood could face. It was one thing when men tapped the latent energies of this land. The Brotherhood was a product of this sort of action. Reaching into other spaces, other dimensions was something that, as far as he could determine when he examined the shared memories of his brothers, had never been attempted by a colonist. There was that one time…but the memory skittered away before he could grab it. A flash of a face like his crossed through his mind and then was, once again, whisked away as if someone was blocking it from him. For a split second, he thought he heard the flutter of wings. Before he could focus on the sound or figure out why this memory was being kept from him, a squeal cut through the air. Quinn sat straight up and looked around like she'd been attacked.

"You're back and brought Five!" Light Oona threw herself at Shadow. He caught her and laughed. Meanwhile, Dark Oona leaned against the door frame.

Quinn moved close to the dark girl with the bright blue eyes. "Hey, sis. I see you're still taking care of her."

She took her elder sister's hand, which was almost as white as her other. "We wouldn't have his help if it weren't for her."

"She's getting bolder then?"

"Maybe. She's fearful of what's coming."

"We all are, sis."

Before Quinn could say more, Dark Oona bolted across the porch. She pulled her light other away from Shadow. Her curls flew around her/their faces as she jumped from the steps to the path and skittered to the gate screaming.

A young man sauntered up and leaned over the gate. "Are you

open for breakfast yet?" Shadow recognized him as the fellow who had been on the wagon earlier. Behind him trudged the man who had to be the driver, and a beautiful woman with dark eyes accented by a multi-colored scarf around her head. A few strands of brown hair streaked with gray peeked out. Her skirt was red and swished around her with every step. She looked tired but kind.

The Oona(s) tore open the gate to get to the gangly fellow asking for vittles. "You're here. You're finally here!"

The older man behind him adjusted a wide-brimmed hat on his clean-shaven head. "They know the boy."

The tired-eyed woman joined him and took his hand. "Of course, they do, my love."

Shadow remembered his partner's story of the show people she'd met. He followed the girls to the gate. Faint music rose from somewhere, and the girls began to dance as she welcomed the visitors.

"Are you making the music, Three?" The paler girl skipped around him as he entered.

Dark Oona rolled her eyes. "Has he ever made music before?"

Light Oona punched her other and giggled. "It's been two years. We've all made changes. Ain't that right, Three?"

"Isn't. And it's his mother. She's the one making the music, silly." Dark Oona punched her back.

The light girl stopped dancing around her brother. She held the gate as the older woman crossed through, then took Seth's mother's hand and leaned into her. "I like you."

The door slammed hard from the porch, and everyone stopped. Thirteen stood at the top of the steps, hair braided tight, hands and arms covered in flour. "What's all this about? You're going to wake the entire..." she said. She put her hands to her mouth and dropped to her knees. She tried to get back up but dropped to her knees again.

Seth ran and knelt in front of her. "Is that any way to greet your brother?" he asked.

"You're here. You're really here," she said. She started weeping and he pulled her close. The boy's parents stood behind them. The mother stepped forward and touched Treze's shoulder without a word. The Oona(s) circled around her/their sister.

After a few moments, Thirteen looked up at her brother and asked, "How'd you find me?"

The boy grinned and said, "Oona and dreams. Oh, and that nice Pinkerton lady we met."

The girl frowned and glanced in Shadow's direction.

The boy's father followed her gaze and glared at him. "You one of 'em too?"

Kate's assessment of Thomas Lazarus was right. Shadow offered his hand and said, "Andrew Jones, Pinkerton's. At your service."

The man cut his eyes at the woman in the scarves, but she was focused on Seth and his sister. He grabbed Shadow's hand and shook it with the firm grip.

"Thomas Lazarus," he said. "Let me introduce you to my lady." He led Shadow to his wife who was smiling down on the two siblings like they were both her own. When Shadow took her hand, she shuddered and stepped back. Her eyes narrowed.

Oona skipped over and took the woman's hand. "He's not bad, ma'am."

"He is like another I have known," Deborah whispered. Another look passed between her and Thomas.

Shadow asked, "You've already met my partner, Mrs. Warne, so yes."

"Do not play stupid with me. I know you walk the Paths," she said taking another step back.

Shadow searched the memory of the Brotherhood, but he did not see her face or find her traces along the Paths.

"Ma, is something wrong?" asked Seth, stepping between them.

"I knew that woman was sent. She was no Pinkerton. She was one of your father's minions," she said, pushing past her son.

The gangly detective said to Oona, "What is she talking about?"

Both Oona(s) shrugged.

Horace asked, "Is there a problem?"

The old showman pulled a pistol from his sleeve and said, "I thought he'd get the message when we got rid of that last creature who came after us."

Shadow raised his hands and said, "Yes, I believe there is a problem, sheriff."

"Sir, don't make me have to fight before I've had my coffee," said the lawman, stepping closer.

Thomas didn't flinch but continued, "So, you got the local law on your side with that Pinkerton act. Your boss's got some nerve."

"Pop!' Seth said, joining the older man.

Light Oona said, "Your real father's after you, isn't he, Three?"

The boy nodded.

Everyone got quiet. The girl pushed past her brother and stood in front of Thomas's gun. "He was one of Shadow's brothers," she continued.

"How do you know this?" asked Shadow. "I don't remember this woman. We remember all of our companions."

"He told me he left his family years before I met him," said Deborah.

Shadow reached into the shared memories of the Brotherhood. There was a moment when those thoughts were fuzzy and there was nothing to grab onto.

Dark Oona took the woman's hand and closed her eyes. "She speaks what she believes is true," she said.

The snake-oil salesman cocked the pistol and said, "Let's make sure you and your brothers remember this warning."

Horace stepped next to the older man and said, "There ain't goin' to be no shooting today, old man."

Deborah's husband lowered his gun and said, "Who you callin' old, kid?"

"The girl, she shows me your light, Shadow of the Brotherhood. I was wrong. You are not his minion," said the woman, pulling away from Dark Oona. She approached him. "I am Deborah, and I am sorry. Now put your gun away, my love," she said, waving her husband aside.

Shadow shook her hand and before he could reply, a whoop ripped through the scene.

"THREE!" shouted a younger boy who pushed his way through the gathering and jumped onto his brother's back.

"You look like a train hit you, Two," said Seth once he'd pried the boy off his back.

"If it had, I'd'a kilt it," said the boy. "Hey, mister?" He turned toward Shadow. "Did I attack you earlier?"

Shadow nodded and said, "You were quite angry when we found you."

"And you and that bearded guy lived?" said the boy with wide eyes.

"If it hadn't been for your sisters, we'd no doubt be dead as doornails," said Shadow.

Thomas's voice lifted over all the chatter. "Now that we've figured out that the Pinkerton is okay and no one is gonna die, how about we go have some breakfast?"

Everyone laughed and Seth said, "As always, my pop is ready to eat."

They all began making their way inside. The Oona(s) squeezed close to Deborah, who held their hands. She glanced back at Shadow and he saw concern rather than fear now.

A large hand landed on his shoulder. The showman said, "I apologize for the gun in your face back there. That woman," he nodded toward his wife, "was put through hell by someone who claims to be one of your folks. You can understand my concern when she said you were like him."

"My brothers and I were created to protect, not harm, so your wife's story concerns me as much as it concerns you, sir," said Shadow.

"And you don't know a thing about this fella?"

Shadow shook his head. "I have no memory of a fallen brother," he said. The abominations had never been part of the Brotherhood, though there were those who tried to make it otherwise. He'd given a part of himself to make sure they never flew the Paths or the earth again. Those who made them repented and returned to the collective of the Brotherhood.

The voices of his brothers rose at the back of his mind. He reached for the conversation but before he could connect to it, Oona grabbed his hand and pulled at him. He followed her into the house despite wanting to follow the voices in his mind. The chatter faded further back into a murmur as the little girl pulling him skipped and giggled over the way the morning had dawned.

26

Pikes Peak rose blue-gray and imperious over Colorado Springs, which spread like a long, well-set table across the flat, red dirt landscape. Kate began to prepare for the imminent landing behind the grand hotel that decorated the foot of the mountain. A knock on her door interrupted her last-minute packing. Mr. West entered. She caught a troubled look on his face as he entered, but he put on a smile as he entered her cabin.

"Will you be joining me?" she asked as they sat down.

"No. There's some business I need to tend to while you speak with Mr. Tesla," said Mr. West. "I've arranged for one of our local brothers to take you to the laboratory."

Kate didn't press him concerning this matter. The Brotherhood handled many cases all over the United States and parts of Canada. She didn't find it odd that he'd be distracted by other issues.

A bell rang, indicating that they had docked. She gathered her things and made her way to the exit. Once she was out, she made her way down a spiral staircase inside a domed tower on the back side of building. No one noticed as she made her way past the bath house and recreational rooms toward the massive main lobby. The ceiling was decorated in red and silver tin tiles which added to the opulence of the arched doorways and large windows that allowed the morning light into the space. A massive fireplace was at the center of the lobby, being kept by a man wearing a coat that matched the rich red of the ceiling. The heads of various antlered game lined the walls. People bustled in and out, some carrying bags, others being followed by young boys pushing carts. The scent of cedar mixed with the heavy scent of cigars caused her to cough as she passed two massive wooden doors that were guarded by yet another man in a red coat. This was much more than she expected from what was supposed to be a western mining town.

A redwood porch stretched along the front of the hotel, lined with heavy rocking chairs where guests could sit and visit after meals. Kate spotted a man seated on a wagon who sported the same face and familiar bowler hat her partner wore. His suit, despite the dust that rose from the road as the horses pulled the wagon forward, was impeccable and black. She waved him down when he drew near, and he nodded. In the entire time she'd been at the hotel, he was the first to see her.

"How far to the laboratory?" asked Kate as she settled next to him.

"Not long, about ten or fifteen minutes from here," the Brother replied.

They headed down the wide dirt street leading away from the hotel. She turned to look back at the mighty mountain. It cut a jagged, snowy figure over the city, and the sun seemed to only touch the very peak.

"How does anyone manage to work with such beautiful scenery?" she asked.

Her driver said, "I'm not sure I know myself."

They passed by wooden houses and several large brick buildings. Just before the wagon stopped, they passed a brown brick gothic-style building with an arched door at the front. The large placard with black letters read "Colorado School of the Deaf and Blind." Several children were seated outside on the wide stairs going to the building, and Kate could see some of them making signs with their hands. Others were jumping rope or sitting on benches sliding their fingers across the page of a book. While the winters had to be difficult, and some children were probably homesick, there was no sense of sadness or fear. Instead, the children seemed content. Kate set her jaw and decided then and there that those children back in Brainerd would be given the same gift of peace. She just hoped that Mr. Tesla would be able to help her to make this happen.

The wagon made its way up a hill topped by a tower with a dome on top. As they drew to a stop, a hum hung in the air, which tickled Kate's nose even as she faded to the Outside for a moment to gather herself before following Mr. West to the door. Before he could knock, a man with hair that rose around his flushed face like a greying lion's mane answered. The scent of whiskey wafted off him and made her eyes water.

A puzzled look crossed the man's face. "Are you the liaison?" He leaned close to Mr. West, who backed away to give him space.

"We are here on his behalf," said the Brother.

"We?" The man rubbed his eyes. "There's only you, mister."

Kate remembered to concentrate. The man's eyes widened as she appeared before him on the doorstep.

She took a card from her bag and pushed it into his hand. "Kate Warne. Pinkerton's Investigation. I believe Mr. Tesla is expecting me."

He examined her card and then looked down at her and then examined the card once more. "You're not the liaison?"

"No. That's my partner. We're working on the case together." She moved forward, and he let her enter without taking his eyes off her.

Mr. West did not follow her. "If you are going to handle the situation, Mrs. Warne, I shall go back to the ship and update my Brothers."

She nodded and he took his leave. The man who'd greeted them shut the door and led her deeper into the house.

The lady detective studied her new companion "Sir, you look familiar."

The man paused and offered his hand. "Sam Clemens."

"You mean Mark…"

"Yep. One and the same. Come on. Nik…Mr. Tesla will be interested in speaking with you." He led her into a large room with a few tables and lots of various gadgets and tools organized on them.

Mr. Tesla did not shake her hand. "I see Mr. Pinkerton received my message."

Kate nodded as Sam pulled out a chair for her. We know that you rescued those children, Mr. Tesla. Did you know that Mr. Harry is hunting them?"

The young scientist's dark eyes got darker, and he sat down. Mr. Clemens started to pour him a drink, but he waved him off. "If he is hunting them, I am not sure gathering them is a good idea, Mrs..." Sam passed her card to him. "Ah. Mrs. Warne."

Kate proceeded. "It would seem that they are gathering on their own. Why would Mr. Edison be holding thirteen children in cells underground? Is this another scientific experiment?"

The young inventor sat down across from her. "Mr. Edison doesn't care about science, Mrs. Warne. Those inventions, they aren't about answering questions or discovering ideas. They are tools to make money and give him power."

"And the children? Are they tools as well?"

"He brings people to Raritan only when they are useful to him. If he knows about the children, and I'm not sure I can say if he does or not, I have no doubt they were meant to be used for him to gain power in some way. It is the same for the scientists. He brings them in, lets them do their work in his facility, and then the moment they balk or discover he is going to take what is theirs, he keeps their work and shoves them out the back door." He slammed his hand on the table and she and Sam jumped.

"Now, Nik. Ain't no need to get all riled up. Mrs. Warne here is just trying to help." His friend set a glass on the table in front of him and the man took a drink.

"Mr. Edison changed in the time I worked at Menlo Park. When I first arrived, he treated me like a prince. He listened and let me work. I thought this was good. I got to work with a genius like myself."

Kate leaned close. "When did he change?"

"It was slow at first. He spoke less, which I didn't mind. I prefer less talk. Then he introduced me to a new assistant."

"New?"

Tesla nodded. "He brought in Mr. Harry. I thought he was odd, which is saying quite a lot. Not long after, I saw Edison poring over old books late at night."

Kate pulled the mysterious book she'd fought not so long ago out of the bag it now stayed in and dropped it on the table in front of him. "You mean like this one?"

The inventor's eyes got wide, and his hand shook as he reached out to touch the book. "How did you get this?"

Kate smiled. "Mr. Tesla, you will find that I hold my own quite well in most situations."

Sam blew a smoke ring and leaned in to get a better look at the artifact. "Most women I've known hold their own quite well in most situations. That didn't answer the question, ma'am."

"It attacked me, and I won."

"What does that mean?" asked Tesla.

"It means the book attacked me and then sent tentacled creatures to come after me for taking the book."

The inventor raised an eyebrow. "You spin tales as large as Sam's."

"I assume you and your partner killed those creatures. Otherwise, we'd be fighting them now." Sam eyed the book as though she'd set a rattlesnake in front of him.

"One dead. Mr. Harry, however..." The lady detective flipped through the book, which was no threat now.

Tesla tapped the table next to her. "Stop. Go back."

She turned the pages back till he tapped the table again. The alligator man with tentacles filled the page in hand inked color. The painting reminded her of some of the creatures from *The Book of Kells*.

"What is he doing in this book?"

Sam moved closer but not right at the table. "Who are you talkin' about, Nik?"

"Mr. Harry."

Kate moved to one side to make room for the author, but he didn't move. "You've seen him like this?"

"I thought it was a trick of my eyes. I came to Mr. Edison's office and heard a heated discussion. Before I could enter, the door opened and for a half second, I saw him like this."

"What were they discussing?"

"I do not know for certain, but I am sure it had to do with Edison's troubles with Mr. Westinghouse. Edison seemed more bent on beating Mr. Westinghouse after Mr. Harry arrived. Everything was about more power in more places."

His friend moved to the whiskey cabinet. "I think we're gonna need a drink." He pulled out an empty bottle. "Good grief, man. It's not even four o'clock yet." He stomped off and then brought back a new bottle. Popping the cork, he poured three glasses, and knocked back his own shot.

"He's an alligator man? There were tales of these folks all up and down the river when I worked on that paddleboat. Never saw one, so I thought it was just shenanigans made up by a bunch of drunk sailors. Of course, there are frogmen in California, so I ain't surprised."

The lady detective ignored her shot glass. "I'm not sure Mr. Harry is one of those folks exactly."

The older man picked up Kate's shot and gestured at the book. "He looks just like how they were described to me down in New Orleans."

"We think he's an avatar for a god." Kate turned the page and pointing at the tentacled creature in the center of the page.

Sam dropped the shot glass and started laughing.

She continued. "The book calls the god Yog-Sothoth."

The scruffy man cleared his throat. "This is a fine story, Mrs. Warne, but folks like us and Mr. Edison don't exactly believe in gods."

"I saw this Mr. Harry change before my eyes, Sam." He pushed aside his glass, untouched and stood up. "He was this alligator and then he was a man again. Perhaps our assessment of god is wrong?"

The young scientist left the room, the lanky author in tow. "You okay?" Sam asked once they were out of earshot of the others.

"Yes. Just wanted to get my…" He walked over to a rack where he kept several types of headgear. He quickly grabbed a small rectangular box and opened it. Inside were wire-rimmed glasses with four extra lenses attached that moved up and down. "Glasses."

"You aren't scared?" asked the writer.

The young man turned, and his eyes were magnified by the spectacles, which were now perched on his nose. He looked a bit like a bug. "Of course, I am scared, but there is something in that book that I have not seen before. A wonder."

"A wonder that may kill all of us." Sam crossed his arms.

His friend walked past him back toward the table and the book. "I thought you didn't believe."

"You seem to take it for serious." The lanky author reached out to grab his friend's shoulder and then hesitated. "If this thing is real and you go after it, whatever it is, then you may get yourself and everyone else killed. I like gambling, but I don't like these odds, Nik."

"Someone I know once told me something he thought was wise concerning adventure." A wry smile passed over the scientist's face.

The author nodded. "Yes. Adventure. Have adventures. This was not what I meant."

"Only because you did not know it existed. Come, old friend, I want to look into its face." Bug-eyed Tesla exited the room. Sam followed.

Nikola leaned over the book once more, looking every bit like a fly about to drink sugar water. He flicked down the extra lenses.

"Fascinating," he said and looked up, "And it is not from this world?"

Kate leaned over his shoulder. "I'm not sure the book or Mr. Harry are from this world. The book attempted murder. Mr. Harry told me that he was The Gate."

"Is he holding something back or allowing something in?" Sam peered at the book from the other side of his friend. "What do you see, sir?"

"There is writing on the tentacles." The young man glanced up at the detective. "Get me some paper and a pencil."

Once she brought them, he sat down and ran his finger along one tentacle.

"The numbers are Arabic. The rest are just symbols that I don't understand." He began to jot down a sequence of numerals in a long, fluid print.

430 9 6 2 7 90 3 77

"Maybe they relate to the numbers in the circle," said Kate, pointing to the Roman numerals. "We think these represent the children you rescued, Mr. Tesla."

Sam pulled the paper from his friend and tapped each number, one by one and muttered to himself. He counted them several times, then scrounged in his pocket, and pulled out a pencil. He put a slash between the 2 and the 7. "These look familiar."

"Of course, they are familiar. Don't be ridiculous," said Tesla. "You watched me write them."

The old writer didn't respond but counted the numbers once more. Then he made a single mark after the second number in each set, like this:

43.0962 79.0377

Nikola leaned over and flipped up three of the lenses from his glasses. "Why the points, my friend?"

Sam picked up the sheet. "If I'm right, these here are longitude and latitude markers."

"How can you be sure?" Kate walked around the scientist and took the paper from the lanky author.

"Because before I wrote those outlandish stories you folks like to read, I was a steamboat pilot on the Mississippi. You got a map, Nik?"

"I do not."

Sam took the paper from Kate's hand, folded it, and put it in his pocket. "Colorado Springs has a newspaper. I bet the editor has a map."

"One problem," said the detective. "Don't we need to know the directions connected to the numbers? I mean, are they north, south, east, or west?"

The older man crossed his arms and leaned back. "You're pretty clever, my girl."

"I am quite clever, but I'm not yours or anyone's girl, Mr. Clemens."

Nikola coughed hard and moved the book toward them. A smirk danced across his face. "There are marks on four sides of the creature." He handed the glasses to his friend, who perched them on his nose and gazed.

"Could be a directional star like you see on a map." The scruffy author pointed at the top part of the huge cluster of tentacles. "The first set of numbers are all clustered in this area of the creature seem to be pointing North." He slid the pencil left on the page.

The lady detective leaned close to the page. "That would be west then, correct?"

Sam pulled out the sheet from his pocket and scribbled a W above the second set of numerals. He grabbed a woolen coat from a hanger by the door. "I'm going to go meet the editor of the Gazette." The author folded the sheet once more and tucked it in an interior pocket. "Once he's discovered who's visiting his fine establishment, I'm sure I'll be able to procure a map."

He exited, then returned, and handed the young scientist his glasses before exiting once more. Nikola perched them on his nose and once more leaned over the book. "If only we knew when the event this page references is going to happen."

Kate took her seat next to the handsome younger man once more. "My partner says the children say its soon."

"Yes, but soon is not a precise time and date, now is it?" He ran his finger around the decorative border of the page. Then he turned the page and there was another border. "This border is curious."

Kate examined it. "It looks like a lot of borders I've seen in books. The shapes are repeated."

"That is true. There is repetition in the pattern, but not like one would suspect." He pointed at a group of lines and circles. "Look here."

"In some places there are more circles grouped together, and in others the lines are grouped."

"Yes, but what if those aren't lines and circles?"

Nikola drew the pattern onto another sheet of paper. Once freed from the border, the circles and lines became another numerical sequence:

01101 00010 10010 01101 00001 00100 10000 10000 00111 01000 10010 10110 01101 01100 00100

"More numbers." Kate examined what he'd written. "What do they mean?"

"Have you read *Explication de l'Arithmétique Binaire*, miss?"

She looked at him blankly.

The scientist continued as though he expected this response. "The author, Gottfried Liebniz, was much like DaVinci and myself—brilliant in many fields, including mathematics. Many say he rode the coattails of Newton, much as Edison claims I ride his coattails. In this article, Liebniz discusses an arithmetic that only uses zeros and ones. He claims that these numbers have spiritual values that the Chinese harnessed in the *I Ching*."

"So, this thing Mr. Harry is the gate for is Chinese?"

The young man stared at her for a moment as if she were baffling. "Forget the *I Ching*. It's the spiritual values that matter. Considering that this creature is supernatural...perhaps the spiritual values create energy?"

Numbers containing spiritual energy was not something she'd considered. Her fingers tingled as she moved them across the chain of numbers on the paper. She moved to the book and traced the border as well. A flush of warmth rolled through her, and the room became brighter for a moment.

Tesla's baritone voice cut through the moment as he continued. "Francis Bacon, before Liebniz, he discussed how letters of alphabets could be ones and zeros and then hidden anywhere. It is possible we have found an example of such a thing here, no?"

Kate sat back, still giddy from interacting with the sequence on the page. "If that's what this is, how do we translate it into something that could be understood?"

"Let me look in my books. I seem to remember seeing a discussion of Bacon and his cipher in one of them." With that, he walked away from the table muttering to himself.

"I wonder how much Edison understands about this book. Perhaps he is almost as ignorant as we are," said Kate. Tesla didn't reply.

With nothing to do for the moment, she wandered around the lab. It was filled with tables and various tools, but uncluttered. Everything had a place. There were several projects that looked like works in progress, including a small metal tower that looked a bit like the one outside and a large wire circle close to the back wall. She touched nothing for fear of disturbing the neatness. In an odd way, the place had the feeling of a sanctuary, balancing serenity and a sort of joyful energy. That energy was augmented now by what she'd experienced moments before.

She opened the back door and saw an odd glint come from the incline of the hill. The beauty of the afternoon drew her outside to investigate. Fields were supposed to be filled with flowers or grasses. This field had those things, but it also glinted with rows of unlit incandescent bulbs. She wasn't sure what to make of this. Was this the madness Edison was talking about when Shadow interviewed him? Before she could follow this train of thought, she heard something above her.

Looking up, she saw a bird with large black wings swoop past her toward the hotel. For a moment it looked like a man. She shook her head and remembered some Cherokee stories she'd heard about men having wings. Some may have been true, but most were just sightings of local hawks. At certain angles and with certain lighting and distance, a hawk looked like a man with wings. A chill passed over her in the creature's wake. She continued to watch it for several minutes.

Most birds swoop and dive as they ride the wind, but this one cut through the wind currents as if they didn't exist. Then it began to descend with the same sort of flight line. Before the lady Pinkerton could see where it was going to disappear, she heard a whoop from the front of the building. She ran around the lab and saw Sam with a round case over his shoulder.

"I've got it! Come, look!" He waved her to him.

Once inside, he spread a map of the United States and territories on a table and used a new bottle of whiskey he had in another bag and several shot glasses to hold it down flat. The author glanced at Kate. "Where's Nik?"

From behind them his friend said, "What is all the fuss about?" The scientist came around to the other side of the table. "You found something, didn't you?"

"I know where we're going. You're gonna love this."

Sam tapped his finger near the top of the United States.

"Lake Ontario?" asked Kate.

"Better..."

"Niagara! Niagara Falls! Of course!" Nikola's eyes danced and he threw up his hands. "It is a great source of power. Mr. Westinghouse and I have a project there. It is a powerful and mysterious place."

The detective said, "My partner would say that it holds a great deal of supernatural power as well."

Sam took a drag off his stogie and puffed out yet another sad looking smoke ring. "If you believe in that sort of thing."

"You don't?" Kate arched her eyebrow at him and faded to the Outside.

The scruffy man cleared his throat.

The young scientist drew a circle around Niagara on the map. "If this Mr. Harry is indeed an...what was the word you used, Mrs. Warne?" There was a look the scientist gave her that said he knew the word but didn't want to say it.

His discomfort tickled her for some reason. "Avatar. He's an avatar for this Yog-Sothoth in the book."

"Then maybe we should start believing soon." Nikola laid the book down on top of the map.

"What are you talking about?" asked his friend.

"Maybe this." The younger man pointed at the tentacled creature at the top of the page, "is the actual god who is coming."

"It would make sense. When the book attacked us, one of the creatures sent had tentacles." Kate shivered for a second at the thought of that thing around her.

"Imagine if we could tap energy more powerful than electricity. The falls have great energy as well. Perhaps this Mr. Harry will use the power of the falls and the children to draw this creature and enslave him," said the inventor.

Kate had not considered such a notion. "Why would an avatar turn on his own god? What would he gain?"

"Dominion," said Sam. "He who has the power, makes the rules."

"Couldn't he do that without Edison?" asked the detective "He's a god."

"No. He's a representation of a god," Sam replied.

It was Nikola's turn to arch an eyebrow. "How does someone who does not believe in God know these things?"

"I read," said his friend. "Don't you?"

"I read science, not about supernatural." Nikola took one of the shot glasses and poured whiskey into it. "I can't believe that Edison does not know what is happening here."

"Should we warn him?" asked Kate.

He knocked back one shot and poured a second one. "That is not what I mean. I mean that I believe Edison is a part of this. It is what he dreams of."

Sam started laughing as he reached for the whiskey bottle. "He dreams of gods taking over Niagara Falls?"

"No," said Tesla. "He dreams of great power. Of enough energy to light the entire planet, Sam."

Sam stopped mid-pour. "Think of the money."

"All things are possible in America, no?"

"You're serious, aren't you?"

"I swear to God Himself."

"That would mean a whole lot more if you believed in God Himself, Nik."

"We know that whatever is going to happen will happen in Niagara Falls, New York, correct?" Kate redirected the conversation before they were overwhelmed in philosophy. "The children keep saying this is going to happen soon."

"They are right," Tesla pointed to the border that followed the edge of the page. "And so was I. This is Baconian code."

"Did you translate it?" she asked.

"It takes time, but I did manage to figure out one word." The inventor scribbled one series of zeroes and ones on a scrap of paper. Underneath the numbers he wrote in slanted, fluid letters "October."

27

"What do we do?" asked Sam.

"You always tell me to embrace adventure, no?" Nikola poured a third shot for himself. "I say we go to Niagara."

"Edison is right. You are mad." His friend snatched the whiskey bottle and took a long draw from it.

"Why are you scared? You said you don't believe in gods," said Kate.

Sam staggered a little and sat down hard in a chair. "I ain't drunk, ma'am."

"If you think I'm mad and don't want to help me, you can go home. I'm sure Olivia will be happy to see you," said his best friend.

The writer winked at Kate, leaned back, and stretched his legs. "Nik, I'm a simple spinner of tales. That particular skill set is not exactly conducive to facing men who are trying to summon monsters to America." He reached for the bottle once more, but Kate shifted it out of his reach. "Even all of this doesn't incline me toward belief in gods, Mrs. Warne."

Nikola sat down across the table from him. "You are my only friend in America, Samuel. Look into my eyes." He pointed at his own dark brown eyes, which reflected the sharpness of his voice. "Are these the eyes of a madman?"

"Yes."

The scientist stood up and turned to the stove.

The older man threw up his hands. "Aw dammit, Nik. You're an inventor. All inventors are mad. DaVinci was mad. Edison is mad. You're mad. That's part of why you're my friend."

The frustration dropped from his friend's eyes as he turned and smiled. "But you are going to help me, aren't you?"

"What do you plan to do once we get to Niagara?"

"I want to kill Edison and stop Mr. Harry from calling the monster," said Nikola.

The author's cigar dropped to the floor. He mouthed the words "kill Edison" several times.

Kate said, "Killing Edison is not such a good idea, Mr. Tesla. We aren't even sure he's part of this plan."

She saw fiery anger turn his eyes from brown to black and shivered in spite of herself. "Do not underestimate the man. He's not as... what is the word...philanthropic as people think."

His friend said, "I'm too young to hang, so are you."

"You are saying to me that I need a sense of adventure. Always! Now I get a sense of this adventure and you say no," said the scientist.

"Murder is not adven—"

"It's not murder," said his friend, "if we save the world!"

Sam stood there a moment. "You have a good point. Wait---save the world?"

Kate moved the bottle to its shelf away from the men. "If this monster is called, who is to say that others will not follow?"

"Or that this monster will not be more than this Mr. Harry can contain?" said Nikola.

Sam sat down and stretched out his long legs. "Of all of my friends, I never dreamed that you, Nikola Tesla, inventor and scientist, would be discussing monsters from other worlds."

Nikola grinned and said, "I have you to thank for that, my friend. Who told me of the Froggy Men?"

Kate sat back down between the two men. "What is your plan, Mr. Tesla?"

The young inventor grew serious. "I have a lab near the falls, thanks to Mr. Westinghouse. I...we," he gestured at Sam, "will go there."

"That's not much of a plan," said Kate. She had hoped for a lot more from the man. "We don't have time for you to go hole up in your lab."

Nikola walked past her and then held open the back door. "Come, I want you to look at this field I've planted, Mrs. Warne."

Kate followed him. "I saw this earlier. Aren't those some of Mr. Edison's incandescent lamps? Why did you put them in the ground? I don't understand the relevance."

"Sam, could you pull that lever next to the door?" asked the scientist.

Kate was surprised at the blanket of stars that crossed the cobalt evening sky. The shadow Pikes Peak cast over them with the last of sunset behind the great mountain. She heard a clunk and a golden haze rose from the field and drove the shadows of the evening gloaming to the bottom of the hill and the roadside.

Sam joined them and whistled. "Nik, you've outdone yourself."

If Kate hadn't known better, she might have thought it was a gathering of wee folks even though there were none on record west of the Mississippi. "Underground wiring? I know that is how the Menlo Park house is powered, but I don't understand how a field of incandescent lamps will help our current situation."

Tesla stepped away from her side and crossed his arms. "Do you think I would show you such inept technology? It is for children. No. There are no wires."

"But how?"

He pointed to the domed structure that dominated the hill.

Kate said, "I don't follow."

The young inventor was silent for a moment, and a note of frustration crossed his face. "Wireless electricity can be used in many ways. I have something I've been working on at Niagara that could help us. I cannot explain more without sounding even more mad than people think."

"We're going to kill the monster with science?" said Sam.

"Yes, you could say that." The dark-eyed man leaned against the house.

Sam got close to his friend. "Promise me something. Don't kill Edison. That can't be part of the adventure."

"I can't make that promise," Nikola backed away.

"We only have circumstantial evidence to connect Mr. Edison to all of this. He may be blind to the part of the plan involving the children and the monster," said Kate. "You are a logical man, Mr. Tesla. Don't let your anger guide you now."

The young scientist turned from them. "Edison wants one thing. He wants power. He wants to control all access to electricity, which should be free for all people, just like the air we breathe. People like him are dangerous. They enslave others to get what they desire."

Kate moved to the stairs on the back stoop. "I can't prove he has done more than try to help those children. Nothing connects him to that book."

"Mr. Harry does." Tesla stared out over his garden of light.

"Nik, just promise me." said Sam.

Crickets begin to chirp as the silence that followed stretched for a spell.

Finally, Nikola Tesla spoke. "We have a monster that is coming sooner than later. I suggest we join Mrs. Warne and make our way to Niagara. We will know what needs to be done by the time we arrive, no doubt."

He stepped past his dearest friend and went inside. After a second *clunk*, the lights along the hillside were extinguished, revealing even more stars along and above the horizons. In the full darkness, they shone as bright as the manmade stars on the ground.

Kate studied the book while Mr. Tesla packed and tinkered with various items on the tables around them. She searched for a drawing, margin notes, a secret page or anything at all that would connect Thomas Edison in a provable way to the monster or Mr. Harry's plan. Thirteen seemed to be the closest connection in all of this. She was the only child he talked about in a specific way. Why was the girl important enough to involve Allan in the search for her? She looked at the page with the Roman numerals and creatures. The Roman numerals were set like a clock face and XIII was at the center where the arms of the clock should be attached. She touched each number and then noticed that some of the numbers were faded. There was also a new figure near the III. It was black and had large wings.

2 8

Breakfast at the boarding house was a loud affair this particular morning as the children reconnected and the adults got to know each other. Shadow drank coffee and listened to the various stories the children told one another. None of them acted shocked at the fantastical things that had happened around them. Thirteen kept to her task of providing breakfast but a soft smile lit her face for the first time since he'd met her.

"What's the plan, Pinkerton?" a voice cut through Shadow's concentration. He glanced across the table at Thomas, who was cutting open a biscuit with the tines of his fork.

Shadow sat down his cup. "I'm not sure there is a plan at this point."

The showman plucked a few slices of bacon from a plate and placed them on the biscuit. "Sometimes that's for the best. Never know when things will go sideways."

"My partner is in Colorado Springs and should be able to provide more information that will help build our plan," said the detective. "I will contact her after breakfast."

"Mrs. Warne is going to have to hurry." Seth, who sat across from his pop, took more bacon for himself. "The Time is coming."

The rest of the children nodded in unison, even Thirteen, who shivered when her brother said this, and hurried out of the room.

Horace poured himself more coffee from the blue metal coffee pot. "Do you know what happens then? Thirteen has said the same thing, but I don't understand."

The Oonas glanced at one another and looked down at her/their plates.

Two studied Seth, and Quinn trembled a little, but she spoke up. "He thinks it's good. That when The Calling happens, everyone will be thankful."

Shadow frowned. "Edison?"

"The Calling will not be good," whispered Light Oona.

Her other kicked her under the table. "Hush."

Quinn ignored her sister(s) and focused on the detective. "He wants the entire world to have electric light. He says it's the greatest single gift he can give."

"What about you all? How do you fit into this?" asked Shadow.

Thirteen came back in with more biscuits and slammed them on the table. "We aren't supposed to talk about The Calling.

Seth took her by the hand. "Those rules don't matter anymore."

The girl sat down next to him. "Without the rules, some of us hurt people. We don't mean to, but we do."

Two grabbed two biscuits and then reached across Thomas for bacon. "Maybe it's time to learn to make our own rules."

"Mr. Harry says we are children of gods," said Light Oona. Her darker self's eyes got wide.

Deborah, who'd been quiet to this point spoke up. "My Seth, his father was no god. He has magic, but he is no deity."

"Why would he want to surround himself with demigods?" asked Shadow. "Wouldn't you be competition?"

Horace cleared his throat and sat back. "This sounds like a lot of bunkum to me. There are no other gods. There is the one God, but no others."

Treze pulled from Seth and poured herself some coffee. "After what you've seen since I've been in Brainerd, are you sure you want to make that statement, Mr. Stewart?"

He scratched his beard. "That was magic, but not God-stuff."

She looked him, but not quite in the eyes. "How do you know?"

He gazed down into his own coffee cup. "I don't."

The table grew silent, and the Oona(s) fiddled with her/their forks.

Treze sipped from her cup and continued. "He needs help when he opens the gate. He can't control what's coming."

Shadow leaned forward, but the girl refused to meet his gaze. "What's coming?"

"I don't know."

He pulled out his notebook and opened to a page where he'd copied part of the drawing from the book. "Does it look like this?"

All of the children got up and gathered around Treze. She took Seth's hand again as her face paled as white as her dark sister's hair.

Light Oona started trembling and tears ran down her face. "Mr. Edison thinks it will save us all *Divi surya sahastrasya bhaved yugapad utthita Yadi bhah sadrashi sa syat bhasastasya mahatmanah.*"

Her dark double backed away from her. "Stop it, sister."

"What is she saying?" Horace dropped his cup, and coffee splashed everywhere.

Dark Oona balled her fists and closed her eyes. "If the radiance of a thousand suns were to burst at once in the sky, that would be the splendor of the Mighty One."

Treze fainted, and her brother caught her. Horace moved to her side. Meanwhile, Deborah and Thomas leaned to gaze at the drawing.

The showman pointed at a figure on the page. This Mighty One looks like some sort of sea monster."

Light Oona continued. *"Kaalo asmi loka kshaya kritpraviddho."*

Dark Oona took her double's hands. "I am death. The destroyer of worlds."

"Where did you get this drawing? How did you know about this?" Seth picked up the page. His face was crossed with curiosity rather than anger.

The detective said, "We found a book at Menlo Park."

Two stood close to him. "And it didn't kill you?

The liaison shook his head. "It damn near tried. Once Mrs. Warne and I subdued it, we found this with other drawings and notes inside."

"Then you know that thirteen of us are supposed to be a part of The Calling." The boy hugged Treze close.

His mother gestured for her son to follow her. "I will care for her in the kitchen. She does not need to see the drawing again. Old man, hand me my bag." Her husband grinned and tossed her a small patch-work bag. She caught it midair and then exited with Seth.

"How do books try to kill folks, Pinkerton?" asked the sheriff. His eyes were wide with bewilderment. The room got quiet. "Look, I'm the sheriff of a town where not much happens. Now my town is filled with people who turn into raging beasts, become two people instead of just one, and fight books."

Thomas started chuckling and then laughing. After a minute or two, the old showman pulled back from his mirth and said, "At least you ain't bored, right?"

Darkness crossed the lawman's face for a moment, but then he got a sheepish grin on his face. "It has been pretty exciting these past few days. Hell, I don't know what's gonna happen from moment to moment," he said, beginning to chuckle. "Just tell me I'm not crazy."

"I can't tell you than, son," said the older man. "I can tell you that it ain't gonna get any better for now." Seth returned with a cup of coffee he set in front of Thomas.

Shadow refocused the discussion by asking Seth, "Why Thirteen?"

"I don't know, sir. I just know that we were supposed to help," said Seth. "Now that some of us are gone, I'm not sure how he can use us."

"Maybe the number isn't as important. Perhaps he just needs extra power to hold the gate open," said Shadow. "Without thirteen of you, maybe the gate won't be as large?"

Horace took a biscuit and slathered it with some blackberry jam. "Why is Treze afraid? I've only known her a little while, but I've never seen her scared enough to faint."

Dark Oona spoke up, "She will be the sacrifice."

"You weren't supposed to tell." Fear crossed her lighter self's face.

"You weren't supposed to know." The darker girl sat back from her other while some of her/their siblings gasped. Two stood up and balled his fist. All the children gaped at their sister who was two but one. "And by the look of things, none of you knew either."

Their eldest brother looked down at his plate. "She never told me."

"Why is there to be a sacrifice?" asked Shadow.

Quinn rolled her eyes as if the detective were a stupid boy on the playground, "Gods always need sacrifice. You've read the stories of the gods, surely, mister."

All of the children started talking at once until Seth hit the table with his fist. "There won't be a sacrifice now. None of us are going to be a part of this."

Dark Oona looked around the table. "Are you sure that's a good idea? I'm not sure I can take all of you to my safe space."

The detective put his elbows on the table. "We can't just hide, Oona. My job is to protect people, just like you protect her." He nodded to her lighter self. "I have to be here to do my job."

Seth leaned close to his sister(s). "I don't want to hide either. That's not what I meant."

"We could fight." Two shook with anger. His older brother put a hand on his shoulder for a moment before the boy decided to take a seat once more.

Quinn came around the table to sit with him. She took his hand. "Maybe we could.

Thomas stood up this time. "You're children. How are you gonna fight some god? And you," he pointed at his son, "you got your own problems since your father is after you. Do you think he's gonna leave you alone while you go fight this thing?"

"Pop."

"Don't 'Pop' me, son. I brought you to come help your sister."

Seth threw up his hands. "This is part of helping her, and I haven't said I was going to fight yet."

"But you will because of all of them," the showman pointed at each child. "I don't want to lose you again, boy. I need you to move boxes and set up. Can't pay for that, you know." He sat down hard in his chair and drank his coffee. Deborah touched his arm, but he shrugged her off.

The frustration on his son's face softened, and he grinned. "I promise you won't lose me."

"How will you fight this?" asked Shadow.

The boy looked around the table at his siblings. "I have no idea. How about any of you?"

The children murmured amongst themselves until Quinn said, "We have a little time to figure it out, I guess."

The snake-oil salesman leaned back in his chair. "I feel so much better knowing that we have a plan."

"We?" asked Seth.

"Did you think I would let you bunch go alone? What kind of pop do you think I am, boy?"

"The type who can't resist a big adventure." The boy made his way around the table and wrapped his arms around the older man. His pop made a show of struggling against this show of affection, but everyone could see the spark of excitement and joy in his eyes.

2 9

There ain't no reason to take all this back to Niagara, Nik." Sam followed his friend as they made their way through the ornate lobby lined with the heads of everything from deer to enormous moose heads followed by a line of porters pushing various boxes and trunks on rolling carts.

Nikola turned to face the lanky author. "Are you the scientist, Sam? I need my tools."

"We can't even say if what you have will help us fight whatever this thing is that's coming."

"And we won't know if we don't have the tools," said the young scientist.

Kate and Sam boarded the *Eclipse* before sunrise, leaving Nikola to direct the porters as they began to load his belongings on the airship. Sho's eyes widened when he came out and saw the spectacle.

"Mr. Tesla, what are you doing?" He scurried toward the young Serbian, who continued to direct the porters.

The scientist continued to direct the porters, who organized the boxes and took them aboard. "I'm telling these men where to put my supplies,"

"They have no business loading anything into my ship." He shooed the porters away from the ship.

Nikola motioned for the men to stop and turned to face the man, who he towered over. "Who are you anyway?"

"I'm Sho, and I pilot this beautiful lady." He stepped toe-to-toe with the man. "Not one box more is going into her cargo bay unless you don't plan to get off the ground." He turned to Kate. "You didn't say he was going to load an entire laboratory."

The young scientist cleared his throat. "There is no need to worry, Úr Sho. I calculated the load weight and sent some of the boxes back. You should be able to fly with no trouble."

Sam attempted to step between them, but there was no way without touching his friend. Instead, he just stood close to both of them. "Please excuse my friend, Mr. Sho. His brilliance counteracts his ability to be considerate."

"Did you consider that we may be picking up others along the way?" The pilot crossed his arms, ignoring Sam.

The scientist nodded. "I even calculated for extra cargo."

"You missed one vital detail, Mr. Tesla."

"And what is that?"

"You didn't ask." The Asian reached out his hand. "Where's your manifest?"

Without blinking, Nikola reached into his coat and pulled out two sheets of paper. The smaller man studied the first and then the second, nodding. He pulled out a pencil and scribbled on the margin.

Kate tapped her foot and rolled her eyes at Sam, who held back a laugh. "How soon can we launch?"

The pilot continued to scribble. "In just," he paused to make one last notation, "a few moments." The man handed the paperwork back to his dark-suited passenger. "Mr. Tesla, your calculations are impeccable."

Nikola nodded and moved up the steps. His best friend shook his head and followed.

Mr. West stood on the platform at the top of the steps. When they joined him, he reached out to shake Nikola's. When the scientist demurred, Mr. West shook Sam's hand and turned to Kate.

"Have you heard from Shadow?" she asked.

"Not at all," said Mr. West. "Perhaps he is involved with affairs at Brainerd."

"Perhaps," said Kate. Mr. West entered the airship without more conversation. She thought she saw a blur around him for a second. She blinked. The blur was gone.

"Ain't that odd?" Sam whispered from behind her.

"You saw that blur, too, then?" She slowed her pace.

The author slowed with her. "I was talking about how he tried to shake Nik's hand. What are you talking about?"

"When he went into the ship, there was a blur around him. Just for a second."

"You know, I've heard some of those spiritualists talk about auras. Could that be what you saw?" her companion asked.

She held up her hand. "I don't believe in auras."

The author laughed. "Now that's rich."

"People don't glow like Edison's lights, Mr. Clemens. They also don't have blurs around them." She began to walk again.

"You would be the expert, I suppose."

"I'll try to talk to him once we lift off."

As they made their way down the corridor, she noted that the pilot and Nikola were deep in conversation. When they arrived at a ladder on the wall, Sho invited the inventor to go up to the control deck with him, but the young scientist said he'd visit at a later point in the trip. Sam joined his friend and they moved ahead in search of their cabins.

As soon as they'd moved on, she stopped Sho herself. "Have you noticed anything odd about Mr. West?"

Sho gave her a quizzical look. "All of the Brotherhood is odd, ma'am. You should know that."

She couldn't help but laugh. "Yes, but what I'm referring to is odd even for one of the Brothers."

He scratched his head. "Not really. He missed a couple of meals, but I thought he was either with you or on official business of some sort. I'm just the pilot, not a Brother, so I'm not privy to all their goings on."

"I find that hard to believe, Sho." She crossed her arms.

The small man said, "I'm really not a Brother."

"You know that's not what I mean."

"In this particular case, I was not privy." He winked, but she saw concern pass beneath his playful demeanor.

She pressed for more information. "Did he mention my partner? Or anything about the children in Brainerd?"

The pilot shook his head. "He has seemed more distant though. This morning, for a moment or so, I didn't think he knew who I was. Then he asked about the war, and we talked about that. Seemed normal after that. Why are you asking?"

Kate looked around. The corridor was empty, but she didn't want to be overheard. "I saw something around him, like an aura, but then it was gone."

"The Brothers are different, ma'am." He climbed up, away from her.

"Have you ever seen an aura around one of them?"

He shook his head. "That doesn't mean he couldn't have one, but you're right, I think I would remember something like that.'

Sam appeared at her side with a small box under one arm. "Nik is getting settled. I thought I'd visit the control deck, if that's okay with our pilot."

"What you got there, Sam?" The pilot nodded at the small wooden box.

The warm scent of fresh tobacco wafted up as the author popped open the top. The pilot grinned.

"Cubans. An admirer sent them."

"People admire you?"

"Much to the chagrin of my dear Livvy," said the older man.

Before heading to his work, the pilot said to Kate, "I'm sure Mr. West is fine, ma'am."

She stepped back to give larger, scruffy man space to follow Sho. "You're most likely right."

With that, she went to her cabin and called up a cup of tea. As the ship began its ascent, she began working on her report for Allan. The blur around Mr. West was wrong. It was though someone was trying to fade into Mr. West's shadow the way she'd seen her partner fade into the darkness in the corners of her office. She had no idea if that could be done or why that would be necessary.

There was only one way to find out. She made her way to the parlor. Sam's laughter echoed from above. The author made friends because of his gregarious nature and genuine enthusiasm in curiosities. She passed the parlor at first because the door was closed. Just as she touched the ornate doorknob, wrongness flowed over her. She shivered.

Mr. West's voice cut through her discomfort. "We were built to protect the colonists." Shadow had repeated these very words many times before.

A cold, hard voice responded. It sounded almost the same as Mr. West when he was angry. "You were built to protect the colonists from their own short-sighted stupidity. The last war proves that their experiment and your protection has failed. I am the answer to that failure."

Someone stood up and started to walk around the room. "Don't be predictable. How many other entities before you believed that they were the solution to the shortsightedness of humans? Come now, you can do better than that."

A flutter rose as if one of them were winged like a large bird. Kate thought of what she saw back at the lab the night before but pushed back the thought so she could focus. "Protection is one step away from dominion."

"Only a fraction of the Brotherhood would be willing to join you. The rest call you an abomination," said Mr. West.

Humorless laughter emanated from within. "*Ab homine...*away from man. That's what they mean, and yet, they are not man either." There was a brief pause. "You could release more of us. I know my brothers who were locked away are ready to take their revenge."

"I can't. Not alone. Not now." Footsteps passed the door and stopped for a moment. Kate moved to one side lest the door was opened by someone on the other side. After a moment, the person, Mr. West, perhaps, moved deeper into the room once more.

She wanted to know more but wasn't sure this was her concern. Shadow was her partner and it sounded like something he would need to know. Maybe he already knew. Another wave of wrongness passed over her. This had to be another secret. For her partner's sake, she made her decision.

Kate entered the Outside and passed through the wall and into the room. It was well-furnished, containing a desk and dark stained chairs carved with dragons. A large mass of darkness hovered by the window of the parlor.

The cold voice emanated from the undefined pocket of darkness. "You released me because you were sure your brothers were wrong. Where is that fire now?"

Mr. West stood up and slammed down his fist, "I released you with the hope that you would find peace and rejoin the Brotherhood."

The darkness sharpened for a second and she was sure she saw wings with stars twinkling inside their canopy. "Isn't that kind of you to hope for me. If my own brothers can't forgive me, how do they expect me to find peace?"

The wings unfolded, stretching across half the length of the window, hiding the sky behind them. What the lady detective thought were twinkling stars in the creature's wings were eyes. Mewling and growls rose as he backed Shadow's brother into the corner. Before Kate could move, the wings wrapped around him. A high-pitched scream cut through her and then the ship listed to one side for a moment, throwing her to the floor. A puddle of black and green ooze dropped onto the floor. Kate covered her nose and felt her bile rise as she began to back out of the room.

The creature locked eyes with the lady detective. "Tell your partner. He'll understand."

I n seconds, she was opening the hatch. A wave of cigar smoke and laughter washed over her.

Sam took her hand as she pulled up onto the deck. "Mrs. Warne, you look terrible," he said.

She got to her feet. "Mr. West is gone."

The pilot glanced over his shoulder, "You of all people should be used to this."

"He isn't on the Paths, Sho. Something ate him right in front of me in the parlor," she said.

His dark eyes widened. "The abominations have gotten more powerful," he said. "Or at least this one has."

"All that was left of Mr. West was a stinking puddle. If the monster hadn't needed me to tell Mr. Jones what had happened, I would have been next, I suspect," said the detective.

Sam tapped ash into a brass tray attached to the arm of a chair. "I imagine the dead aren't as filling, my dear."

This one comment abruptly stopped all the thoughts tumbling over each other in Kate's rushing mind. This was no laughing matter, but she couldn't help herself. The author took her by the arm. "Let's go have a look. I'll report back, Captain."

He went down first, and Kate followed. In a moment they were standing where the parlor door had been moments before. Only smooth red wallpaper striped in blue greeted them.

"I would be doubtful of your knowledge of the ship if I didn't know that you'd traveled on it the same as I had." Sam ran a hand along the new length of wall in front of them.

Kate leaned out through the wall. The great barrier of the Rockies stood stark against a startling blue sky. Clouds fluffed up beneath the ship. The sunlight made the peaks of the mountains sparkle like quartz. If there hadn't been a parlor and her partner's Brother there moments before, she might have been enchanted by the view a bit more. Stepping back into the corridor, she said, "We have some explaining to do, I suspect."

Moments later they were back on the control deck.

"I swear this ain't a joke, Sho." Sam paced across to the wheel and took it for a moment.

The pilot said nothing but clicked a few brass switches and kicked out a stand to hold the wheel steady. As he passed Kate heading to the hatch on the floor, a whirring caught her attention. He stopped to adjust something on the side of one leg and then slid down the ladder to the corridor below. The lady detective had to float to keep up with him, while Sam strode behind her. Once they arrived where the parlor had been minutes before, he ran his hand across the wall.

"So, this thing ate Mr. West and an entire room out of my lady?" said the pilot.

"It did have the courtesy to redecorate to match the rest of the hall. It also didn't try to kill the rest of us, which is better than I expected." Kate leaned against the wall as the Asian continued to examine the area where the arched oak door had been.

Nikola moved around Sam, who watched from the middle of the corridor. The scientist knelt next to the pilot. "Why are you touching the wall, Mr. Sho?"

"My friend, Mr. West, has been eaten by a creature." Kate answered. The young man stood up and backed away.

The Asian frowned. "And it took part of the *Eclipse* with them. Why take the room?"

"What sort of creature?" The scientist moved closer to Kate.

"I'm not sure. All I saw was darkness and massive wings that had eyes and mouths" She stretched out her arms as she explained.

"I have seen this thing flying over Colorado Springs before," said Nikola.

"What is it?"

The inventor shrugged. "I do not know. I have seen many strange things in this country. One more was not worth investigating."

Sho's eyes widened. Then he hung his head. "It was a Brother."

Kate moved to his side. "It mentioned that to Mr. West. I don't understand."

"There was an experiment at the beginning of the war. The president wanted to have power on the land, in the water, and he got this idea that having power in the air could work too. I was recruited to be a part of that plan and, of course, the Brotherhood was already involved," said the Japanese man. He patted the wall with a gesture of fondness and continued, "That's how I was able to build my beautiful lady here."

Kate nodded. "Some of our investigative teams were dropped into enemy territory from some of those early ships during the latter half of the war. I had no idea who was involved in the program."

"You were a spy, Mrs. Warne?" Sam arched a bushy eyebrow at her as though he didn't believe her.

His challenge didn't surprise her. Most had no clue about the women of the war. "Many women were. It was a peculiar time, was it not?"

"Indeed." He softened his challenge with a gentle grin.

Sho interjected. "The president wanted to recruit more of my family because we have a knack for this flying but Tenno Komei, the emperor himself, refused to allow such a thing. The Brotherhood offered a solution instead."

Nikola gave him a curious look. "It was not another airship?"

The pilot's gaze hardened, and he shook his head. "They tapped into the power that makes them what they are and attempted to repeat what was done on Roanoke Island."

"I don't understand," said Kate.

Instead of answering, the pilot led them back to the control deck before continuing. Once he'd checked the various dials and navigational tools and his remaining passengers settled, he continued his story. "They tried to make a different version of themselves. You saw the result."

The lady detective sat down near one of the windows on one side of the deck where the Rockies towered in the distance like a marbled blue wall that protected all that was west of them. The barrier they created was evident even as the ship turned back toward the east. "The Brotherhood is based on honorable traits. They serve to protect. Why wouldn't this version be the same?"

"The Brothers were made?" Nikola gazed at the instruments around him and scribbling notes.

The pilot took the wheel and turned it and the nose of the ship away from the Rockies. "You would say it was impossible, Mr. Tesla."

"No one has created life. Birth, yes. Created from nothing, no," said the scientist. "Now you say to me that they were created."

"You said you have seen many strange things? Well, this is one of those strange things. They were created to protect folks like you and Sam and Kate. Except when this new version was attempted, it was created for war." His face hardened and his eyes got darker for a moment.

"Soldiers?" asked Kate.

"And spies. When the war ended, the winged brothers decided that humans were too stupid to deserve protection," said the pilot.

The lady detective said, "Neither Shadow nor Allan mentioned..."

"Do you think they would have?" said Sho.

"I was head of the female spies—"

"Who had no need to know about these creatures," said the small man.

Kate wanted to shout that her partner never lied or held back information from her. She wanted to hold to the idea that Allan, once

her best friend, would never keep this from her. They shared everything at one point in their relationship. War, however, often created
contrary circumstances that no one wanted to accept or would even
consider in peacetime. There was a good reason, she was sure. There
had to be.

Sho continued, "Once the war ended, the Brotherhood attempted
to go on as it had for two hundred years. The winged ones only
knew dissent and destruction and had little patience for the
colonists. After Lincoln was murdered, they wanted to attack what
was left of the south, breaking the treaties signed by the generals in
Virginia."

The days after the president passed were frantic at the office. Allan
sent investigators to D.C. to assist in the search for John Wilkes
Booth. Shadow was called back to join The Brotherhood, but he left
before Kate could ask him why. Allan told her he was on a special
mission to chase demons a medium claimed controlled the wily
assassin when he shot Mr. Lincoln. It seemed a bit ludicrous at the
time, given the continued tensions that the nation faced in those early
days after the end of the war, but she never considered that her lover
would lie about her partner's whereabouts. Instead of raising questions, she accepted the story and never asked more. It was, after all,
her partner's mission, not hers. Sho's explanation made her wish she'd
pushed for answers instead of accepting everything he told her like
some sort of lovesick schoolgirl.

Sam leaned close to the pilot, with a look of avid curiosity that
reminded Kate of every newsman she'd ever met. "There are more?"

"There were more, but not now. Most were killed trying to take
Savannah. And no," the pilot puffed the fresh stogie, "there is no
record among you folks concerning this."

"Members of the Brotherhood don't die," said Kate.

The Asian tapped ash into a metal ashtray. "Okay. They faded
away."

"This is utter nonsense," said Nikola. "No one fades away. They are
alive or dead."

Kate faded to the Outside. "Are you sure about this, sir?"

His eyes widened while he stepped back from her. His best friend laughed. "I guess your definition of nonsense has shifted."

"If you are speaking of humans, you are correct about being alive or dead. I happen to be dead. I choose to live here and work." Kate returned to the Inside and a more solid form.

"Aren't your partner and this Mr. West human?" The scientist took a seat near the window.

The lady detective paused. She'd never considered what Shadow could be except one of The Brotherhood. "I'm not sure. He does say that they don't die. But I assumed that the fading away quip was just that—a joke.'

Sho leaned back and puffed a smoke ring that soon circled the room. "The Brotherhood employed Union mages to help them hold off an attack by the winged ones on Savannah, Georgia, an important port to the state, which was beginning the process of restoring things."

"Wouldn't they have supported the attack on Savannah?" she asked.

Sho turned the wheel a bit and said, "No. After Appomattox, the members of the Mage Corps disbanded and most wanted nothing more to do with fighting or war. You know how bad it got, Mrs. Warne. Many who'd put their faith in the Brotherhood pulled away. When they got wind of the possible attack, they had to act. If the winged ones succeeded, the country would be plunged into another terrible war."

Sam leaned close to the pilot. "What happened to them?"

"The mages, with the help of the Brotherhood, managed to lock the creatures out of The Paths and away from this world." The Asian checked a few gauges on the walls. "I'm sure this visitor was a shock for Mr. West."

Kate conjured a cup of tea for herself. "They seemed to have plans together and were well acquainted enough to discuss the winged one's son.

The pilot's eyes widened, "Do you think one of those children you've been tracking is his?"

The detective considered Seth from the medicine show and the story his mother told them in the wagon that evening. "I definitely think one of them is his child," she said. "And I think this creature wants to use him and the Brotherhood to take over the country."

Nikola frowned and said, "But Edison..."

"Of course, the boy's sister and your concerns take precedent, Mr. Tesla," said Kate. "Just the same, we need to alert the rest of the Brotherhood of this additional threat. Unless they already know?" she gave a questioning look at the pilot.

"I can't say what they do and don't know, ma'am. I'm just the pilot of their finest airship tasked with taking you where you and your entourage need to go," said Sho. "I can, however, put you in touch with your partner or with the Brotherhood itself."

"What if that winged one comes back?" asked Sam. "Do we shoot it?"

"Shooting is not always the answer, my friend," said Nikola, shaking his head.

"It took a whole room off this thing," said the author, "What'll happen if it comes back?"

"We won't be shooting anything if we're up in the air," said the pilot. "That's an order."

Kate said, "I don't think it is coming back. It got what it wanted."

The ship began to shake and bump, throwing Nikola and Kate to the floor of the deck. Sho held the wheel while Sam peered out the observation window.

"You might want to hold that thought, ma'am," the scruffy-haired man said as a dark figure with wings swooped past the ship faster than she'd ever seen anything move.

A streak of darkness followed the creature across the open sky as it turned and dove toward the ship. Its ebony wings blinked with the many sets of eyes as it kept pace with the moving air vehicle.

"You've hidden my son, Spectral." A voice cut through the drone of the engines.

Kate approached the window and gazed into its featureless face. "I've done no such thing. If you can't find him, that's not my problem."

Sam pulled her back and leaned close to her ear, "Ain't no need to provoke it."

"Well, what would you suggest?" She stepped away and out of his grasp. The ship lurched to the side, throwing her and Sam into the wall and each other.

"What was that about shooting it? I distinctly remember—" started Nikola as the ship rocked hard once more.

Sho raced around them to the control panel covered in brass dials. He pulled a dragon-headed lever set on the floor next to the panel down hard and a sharp hiss rose above the din of the turbulence and now groaning engines. The airship dropped from beneath them. Without losing his footing, the pilot pulled a second lever and brass shades fell over the observation windows. "As I said, we won't be shooting anything while we're in the air."

As the ship continued to lose altitude, Kate crawled to the wheel that was useless in this descent and held onto it. The small captain of the ship twisted the dragon lever, releasing another sharp hiss. He shouted to her, "Pull the throttle!"

Using the wheel, she got to her feet. "Which one is the throttle?"

"The big handle next to the wheel," barked Sam. "Push it forward."

The detective pushed the shining handle forward. The engines growled as the ship's nose lifted, and she felt her feet slipping out from under her.

"Steady, my girl. Steady. Pull back slowly now," said the author as he joined her at the wheel and put his hand over hers.

"I'm still not your girl, good sir." She nudged him and yanked her hand from under his. "Where were you a minute ago?"

"It doesn't matter. You took to this like a natural, wouldn't you say, Sho?" said the bushy haired man.

The pilot was peering into a brass tube that also looked a bit dragon-like. It went up into the ceiling. Kate was reminded of the submarines she'd travelled in during the war.

"Where is he?" She left Sam to tend the wheel and joined Sho.

"The dragon's breath makes it hard to tell, ma'am," said the small man as he turned the viewer to portside.

"Dragon's breath?" asked Nikola. "What is this you speak of?"

"It's a little surprise I made up for moments like this, Mr. Tesla," said the pilot.

"You are a chemist as well?" The inventor arched his eyebrow and doubt crossed his sharp eyes.

"I dabble. This is an old family recipe I'm using in a modern application," said the Asian, continuing to monitor the sky.

Kate asked, "Poison?"

"No. That would hurt our fellow air creatures," he said as he backed away from the periscope and offered Kate a chance to look. "All I wanted to do was confuse him a bit and give us chance to get some distance."

A dense, almost black cloud hung in the sky near what Kate thought was their last position. Lightning flashed near the center of the cloud in one spot over and over again. It reminded her of some of the mage tactics used during the war.

"Did you create the lightning in that cloud as well?" asked the young inventor.

"That must be our friend fighting to escape," said the pilot. "Lightning isn't my weapon of choice. That's my cousin, Rairū's department."

"Couldn't he just fly out of it?" asked Kate as more lightning crackled around the edges of the iron-tinted cloud.

Sho chuckled and said, "There's more in that cloud than meets the eye. He won't die, but he will be confined."

Sam arched his eyebrow. "Confined?"

"It will close in on him as long as he fights. In the meantime, we can escape," said the pilot as he increased the speed of the airship, taking them farther away from the mountains and the heavy flashing cloud.

"He'll find us again," said the lady detective, stepping away from the periscope, allowing Nikola to peer out into the sky for the moment.

"No doubt. You managed to upset him, ma'am, no offense," said Sho. "Have you hidden his son?"

Kate said, "No, but I know who has. If he takes time to think, he'll know as well, which means that we now have two problems."

Sam said, "Isn't this a Brotherhood issue?"

"It would be, but his son is one of the thirteen children Nikola rescued," said Kate, glancing over at the scientist.

"Seems like you have caused all sorts of mayhem, my friend," said the author with a grin.

Nikola stepped back from the brass periscope and said, "All of your learned instruction in this matter has paid off, no?"

"Are you making a joke?" said Sam laughing. "If you smoked, you son of a gun, I'd offer you a cigar and congratulate you."

"If you laughed, then yes. Congratulate me with some whiskey instead," There was a glow of delight in the scientist's eyes and a wry smile spread across his face.

"I should warn Shadow. I have a feeling you should warn the Brotherhood as well," Kate said to Sho.

The pilot said, "Once I inform the Brotherhood, he should know."

"I'm not so sure anymore," she said.

The Asian man nodded and pulled a map from his pocket. "There's a small air station about four hours ahead of us. I won't need fuel, but we can stop so that you can contact your partner. I'll take the time to assess any damage that may have been done from the loss of the parlor. It's not often you lose an entire section of a ship midair."

He turned the wheel and the ship turned with it. Clouds passed the observation window and Nikola continued to watch out the periscope. Kate paced for a while, as Sam continued to smoke and follow Sho's commands as they made their way to their next stop. She pushed back the worry that the creature might get to Shadow before her message did. There was nothing worse than feeling helpless, but there was no quicker way she could reach him. The pilot and her companions were doing all they could to help, and that counted for something. In the meanwhile, all she could do is sip her tea and wait.

32

MR. ANDREW JONES

BRAINERD, INDIANA

AIRSHIP ATTACKED MR WEST EATEN BY WINGED CREATURE SHO SAYS ITS A BROTHER WE SHOULD ARRIVE IN BRAINERD TOMORROW WILL EXPLAIN MORE THEN DONT WALK THE PATHS BE SAFE

KATE

The news concerning Mr. West was old by the time the telegram reached Shadow. The snuffing out of his being had echoed through the collective when it happened. Kate had to be shaken to not consider this. He was sure that Sho had explained the intricacies of what she'd witnessed although he was certain that his partner was clever enough to figure out most of it on her own.

At least it'd decided to not destroy the airship.

"Who released the abominations?" Shadow asked his brothers.

The collective grew silent. They all knew, as he did, that it was Mr. West. Speaking his world name and acknowledging his actions in this matter would make them all culpable.

"As one of us acts, all of us acts," said Shadow, reciting a teaching from the early times.

Another voice spoke, "Says the Brother who keeps secrets, Mr. Jones."

The collective began whispering. He knew that this day would come.

"And yet I continue to follow the orders given to us on Roanoke Island. Did I not lock away the abominations for you? Do I not keep the pledge to protect the people of this land?"

"The Brotherhood is changing," said another voice.

"Why is that bad?" asked Shadow.

The odor of burnt flesh and sulfur from the cannons surrounded Shadow, and he could see bodies for what seemed like miles across a field being picked over by giant spiders. A steel gray storm cloud sat at the top of the mountain, lightning striking cannons and men at will. A flood of anger and shame flowed over him.

"We did what we thought was right and failed," said Shadow.

A voice said, "Failure isn't an option for the Brotherhood. You have been with the colonists too long."

"Remove me as liaison. Send someone else. Maybe one of you would like to step up and take care of this mess."

Silence prevailed for several minutes. He knew the answer, but that didn't stop the disappointment that rose in him.

"I see."

A wave of assent flowed over him, followed by a heaviness that was his own. He was the liaison, the only liaison between north and south. It had been so since the treaty was signed in Gettysburg twenty years before. The other liaison had been sent west in order to stem the Splintering, and now the fruits of that choice were ripened.

"And if I fail?"

There was no response. Someone touched his shoulder, and Shadow came out of the trance.

"Are you okay, Mr. Jones?" asked Horace.

Shadow ignored the question and handed the young sheriff the telegram. He said, "Kate, my partner, will be here tomorrow. Does this town have an air station?"

Horace shook his head and pointed behind the boarding house. "There's plenty of fields where an airship could land back that direction, although we haven't had one land out here before. What's this about winged creatures?"

Shadow saw Seth hesitate at the front door at the term winged creatures. The youngster glanced back into the house, and then slipped out onto the porch to join the two men.

"You've seen my father?" The boy's fear was palpable.

Horace passed the telegram back to Shadow. "What're you talking about?"

"Does that telegram say something about him?" Seth reached for the paper but stopped himself and looked down at his feet. "I'm out of turn here. Sorry." He started to leave, but Horace took his arm.

"Mr. Jones, what does the winged creature have to do with the boy?" asked the sheriff.

Seth pulled free, though not in an angry way. "That creature is my father. My real father."

Shadow said, "That's just not possible. They weren't made like that."

The boy crossed his arms. "Say this to my mother."

Thomas came out and stood behind Seth, "Say what to your mother?"

Seth handed him the telegram. Thomas twisted his mustache as he read, then handed it back to his son. "Why would he kill this Mr. West? Is he another one of his children?"

Shadow said, "West is part of the Brotherhood, and so am I." The boy handed the telegram back to him.

The snake-oil salesman scratched his head and squinted his eyes. "I remember y'all from the war. We thought you were all part of one big family because y'all looked alike."

"In a way, you were right. We are all one," said the detective. "Or were until the war."

Thomas sat down next to him, "I remember the winged folks too.

They rained bodies from the sky at Kennesaw Mountain. Between them and those infernal spiders, no one had much of a chance even though Johnston claimed the victory."

"The attack was meant to be focused on the Confederate mages on the side of the mountain. Instead, the winged ones attacked all the mages and then executed everyone the spiders didn't get to," said Shadow. "Until then, we didn't know that they weren't like us. The schism that began when you all began to secede was deepened by this one battle. Once the war ended, we had to face our error. The treaty at Gettysburg gave us no choice."

The older man nodded. "Both sides swore off mages."

"The treaty outlined more than that. Part of the agreement was that the Brotherhood would remove the abominat—the winged ones —from this reality for the protection of all."

The showman snorted. "You missed one."

Shadow put his head in his hands for a moment. "No. Worse. Someone released one. Possibly to finish breaking the Brotherhood."

"This Mr. West?" asked Horace.

Shadow sat up. "I don't like jumping to conclusions, but I fear that is the case."

The sheriff's eyes got wide. "Wait. Treze says something is coming. Is this it?"

Seth said, "No, but it could be connected in some way. It seems more than coincidence that my father has come for me right now."

"I see no connection," said the detective.

The old showman stretched out his legs. "Deborah says there are no coincidences. Why didn't this winged one try this sooner? He's been free at least fifteen or sixteen years. The war was done eighteen years ago."

Shadow stared out over the porch. "I have no real answer here. Maybe he was building support or strength."

"Your Brothers have to have some answers. This is their making." Thomas's voice rose as he continued. "One of your own let him go. How could they not have answers?"

The detective kept an even tone. "My brothers are silent on this matter except to expect me to lock that thing up once again."

"Is that what you are going to do then?" asked the sheriff.

"I am the liaison for the Pinkertons, that hasn't changed. The children and whatever plans Edison and Mr. Harry have are my priorities." He folded the telegram and put it in his pocket. "Dr. Lazarus, we may need your war-time expertise as things move forward."

Thomas's eyes sparkled with a mischief that the detective appreciated. "I'm proud to offer them."

They both rose from the swing and the old showman punched his son's arm. "Go tell your ma I'm off with the Pinkerton. Don't tell her about your father though. She needs to rest."

The boy moved toward the door. "You know she knows."

His pop leaned in close. "Let's pretend she doesn't for a bit. She enjoys knowing before we do."

As Seth headed inside, the sheriff made his way down the stairs. "I should probably head back to my office, Pinkerton."

Shadow stopped him. "You're part of this too, Mr. Stewart, so don't leave yet."

Horace fiddled with his hat and then scratched his beard. "Not so long ago, I didn't believe there were supernatural things. I thought they were stories folks told at Christmas for fun. Since I met Treze, all that disbelief has been turned over. I don't know anything I can do to help at this point."

The old snake-oil salesman clapped him on the shoulder. "Son, if I'd not done anything when I learned that there were oddities in this world, I wouldn't have a family. Just do your job, same as always." He clapped an arm around the young sheriff and continued, "Besides, you've got two old pros to guide you, ain't that right, Mr. Jones?"

33

Kate fidgeted with the handle of her bag as she felt the ship descend. Even though she sent a telegram, there was much to share with her partner before they headed to Niagara. She should have telegrammed Allan, but just couldn't bring herself to do so. Every message she sent was responded to with sentiments she couldn't return anymore. How could she explain that she loved the job more than she loved him? She had no desire to see a grown man cry over the likes of her again. He'd done that at her bedside and funeral.

The airship bumped once and Sho's voice came from a pipe in the room, "Last stop, Brainerd." At that point, she shifted her wardrobe from her more comfortable denims and men's shirt, to a simple floral skirt and blouse like she'd seen out west. As she made her way out, she adjusted her hat, which was adorned with the same small flowers as on the skirt.

When she stepped out onto the platform, Shadow waited with a smile, which did not conceal the worry in his eyes one bit. Whatever he knew or had surmised about their situation was worse than she thought. Kate's shoulders relaxed for the first time in days when he took her hand at the last step despite what she saw in his face.

"Peaceful trip?" He took one fluid motion from her hand to grab her bag.

"You know, there's a hotel in Colorado Springs who could use someone with your skills, sir."

"That doesn't answer my question, Mrs. Warne."

She shivered and then chastised herself for being afraid. "That thing took the entire parlor off the side of the ship midair without shaking us at all. I guess that could be classified as peaceful."

"Why would he take the entire room if he just wanted to kill Mr. West? I'd say he lacks finesse." Shadow offered his free arm.

She accepted and continued. "Sho says the creature is one of you."

Shadow stopped. The air felt heavy around them for a moment then settled. "Does Mr. Tesla know?"

She nodded. "And Mr. Clemens. The real question is why *I* didn't know. We've been partners off and on since before the war. I heard rumblings in the Confederate camps about winged men, but you never said anything."

"There were many secrets we both kept as I recall."

"If I had known the rebels had created something like them, I would have shared it with my partner. Hell, I would have shouted it from the top of the White House." She shook as her unexpected anger rose.

"You wouldn't have had to. They made themselves perfectly clear at Kennesaw Mountain."

Kate's frustration rose at his at tone, which made her feel childish. "I asked you about this after I heard stories from the Rebs. You assured me they were telling tales." She flickered to the Outside. The air was cooler, and her partner's skin was paler from this place. She forced herself back Inside. "Partners don't lie!"

He closed his eyes and gripped her arm as if to keep her from going Outside again. Arguments between them were so rare, it took Kate a moment to register that he was as upset as she was. "The President ordered us to secrecy," he said in a low tone. "You of all people know what that means."

The heat of her anger ebbed at those words. She did know. They were working for the good of the Union. There was no arguing if the President told you to keep a confidence, even if it was a world-altering confidence. She felt Shadow's grip loosen as they walked in silence for a small moment.

Finally, he continued. "The president wanted a weapon that would end the war before the winter. We provided what we thought could achieve that. If I could have told you, I would have, but..."

She leaned into him and patted his arm. "I can't argue with the president."

"Friends again?"

"Partners, too, if you don't mind." Then she added, "So what do we do with this winged Brother?"

"He nor the rest of those things are my Brothers."

"Sho said—"

"We broke bonds the moment we locked the abominations out of the Paths and away from this world. It is not my Brother."

Kate pulled away. It wasn't like him to talk over her. "What he said was that some don't agree with your assessment."

He looked down at his polished shoes. "That disagreement is breaking the Brotherhood."

"It's possible that it killed Mr. West to exacerbate that disagreement."

"If that was the goal, it succeeded. The one thing the collective agrees on in this matter is that I'm to take care of it since I'm the liaison."

"That seems unfair."

Shadow said, "This isn't about fair and unfair. This is about duty. I put it away before. Now I have to do my job again."

"What about the children and Niagara?"

"Niagara?" Her partner offered his arm once again and Kate took it.

She kicked at a rock as they continued. "Sam and Nikola figured out what some of the drawings and symbols meant in the book. We believe the event the children have been talking about is happening at

Niagara Falls. If the dates we saw are correct, we have less than a week to get there and stop it."

"Have you figured out what the event is?"

"Mr. Harry and Edison are calling a god. The god Mr. Harry represents, we think." When she said it out loud, the whole situation seemed ridiculous. Her partner, however, took in the information like nothing was out of place.

"Edison's involved, then? But why?" he asked.

"Mr. Tesla is convinced that Edison wants to find a new power source. Maybe to augment electricity."

"That's mad." They'd made it to the boarding house. He led her up the step although both of them knew she needed no assistance.

"No madder than a flying abomination removing the parlor from an airship midflight and killing one of your brothers," she said.

Her partner set down Kate's bag. "And the children?"

"The best I can figure is that Edison wanted to use their powers to help control the situation when the god came through to our world."

"This is officially madder than removing the parlor from the airship midflight. Those children aren't powerful enough to handle a god."

"You have seen the havoc they've wreaked since they've been out. It's possible they could." She sat down on her bag and shook out her skirt even though she didn't have to.

"This is blood sacrifice you're talking about. I can tell you the Brotherhood won't stand for it." He paced back and forth. "They are children. We can't just take them to Niagara to feed whoever is coming through that gate,"

Kate leaned her head on her hand. "Does the Brotherhood have a contingency plan for dealing with a god who is being pulled into our world against his or her will?"

The porch swing creaked when her partner settled on it. "No."

Treze interrupted from behind the screen door. "Tell your Brotherhood it's not their choice or concern. We are doing what we were raised to do."

Shadow got up and met the girl at the door. "There aren't thirteen of you anymore. The book shows all thirteen."

The girl's eyes glazed over. "We are a family, Mr. Jones. Together we can do anything."

Kate joined her partner and placed her hand on the screening. "Do you believe that or were you just raised to say that?"

The hard surety in the girl's demeanor faltered. "I don't know."

The lady detective reached for the girl, but she backed away into the cool darkness of the room, eyes down at her feet. She turned and ran into the warmth of the kitchen. Two voices in tandem said, "You shouldn't upset her."

She leaned against back wall of the porch. "That wasn't the intent," she said, as two girls, dark and light, skipped past her and sat on either side of her partner, who settled on the swing once more.

"It's time." Dark Oona kicked her legs back and forth. Dusty black boots with ornate metal buttons up each side tipped from under her skirt as the swing moved.

Shadow sat his bowler on one knee, stopping the swing. "We know."

The lighter version of the girl grabbed his hat and turned it her hands before putting it on her head in a cocked, jaunty way. "We could take everyone back to the safe place."

He frowned. "But you told me—"

"We lie as much as adults. Didn't you know that?" The darker girl giggled.

Light Oona became solemn. "We can't run this time, sister. Thirteen is right. We can face anything."

Kate walked across the porch and knelt in front of the girl with white hair and crystal blue eyes. "Do you believe that or is this something you were taught to say?"

The girl's demeanor shifted from solemn to something much darker. The detective shivered as if it was the dead of winter. "Those two monsters who hurt me, hurt us, didn't teach me a damned thing, ma'am. Maybe it's something they taught the rest of them, but not me.

I know we can face this together." The pale-eyed child turned to Shadow. "Tell your brothers it ain't—"

Her dark other finished from his other side. "—isn't their choice."

The brother took his hat off the lighter girl's head and placed it back on his knee. "Are all of you of one mind in this?"

Light Oona jumped off the swing. "Only one way to know." She called out into the house as she skipped toward the front door.

Her dark self stayed behind on the swing. "It won't matter if we have consensus or not. We have to face this."

"Then why bother asking?" Kate joined her partner where the girl's other had been.

"This gives her a way to not be afraid." The black-haired girl kicked her legs again and Shadow pushed just enough to make the swing move just a bit.

34

There are only five of us to face down this thing," said Seth. He leaned over the pages of the ancient book and continued, "The book shows thirteen people in the circle."

"Maybe the rest doesn't have to include our family," said Duo as he whittled. Shavings scattered around his chair. Kate wasn't so sure that giving the boy a knife was wise, but he seemed docile enough for the moment.

"That's not what we were taught." Treze paced, arms crossed.

Quinn poured herself some water and offered her sister a cup. "A lot of things we were taught is nonsense. You of all people should understand that."

The older girl looked down at the floor, hands clenched. "That thing they're calling isn't nonsense. If we aren't all there as a family—"

"Maybe that monster won't be able to come in. What if Edison wanted to stop it from coming?"

"Now who's spouting nonsense?" said Duo, continuing to work. "You realize he and Mr. Harry are friends, right?"

Dark Oona rolled her eyes and looked up at the ceiling. Kate felt her/their impatience. The children had been going around about Niagara and what they should do for an hour or more.

"The adults should have a final say," said Light Oona, who kicked her legs back and forth and fidgeted, expressing her own impatience.

All of the children got quiet when Nikola and Sam came downstairs to join them at the table. The lady detective saw a similarity between them and Oona in that moment. Tesla was trim, wore a dark suit. His hair was parted in the middle and curled at the ends. His mustache was trimmed thin and sharp. He was handsome in a most precise manner. He surveyed the children for a moment, and his eyes shone, revealing a mixture of intelligence and wit that rose above the common. Sam wore a white suit that matched his wild white mane and mustache. His smile was more mischievous and childlike than his friend's, though he was as uncommon.

"These are the children you rescued?" asked the author.

"Not all of them," said the scientist, craning around the group to see if there were more. "Where are the rest?"

Treze curtsied, keeping her eyes low. "We don't know, sir."

Sam shook his head, his mane of gray whisping around his face. "Young lady, you are more formal than needed. We're just a pair of rogues here, eh, Nik?"

"We owe him our lives, mister. What's wrong with a bit of courtesy to our rescuer?"

Oona, both of her, ran to Nikola and before he could say no, embraced his legs and said in unison, "Thank you."

Seth, on the other hand, stared at Sam with his mouth agape. "Mr. Twain."

The scruffy author tipped the bowler he was wearing. "In the flesh, young man. I assume you've read my tall tales."

The boy grinned and nodded. "My pop has a few of your books. Can I shake your hand?" He came around the table and reached out.

The older man grabbed the boy's hand. "Your rescuer brought me into this little escapade. You can thank him."

Duo stood on his chair and roared. The room got quiet, and Shadow reached beneath his coat before he could stop himself. The boy crossed his arms as all eyes fell on him. "While this is all very charming, no one has suggested our next step."

Nikola went to the book. "It's obvious we need to stop your captors from allowing that thing into our world."

Quinn joined the man. "If all we need to do is stop it, I could do that in my sleep."

The young scientist arched his eyebrow. "I fear you are not as powerful as that, Miss Quinn. It won't be enough to hold it in place. We need to push it back into its own world."

"Isn't it already sort of here in the form of Mr. Harry?" Sam patted Seth on the arm and moved to take a place by the book, and the boy sat down, eyes never leaving his idol.

"I've been considering some things." Tesla tapped his head. "I don't think Mr. Harry is an avatar. He's a god in his own right and with a separate agenda."

Kate moved next to the scientist. He stepped to one side to give both of them more space. "Well then, why would he want to open the gate to let another god into this realm. Aren't gods notoriously jealous?"

"They do seem to want focus on themselves alone." The author scratched his head. "Perhaps that's it though." He nudged the sharp-dressed scientist, who flinched. "I think Nik here may be on to something."

"Of course, I am." Nikola's eyes sparkled like a kid at Christmas time. "Mr. Harry is fulfilling two needs in one step. Mr. Edison wants to use the god's energy. Mr. Harry wants to trap this god. Maybe it's a power play, much like when Zeus killed his father. He wants to ensure that this planet is his, so he takes out someone bigger while he can."

The lady detective leaned down and pointed at the page. "But why the children?"

Seth reached across the table and tapped the edge of the book. "Magic? Maybe our powers combine."

"That's never happened before." Duo jumped down from the chair.

"Maybe it only happens in that time and place." The older boy scruffled his brother's hair as the boy plopped down next to him on the bench.

"We all have our jobs and strengths." Treze recited in the same monotone she'd used at the screen door.

"Stop saying those things!" Quinn screamed and tears streaked her face as she lunged across the expanse of the table between them. Seth got up, but his younger brother caught him and shook his head.

If their older sister had been Medusa, everyone would have turned to stone. She took the girl by the chin and forced her to look into her eyes. "No matter how much you hate all of this, we have a job. All of us." Quinn skittered back off the tabletop, eyes closed. Seth held her close as she composed herself. Their sister stood, head held high, eyes far away.

"So, you're saying we go and help those two monsters call this god that will most likely kill us all?" Duo carved a piece of wood in his hand. A shape was taking form and he never paused even as he spoke.

Treze ignored him and went to Quinn She took her hands in her own. "All of those things we were taught, all of those things that they did to us we can use against them as well as for them."

Quinn turned red but looked her sister straight in the eye. Treze continued, "I—we" she nodded at Seth, "tried our best to protect all of you. We were the oldest, but we were children too. Some of the sayings are true though. We are family because we don't have anyone but each other. We have jobs and strengths. Our powers are all different. We have a choice. We can stand here and quarrel, or we can go to Niagara and stop Mr. Edison and Mr. Harry from calling this god."

Duo laid his carving knife on the table and grinned. "Oh good. A fight."

His older brother picked up the knife and fiddled with it. "But we aren't complete."

"Says who?" Thomas entered the room. Seth passed the knife back to the younger boy and nodded at the open book.

"Pop, the drawing..." said Seth.

The old showman pulled it to him and whistled. "That's one hell of a monster and y'all're planning on fighting it? Seems awful foolish. Five children facing a monster." He gave Kate a sharp glare. "You gonna let them do this?"

The question took her aback. She'd almost forgotten that they were children. "Mr. Lazarus, I have a feeling that none of us can stop them."

He nodded and stroked his long mustache with his fingers. "I've found that to be true of my boy. Once he puts his mind to something, he's hard to hold back. Much like his pop." He clapped Seth on the shoulder. "Son, are you thinking that you and your brother and sisters are going to go face whatever this thing is on your own?"

The boy glanced at his brother and sisters. "Well, I know you'll balk at the idea, so I was thinking of inviting you and the other adults to join us."

"That's some slick talking, boy, and a fine idea. I was worried that I'd have to explain to your ma why you had left her."

"She probably already knows."

"When do we leave?" asked Thomas.

Shadow entered the room, and Kate faded to the Outside only to re-emerge next to him.

"Any word from the Brotherhood?"

He walked them both back out of the room and closed the door.

"Our predicament is secondary to the abomination."

"Those children in there are prepping for all-out war, secondary or not."

"Allan would say you completed your part of the assignment when you found the girl." Kate started to protest, and her partner put up his hand. "I didn't say that was what I would say, but I'd like to point out that your mission isn't the same as mine anymore."

"The hell you say!" She turned her back on him to contain her aggravation. "The moment you became my partner, all of our missions are the same. Don't think you can put me on a train back to Chicago while you go gallivanting off with a bunch of ill-prepared children."

He took her hands. His quiet voice cut through her rant. "I wasn't telling you to go back to Chicago. You and I both know that even if Allan told you to come back, you'd end up in Niagara. I just wanted to remind you of your options."

"What if your brothers don't come to a consensus?"

"I'm going anyway. That boy's predicament is my fault. I should have made sure no one could bring those abominations back here."

She squeezed her partner's hands. "The Brotherhood is to blame, Shadow. Besides, the bigger problem is coming through that gate at Niagara. We'll figure out the abominations when they come at us."

He grinned and winked at her. "So, no game plan, huh?"

"Not a clue besides making sure that those children don't kill themselves once they get where they're going." Kate stepped back. From the next room, Thomas's voice pitched above the chatter, though not in an aggressive way.

"What about the adults?" asked Shadow.

She reached for the door. "They're on their own, I suppose."

"Will there be enough room on the *Eclipse?*"

The familiar voice of the pilot rose from the porch, "Enough room for what?"

I'm not sure the Brotherhood will approve, Mrs. Warne," said the pilot a few moments later.

Kate opened the screen door to allow her friend in. "Are we not completing a mission to protect the United States?"

"Well..." The Asian man scratched his head while looking at Shadow for some shred of support.

Shadow ignored the silent plea for help. "Can we all fit into the *Eclipse?*"

"Yes."

Kate kissed the pilot's cheek. "You are doing the United States a huge service, sir."

He turned and headed for the dining room. "No, I'm putting my job in jeopardy for the likes of all of you. If anything happens to my lady during this little escapade, Pinkerton owes me."

"I'll make sure he knows." She had no idea how she would convince Allan to pay the man back if the ship was destroyed, but compared to the coming of a god, that problem was miniscule.

The room buzzed with chatter and children skittering around when they entered.

Sho raised his voice above the din. "Hey, you Goober Pea Bummer, what you know?"

The old showman jumped and turned to face his attacker. Anger burned in his eyes till he laid them on the small Asian man in leathers. He made his way across the room and picked him up in a bear hug. "You old heathen, you!"

"I should have known you were involved in this. Where's Sarge?" Sho struggled to make Thomas put him down.

"At home with the wife, I suspect. Doesn't get out like the old days." The larger man put Sho back down.

"He's going to be awful upset when he finds out about this little caper." The Asian clapped his friend on the shoulder. "It's good to see you didn't die out there."

The older man led him to the table. "The whole of your Union army made a hearty effort to get rid of us, that's for sure. It's good to see you too."

The pilot looked around the table at each of the children, even Treze. "All of you want to fly to Niagara in my ship, is that it?"

The room erupted as all the children began talking at once.

"QUIET!" bellowed Thomas. "Let the eldest ones talk right now."

Seth reached out and shook the small man's hand. "How much do you know about this already?"

Sho shrugged and followed the boy, who led him to the book on the table. "I know there's something going on with Mr. Edison involving powerful god-level magic at Niagara Falls. I also know that you all are somehow a part of this mess and that I'm going to end up taking you to Niagara. The only thing I don't know is how soon we leave."

"How fast does your ship travel, mister?" Treze joined her brother and looked dead on at Sho. "We don't have long."

"You don't have a plan either," said Kate.

"And you do?" said the girl.

Kate ignored the question. "What were you supposed to do? What did they tell you to do when you got there?"

"Well, we were supposed to have twelve in the circle and one in the center. Each of us were to use our strengths and powers to help after the gate opened." The girl pointed at the book. "It's all right here. You've read it same as me."

The lady detective remembered something Edison's assistant said to her. "Mr. Harry said he was the gate. Is that true?"

"He says that a lot, but we aren't sure what he means," said Light Oona.

Duo finished his carving. It looked like a figure of some kind. "I think that god is coming through him."

Quinn sat down next to her brother and played with his knife. "We should kill him before that happens. That should be the plan."

Shadow took the knife from the girl. The blade shone like a star for a moment as he gave it back to the boy. "Maybe it won't come to that."

Kate saw a look ripple through all of the children that said what she was thinking. It would have to come to that.

She said, "We shall have to see, won't we?"

Stars spread across an early morning sky painted in shades of blue and purple when Kate made her way out of the house toward the ship. The gondola lights hadn't gone off all night, so she was sure that the pilot was awake. She wondered if the man slept at all.

"Coming to see what Sho's up to?"

She grinned. "You too, huh?" Her partner joined her on the rocky path. The starlight made him look paler and more striking. The lines of his shoulders were sharp when he should have just faded into the darkness.

They both laughed. "Have you sent that telegram to Allan yet?" he asked.

"The fellow at the train station was asleep when I went by earlier. I hated to wake him. He looked peaceful."

"You could have telegraphed him yourself and no one would have known," Shadow offered his arm, but she declined. "Why are you avoiding Allan?"

"I'm not."

He held up his hand. "But you are."

The look on his face told her just how much he understood about this situation she'd created for herself. She'd never told him anything and he never pried, but it was clear he knew enough about her romantic entanglement to have an opinion.

"He needs to let me go."

"Why?"

She faded into the Outside and then returned, "I'm dead and buried."

Her partner stopped on the path. "Except for him, the moment you came back to work, you weren't dead or buried. He sees you and sometimes he can touch you. Did you expect him to turn off his heart like one of Edison's incandescent lights?"

She hung her head. Shadow was the one person in her life that could cut right to her truths. It should have made her mad, but instead it made her appreciate him more. "I didn't consider any of that. When I learned I had a choice, my first thought wasn't about coming back to Allan. It was about the work and how being dead could help with the work. That's when I figured out that I didn't love him as much as I loved doing what we," she pointed at Shadow and back at herself, "do out here in the field."

"Did you tell him that?" He passed her his handkerchief.

She took it but refused to do more than fidget with it. "How do you tell someone who sat at your bedside for days and wept like a child at your grave that you don't love him?"

Her partner took the bunched-up square of cloth from her hand, tilted up her head, and wiped away her tears. "Kate Warne. You are one of the smartest, toughest women I've ever met. You are also one of the thickest when it comes to Allan Pinkerton. You love him. Otherwise, you wouldn't be so disturbed by all this."

"Maybe once this mess is done, I should just resign and go back to the Outside. I can't continue to torture him like this."

"Kate Warne doesn't rest on her laurels. You'd be back within a month."

"When I got to the Outside, I thought it meant that people got to become better and have a chance to live in a better way. It was a sort of second chance. My better chance was to choose to live in both realms and help people. Remember that boy that Quinn put in a tree?"

He nodded.

"I went searching for him in the Outside to hear his side of the story. He attacked me."

"It's not the first time you've been attacked."

"The attack isn't the point. He made it clear that he was thrilled to be dead because he could hurt more women in the Outside. After I put my boot in the boy's throat and ran him off, his grandfather came to me apologizing for the boy like it was his fault. Bad things can happen in the Outside, so I'd not be resting on my laurels."

"Are there detectives in the Outside?"

Kate took his arm. "I don't know, but there could be. I've done this work for most of my adult life. Maybe I could talk Allan into letting me open a Pinkerton's branch there and broaden our supernatural division. It won't be an exact resignation, but the separation will give him a chance to move forward."

"Separation won't change how he feels about you." He patted her hand as they began to walk.

"At least this way he won't see me in the office all the time." She stopped again. "I should go send that telegram."

"I can do it for you, and you can head for the ship.

She shook her head "Time to pull up my pantaloons and do my job. He's expecting an update, I'm sure."

Shadow headed toward the airship while Kate went to the train station to send her report. No doubt there was a telegram waiting for her as well.

36

Shadow came around the side of the ship where Sho leaned over with his hands on his knees gasping for air while Thomas shook the room with his larger-than-life laughter, his eyes revealing the mischief that seemed to drive him at all times. When the older man spotted Shadow, he stopped laughing, and he tapped the pilot on the shoulder.

"I swear that Sarge has his little treasures hidden all over this land," He ignored his friend and gasped between phrases.

Thomas said in a loud voice, "Yeah. I'm so glad that someone else didn't find it first."

The pilot continued, not hearing the danger in his friend's voice. "Good lord, there would have been no town. It'd have been one big FLABOOM!" He rose up to follow through on his mock-explosion and found himself facing Shadow in the early morning light.

"I'm not going to say a word. I trust your judgement." The detective sat down next to the old showman, while his drinking companion cleared his throat and looked at his feet.

"That's mighty good of you. This was my idea. Sho here had nothing to do with it beside helping me load a few boxes."

"The Brotherhood—" Worry crossed the Asian's face.

"Let's just say that I can keep secrets when I want. They won't find out until I file a report when this is all over. Just make sure the airship doesn't blow up."

"Don't mention this in front of Deborah. I'll never hear the end of this."

His friend fiddled with an empty liquor bottle. "You told me she sees all. Have you been lying to me all this time?"

Thomas laughed and waved his hand. "She probably knows everything, but I'd rather not mention it just the same."

"Mention what?" Seth came around the gondola with a cup of coffee in his hand.

"Is everyone awake now?" Thomas looked past the boy. "Where's your mother?"

"What are you up to?" His son sipped from his metal cup.

"I added some insurance for this little excursion of ours."

"Pop, Thirteen—I mean Treze, Oona, all of us have prepared for what's coming most of our lives."

"You think you all can manage a god with no help?" said Thomas.

"That's not what I meant." The boy offered the half-drunk cup to his pop. "I'm not sure any of you are going to be able to help us once that gate opens. I don't want you or Ma or any of the rest of you to end up dying because of us."

"We've already had this discussion once, so stop." He took the coffee from the boy, drained the cup, and handed it back. "Now go help your ma while I finish here."

The boy looked as though he wanted to say more, but settled on, "Yes, sir," and ran back to the house.

"If what you told me about him is true, you shouldn't worry, old man." Sho pulled out a wrench and gestured toward the retreating figure. "He's a good kid."

Thomas looked down at the ground. "We just got him back a few years ago. If his little trick doesn't work when we get to Niagara, his mother will come unhinged and then we could all be in trouble."

"Worse than what Edison is calling?" said Shadow.

The older man considered the question, then responded, "That's a tough call."

The pilot laughed despite the seriousness that faced them. "Where's Miss Kate?"

"Telegraph office. She is sending a report to Chicago so that the Pinkertons are up-to-date on our whereabouts."

"Any hope for reinforcements?" The pilot adjusted a gear on the side of his leg and then climbed up and opened a box on the side of the gondola. Thomas joined him and opened a toolbox on the ground.

"From the Brotherhood? I'm not sure. From Pinkertons? I have a feeling someone will meet us at Niagara even if Kate requests otherwise. Let's hope those reinforcements don't complicate matters," said Shadow.

"And if the boy's father shows up wanting another piece of Sho's ship?" The showman picked up a tool with an odd basket-like widget at one end. His friend took it without looking and continued to work. "Will the Brotherhood want to be involved then?"

"The Brotherhood is struggling with the answer to that question, Thomas Lazarus." Shadow's voice echoed as many were speaking through him at one time. His vision blurred and his head felt like it may explode.

"Hey, I got their attention." The older man's eyes darkened and revealed a hardness that Shadow had faced before. "Look, I don't know all the complexities of your organization or even who you are, but one of yours managed to father a child and is now hunting that child. I'm sure Mr. Jones here has explained by now why that child is important to me."

"Neither are one of us." Shadow fought back against the others who were using him as a conduit. He wanted to deny this, but they forced him back.

"Sho was telling me this. Y'all cast him and some of his closest friends out and locked them away except you didn't do a very good job of it since he's been out running around for at least fifteen years." Thomas's fists clinched and his shoulders tightened. He stepped closer to Shadow. "Fifteen years and none of you knew he was out hurting folks."

Sho grabbed at his friend's broad shoulder, but the showman pushed him away.

"We didn't know that some of us could keep secrets." The Brotherhood spoke through the detective. "We have learned different since that time."

"All of you are holding back help for my boy because you didn't know one of your own was a liar? Which one was it? Do you even know?" The older man drew his pistol and cocked it as he stepped closer. "Was it you, Mr. Jones?"

The pilot stepped between the two men. "There's no use for violence, Thomas. Think of the children."

"I am."

Shadow pushed past his brothers and found the barrel of a gun in his face. He raised his hands and said in his own voice, "It was another, but it was all of us. We were so sure of ourselves then even after turning out the abominations. Please lower the gun."

Thomas lowered the gun. "So that's what you call him—abomination. What does that make Seth?"

"I'm not sure."

The pilot turned to face the detective. His relief was palpable. "Based on what Thomas has told me, the boy is one of you."

"The Brotherhood was made, not born. We aren't even supposed to be able to—"

"And yet, here we are, my friend." Sho threw up his hands "Seth is the first-born Brother."

Words failed Shadow for a few moments. The idea of a born brother was a lot to take in. He could feel the collective's muttering tickle at the back of his mind. He pushed them farther back but was unsure if that would be enough to shut them out. "We need to keep this under our hats for now." He extended his hand to the old showman. "I'm so sorry for all of this."

Thomas stared at it for a long moment. The pilot nudged him, and the older man shrugged before taking the detective's offer. "Don't apologize. Help me put my boy's father down for good."

"I see we're all working to get this ship off the ground," said Kate as she came up the trail. The sun was painting golds and reds across the sky.

"How was the report?" Shadow turned at the sound of her voice.

"Short. I mentioned that we were heading to Niagara."

"And the rest?"

She crossed her arms. "Mr. Jones, you are rather nosy today, aren't you?"

"Just concerned."

"Your concern is noted. Allan planning to come to Niagara. It is not what I want, but he is the boss. Now tell me what those two have been up to." Thomas and Sho were heading into the airship.

Her partner offered her his arm. "Just planning and packing. Let's go make sure that the children are ready, shall we?"

She took his arm as they headed toward the house. The windows from the kitchen were already lit up and Treze was hustling in with a bucket of water. The girl's bag was on the back step. The Oona(s) came skipping out from the back door of the kitchen and sat her/their bag next to her/their sister's. Kate wasn't sure she was ready to talk about her conversation with Allan, nor was she ready to talk about the decision she'd made concerning their problem. All that mattered for now was making sure that these children didn't end up dead or worse, helping to invite in something that could make her personal problems a moot point.

3 7

E verything's so tiny," said Dark Oona.

"It doesn't look real," said her other.

Kate nodded as the girls watched the world below rolling out before her/them as the airship made its way to Niagara. The trees and towns, cities and rivers created a green, gold, and brown quilt that spread toward the horizon. Wagons and trains moved like ants across a picnic spread. She could understand why the girls couldn't believe it was real.

Treze said, "It's all real. Even what you can't see." She joined her sister(s) at the panoramic window.

She said in unison, "Especially what you can't see."

The older girl leaned closer to the glass. Her shoulders dropped a little as she continued to watch life in miniature below. It was good to see her relax even for a moment, Kate thought. Dark Oona caught Kate's eye and winked as if she'd heard the thought. Truth was, the girls probably had. She was glad that they were distracted by something so simple. In just a few hours, if the book was true and they failed to stop what was coming, all of the things that were real below would be traded for a new, darker reality.

The lady detective asked, "What do you see, Oona?"

Treze's shoulders tensed, and the girls looked at one another.

Light Oona fiddled with the blue bow in her hair, twisting one end around her finger. Her dark other stopped her, shaking her head. "You've seen the book."

"Yes, but is there more?"

The oldest of them turned, fist balled and face hard. "What my sister is telling you is that she doesn't want to talk about it right now."

"I can talk about it." The pale girl in blue stepped between Kate and her sister. "The world could become a battleground, ma'am,"

Dark Oona looked as if she'd never seen her lighter self before. "You're not afraid?"

Light Oona tugged at her other's ebony hair. "The vision is changing. Before it was just us. When we called Shadow, we got help. I'm not so scared now."

Treze said, "Are you saying we can fight that thing now?"

"I don't know." Light Oona shrugged and shuffled her feet. "I just feel hopeful."

Her sister in black fiddled with her own bow now. "Wishful thinking isn't going to destroy what's coming. We must be practical."

"Tell me what's more practical—hiding in our safe place while that thing eats our world or fighting with all our might?" The light girl took her other's hand.

"Hiding seems pretty practical."

"We already made the decision to go fight, so this discussion is sort of moot, right?" Treze turned back toward the window. Kate noticed that the number on her neck looked red around the edges.

Her pale younger sister stood behind her and played with her sister's hair until it covered the number. "The point is that our chances have shifted in a positive direction."

Dark Oona said, "And what about Mr. You-Know-Who?"

The light girl's eyes widened, and her hand shook. She closed her eyes and clenched her fists. "You and me, we can take him down."

Her dark other stepped back again. "Good lord, you sound like me."

The paler of the two skipped around her other. "I guess you're a good influence. I am hopeful and less afraid." She giggled, joined arms, and skipped out. One of them said something about Sam and cookies as the door slid closed.

Maybe her/their older sister had answers though why the girls were so important to Edison or why he would hire Pinkertons to find a child that his godlike assistant had already located on three different occasions was a mystery.

Kate joined Treze at the bay window. "Why would Mr. Edison hire us to just find you?"

"Your partner said he was using me to track the other children."

"Mr. Harry can find them, so that idea doesn't make much sense, now does it?"

"I didn't answer Mr. Jones." A look of disdain crossed the girl's face as it reflected in the window. "What makes you think I'll give you an answer?"

"I don't know." The lady detective sat on large windowsill and gazed down at the verdant landscape that passed below them. "I can see him wanting to come after Seth or even Oona, but not you."

The two of them sat in silence as the ship passed through some fluffy clouds that obscured their view. The detective rose to leave the room. She wouldn't force the issue even if the answer could help. The girl didn't trust them as it was. Just as she slid the door and stepped out, she heard Treze's skirts rustle.

"He ate some of us, you know," said Thirteen in a soft matter-of-fact tone.

Kate paused and turned without meeting the girl's gaze. "Mr. Harry?"

The girl nodded and sniffled. "When he can't find Spectrals, he eats the children in the facility."

"But there were only thirteen of you when you Mr. Tesla rescued you. Haven't you always been the same group?" The detective sat back down. She wished for tea but didn't want to upset the girl more by conjuring a cup in front of her.

"We were the strongest. He told Edison to keep us and help us learn about our powers. Edison had no idea how to help us, so he did what he does best—experiment. He'd figure out what we could do and then use us to help him with all sorts of strange things. Seth kept us alive. Mr. Edison was fascinated with my ability to cause bad things to happen and experimented with me many times. The weaker children weren't treated the same. They were given to Mr. Harry, and we'd never see them again." The girl turned her head. "Once, I offered myself in exchange for a little girl who had come to our group but wasn't strong enough to keep up. Mr. Harry said I wasn't meant for him and took her from us." She clenched her fist. Kate offered her a handkerchief.

"Who were you meant for then?"

Treze ignored her offer. "At first, I thought I was meant to guard the others, but after she was taken from me, I wasn't sure. Then I saw the book, and Mr. Edison began to explain our roles in the event. Each one of us had a job."

"And then you were taken away from all that."

The girl stared out the window. "The best day and worst day of my life was when Mr. Tesla put us on that train. We were free, but I had to let go of the only family I ever had piece by piece. Then I had to figure out how to not hurt people."

"Did Mr. Edison want to find you to protect people? That's what he told Mr. Jones."

Treze's laughter was harsh and tinged with bitter disappointment. "Mr. Edison? Protecting people? You must be joking? He never protected us, not once. Think about that book for a moment. Where is the thirteenth figure?"

"In the middle of the circle. Are you a focal point for magic?"

The ship moved into some gray clouds, casting a shadow over them both. Kate's companion closed her eyes and her jaw tensed. "I'm the sacrifice."

Kate was stunned and enraged at the same time. She wanted to scream and throw things. That anyone would want to use a child to placate a god. Instead, she choked back and coughed. "I'm sorry."

"Don't feel sorry for me." The girl said as she hit the window with her fist. "Seth thinks he can save me, but he's wrong. If I'm sacrificed, then I won't go where he can save me."

"I don't understand."

"When Seth dies, he goes to a place where there are doors. He's told me that there are doors for all thirteen of us. If I go there, he can unlock a door for me to return to the Inside."

"That thing Harry's summoning eats souls, doesn't it?"

"If it's like Mr. Harry, I fear so. I won't go Outside or to Seth's room of doors if I'm sacrificed."

"Oona doesn't know?"

"She sees a lot, but she hasn't seen this."

"How do you know this is the plan? That figure could be anyone at all." The detective knew she was grasping at straws.

Treze turned to Kate, her eyes were on her boots. "Mr. Edison told me right before Mr. Tesla released us. I felt important and relieved,"

"Relieved?"

"If I was sacrificed, I couldn't cause more bad things, don't you see?" She threw up her hands. "I wouldn't hurt other people anymore. I want to be free of myself. I'm bad for everyone. The only real way to be free of myself and the bad luck I spread is to die."

The clouds grew denser and darkened to a steel color. The ship shook as though it was a stagecoach on a rough patch of trail. Pellets of ice cracked against the window. Lightning flashed and the ship tilted to one side, throwing both women to the floor.

Kate pulled herself up and offered her hand to Thirteen, who ignored her and pulled up on one of the chairs instead. The ship rocked, throwing them both toward the bar in front of the window.

"I'm sorry. I swear I didn't look at anyone or think bad things about any of you."

"This isn't you," said Kate.

Treze raised her arm to her face as more ice blasted across the glass. "How do you know?"

At that moment something dark rushed past the window and into the storm. Kate was sure she heard laughter as it passed.

"Do you know Seth's father?"

Thirteen frowned. "I've met Dr. Lazarus, of course."

"Dr. Lazarus is not his father." A dark figure with wings came at the window and then pulled up hard. The ship shook once again, throwing them both against the furniture. "That thing is."

38

Shadow climbed through the open hatch of the bridge as the ship rocked hard to one side.

Sho pulled levers and spun a few wheels along the wall. He glanced back at the Pinkerton. "I didn't know the Brotherhood could call up storms."

The engine coughed hard and the pilot cursed under his breath.

"We can't."

The abomination swooped out of the heavy cloud and clapped its hands. The windows around the bridge rattled hard and the ship listed to one side throwing everyone to the floor except Sam, who clung to the wheel.

Thomas popped up through the hatch. "Is it time to pull out Sarge's surprise?"

The ship dropped out from under them, and the sky went from dark to bright blue in a matter of seconds. The engines coughed once more and then smoothed out. It was as though nothing had happened.

Sam held the wheel steady but tried to look out of every window. "Where did it go?"

Kate and Treze held on to each other until the ship stopped shaking and the sky blazed blue through the windows.

They both stood up. The detective said, "We need to find the others."

They found Seth in the hall heading toward the ladder to the bridge. Fear darkened his usually kind eyes. "Ma's in a trance. She won't wake up. She's fighting him. I know it."

Treze grabbed her brother's arm. "That thing's really your father?"

"Yes. If I don't get out to him, he's going to kill Ma and maybe all of you to get to me."

Kate held on to one side of the ladder to steady herself. "How will you get to him?"

The boy shrugged. "I don't know. Maybe I'll just call to him. If he gets me, you all will be safe."

"We can't leave you with that thing." His sister didn't let go.

"I don't think you get that choice." He shook out of her grip and looked her dead in the eyes. "Please watch over Ma. I'm going to find Pop."

He climbed the ladder and left them alone in the dim corridor.

The girl turned to the lady detective. "Aren't you going to try to stop him?"

"How'd that work out when you tried?" Kate stepped past her and headed toward the passenger berths. "Go find the others. I'll sit with Deborah and try to figure out how to help her."

"Pop!"

Thomas rushed to his son as he made his through the hatch. "I thought for sure you'd be gone."

"Ma's fighting him. She dropped into a trance when the storm started."

The panic filled the old showman's face. "She can't! She's terrible weak. That crazy woman."

"I need to get out to him. He wants me." The boy ran to the window and gazed out into the blue.

Shadow joined him. "Why does he want you? What use are you to him?"

"It's the keys. He wants my keys."

"What sort of keys?" He'd never heard of any of the Brotherhood needing keys for what they did.

"There's no time to explain. I have to get out there before he kills her." The showman's son started pacing. Shadow wasn't sure if he or Thomas was more upset.

Thomas grabbed his son's shoulders. "Is flying one of your powers, boy? How do you expect to get out there?"

"I don't know."

Sho looked thoughtful and made his way to the opposite side of the deck. He opened the door to a black metal cabinet and nodded at Thomas.

"Hey, grayback."

The showman's dark brown eyes widened when he turned to respond. "Holy hell, Sho."

The pilot eyes sparkled with delight. Inside the cabinet were three leather suits hanging on one side. On the other side were three metal contraptions that looked like soldiers' backpacks made of copper.

Tesla pushed past Thomas and examined the backpacks. "They are engines, yes?"

The pilot pulled out one of the suits and held it up. "They're just to get you off the ground and up into the air."

Thomas joined the men and took the leather uniform from his friend. "He's being modest. The Federals used these contraptions to scout ahead as they made their way to Atlanta and then the sea. They flew high enough that our boys couldn't shoot 'em down. You're the bastard behind that, huh?"

"When the abominations failed, the president had no choice but to accept my secondary plan." The showman gave the small pilot a dark look.

Shadow felt a tension he'd felt many times since the war. "You okay, Dr. Lazarus?"

The older man didn't respond. Instead, he examined the suit as if looking to see if he would die from touching it.

"Pop?"

The Asian hung his head. "I'm sorry, Thomas."

"It was wartime. You did your job just like I did mine," he said.

Nikola cleared his throat and tapped one of the metal packs in the cabinet. "And they are in working order?"

Sho shot a look of surprise at the man. "Of course, they are. I tinker with them and clean them as much as I can."

"I could fly that up into the cloud." The boy sauntered up to the group. He took the suit from his pop. Thomas was not amused.

"No."

Seth threw the suit down. "Ma is up there fighting him right now. I thought you loved her!"

His pop turned on him, tears in his eyes. "Don't you ever doubt my love for your ma!"

"But—"

"Hush boy. You aren't going," The boy gestured to the window and started to protest. The showman waved his arm. "Not alone. I'm not going to let that thing come after the two dearest people in my life and not take a stand. Excuse me, Mr. Tesla."

He reached past the scientist and pulled out one of the other suits. "You Feds were kind of small."

The pilot laughed. "Deborah feeds you too well, old man."

Thomas joined his friend. "You speak truths. Show us how these things work so I can go get my woman back."

A little while later, Thomas and Seth were suited up and standing at a door that opened into the sky. The storm cloud far above rumbled as parts of it lit up in different places at different times.

The snake-oil salesman glanced up at open sky. "She must be giving him hell."

Seth grimaced. "That should be me up there."

"Well, now's your chance, boy." He flipped a switch, closed his eyes, and jumped. Shadow leaned forward at the window close by as the older man dropped below the airship. He heard what he thought was an explosion below them. This was followed by a whoop as Thomas rushed up and hovered like a hummingbird.

Seth pulled down his goggles, took a deep breath and stepped off into the open air as the storm rumbled around him. The engine on his back coughed and then yanked him up as well. With just a little maneuvering, the boy managed to hover next to his father. Both gave little salutes to Sho before flying toward the cloud.

Kate's eye was caught by something flying past the window of the berth where Deborah lay. She rushed over and leaned to get a better look. Two men in brown leather suits were flying up to the storm cloud.

"Dammit."

A sharp gasp made her turn away. The witch sat up. "I am on the Inside, no?"

The detective took the older woman's hand. "Yes. You're back on the airship."

"Oh, the ringing." She held her head in her hands then glanced around the cabin. "Those fools."

"Who, ma'am?"

"My boys." The woman began speaking a different language. From her tone, Kate imagined she was cursing.

Treze slid the door open. "Mr. Jones sent me to tell you—"

The witch waved the girl in. "They went to the cloud."

The girl sat down opposite Kate. "To get you back."

Deborah fell back onto the bed, her dark hair spreading out behind her like a veil. "You old fool," she muttered. "He will kill you both for those keys."

"Keys?" The lady detective leaned forward.

The girl took the older woman's hand. "Remember that room I told you about? The one where Seth can come and bring us back."

Kate nodded.

"It has to be the keys to those rooms. I'm not sure why anyone would want them. They just save those of us who are family."

"Did he go and bring back any other creatures from the dead when you were at Menlo Park?" asked Kate.

The girl cocked her head to one side and frowned. "Not that I know of."

Before the lady detective could ask more questions, Shadow entered the room. "How is Deborah?"

The older woman sat back up and pointed at him. "Deborah, good sir, is aggrieved because you let her menfolks go off on a foolish mission." She broke into her second language and tried to stand.

Shadow offered his hand to the woman, and she became more agitated. "Thomas said you'd be angry."

Deborah pushed past him and almost fell against Treze. The girl took her by the elbow and steadied her as she stumbled to the window. She gestured to Kate. "I must go fight again."

"I can go with you." She joined the witch and the girl marked thirteen to gaze into the sky.

Kate's partner cleared his throat and broke into the discussion. "This is my fault. I should go."

The older woman turned back to him. "Will the Brotherhood stop you?"

He slid the door behind him shut. "They want me to fix this problem, so my guess is no."

"You haven't asked them?" The look of defiance answered her question.

The witch took his hand and began to sing. The lady Pinkerton tried to get between them, but her partner closed the gap by taking Deborah's other hand.

"Get the rest of the crew to Niagara. Allan is expecting you. He'll be livid if you don't arrive."

Kate put her hand on his shoulder. "And if things go badly?"

He adjusted his hat and his eye twinkled in that way they did when there was work to be done. "Mrs. Warne, they won't."

Slanted rain pelted the windows in spite of the robin-egg blue of the sky around them. Deborah slapped at her new companion. "Enough talk. We must go!" She began her song again and a rift in the wall opened to roiling gray clouds. Both of them stepped out and the rift closed.

39

Silver lightning crackled as the Brother and the witch stepped out into a roiling gray space. Thomas and Seth were hanging by tendrils of mist that twisted and tightened when they struggled. The older woman trembled, and her eyes went black. This was no fearful tremble. She began singing under her breath. Shadow wasn't sure which was more terrifying.

The abomination, for Shadow refused to speak its name, stepped from behind his captives. A grin split across its shiny onyx face. "My beloved, you've returned and brought me a gift. How unexpected." It reached for the detective but drew back as a ring of fire blazed up around its visitors. The fire jumped, as if living, lit its fingers and ran up its dark arm.

"Damn you, woman."

Deborah continued to sing as if she'd neither seen nor heard a thing.

Thomas rocked hard against his wispy binding and swung back and forth as if connected to the top of the sky itself. "I'm not sure she's the one who's damned."

The abomination threw the fire on its arm at Thomas. The witch cried out and the fireball as well as the protective barrier around her dissipated. With a twitch of the creature's wrist, Deborah gagged and kicked. Her eyes rolled for lack of air.

"I never liked her songs," it said.

Seth screamed. Shadow moved past his companion and grabbed the thing's arm. "Put her down. She's done nothing to you."

It flexed its wings and pushed the Brother back hard enough to make him drop below the group floating in the storm clouds. "She made a deal with me a long time ago that is not your concern, Mr. Jones."

"My boy made his decision," Thomas said. As the detective rose back up, he noted a twinkle in the older man's eyes that seemed out of place in such a dire moment.

"Patience was never strong in your kind. Put her down. I'm sure something can be worked out." The detective stopped in front of the winged creature, angled where the old showman was blocked behind him. He wanted to give the showman some time for whatever he was up to. "Deborah says you want keys, and the boy can give them to you, is that right? Why didn't you come to the one who locked you up in the first place?"

"And have you just toss me back into the Between? Children are malleable. All of this would have been easier if my darling hadn't run away with that peddler."

"You're just like him!" said Seth.

Thomas said, "Hush, boy. Yeah, let's work something out where Deborah doesn't die."

The detective was glad the boy's father caught on fast. He heard the man's wife gasp hard as if the thing had relaxed its grip.

"Phalanx."

"Oh, you do remember our name, Brother. How quaint," said the creature. It dropped its arm and Shadow heard the flutter of skirts and another hard gasp from the woman behind him.

Shadow pulled an ornate key from his jacket. "Let them alone forever, and I'll release all of you." He heard the showman moving around some more and there were some whispers. Out of the corner of his eye, he saw the glimmer of metal. Even though the thought of offering it the key made him sick, he knew the possibility would distract it.

Phalanx's eyes narrowed and the stars that glittered across his skin turned to pinpricks. Then it laughed. "Why would you do that, Brother?"

"What we did to you was wrong. I could convince our brothers to take you back. We could help you return to our code—"

Phalanx laughed harder. "My Brothers are creatures of chaos. If we controlled your colonists, we could wage war on every continent. The bloodshed would be delicious."

"You couldn't stop your own brothers from locking you up. How do you expect to control an entire army of men who have fought to be free all this time?" Shadow moved closer to his once-brother.

The creature met him toe-to-toe, forgetting the family that had been his prey only moments before. "For all your so-called honor, you lied to us then. We were victorious, just like you wanted. Instead of celebrating, you threw us into a hole like so much war garbage."

"We did everything we could to keep that from happening."

It snarled and opened its wings. "How would we know? We were cut out of the collective after our glorious victory at Kennesaw Mountain. The silence was painful. And you, Brother, led the way for it all."

Darkness surrounded Shadow, but he couldn't open a way to the Paths. All he could see was eyes of all shapes staring at him. Mewling voices rose around him, piercing his mind, cutting him off from his Brothers. "How does it feel to be alone?"

Before he could respond, the voices were cut off by a huge boom from outside this pocket world. The force of an explosion shook him hard. The eyes around him faded and he fell backward into the Paths. His head hurt, but he could feel the collective of the Brotherhood in the back of his mind once more. Light shone in on him and he saw that Phalanx was arching backwards from the explosion. It steadied itself midair and swooped down, attacking Seth from behind. As it wrapped its smoldering wings around the boy, it screamed like a bird of prey and faded away. The showman's son dropped on a cloud like a broken marionette.

"Well, shit," Thomas scrambled to his son's limp body.

Shadow crawled out of the Paths and made his way to the small family. He checked Deborah, who was unconscious but alive. He knelt beside the snake-oil salesman.

"Where did that thing go?" the older man asked.

The witch sat up, eyes wide. "He's in my boy! Thomas, he's got him!"

A sardonic grin spread over the boy's face. He screamed.

She crawled across the clouds and latched onto the detective's arm. "We will go after them. Now."

Thomas moved to her side and said, "My love, you are too weak."

She gave him a look that could wither flowers at fifty paces. The force of that look scared Shadow as much as it seemed to scare her husband. She yanked his sleeve. "We will go now." A song that sounded stronger than she looked rose from her throat. Her voice was hoarse and raspy, but forceful.

"Where?" Darkness rose around them, and the detective embraced it.

"The Between, of course," she said between stanzas.

He raised his hand to try to make her stop singing. "You can't go there." She ignored him and used his arm to get to her feet.

She continued the tune and sang to him. "I go where I like, Mr. Jones. Now we will bring Seth back. Will you open the Paths or shall I?"

Shadow looked over at Thomas who backed away, hands raised in a sign of defeat. "You can argue, but you won't win."

The witch moved close to her husband and took his face in her hands. "You take that deathtrap on your back and fly back to the ship. I will bring our son back soon."

He leaned down and kissed her. "You're trembling."

"Don't worry over me, you old fool."

"If you die, who's going to fix my breakfast?"

She swatted him. "I imagine you'll survive on burnt eggs and bitter coffee, no? Or maybe find one of those pretties that come to your shows who will cook for the starving old man?"

He took her hands and looked down at his feet. "It should be me going."

His wife kissed each of his rough, heavy hands and released them. "Sarge will be upset if you don't use those explosives at Niagara."

Thomas grinned at the Pinkerton. "I told you she probably knew."

Shadow offered his hand to the man. "We'll be back with the boy soon." It was a promise he hoped to be able to keep.

Thomas shook his hand while never taking his eyes off the woman he'd loved for decades. He cranked the pack on his back and hovered until the detective and his wife stepped into the dark portal that was open behind them.

"Seth!" The old witch paused and covered her face. Her son was draped in stars and darkness. Anger, pain, and sadness flowed from him and echoed in the space that was the Between. He screamed, but this faded into a mad laughter. Shadow reached for his companion, who'd sunk to her knees in anguish. She peeped up from behind her hands. Her eyes were dry and had a sharp cast to them.

"He is one of us now, woman." Phalanx spoke through the boy.

Deborah stood and muttered under her breath. Her delicate hands glowed, and her eyes turned black. The muttering became a shout and blue lightning crackled and lit the dimness of the Between. It struck and went through the boy but didn't seem to faze him.

More mocking laughter rose around them. "You see, my boy? She attacked us. She doesn't love you."

The laugh was cut off by another scream. The figure doubled over as if in great pain. Deborah ran to go to it, but Shadow held her back.

When it stood up again, they saw the boy's face where once there'd only been darkness. "Let me handle him, ma. He wants to waste all of your energy and kill you." His voice choked off and his face melted back into the starry darkness.

"Let our boy fight, woman, if that's what he wants. I'm bored with you anyway."

Shadow reached out to the darkness of the Between and opened a hole in the floor beneath the abomination. Phalanx tutted at his brother. "This isn't your concern." The opening slid across the floor under the detective's feet. Had he not embraced the darkness the opening would have closed him off from the Between.

When Shadow reemerged, his once-brother was covered in purple flame and a faint but familiar song echoed from everywhere and nowhere at the same time. Deborah was crouched as if ready to attack, but she wasn't singing nor was any of her usual music flowing from her. The tune grew louder, and the heat of the magical fire intensified. He stepped in front of the witch to shield her, but had to back away. She never flinched, and the fire never spread.

Pictures formed in rising flames, becoming more distinct with each new verse and stanza. There were no words, only music. Thomas appeared first, dressed in his robes and turban as if it were show time. His laughter filled the room as a picture of him giving Seth books rose and then faded. Next were the children, some of them Shadow had never seen before. Treze came into view, her face as plain and strong as ever, holding Seth's hand. The final image was Deborah, singing and walking through stars and flames, reaching out toward them.

The song rose in volume and a sense of joy overcame the despair that, till this point, had flooded the space. The Pinkerton saw tears flowing down the old witch's face, but she also smiled. He couldn't help but smile himself. The figure that had been Seth faded into the darkness of the Between. The song stopped.

"What's happening?" he asked.

Deborah wiped her face with her sleeve. "He's gone." She took his hand and started to sing the song to open the portal back to the Inside.

Before she got through her verse, a blinding light cut through the darkness and a series of white doors formed a wall around them. Each one of them had a number, one through fourteen. Shadow let go of her hand and checked each one. They were locked.

A heavy thump followed by a groan and a cry from the older woman caused him to turn. Seth was crumpled, scraped up and naked, on the almost blinding white floor. The boy scrambled to his feet, looking less human and more like a wild animal being hunted. In his right hand was a large ring filled with keys. Deborah started for him but a too-familiar whoosh came from above, knocking her down. Phalanx dropped near the boy and wrapped his wings around him.

The boy's mother began whispering to herself. The detective couldn't make out any part of her words except, "Focus on the light, my little one."

Phalanx laughed and flipped one wing at her. She rolled back hard against a door marked with the number thirteen. "He's one of the Brotherhood. Shadow knows, woman. Our boy walks in the darkness because he is darkness. He can't focus on light."

"Without light, there can be no darkness." The detective recited. He didn't understand how his opponent had forgotten this part of the law.

The mirth on the abomination's face vanished. At first, Shadow wondered if his response was to blame, but then Phalanx fell backward as the boy pushed from between the star-flecked wings that held him. He held a key ring high above his head as he tripped over his own feet, blinded by the glare of the doors. The boy hit the floor and skidded until he bumped against the one marked with the number that was his given name. His winged progenitor sprang to his feet. Shadow could sense the fury inside the creature.

Phalanx towered over his son who clutched the keys needed. "Where are we, boy? Are we in your mind?"

Seth slid along the curve of the wall out of his father's reach.

"You had your chance. When I catch you, I will take the keys and kill you for good." The creature's wings mewled and groaned like hungry cats.

Seth stopped at a door with a golden 14 emblazoned on it. His mother squeezed his hand and then scrambled toward the detective, who was not sure what to do.

"Brothers can't die. You said so yourself." Seth reached for the knob and pulled himself to his feet.

Shadow spoke up. "He's right, Phalanx."

"I killed our Brother, Mr. West. Right in front of your lovely partner, I might add. All I left was mush." He stepped closer to the boy, who refused to break eye contact with his father.

The detective pursued the discussion. Maybe this would distract the thing long enough to allow Seth to do whatever it was he had in mind. "You killed his form, perhaps. He hasn't left us. I guess when you were made, you didn't have much time to learn the nuances of our people or maybe you just didn't pay attention."

The abomination turned to focus on his brother, eyes narrowing. "I know all that every Brother knows." Phalanx opened its mewling wings, revealing eyes of all sizes. They all glared at the detective as he got as close as he dared.

"Are you sure? We were in a bit of hurry when we created our new brothers. I'm sure you learned everything though. We are people of precision, after all."

Seth ran his fingers around the ring, touching each key till he came to the last one. His eyes widened. He took the key and slid it into the lock of door 14, and he opened the portal.

A hot, dry breeze blew into the room. The door opened onto a desert scene that had as its centerpiece a red stone tower with a flat top. The sky was striped with a blue and orange sunset. The breeze became more intense as it whipped around Shadow, pulling him off his feet as the wind tugged him toward Phalanx and the exit behind the creature. The wind shifted and dropped him to the floor as it recentered around the creature. It opened its wings, but the wind howled and wrapped them around its body.

Seth stepped around, gazing up at Phalanx like it was a pinned insect. "I can't kill you, Father, and I don't believe you can kill me. I can, however, protect everyone else from what you want to do."

A whirlwind of red sand rose on the other side of the door. Shadow heard Deborah gasping hard as if the air was being sucked from her. The cyclone of sand, looking every bit like whirling blood entered the room and circled around the winged creature. As it whipped around him, the Pinkerton could see cuts forming on its face. Seth stepped back as the mini sandstorm paused at the threshold.

Phalanx's voice rose above the scream of the sand and wind, which took on the shape of its face and body. "Another war is coming, my Brother. Only not just between those ridiculous colonists you love so much." The abomination-shaped sandstorm turned to the boy. It shook hard and a raw, bloodied hand reached out, stripped of skin. Clean bone showed at the joints. "We could stop this war together."

"I like being just me." With that, the boy kicked the winged former brother as hard as he could. His father's screams mixed with the howl of the red sandstorm as it pulled him through to the other side. The door slammed, cutting the painful shriek off, leaving them abruptly in silence. Deborah crumpled to the floor, gasping.

Seth scrambled to her and hugged her close. "Ma, I didn't mean to hurt you. I didn't know."

The old witch reached up and patted his cheek. "Hush, now. You are naked. We will find clothes."

He turned as red as one of her scarves and turned away. "You can't see me like this!"

She started laughing and sat up. "As if I've never seen my baby without clothes."

Shadow offered his coat, and Seth wrapped it around his waist. "Don't tell Pop."

His mother laughed some more as she got to her feet and brushed off her skirts. "He will tell the story of how you defeated that creature with no clothes on, my son."

"That's what I'm afraid of!"

She embraced him, coat and all and whispered a song. The air shimmered and a rustic shirt and some pants formed around the boy. A small bowler finished off the outfit. "Now that you are decent, I think we are ready to leave, no?"

Seth handed the Pinkerton his coat. The white room faded out as the boy took his ma by the arm and their companion took her arm on the other side. Together they parted the darkness and stepped out onto a field of grass. A steady roar filled the air and a cool white mist rose around them. In the distance, people strolled and picnicked in the silvery sunlight of a mild fall afternoon.

"What is this place?" Deborah shaded her eyes against the brightness.

Shadow said, "Niagara Falls."

40

Kate helped Thomas when he stumbled through the side entrance of the hovering airship as he turned off the pack on his back.

"Where are the others?" she asked as he pulled up his goggles and began to take off the leather flying suit.

"Your partner and my wife went somewhere called the Between. Said I couldn't go, but that Seth was there."

Kate had heard of a place that wasn't Inside or Outside. She'd thought it might be like what the Catholics called Purgatory.

She pulled the door shut and spun a large wheel to lock it. "We can't wait for them. That thing in Niagara is coming and we have to be there."

"And my boy and wife?"

"My partner will get them to Niagara as promised." The lady detective reached to pick up the tanks, but the man waved her off and grabbed it and the suit from the floor.

"If he and Deborah can go to this Between place and live, I suppose they can get there as well. I'm pretty sure there's nothing that can stop my beloved if she puts her mind and magic into it." He headed up the ladder that led to the living quarters of the ship. She waited till he was clear and followed. The older man offered his hand once she'd made it to the hatch.

Taking hold, she allowed him to pull her up. "In the meantime, we need a real plan. Let's go find Nikola and Sam. I have a feeling they are already up to something."

Duo ran up to them as Thomas gathered the suit and tanks.

"I can't find the girls." He grabbed hold to Kate's arm.

"Maybe they went to visit Mr. Sho?"

His grip tightened. "I've looked everywhere, ma'am." As he spoke, he faded as though he was going Outside.

Kate put her hand over his. Pain seared through her head as one word echoed: "COME." The boy solidified for a half-second before the pain, mixed with rage, confusion, and fear, became too much. She screamed with Duo as they faded and fluttered like a dying incandescent light. He disappeared as she regained her form on the Inside and fell back into Thomas.

The old snake-oil man caught her. "What just happened?"

The lady Pinkerton steadied herself with his help. "The children are being called to Niagara. I'm pretty sure I know how and by whom."

"How close are we?"

The ship began to descend as if on cue. She brushed off her skirts and patted her companion on his broad shoulder.

"I would say very. Let's see if our geniuses have come up with a plan."

Tesla looked down at the spread of river flecked with small islands. The voice of the falls could be heard on the bridge. Mist formed on the outside of the windows surrounding him and his companions. "I will need to get to the power station on the mainland."

Sam passed him a shot of whiskey. "That's at least a mile or more away from the island. By the time we go there and try to get on that island, everything will have gone to hell. Whatever you plan sounds impossible."

The young scientist knocked back the potent liquid. "Have you learned nothing during our friendship? I do the impossible on a regular basis."

The scruffy author rolled his eyes. "I was afraid you'd point that out."

Thomas came up from the hatch, suit and tank in tow. He gave the pilot, who'd come to help, a bear hug and the men headed off discussing what had happened. Kate followed but turned her attentions toward Sam and Nikola. "What is this genius plan, Mr. Tesla?"

The scientist offered her a shot, and she took it without hesitation. Today was a day for stronger spirits. They turned back to the fogged window.

"You will have to see it to believe it."

Sam poured another drink and laughed. "He always does this when he has a newfangled toy."

The younger man shot him a dark look. "It's not a toy. It is a tool that will end all wars."

Thomas joined them. "That's a mighty big claim, mister." He took the whiskey and poured himself and Sho a shot. The pilot raised his hand, and the old showman took both for himself.

"I am smart enough to make such claims, Mr. Lazarus."

The older man took one shot and then the other. He wiped his mustache with his sleeve. "So are the rest of us supposed to just sit back and let you use your tool then?"

Kate set her empty glass on the window seal. "No. We aren't going to just sit back. Mr. Jones has to already be on Goat Island. I am sure that he's managed to clear the tourists from the area. Allan called the air station, so maybe he got some help in that department."

"What about Deborah and Seth?"

"If they are with my partner, I'm sure they are safe."

He scoffed. "I'm sure they are right in the middle of this madness. If the other children are gone like that boy said, Seth is too."

Sho tapped the glass. "Y'all need to see this."

They looked down at the river below. One part of the falls was straight, but the rest curved like a horseshoe. At the edge of the largest of the islands was a glowing blue archway. Inside was darkness speckled with distant stars and galaxies.

Kate's head spun and the Inside began slipping out from under her. Something pulled at her like that box had back in Raritan except this was far more powerful. She took Sho's hand but couldn't feel it as her own hand slipped through him. For a half-moment, she could have sworn his hand was white and clawed. She remembered how she'd had to concentrate when she'd first re-entered the Inside after her death and the pilot put his hand/claw over her own. The detective willed herself Inside and squeezed her friend's small hand. None of the other men noticed her struggle. She asked, "How soon do we land?"

The small man, following her lead. "I'm not sure we can at this point, Mrs. Warne. My compass is going crazy."

Sam peered at the cabinet. "You got any more of those flying suits, Sho?"

"I do, but I'm not sure—" The pilot took his usual place behind the wheel after checking a few dials on the wall behind them.

The author pointed at Thomas. "If that high binding Greyback can handle them, I imagine Nik and I can too."

"Mr. Clemens's argument is logical." The scientist was already opening one of doors and taking out a suit. "It will be a short journey. I can see the power station from here."

The pilot stopped what he was doing. "You'd trust my work, sir?"

"I see your handiwork around us. You aren't as clever as I, but closer than Edison ever dreamed of being."

The Asian stepped away from the wheel and offered his hand to the dapper scientist, who waved him off.

Sam shoved a note into Sho's pocket as he joined Tesla. "If we don't make it, please give Livvy this for me. Tell her not to fuss until after she reads the letter."

Nikola passed him a suit. "We are not going to die, my friend. Now come. We have work ahead."

Before Kate could add anything, the scene in front of her was torn away and she was yanked from the Inside. She tumbled through the wall of the airship and found herself midair above the raging pit of water. A familiar tingling at the back of her mind grew as she dropped toward the island below. She passed through a swirl that screamed and moaned and she felt the pull grow stronger.

As she dropped closer to the island, she saw a box much like the one she'd seen back in Raritan, except this one was much larger. A wheel on its side turned on its own and steam puffed from the back. The center of the swirl that she was now a part of was being pulled into the box.

She grabbed at a fellow Spectral who was near her. He wasn't screaming like the others around her. His eyes widened as he focused on her.

"You're stronger than the others."

Kate said, "It doesn't matter, we're all heading down there, I'm afraid."

"The gods are culling us from this place. They used to come here long ago and feed. Now they return."

Despite the speed they were swirling and falling she tried to continue the conversation. "Why did they stop?"

"I don't remember. It is so long that I've been Outside. The gods don't come to the Outside."

Something solid hit her leg once, and then again. The pouch she wore on her belt was swinging back and forth hard. At first, she thought this was caused from her going around and around. It didn't move like that, however. Instead, it struggled like a small kitten trying to escape. Then the ornate bag tore open and the same antler-handled knife that she'd used on Mr. Harry back at the hotel flew into her hand. The blade shone like it'd been sharpened by cutting the bag. At some point, she thought to herself, she'd have to pay another visit to Don the Knife back in Savannah to thank him for such a gift. They were close enough now for Kate to see a belt that connected the large wheel to the steam engine that kept it moving.

Her companion disintegrated around the edges as he pulled ahead, gaining speed as they got closer to the whining box below. His voice sounded buzzy and echoed as he whooshed down. "You carry a godslayer."

The knife yanked her arm up and her own journey slowed. Seconds later, her arm released and the blade spun down, gaining momentum as it targeted the machine and then cut the screaming belt that moved the wheel. She missed the Spectral who'd spoken to her by only inches. Parts were thrown in all directions, and a massive cloud of steam and what looked to be parts of Spectrals surrounded and blinded Kate.

As the steam cleared, she found herself surrounded by hundreds of Spectrals, some disappearing while others searching the Outside for others they knew. The knife flew up and orbited her till she grabbed the handle. A tingle ran through her arm, and she was sure she heard laughter.

Kate floated above the group. "Go now, my friends. Leave the island like the Insiders."

Most nodded and faded out with their friends and family members without a question. She had no idea why they didn't ask questions, but in this moment, it didn't matter as long as they were safe.

The Spectral who'd spoken to her stayed by her side. "Now I remember."

"What?"

"There was one long ago, when I lived, with a knife that shone like yours. This person made the gods leave."

A scream pierced through the conversation. She hugged her new friend. "I need to go. I will find you when this is over." He faded out and she rolled the knife in her hand. If this knife was some sort of godslayer, it may be more useful than she'd ever suspected.

Seth doubled over as he walked with Deborah and Shadow across the red wooden bridge that led back to Goat Island. Before Deborah could get to him, he vanished.

"He's calling them." The old witch held her head and tears flowed down her face.

Shadow guided her past groups of people who looked frazzled and hurried. "You can hear him?"

"No, only the echo of pain from the children. He's claiming their minds."

The Brother took her arm and let her lean on him. "I can take you back to the mainland, ma'am. You're weak."

She stood up straight and pushed him aside. Her dark eyes turned black and for a moment, her hair lifted around her head as though a strong wind was blowing up the river. "My son will not be claimed. He has proven that once already." Then she began to sing. Her rich contralto notes wrapped around the lanky detective. His shoulders relaxed and the constant roar from the falls softened and faded to a whisper. Movement on the island below them slowed to a crawl.

The song continued as Deborah turned to the detective. "This will give us time. If the children listen to my words, they should be able to resist."

Nikola and Sam landed outside the Westinghouse Power Station with only a minor incident involving a flock of Canada geese.

Sam removed his suit, which was covered in bird droppings. "Foulest creatures in the world."

His best friend pulled up his goggles. "They attacked only because you decided to try and join their formation."

"It seemed like a good idea at the time." The author took the tank Tesla handed him as the scientist struggled out of his own suit. "So where is this new toy of yours?"

"It's no toy." The dapper young man led his friend around to the back of the station and up a flight of metal stairs. Once inside, he pulled out a flat rectangle of metal and slid it into a thin slot in one wall. The door glided sideways, and the two men stepped past a massive generator. The corridor led to an open room filled with dials and levers. The ceiling was glass and above them was a massive tower with a globe at the top.

Sam leaned against the wall and took a puff from his stogie. "It kinda looks like the tower in Colorado Springs."

"They are very much the same." His best friend picked up a clipboard and began turning dials on the wall.

The generator began to hum in a sort of deep baritone that rose to a pleasing tenor as Tesla pushed a few levers. The building shook and rattled hard enough to throw the author to the concrete floor.

"That's a hell of a lot of power, Nik." Some panes from the glass ceiling fell and shattered behind them. "You may want to turn it down?" Sam got up and brushed off his pants even though there was no dust to be seen.

The scientist made a circle around the room, checked some gauges and took notes as if nothing had happened. "That's not my machine. Perhaps it is something outside."

The scruffy writer ran up the spiral staircase that led to a platform at the ceiling window. The arched azure gate on the island had changed to a translucent pillar of ultramarine that reached up into the upper limits of the sky. An undefined shape writhed and grew inside the cerulean column. It pushed against the light that contained it, revealing a pattern of scales that resembled those of a giant rattlesnake. The coil's narrow end flipped, and rows of circles flattened and glowed, turning that part of the pillar green for a moment. Lines of green-gold moved up the lower length of the coil and the snake-creature's long body split. It flexed hard as a bellow exploded across the land and water and shook the station hard enough to make Sam hold tight to the rail at the top of the staircase. The light-container cracked and pieces of it dissipated at the top. A face with thousands of eyes gazing in all directions peered out toward the station. The creature shook and roared. More of the light melted away, revealing a massive maw containing row after row of shark-like teeth, large, black and sharp-edged. Sam was frozen in place with terror. A part of him withdrew for a moment and he felt like a small, helpless child. He pulled out his flask and took a long hit, letting the whiskey draw him back to the present. He closed his eyes and almost stumbled down the stairs. "I think we'd better hurry, Nik."

41

Shadow spotted his partner about the same time the cerulean pillar rose up out of the curve of Horseshoe Falls at the other side of the island. She waved and ran to join him and Deborah.

"You missed all the fun." Kate tucked her knife into a sheath that appeared at her waist. The island shook hard, but they managed to stay on their feet.

Her partner nodded toward the old witch. "Don't count on that. Shall we go help the children?"

A rage-filled bellow echoed from the falls and all three of them were thrown to the ground. A tentacle thrashed and shredded through the veil that separated the Inside from the Outside. Shadow crawled over to Kate and grabbed her around the waist as her vision began to flutter. She leaned her head on his shoulder as things around her began to solidify once again. They both reached out and found Seth's mother, who was scrambling to her feet. She pulled them up.

"We need to hurry. It's breaking free." The snarling thousand-eyed creature struggled against what was left of the pillar of cosmic light. As they approached the side of the island, a half-circle of three children stood around Treze. The girl's skin was pale and her lips were blue. A splash of red and brown went up the slashed sleeve of her blouse and her skirt was spattered. A fourth child with the face of an alligator crouched at her feet. Only the calico dress gave any sense of who the child might have been. Her claws and arms were covered in something brown and thick. They were all soaked from the ever-rising mist from the falls just beyond them. Their skin reflected the cerulean cast provided by the massive column that contained the god-monster who continued to struggle.

Dark Oona stepped out right beside Shadow and took his hand. Tears streamed down her face.

"They've taken her blood already."

The alligator child scrambled to where Edison and Mr. Harry stood and held up her claws. Mr. Harry scooped her up and hugged her like he was proud of her.

Shadow knelt beside the dark girl. "How did you escape?"

She wiped her face with her sleeve. "He has no idea I'm here. I'm surprised Deci didn't tell on me. Guess she's excited about the blood."

Treze fell to her knees. The moment she touched the ground, the island shook once again. Kate saw what looked like the child's Spectral form rise above the group for a second, and then it yanked back and returned to her kneeling body.

Dark Oona turned from the adults and faced the monster inside the column.

"The Calling is now."

The pillar shook hard as cerulean shifted to ultramarine. More pieces of it fell away and dissipated as the creature struggled against its binding. The remaining enclosure darkened casting a massive shadow across Horseshoe Falls and then followed along the curve of the island to connect with Bridal Falls. The usual raging white waters turned black and then blood-red. The creature grew, pushing upward toward the sky which had turned from bright and clear, to cobalt and filled glowing cobalt eyes that gazed down with a deep-seated hunger. Kate turned away, ashamed of the terror rising inside her. She saw Mr. Harry take out a familiar box and begin turning the handle on its side. She nudged her partner. "What is he doing? There's no way he can control that horror."

Deborah ran ahead of them and pointed to the children at the rim of the falls. "Can you see them?"

At first, Kate was confused. Of course, she could see the children. They'd stayed in place through the ground shaking and the massive god fighting right at them. A chill flooded through the lady detective. Then she saw what the witch was pointing at.

There were more children in the half-circle now. They appeared one at a time, some older like Seth and Treze, others barely toddlers. She couldn't see their faces, but their sorrow and fear hung heavy in the air around them. Dark Oona took her hand and squeezed it. Shadow passed her a handkerchief because tears rolled down her face afresh. "They are our family. No wonder I couldn't find them. No wonder Seth couldn't find them."

Kate also cried. "I thought Mr. Harry ate Spectrals."

The girl passed the handkerchief to her. "We're special. He and Mr. Edison always said so."

The spectral children began to sing, and strings of darkness flowed from their faces toward the blood red column, mixing with the light. The creature's tentacles writhed and splashed against the top of the falls until the darkness wrapped around them and held spread mid-air. Even as it struggled, the children did not move, but continued to sing.

Seth's mother pulled her dark red crocheted shawl tight around her shoulders and shivered as the air chilled. "How do they know this binding song?'

The monstrous god pulled hard with one mist-coated tentacle. A Spectral child flew up, connected to the rope of mystic darkness. The strand stretched, sending the tiny girl high above the head of the creature. It leaned back, opening a mouth that was filled with rows of sharp, crest-like teeth, and she dropped right in. There was no time for even a scream. The other children tried to step back from the edge, but they were bound to the flailing arms of the god in the pillar.

Dark Oona ran toward the circle, but Shadow grabbed her from behind. She fought to free herself. "I can't let her get hurt. Let me do my job."

The detective held onto her as she continued to fight. "If you die, you can't help her, now can you?"

Another child lifted off the ground and toward the maw of the god.

Kate couldn't move. She had a million things she thought she should do, but she couldn't will herself to move from her spot. The idea that someone would sacrifice children, even the ghosts of children, was more than she could take. Deborah snapped her fingers in front of her face. "Come on, detective. There's no time for foolishness. My husband says you are tough, but you stare like some sort of schoolgirl."

Kate shook her head and wiped her tears. "What do you need?"

The witch pointed at the knife on the lady detective's hip, "That right there will do nicely."

Without hesitation, she handed the older woman the God-Killer. The witch marched out a few paces from her and cut into the ground. A hum rose as she walked backward, dragging the blade through the rich soil of the island. It rose as she finished the first half of what was going to be a circle. A huge smile crossed the woman's face, and she sang a few notes before continuing. The crescent she'd cut began to fill with golden light. Warmth tickled around them as she made her way around. Kate felt safe in a way that she hadn't in a long while. The dark girl in Shadow's arms relaxed and stopped fighting as she turned to watch Seth's mother pass them. The light turned the girl's ponytails blue.

Once the witch closed off the circle, she scooped something out of her skirts. As she whispered words the lady Pinkerton didn't understand, she sprinkled white crystals into the circle of light, making her way around a second time. Facing Kate, she took the God-Killer out once again and wrapped her hand around the blade. She winced and let her own blood drip inside the circle. A song flowed from the knife and Deborah sang a counter tune. Their notes wrapped around each other and became fierce words, rising like a call to arms. She pointed her bloodied hand toward the raging monster, who was dangling another child above its serrated mouth. The song stopped, but her eyes were now as silver and sparkling as the blade in her hand.

A voice larger than the old woman boomed across the expanse. "You will not take our children. I forbid this."

The children's song stopped midstream. Shadow, Kate, and Oona stepped away from her as stripes of green and purple appeared on her cheeks. With a flick of the woman's wrist, a slash of blinding light cut the darkness binding the children to the creature. All of them, living and Spectral, fell to the ground. The remains of the ropes turned golden, and the creature howled as the light seared into its flesh. The stench of burned flesh overtook the comforting scent of the falls. The creature broke down more of the pillar, fighting to rid itself of the agony of the light that danced along its arms.

A tentacle lashed across the island and crossed the golden flames of the circle. Shadow and Oona backed away from it. Kate grabbed for Deborah, but the woman shoved her back and muttered "Don't touch me, child." Even as the arm was engulfed in magical flame, it wrapped around Seth's mother and pulled her up and out of the circle. Using God-Killer, the witch stabbed at her captor. An outraged howl shook through the creature, and she dropped the knife inside the now devastated circle. It fell at the lady detective's feet, blade piercing the ground. Light and song were both rising from the old woman even as she was being lifted ever higher from the safety of earth. Kate grabbed God-Killer and sheathed it.

Shadow turned her around to face him. His hands trembled as he gazed up after the singing witch. He was as white as the foam that rose behind them. "We need to get to the children and stop Edison from doing anything else rash." Dark Oona crouched behind him, holding the edge of his coat.

"What's more rash than calling a god and binding it with children?" Kate glanced around, not sure what to do next.

Her partner ran toward the broken circle of fallen children, Dark Oona in tow. "If I find out, I'll let you know."

For a moment, the lady detective hesitated, then raced to catch up with them.

Sam cursed as he ran back up the stairs to the window. "Why the hell didn't you build a periscope, Nik?"

The creature's long tentacles were flailing out over the island as the pillar of light cracked and continued to change from blue to red to black. One of them caught on fire as it touched the ground. It yanked back and the creature roared in what seemed to be agony. Then the author spotted two or three bright colored pieces of fabric floating down from it.

"Holy hell. I think it got Thomas's wife!"

Sam heard a click and a drop of a lever. His friend's voice came from the pit below. "Cover your eyes."

The scruffy-haired man was sure he heard music over the bellows of the creature as he covered his eyes. "Didn't you hear me? If you shoot that thing, you'll kill her!"

The entire building vibrated, and the writer grabbed for the railing behind him. If he hadn't been so scared for Deborah, it may have been relaxing. The air around him began to tingle and then his mountain of hair began to rise as if by magic. Even his bushy mustache rose above his lip, tickling his nose and making him want to scratch. Then the world turned purple, and he was sure that something lifted him like he was a doll. If he hadn't held on tight to the railing the boom that followed would have sent him down to the floor below.

Deborah saw the purple lightning move as if in slow motion toward the creature, and by default, her. Although the tentacle was squeezing her to the point her chest ached, she tried to croak out a few notes to create her song. Silver light crackled around in front of her eyes, but she wasn't sure it was magic or just a sign that she was going to pass out.

A voice somewhere below her rose, carrying the notes that she struggled to control. The song, so clear and pure, was fractured as the entire world around her turned lavender. Her hair rose up, pulling her red head scarf loose. The tentacle that held her flailed, throwing her back and forth like a rag doll, as energy tinted in indigo, violet, and plum danced up and down its length. Above the pain-fueled roars, she heard the song continue as if nothing was happening. She clung to the tune to keep from losing consciousness.

The tentacle froze for a second and released from around the old witch. There was nothing between her and the ground as she gasped for air to join the song. Before she could start, a silver bubble formed around her, floating her away from her captor. Deborah laughed at the surprise that danced in all the thousand eyes of the creature's face. It was as if the thing hadn't expected much of a fight. Another tentacle struggled to grab at her shiny bubble, but she nudged herself out of its reach as energy lit in magenta and amethyst intensified and the creature lost control of its arms. It fell back over the curve of the massive falls just behind it. The spray of the falls turned violet and lavender as it engulfed the writhing grey form that had moments before been a threat. Deborah steadied her magical aircraft to watch the last couple of tentacles crumple and sink under the force of the falling water. One last touch of indigo lit the mist at the bottom of the falls as it churned against itself and whatever was left beneath.

Above the ever-present roar of the falls, the song that rescued her moments before rose sung by one and many voices. Turning the bubble, she saw the children holding hands. The music was coming from them. Edison and an alligator man ran toward the red bridge at the other end of the island. It would have been satisfying to chase them down, but she had something, someone more important to consider. She sang a few notes and guided the sphere toward the children. The bubble popped when she touched the ground.

Seth ran to her, and she wrapped her arms around the boy. "I thought you were a goner, Ma. I didn't know what to do but sing this song in my head."

His mother kissed him. "You saved this old woman."

"STOP!" They both turned to find Quinn, feet spread apart and fists clenched at her side. The inventor and his assistant stood in front of her like figures from Madame Tussaud's.

Deborah went to the statue-like girl. She took her crocheted shawl, which was now tattered, frayed, and wet from being held by a monster, and put it around the child's shoulders. The girl clutched the wrap but stood her ground as the woman stroked her hair. "This is very good, my girl. Now we make sure they cannot leave at all." The witch took out a pouch and sprinkled red brick dust around the two while whispering to herself. She completed her circle in front of Mr. Harry, whose once dapper looks were replaced by the face of an alligator, complete with cold, golden eyes. "You will not hurt these children anymore. If I could send you back where you came from, I would."

The reptilian assistant leaned as close as the barrier the old woman laid would allow and bellowed. The ground began to shake, and a screech cut through the ever-present roar of the falls. Edison's already pale face turned gray, and he backed up to the edge of the brick dust circle. The avatar turned and slashed at the old inventor with its clawed hand, missing by bare inches. Edison dropped to his knees and whispered, "This was not the plan."

Writhing tentacles reached over the raging water that curved around its bulbous body. A face with thousands of eyes rose over the edge of the island as the arms on the land began to dig in, lifting the creature higher than Chicago's Home Insurance Building. The old witch dropped her pouch and started singing once again. Mr. Harry's bellow faded into a deep thrum. The creature answered with a second screech that dropped into a low tone that passed across the island in a wave, knocking Deborah off her feet and across the ruddy circle behind her. The reptile-man grabbed her by collar and pulled her closer to his feet, but his eyes glazed as the drone from the creature rose. His clawed hands dropped as he slipped into a sort of trance. The witch wretched away from him and ran as fast as she could.

Despite her fear, she turned back for a second. Edison was curled up at the feet of the two-legged reptile in a suit. Neither seemed to see her anymore. Before she could continue, a hand latched onto hers and pulled. It was young Quinn, who pointed toward Seth. The woman began singing under her breath once again as they made their way across the island toward the boy, their captives free and forgotten for the moment.

Kate fell over Treze when the ground shook the first time. The sky darkened as the creature she thought Mr. Tesla had taken care of pulled itself up and above the falls, glowering down on them all with those eyes. So many eyes. If the scientist's weapon hadn't worked, she wasn't sure anything else would. She pushed the dread that rose in her as large as the monster they faced and focused on the girl beneath.

She got up and reached for her companion. "Can you stand?"

The ground shook again, but this time she willed herself to be steady. The girl pulled ignored the detective's hand and clambered to her feet. Her younger brother rushed up and took her hand.

"It sure has lots of eyes," said Two.

His sister covered his eyes with her hand. "Mr. Harry told me that looking into them would make a person mad."

The boy pushed her hand away, gazing up at the rising god. "Being mad might make it easier for me to tear it apart."

Kate knelt down and took his face in her hand. "You are not to go try to tear that thing apart, do you hear me?"

He turned away. "It would be the first time my powers would be used to help."

His sister hugged him tight. "You shouldn't ever have to rage again, Duo."

Seth joined them, his brown hair tousled and sweat rolling down his face. The girl pointed at their younger sibling. "He thought he'd tear that thing apart with his own bare hands."

"Do you really think you could?" In spite of the seriousness of the situation, the older boy had a spark of mischief dancing in eyes.

His sister put her hands on her hips. "Don't you start. Wait, Duo, what were you saying about eyes?"

Her face hardened and the detective wondered why the girl was angry at her brother. The girl bolted toward the god as it screamed and stretched out more of its scarred and singed arms across the island.

Her brothers chased her and Kate followed. She faded Outside and reappeared in front of the girl. "What are you doing?"

Treze stopped just before running into the lady detective. Frustration crossed her face and she tried to walk through the woman. Kate solidified on the Inside and held her ground against her. Seth ran up and took his sister by the hand. His face was wet with tears. The girl's shoulders dropped, and she gazed away and up at the monster that was shaking the world around them. "Just what Duo said. I'm going to use my powers to help for the first time ever."

Her younger brother skittered up in time to hear this. "You just told me that I couldn't do that."

"I told you that you shouldn't have to rage again. If you raged, you'd have to get close to that thing. It's faster and bigger than you."

Duo started to protest, but she continued as if he wasn't there.

"I don't need to get close."

Kate glanced over at the boys. "Go back to your brother and sisters." The older boy didn't let go of her hand and Duo crossed his arms and leaned back. She could see the fire rising in his eyes. "You both need to trust her."

Seth leaned over and kissed his sister's cheek. Duo kicked at the ground and a growl rumbled under his breath. Treze took his hand and held it against her cheek. "We all have our job to do." He nodded his head. Then he stepped away from her and turned his head. Kate was sure he was crying. The lady detective pushed her knife into the girl's hand. "I want this back, do you understand?" For the first time, the girl looked her dead in the eyes and nodded. A chill flushed through Kate.

Treze tucked the knife in her belt, hiked up her skirts and ran toward the edge of the island. She kicked one of the massive arms that were now embracing the land beneath it. "Hey, beastie, look at me!"

The tentacle arched up and swung toward her. She skipped away as if she was playing a game. As Kate ran to follow the boys, she was sure she heard a merry, childlike giggle behind her. She turned back in time to see the girl pick up a rock and throw it toward the body of the monster. "Look at me! Come on! I'm the sacrifice, remember?"

A tiny blue portal opened just outside the broken brick dust circle and a small girl with blonde braids and the face of an alligator stepped onto the ground in front of Mr. Harry. She walked past him and kicked Edison.

"Get up, old man. We have work to do."

He groaned and tried to cover his face. She got down on her knees, leaned down till her boxy, scaled face was level with his, and hissed.

He scrambled to his feet. The alligator-child skittered to the inventor's assistant and bit his leg. The avatar kicked her into the grass beyond the once magical barrier. She growled and ran at him but stopped short when he raised his foot toward her face. "Don't make me kill you, child."

A thick, gray-brown tail grew out from under her skirts, and she lashed it toward her attacker. He jumped over it, hissed and crouched.

Edison screamed, but neither of them paid attention until he pushed between them and pointed toward the sky, which turned from cobalt to royal purple before their eyes. The air tingled and crackled around them, and the old man's hair lifted and fluttered around his face.

Mr. Harry, forgetting his fight with the girl, backed away from both of them and ran for the portal of summer blue Deci had left open. Edison and the monstrous girl followed.

Nikola turned a few buttons and readjusted some dials. A hiss rose from behind him as he prepared to flip the switch to release another charge.

"Edison should have let me kill you before you got away, Serbian," said a voice.

The young inventor's hand hovered at the switch. "How did you find me?"

A clawed hand grabbed his shoulder and turned him around. He was facing an alligator in a suit. "That electrical blast was a bit of a giveaway." A hiss came from behind the creature and a smaller reptilian person in a dress stepped out.

Sam yelled from the above. "If you're gonna take a shot that's more than a warning, Nik, now might be the right time."

Nikola looked the man-creature dead in the eyes. "My friend. He is excited, no?"

He felt a tug at his waist and looked down to find a pretty little girl with blonde braids and a soft, sweet-looking face. She was wearing the same dress the alligator-girl had moments before. "I remember how you rescued us that night. We were all so scared, but you took us to the train and was so kind. I love you."

The Serbian's mind swirled for a moment and all he could see was her beautiful face. She grabbed his hand, and he flinched. Her beauty was replaced by a hideous creature that took many forms at once and none at all. Past that he saw the calculations he'd been working on before they arrived, shimmering against a starry sky. He slapped her hand away. "I do not have time for this."

A deep bellow echoed around him, but he continued to focus on the plan. He tapped a few buttons, set some dials, and reached for a lever. Behind him, he heard the voice of his greatest foe, Thomas Alva Edison. "No!" There was a single, flat percussive crack followed by a thump. The scientist pulled the final lever and turned.

A small, smoking hole was in the head of the now fallen Mr. Harry. Edison knelt next to the reptilian creature in a suit muttering about lost opportunities. Sam re-holstered a well-kept long-barreled pistol under his brown tweed jacket. The writer gave his friend a nod.

Nikola tried to kneel next to the fallen creature, which was no longer human at all, but the young girl hissed at him as her human features melted away. He backed away. The girl swiped at Edison, leaving the sleeve of his jacket slashed. Blood oozed from his wounds, and he skittered away. She chirped and fawned over the alligator-man, tears rolling down her own long, boxy nose, while Nikola pulled a flask from his jacket and took a long swig.

Mr. Harry convulsed. His reptilian eyes opened and darted around for a moment. The girl chirped louder. Mr. Harry coughed, blood seeping out of his snout and eyes. With a speed that didn't seem possible, he rolled and swiped at the child's face, but she blocked his attack with her small, frail arm. The young scientist was sure it should have broken, but instead, she pivoted and dug her own claws through the sleeve of his shirt. Red blossomed beneath her scaled hand.

"Papa, gods don't die."

A deep, but weak thrum emanated from the fallen creature's chest. It coughed hard, blood tipping the sharp teeth around its maw. "I am the old. You, my child, are the new."

Her chest opened with a sapphire light that faded to look like a spring sky. She leaned in close to the face that was so much like her own and said, "I love you."

The energy of the words wrapped around Nikola's heart, and he was sure that it was his own mother saying them to him. He dropped the flask of whiskey he'd pulled out to take a hit from. His mother wouldn't want to see him drunk. In the distance, he was sure he heard good old Sam saying something, but all that mattered was that he was loved by his mother, who was just behind the door waiting, he was sure. He needed to see her and tell her of his exploits. She'd be so proud.

A massive bellow shook him from his reverie, and an alligator-child stood before him, all teeth and scales. She shoved him hard enough to make him bounce against the whirring generator behind him. "Not you, mortal. I don't love you."

Relief and deep sadness washed over Nikola, none of which was for the creature on the ground but was rather for his loss of opportunity to see his mother once more. He closed his eyes to refocus on his work. There was no time for this nonsense.

A whiff of tobacco mixed with whiskey brought him back to reality. Sam was at his side. "Are you okay?"

Nikola twisted his mustache but before he could reply, the light from the child's chest changed from sky blue to the same cerulean that had surrounded monstrosity at the falls.

Mr. Harry lifted from the floor and merged with the light. His features stretched as his body faded more and more. The girl hugged her papa as they became the same. She was him and he was her.

"I am the gate." The words echoed out of her chest, sounding like Mr. Harry but also sounding like herself. The light turned cobalt and enveloped them. Two rays of gold cut through the blue light. With a roar, the blue veil dropped, and the girl was alone. She gazed up at Nikola. Her once fine dress was shredded, and her eyes were like the sun in autumn. They faded and paled till they once more were more human than reptile. In a small voice, she said again, "I am the gate." She collapsed into a small heap at his feet.

"I don't know what that means."

Sam picked Nikola's flask from the ground and took a swig of his own. "Should we shoot her too?"

The scientist rubbed his back and then checked the dials and gauges he'd been slammed into. "I think not. Just tie her up, will you?"

A screech tore through the moment and the building shook hard. Sam glanced up from his task and his friend gestured at the stairs. The writer scurried back up, taking his abandoned post once more.

"Holy hell, Nik. It's back."

"That's not probable." The young inventor scrambled up to see for himself. He grabbed the flask from his best friend's hand and turned it up. "But apparently, it is possible."

Thirteen threw another rock as it turned all of its eyes on her. "That's right. Look me dead on. Take me in. You're not the only monster on this island."

Her head swam as their gaze locked. The world around her fell away like a heavy curtain and all that surrounded her were stars, blinking and sparkling. They were all gazing upon her, those stars of all colors. They drew closer until millions of faces of all colors and shapes surrounded her. Tears streaked her face as she reached out for one in particular. A woman who wore a braid like her own and had eyes like sapphires.

"Mother?" Before she could touch the woman, whose face now looked red and puffy, pulled away. Her deep blue eyes reflected terror and shame. Then she was gone. Gone. Gone. Just like always. Never to return. Treze screamed. All she wanted in her whole life was this one person. Instead, she was left alone surrounded by faces that she didn't know or care to know that spun around her. They began muttering, low at first and then as they spun faster, their voices raised in a litany she'd heard over and over again.

"Useless child."

"Murderer."

"A danger to everyone around her."

As the accusations continued, the voices became familiar. That man who ended up dead in the creek because he visited her house. The boy who lost his entire family after the house burned because of her. Edison. Horace. Mr. Jones. Oona. Kate. Seth.

She covered her ears when she heard Seth's voice. The words cut her deep. The faces drew closer, and the mutters became shouts around her. She almost closed her eyes to keep from seeing them all gazing at her with disappointment and anger.

Wait. Seth?!

"Seth loves me and has never said an unkind thing. He loves me, and I love him. We are a family. This stops now."

The roar of voices halted, and the silence was as startling as the raging voices. The stars fell from the sky and the voices were replaced by the song of the water that fell to great depths beneath her. A broad, slippery tentacle kept her from plunging to her death below. She had no idea how long before the thing had managed to capture her, but she also wasn't surprised. All thousand eyes of the horrific creature seemed locked on her as if she were some sort of rare oddity. Treze was sure this wouldn't hold forever and that sooner or later she would become one with the mists. Perhaps, however, it would give her siblings time.

Shadow met Kate before she could join the group of children and adults ahead. He gestured toward the girl, who was now above the ground in the embrace of the monstrous god-thing in the falls. "Why did you let her go out there?"

The lady detective slowed her pace but kept moving toward the others. "She seemed to have a plan, and I had none at the time."

"We're supposed to protect them." Shadow stayed in stride with her.

"Consider what she causes." She stopped and crossed her arms. Before her partner could respond, a screech echoed across the island. Her partner stumbled, but she caught both of them.

"I guess it's too late to argue about this now." He steadied himself, and she took his arm.

Deborah and the children circled around them. The old witch was humming under her breath and Kate took the woman's hand with her free hand and squeezed it. A warm tickle moved up her arm. The Oona(s) pulled Shadow away and embraced him as she watched the creature grow and flail at the edge of the land. Her/their sister looked like a soaked rag doll in its arm.

"She did this for all of us," said the Oona(s).

He knelt down between her/them. "Did you know she would?"

Light Oona wiped her eyes and turned from him. Dark Oona nodded. They both said, "It was the only way."

Deborah stopped humming for a moment and snapped her

fingers. "You speak as if your sister is dead, but she is not. She fights. Look at her."

They all gazed up, but the girl didn't look like she was doing anything at all. Neither was the creature.

Kate poked Shadow. "Listen."

Silence. No screeches. No bellows. Even the droning of the falls was gone.

Breaking sound vacuum, Seth's mother said, "Now is the time we strike. We must help!" She started humming once again and made her way toward the tableau of monster and girl. Her boy grabbed her shoulder.

"Ma, you used everything you have. I'm surprised you're standing."

She hesitated and put her hand over his, never turning back. "We must do what we can. She is family."

"If you are determined, then I am with you."

Duo and Quinn came up beside the older woman and the girl took her hand. Her younger brother stared up at the frozen creature, his eyes blazing with a mixture of delight and animal hunger. The girl had to snap to get his attention, and then he took her hand.

Deborah's hum became a chant and then a full-out song. Seth raised his baritone voice and picked up a harmony that was sweet and brutal. Energy flowed from the Outside to the Inside and the lady detective couldn't help but cry because it reminded her of love, loss, and recent decisions. A flush of warmth flowed over her and with it an assurance that her decision would be the right one.

A soprano voice joined in a sharp-edged descant above the main tune. A startled look passed over Duo's face as the high notes passed his lips. He sang in a loud reckless way that joined with the softness of the witch's own notes in spite of their harshness. The urge to tear everything into shreds flooded over her and she reveled in the destruction that could come if she was loosed.

A breeze blew in from the river. The scent of fish, earth, and the slightest hint of salt wafted around them, cooling Kate's destructive longings. Gentle giggles tickled around her, and the voices of the Oona(s) circled around them like yellow butterflies on an early fall morning. The light girl followed Deborah's lead and her dark other harmonized between them and her brothers.

Tenor notes joined and she was sure that she saw what she thought may be the paths that Shadow traveled when he was not with her. Bittersweetness hugged around the circle. She glanced at her partner and he shrugged. Quinn poked the lady Pinkerton and they both added their own layer to the growing chorus of voices, which melded and grew stronger as the old witch led yet another verse. Although the words were unknown, the intent grew clear as a wall of silver that reminded her of the sphere that Deborah had floated in earlier solidified around all of them. Silver darkened to a translucent pewter as the song continued.

Deborah moved out of the circle and lifted her head to the sky. "Thomas!" She shouted his names three times and then raised her arms and chanted.

"Open the door, Sho!" Thomas stood at the ready. "She needs me."

The pilot slid it to the side. "Are you sure about this?"

The old showman hooked a bag on the belt of the almost too-tight suit he wore. He pulled down the goggles. "Can't you hear her?"

"No. I do hear music, though."

"It doesn't matter. I'm supposed to get out there. When I get hooked up, I'll need that tube." He pointed at a metal cylinder on the floor. The Asian nodded and clapped him on the shoulder before he made his way down. The showman clipped himself onto the ladder with some hooks his friend had given him. Then signaled for the tube.

The pilot saluted him as his friend dangled high above the raging waters. "Don't damage my lady, you scoundrel."

The *Eclipse* circled just above the creature's head, but it didn't seem to notice. Instead, all its eyes were focused on Treze as if the girl had put it in a trance. As the airship moved around the god-monster, Kate saw a figure hanging just below the gondola. Deborah's call was answered by a single whoop. The old woman twirled around and laughed as if she were as young as the Oona(s), her scarves swirling like multi-colored clouds around her face and body.

Her husband's feet grazed the edge of the mist that rose from the falls. He took something from a pouch and stuffed it and a few other things in a cumbersome tube and then swung in a way that made the detective sure he would fall.

"Fire in the hole, you bastard!" Flames blew out of the tube and the ladder turned into a giant swing. Thomas somehow held steady.

The creature, however, did not hold steady. The bulbous upper portion of the creature kicked back in opposition to the airship as what came out of the tube impacted. It kicked back a second time as an explosion ripped into its flesh, tearing away half of it head. The mist of the falls turned to a putrid green-brown and a shriek rose, shaking the island and the ship above it. Deborah fell but kept singing. Tentacles flailed as the creature sank into the waters and fell back, but none of them touched the witch or her circle of family.

Duo laughed and said, "I'd say that's some bad luck."

Quinn screamed and pointed at a familiar figure that was now plummeting toward the discolored, roiling falls. Dark Oona kicked her older sister. Panic dropped from the girl's face and the number on her neck glowed. "STOP!" Her command was carried by the notes that rose from the rest of the group. Treze held mid-air, arms and head hanging toward the ground. The creature was frozen in the mixture of water and its own destroyed bits. The older girl in the circle trembled as she put her hands to her head.

A second explosion rattled from the falls, and at first, Kate thought Seth's father had taken another go at the creature in the water. The airship flew backwards in the air as if someone had thrown it like a ball. Thomas and the ladder swung back and forth, but the showman was held to the ladder by something. The old man couldn't have caused this kind of mayhem. Treze's limp body was also pushed away and then dropped, bouncing on the ground below. Kate ran toward the girl, but her partner stopped her and shook his head. Before she could protest, a chartreuse sphere rose out of the river from behind the god-monster.

A ringing tone that turned into another boom rolled across the island. Deborah's song was disrupted by an atonal jangle of notes. The witch ran to the group, covering her ears. The notes tore through the protective magic barrier and was replaced with a cold, desolate wall of energy that closed in on them all. Duo crouched like a wolf ready to defend his pack in front of Quinn, who lay on the ground in a fetal position. He pulled the Oona(s) behind him, but not before the paler of the two slapped his hand. He snarled, and her other pulled her away. A small, but familiar voice echoed around them, "I love you. All of you."

Light Oona balled her fists and her eyes glowed like stars of icy blue. She lifted off the ground while her other reached up for her. She pointed at the churning sphere and over the discordant, painful tones said, "NO, YOU DON'T! Leave us alone!"

A sheet of lightning flashed around them, and rain started falling although the sky was clear. The sphere grew larger, and Kate felt heat wafting from it. More steam and fog rose from the river. The detective scrambled to Deborah, who was near unconsciousness.

The words they were singing before rose in her mind, and she began to sing them herself. Shadow started singing again too and walked toward Duo, who was crouching like an animal. The boy looked up at her partner. At first, he barked and howled the notes but then started, once again, with his young soprano. The darkness inside and around them pressed against them, but as they continued, it dispersed and evaporated along with the fog that had risen.

"Keep singing and don't listen," she said between verses. The old witch sat up, took her hand, and squeezed it. She sang in a whisper, but it was enough to send the last of the fear and despair back toward the river and its source.

A reptilian face looked down from the sphere over the scene. Blonde hair spilled around the boxy face of an alligator-child. The eyes glowed like lanterns into the storm. "This is not over my brothers and sisters. We will come again, you will see."

The sphere dropped down almost past the edge of the island over the fallen god-creature. After a moment, it shot out of the curve of the falls, pulling tons of water up with it. What was left of the monster was now in the sphere. As it shot into the sky, the river that had followed dropped back into the basin, shaking the island and causing a massive wave to flood back onto the land and downstream.

"Treze!" Deborah pointed to the rising waters where the girl once laid

"She's fine, ma. Just fine." Seth approached the group carrying Treze's limp body in his arms. While the girl's dress dripped and her hair stuck to her face and shoulders, he was dry except for his arms. The Oona(s) danced and two stars circled around her/them and their older siblings.

Quinn held back, tears flowing down her face. "I thought she'd be, you know, because of Seth." Duo hugged her hard.

Seth laid the soaked body on the ground. Kate stepped Outside to see if the girl was close by, but no one was around. That sphere could have taken the girl. She shivered at the thought. She touched Shadow's hand and came back Inside. He put his arm around her.

The boy knelt by his sibling and put his hands around her face. He began to whisper words that were unclear. It reminded her of what had happened with the horse. A golden key appeared in his right hand and the number 13 shown along its top. His spectral form separated from his body. He turned and grinned at Kate. It rejoined the boy's body as he kissed his sister's forehead.

Their remaining siblings circled around them, and the dual stars orbited around them. Duo put his hand on his brother's shoulder, and Seth reached up and grabbed it. Quinn stood across from him, searching the sky as if she expected something else. The Oona(s) held each other close, one as pale as the moon, the other as dark as onyx, her/their eyes on her/their older brother. Treze grabbed Seth's arms and squeezed them as she looked at the group around her.

"Did we all die?"

Her brother took her hands and said, "Nope. Not a single one of us."

The Oonas jumped up and down and the stars swooped around the children as if in tune with her/their joy. Duo punched Quinn in the arm. Quinn knelt down next to her sister while the younger boy whooped and howled at the sky.

Seth embraced Treze, his tears mixing with the remains of the water from the river. "You did good, sister."

42

Kate waited in the downstairs lobby as Shadow and another Brother questioned Edison. The Brotherhood recommended that they handle his case rather than the usual authorities. Something about being a national treasure. She thought this was garbage, but Allan supported this view and she had no real say in the matter. Sam and Nikola filled her in about Mr. Harry and his daughter, Deci, and their encounter at the power station. It would seem that a new avatar had been born, and she wondered how long before the ancients would once again attempt to regain traction on Earth.

One of the Brotherhood, Mr. South, led Edison out of the ornate iron elevator. Her partner followed. Mr. Edison was frailer than she remembered him being when they'd visited Menlo Park. His dealings with the supernatural had not been kind to the Great Inventor. There was talk about setting him up with a sawmill in Michigan, and the man seemed agreeable to the idea. The Brotherhood also took the mystic book from Shadow once they'd returned to Chicago. For the moment, it seemed that the inner turmoil of the organization was set aside to deal with this matter.

Edison took her hand in his and said, "I don't believe we've met, have we, young lady?"

She had been on the Outside, so it surprised her that he could see her. Strange changes for sure. "Kate Warne, sir. Pleased to make your acquaintance."

He turned to Mr. South. "Well, we must be on our way if we are heading to Michigan. I hear that Mr. Kingsford needs a design for a factory. I already have some ideas." He tipped his hat to her before exiting.

Once the front doors clicked shut, she turned on Shadow. "You wiped him, didn't you?"

"Neither Allan nor the Brotherhood saw good reason to put him in prison." He headed back to the elevator without offering an arm. She balled up her fists and followed him, slamming the iron gating into its lock before setting the lift in motion.

"He should be there rotting after what he did to those children." She stood toe-to-toe with the tall man. "Why are you determined to protect him?"

"I'm not." He took her hands. "The Brotherhood, however, believes we need him to catalyze a few things that are coming. He is a genius, you know."

Kate shook his hands away. "The last time the Brotherhood attempted to catalyze something, you ended up locking up what they came up with. Is that what you want to happen again?"

The lift stopped and he moved past her to slide the gate to one side. "I am a single voice of dissent in this matter. Even with the destruction of one of our own, their larger plan overrides my view of justice."

"And what about protecting all of the citizens of this country?" He backed out of the way as she exited into the hall. She stomped toward the office door which bore the names Mr. Andrew Jones and Mrs. Kate Warne. Allan hadn't removed her name yet.

"He remembers nothing of this escapade. He only knows that he needs a change of scenery, and that Menlo Park is no longer for him. He's bored, and Mr. Kingsford and Mr. Ford have offered him an opportunity to build a charcoal factory. Wiping his memory is safer for all of us than locking him up while he remembers how to summon ancient gods."

Kate paused and her shoulders untensed. As angry as she was about this decision, the Brotherhood's decision was logical. Edison had a lot to offer when he wasn't destroying lives and threatening the entire world. Maybe a wipe and a change of scenery would make a difference. "My opinion doesn't make much difference here anymore, does it?"

"Did you tell him what you want to do?" Followed her into the office.

"I sent my resignation before Niagara Falls. He's not said a word since we came back"

"He's ruminating, no doubt. You're leaving him twice."

She hit her partner's arm. "That's not fair." It was fair, but she didn't want to admit that to Allan, her partner, or herself.

"No, it's not, but truth nonetheless."

There was a letter on Kate's desk.

Kate tore open the plain envelope and read:

Dear Mrs. Warne:

Thomas and I want to thank you for helping us build our family. The children are doing well and as of yet, Treze's bad luck has not returned. Enclosed is a token of my appreciation. If you should ever need us, this is a beacon. We will respond.

Mrs. Lazarus

Kate pulled out a blue and white glass pendant. It looked like an eye. She put it around her neck. A song whispered around her for a moment before settling into the background. Her partner started humming along but faded out. Then his eyes went blank. The lady detective conjured up a cup of tea and straightened up a bit. It was clear his Brothers called.

A few moments later, her partner's demeanor shifted, and he moved to hang his coat. "Remember that case in Savannah a few years ago?"

She sat down her cup. "Yes. Missing persons on the river front. Someone swore there were Spectrals involved, and we met that charming fellow, Don the Knife."

"Well—" He arched his eyebrow and gave her a quizzical teasing look.

She raised her hands and backed away shaking her head. "Oh no. I'm leaving, going Outside, remember?"

He paused for a moment and his face went blank. "The Brotherhood was contacted by a group of Spectrals. Says that whatever was going on last time has started again. Could be a good way to start your new line of work."

"Why would they ask the Brotherhood for help?"

"Because there is no liaison between any detective agency and the Outside. At least not yet. It would seem that Spectrals have started going missing as well."

"A liaison between them and the Brotherhood or them and Allan?" She called up a cup of tea in the hopes that she could slow down her thoughts and what was happening. The office door opened, and Allan entered.

"Well, technically, I haven't fired you, and a telegram doesn't count as an official resignation, at least not at Pinkerton's."

"Is that a rule?" She sipped her tea without taking her eyes off the man.

He cleared his throat but met her gaze. "It is now. I won't accept one on official letterhead either.

The master detective handed her a folder, but she pushed it aside. "You aren't happy as long as I stay."

He threw up his hands. "Of course, I'm not happy. I won't be happy if you go either. Do you know how hard it will be to find someone to replace you?" He gestured at Shadow, "He'll have to train him."

"Him?!" Kate sat the cup down on the desk hard enough to make it dissolve into the Outside. "What about one of my ladies? Any one of them could take my place. They are well trained and just as…"

"What? Stubborn as you?" The bear-like detective laughed until he coughed. "Why replace you? The entire reason you came back is because this," he lifted his hand in the air, "is what you love." He leaned over her desk until they were nose-to-nose. Didn't think I knew that, did you?" He settled in an oversized blue upholstered chair meant for him. "Listen to me. I'm sad that we can't continue but I'll be fine. Do this one last job for me. No, for yourself. I'll sort myself out. When you return, we can discuss whether you should stay or go."

In spite of all the tangled feelings that centered around the burly man, she couldn't help but be intrigued. She picked up the folder and glanced over the particulars.

Peering over the papers, she saw a wry smile cross over his face. It never failed to melt past her defenses. "Shadow, didn't you say there were Spectrals involved?" Her partner nodded. She laid the papers down. "Please understand, Allan, this has nothing to do with you or your somewhat compelling request."

"You are concerned for the Spectrals involved. Makes perfect sense, Katherine," said Allan.

Her partner grabbed his coat once again. She straightened his tie, as per their ritual. "I'll meet you at the station on River Street," he said as he stepped into the darkest corner of her office. Meanwhile, she tucked the folder in her travel bag and adjusted her hat. Pinkerton stood as she exited, and she was sure she heard him chuckle as the door closed.

One more case couldn't hurt.

The End…for now

AUTHOR'S NOTE

When I began writing this book, I had two separate stories in my head. One involved a plot centering around Edison and Tesla, and the other centered around a girl named Thirteen, who I imagined after my friend, Jeff Racel, introduced me to Johnny Cash's cover of Glenn Danzig's song "Thirteen." I blended the two stories with the intention of Thirteen/Treze being my main character. During those early days, I also discovered that I needed detectives, and I want to create some that would easily connect to Edison and Tesla, but also have experience with the supernatural elements of the version of the United States I was creating. I did a Google search (like any good amateur researcher would) and found Pinkerton's National Detective Agency (yes, the company is still in existence). I read the history page of the company website and discovered Kate Warne. I scribbled her name in my book notebook after doing a happy dance in my kitchen (if you know me, you know this is a frequent event in my home). At the time, I had no idea that she would end up usurping Thirteen, as my lead character, but I was happy that all of the detectives weren't male (I'd had that fear going in).

Then I learned that Kate died in 1868. My novel begins around 1883. What to do? I gave this a few days thought while reading more about her, Allan, and the Pinkertons in general. I learned how tough and stubborn she was, and one day it hit me that she was still in her prime in 1868 (she died when she was 38 years old). Someone with her kind of drive would probably be pretty angry that she was dead and couldn't do the thing she loved anymore. Then the "what ifs" rose up inside of me. What if she had a choice after she passed? What if she decided that she wanted to work anyway? Thus Kate Warne, first female and Spectral detective was born.

The historical Kate Warne, however, was as fascinating, strong, and clever as her fictional counterpart. Not much is known about her prior to her time with Pinkerton's. We know she was born in New York in 1833. She was hired by Allan Pinkerton in 1856 when she marched into the Pinkerton National Detective Agency in Chicago, Illinois to answer an advertisement for a detective position with the firm. She was 23 and a widow with no children. Mr. Pinkerton was unsure this was a good idea until she explained that she could "worm out secrets in many places to which it was impossible for male detectives to gain access" (pinkerton.com). He hired her and made her the first female detective in the United States.

The young woman proved herself in short order when she ferreted out a railroad embezzler by befriending the suspect's wife. Using her charm and gift for conversation, she gained information about the theft and went on to find the hidden cash. Her "tact and savvy served her well in 1861" (Blakemore). Pinkerton discovered "The Baltimore Plot," focused on President-elect Abraham Lincoln led by a group of Southern conspirators who hated his abolitionism that was to take place during a whistle-stop tour from Springfield, Illinois to Washington D.C. Kate headed to Baltimore and posed as a Southern widow and even wore a secessionist cockade (this is a ribbon with a state button at the center) to show that she supported the cause. She was accepted into the fold of the community and began feeding rumors and bits of conversation back to Pinkerton. Soon the plot unfolded. The attempt would take place during a scheduled stop in Baltimore.

The lady detective's responsibilities shifted as a plan to protect the President-elect took form. Pinkerton planned a "complex ruse that

that involved Lincoln traveling in the sleeper compartments of regular passenger trains to evade public notice" (Blakemore). Kate purchased sleeper berths, pretending to have a sick brother who needed complete silence and rest. She then met a disguised Lincoln at a Philadelphia train station. They acted as brother and sister, and she then accompanied him to the sleeper car where they stayed until they arrived safely in Washington. According to some versions of this story, "Warne did not sleep a wink on the overnight trip" and that Pinkerton came up with the company slogan 'We never sleep' as a result" (civilwar/wikia.org/wiki/Kate Warne).

Kate continued her work with Allan Pinkerton throughout the Civil War. At times she posed as a Confederate soldier (one photograph shows her standing by a tent at an encampment). Other times she posed as his wife as they infiltrated various points of Southern society. She also worked as part of Pinkerton's team to set up a military intelligence unit for Major General George McClellan in Ohio.

After the war, she worked several high-profile cases including the murder of bank teller George Gordon in Atkinson, Mississippi, where she went undercover once again and was able to gather enough evidence to discover and convict Alexander Drysdale of murder and the theft of $130,000. Allan Pinkerton would name her one of the five best detectives at his firm, and she became Supervisor of Female Detectives.

Her real-life adventures were cut short when she contracted pneumonia or tuberculosis, depending on which sources you read, on New Year's Day 1868. Allan Pinkerton really did spend every day at her bedside until her death on January 28. There is a lot of speculation concerning the nature and depth of their relationship, but no clear evidence to support a romantic entanglement. There are enough rumors to make it a possibility, and since fiction trades in possibilities, I decided that this was something worth pursuing in this novel and in novels to come. Interestingly, she's buried in the Pinkerton family plot in Chicago's Graceland Cemetery.

WORKS CITED

Blakemore, Erin. "The Woman Who Helped Stop an Early Attempt on Abraham Lincoln's Life." *Time.Com*, Mar. 2017, p. 1.

"Kate Warne." *Civil War Wikia*. https://civilwar.wikia.org/wiki/Kate_Warne.

"Our Story-Our History." Pinkerton.com. https//pinkerton.-com/ourstory/history.

READING LIST

My publisher thought it would be a great idea if I included a reading list focused on the historical counterparts of some of the characters in this book. I was thrilled to make this addition. There are a lot of good resources about Edison, Pinkerton (and his company), Tesla, Twain (or Clemens), and Warne. While this list isn't comprehensive, it does attempt to point out sources that will offer a chance for further exploration. These books can be found on Amazon or at your local public library.

What's excellent about each of the people mentioned in this list is that even if they never faced down cosmic horror like their fictional versions did in this book, they all led extraordinary lives and contributed to the rich fabric of American history.

I am always curious and what draws me to each of these individuals is their native curiosity. Each of them was a student—of life, of science, of people and the world around them. While each were led down different paths by their yearning to know more, each used that latent desire to change the world, mostly for the better.

Now on to the list.

THOMAS ALVA EDISON

1. *Edison* by Edmund Morris (2019)
2. *The Wizard of Menlo Park: How Thomas Alva Edison Created the Modern World* (2010) by Randall E. Stross

ALLAN PINKERTON AND PINKERTON'S NATIONAL DETECTIVE AGENCY

1. *The Pinkerton Agency: The History of Allan Pinkerton and America's First Major Private Detective Organization* (2019) by Charles River Editors
2. *Allan Pinkerton: The First Private Eye* (1997) by James Mackay

MARK TWAIN

1. *Mark Twain: A Life (2006) by Ron Powers*

ACKNOWLEDGMENTS

Writing a book is a bit of a journey, and I have been blessed to have many wonderful people who have helped, supported, and loved me and *Children of Menlo Park* over the last four years. I don't want to miss anyone, but if I do, please know that I love and appreciate you.

I'd like to thank my beta readers who slogged through those initial drafts as I was meeting characters and discovering the actual core of the novel. Darrell Grizzle (who is an incredible author in his own right. Go to Amazon and check out his short story collection, *I Never Meant to Start a Murder Cult and Other Stories.*) and Glenn Price (author of *Space Opera Star Atlas 4 and Star Atlas 7)* were there for the early days and often talked me into moving forward when I was unsure of the direction I was going. Darrell is the one who, after I spent months editing and reediting my first draft, said, "Just send the damned manuscript." Lisa Archen Duncan was the first to read the complete novel and was a constant source of encouragement, comfort, and brainstorming. She also has shamelessly promoted me and my book over the last few years. Without her sharp reading and willingness to tell me when something didn't work, the novel wouldn't be half as awesome as it is. I also need to thank her for connecting me to the best group of women I've ever met (Gale, Celeste, Kris, Julie, Shannon,

Heidi). Maeve Nettles often gave insights into various characters that I didn't see myself. She also pointed out times when I could use better, more inclusive language and when there were holes in my story. Sometimes, she even let me prattle about the book all through our many sushi lunches. She has also successfully promoted this novel to her rather incredible circle of friends.

One person I have to mention Robert Ziegler. During the first draft of the novel, I created a contest on Facebook to help me figure out what to name Sho's airship. I promised that the winner's name would appear in this section of the book. Robert named her the *Eclipse*. I also got a bunch of other airship names and made note of who suggested them, so as more show up in other stories, you may see your name in the acknowledgements of those books.

I also want to extend special thanks to Jeff Racel, who is a good friend and has encouraged me along this journey as well. Without him, I would have never met Thirteen and the rest of the children. In late 2015, I was trying to work on a new horror short story, and he sent me a link to Johnny Cash's cover of Glenn Danzig's "Thirteen." The lyrics captivated me. I listened to it until I could sing it in my sleep. Then I started tinkering and Thirteen in front of a burning house emerged in my mind. Once that happened, I decided that her siblings would also be attached to a song from The Man in Black's discography.

I need to mention the Broadleaf Writers Association as well. If it hadn't been for Broadleaf, I may have never gotten the courage to begin this novel at all. Through Broadleaf and its annual conference (broadleafwriters.com), I got to meet Bill Blume (this is your fault, man), Zachary Steele, James A. Moore, who manages to always remind me to sit my ass down and write the words, Benji Carr (my cheesecake husband now and forever; FYI his novel *Impacted* is AMAZING), and so many other amazing writers. This organization changed so much for me. I found my community and met so many people who were generous and willing to offer support as worked on this project. It's been six years since Bill asked if I was going to attend the first conference. Now I'm on the board and am part of planning the conference. I love all of you involved so much and am so thankful for all of you.

Many thanks as well to all of my friends who have encouraged and cheered me on through all this via Facebook. From the first time I wrote the tag #supersecretproject and started tracking my word count until now, some of you have been right there with me asking how it's going, sending love on days when I doubted myself, and riding this crazy rollercoaster to this point. All of my Facebook fans and friends have been so kind, and I am thankful for each and every one of you.

Thanks to Lynne Hansen, Jeff Strand, Charles Rutledge, and Amanda DeWees for sharing their time and professional experiences with me as I learn to be a professional myself. Each of you have taught me things that I never learned from my Master's program, but needed to know. Y'all are just the best.

Love to Crystal, Kitty, Jessica, Jamie, Benji, and Can from the HWA Atlanta: Coven Critique Group. Each one of you are such talented writers, and I feel honored to get to learn alongside of you. I am a better writer and person because you all are a part of my life. Thanks also to the HWA *Atlanta Southern Nightmares Reading Series* for allowing me to read my short stories to the general public. I also want to thank the editorial team of the Atlanta chapter's anthology, *Georgia Gothic*, for including my story, "You All Gotta Eat."

Of course, without my editor and publisher, John Hartness of Falstaff Books, this novel may not have gotten as far as it did. I doubt he knew what he was getting into when he saw me at the Falstaff table at Jordancon in 2016 and asked what I liked to read. To tell the truth, I wasn't sure either. What I was sure of when I walked away from that encounter was that he was good people and someone I felt comfortable sharing the manuscript with. I had no idea at the time that he would invite me to my first writer's bar at Dragon*Con and then use his minions (like Jeff Strand) to poke me until I finally sent him a draft.

John has been patient and kind as he taught me to be a better writer and novelist. He helped me cut and develop a huge manuscript without making me feel any less than awesome about what I'd created. He's made me cry several times, not out of frustration, but out of pure joy because he loved this story and these characters as much as I did. He's challenged me and given me the tools to make this the best novel it could be. I'm so glad I worked up the courage to talk to him that spring day in 2016.

Last, but not in any way least, I want to thank my family. Mom and Dad, you've instilled a sense of wonder and curiosity in me that is at my core. You also imbued a love for the strange and supernatural. I love you. Maeve Nettles, my fae child and constant beta reader, you are amazing, lovely, and incredibly talented in your own right. Keep writing, painting, and being exactly who you are. Stuart Juhan, my beloved bear child. I revel in your growth as a gamer and a storyteller. I revel in your extra-large heart. You are a good man and make the world a better place for being in it. I love you and am proud of you. Both of you have supported me through my own creative journey, even when you were kids. Amanda Canup, my sister from another mister who's known me since I was "that tall" (no matter that I still am "that tall"). You have held me together through so much over the years. Thank you for letting me talk and rail and rant and be ridiculous, even before I wrote this book, and for building my fabulous website (www.jessicanettlesauthor.com). You are the best of best friends.

I cannot mention everyone I want to mention, or I'd end up writing an Oscar speech (I think I might have anyway). Every single one of you who have been there over the years supporting and sending good vibes or cups of coffee or listening when I babble on and on about my latest bit of writing have a special place in my heart.

ABOUT THE AUTHOR

Jessica Nettles has a B.A. in English and an M.A. in Professional Writing from Kennesaw State University. She is also currently on the board of the Broadleaf Writers Association in Atlanta. When she's not writing, knitting, playing ukulele (not very well), or playing *Dungeons and Dragons*, she teaches English Composition at a local technical college.

FRIENDS OF FALSTAFF

Thank You to All our Falstaff Books Patrons, who get extra digital content each month! To be featured here and see what other great rewards we offer, go to www.patreon.com/falstaffbooks.

PATRONS

Dino Hicks
John Hooks
John Kilgallon
Larissa Lichty
Travis & Casey Schilling
Staci-Leigh Santore
Sheryl R. Hayes
Scott Norris
Samuel Montgomery-Blinn
Junkle

Made in the USA
Middletown, DE
01 October 2023

39731699R00208